# ALSO BY JOHN HERRICK

**Fiction**

Hit and Run

Between These Walls

The Landing

From The Dead


**Nonfiction**

8 Reasons Your Life Matters

# BEAUTIFUL MESS

## A NOVEL

## JOHN HERRICK

SegueBlue

Published in the United States by Segue Blue, St. Louis, MO.

This book is a work of fiction. Names, characters, places, and incidents are the product of the author's imagination or are used fictitiously. Any resemblance to actual events, locales, or persons, living or dead, is entirely coincidental.

Book layout by Ebook Launch

Library of Congress Control Number: 2016959604
ISBN-13: 978-0-9915309-6-0
ISBN-10: 0-9915309-6-9

*Publisher's Cataloging-in-Publication Data*

Names: Herrick, John.
Title: Beautiful mess : a novel / John Herrick.
Description: St. Louis, MO : Segue Blue, 2017. | Summary: An aging Hollywood relic finds a lost screenplay by Marilyn Monroe which catapults him to the top of the A-list. But the opportunity to reclaim his fame and fortune come with a choice: is he willing to sacrifice newfound love, self-respect, and his most cherished friendship to achieve his greatest dream?
Identifiers: LCCN 2016959604 (print) | ISBN 9780991530960 (softcover)
Subjects: LCSH: Monroe, Marilyn, 1926-1962—Fiction. | Actors—Fiction. | Man-woman relationships—Fiction. | Friendship—Fiction. | Hollywood (Los Angeles, Calif.)—Fiction.
| BISAC: FICTION / General.
Classification: LCC PS3608.E7746 B43 2017| DDC 813/.6—dc23
LC record available at https://lccn.loc.gov/2016959604

PRINTED IN THE UNITED STATES OF AMERICA

Dedicated to the memory of
Kim Steele

One day, we'll play together again in heaven.

# ACKNOWLEDGMENTS

Many individuals helped make this novel possible, including those mentioned here...

My family. Thanks for your love, and for understanding that sometimes these books need to be the way they are, even if it's crude or awkward.

Author Howard Roughan gave me strategic advice on crafting my stories. Thanks for your kindness, humility, and for the honor of letting me learn from you.

Eliot Parker, a terrific writer, for the mutual encouragement and respect, year after year. Iron sharpens iron.

Author Steven Manchester, an unexpected new acquaintance and a kind soul. Thanks for your generosity and encouragement behind the scenes. Knowing you has been a blessing.

Maryglenn McCombs, a talented publicist and my personal champion. Not only are your passion and faith in me as a writer genuine, but you have no idea how much that faith has meant to me when things looked dark around me. You're my MG.

Dr. Carla Siegfried — I'm able to write because God worked through your hands. You will always have a special place in anything I write. It's a privilege to have you in my life.

Jackie Ammons, Haydon Spenceley, Pam Rempe, and Christen Santoscoy were my early draft readers.

Phil Lewis provided my first opportunity to write for the public on the radio in 1996. You don't think you deserve thanks. But the truth is, that experience fine-tuned my ability to speak to a specific audience—and you were the guy who gave me the chance. Everything I write today has some roots in your team.

Rose Seifert, Heather Manning, Bobby Schroeder, Felicity Swann, Aisha Ford, Kelly Corday, Marnie Thompson, Karen Robinson — for your encouragement, prayers, faith in me, and the everyday nuggets that add up.

Thanks to the bloggers, reviewers, media people, and everyone else who gives my work a shout-out.

Without a doubt, I've forgotten people here, and I apologize for that. Thank you for those who have supported me— whether I realize it or not.

From the bottom of my heart, thank you to my readers. You don't need to read my material, but you choose to. What an honor for a writer.

Lastly, but truly *first,* thanks to God. I hope I'm doing this Your way.

Much love. Never give up!

# BEAUTIFUL MESS

All the world's a stage,
And all the men and women merely players;
They have their exits and their entrances;
And one man in his time plays many parts.

William Shakespeare

*As You Like It*

Act II, Scene VII

# PROLOGUE

## THE PRINCE MEETS
## THE SHOWGIRL

# LONDON, 1956

*PACK YOUR SUITCASE,* they had told him. *You'll depart for Britain in the morning.* He'd received fifteen hours' notice.

"And don't fuck it up," the studio staffer had threatened the young man, spewing cigarette smoke in his face.

Eighteen-year-old Del Corwyn had gotten himself hired as an errand boy at Warner Bros., where he had fetched coffee and water, delivered telegrams, endured verbal abuse, and completed whatever other menial tasks arose along the way. Del had gotten the job just a few months ago. He'd shown up and they had hired him. Simple as that. He was young and hungry.

And now, as luck would have it, they had shipped him to London.

The studio folks had assigned him to the set of *The Prince and the Showgirl.* They had instructed Del to serve Marilyn Monroe's every whim for the duration of the production. He should consider this an around-the-clock gig, they'd told him. Marilyn calls at midnight? Put your pants on and deliver her a toothbrush.

The current scene took place in what was supposed to be the embassy of Carpathia, a fictional Balkan country. Marilyn Monroe portrayed Elsie, a showgirl who had captured the delight of the Prince Regent.

Marilyn—Elsie—lifted a glass of champagne and toasted President Taft.

"Cut!" yelled a man with a baritone, English accent. Laurence Olivier, the film's director. "Take five!"

At that, Marilyn wiggled as if to shed the showgirl aura from her body. She strode past the camera to a folding chair, the one with her name affixed to it in block letters, and settled into it. A sheen of perspiration had broken through her powdered brow. The hair stylists had given her platinum-blond

1

hair a classic, sexy appeal. Her snug, light-colored dress accentuated her ample bosom and, in Del's opinion, her ample rear end.

"I'm parched from those hot lights," she said to Del as she picked up a script and fanned herself. "Please bring me a glass of ice water, young man. A tall one."

Without a word, Del fetched a glass from a table of refreshments. The handsome teenager returned to find the actress eyeing him with curiosity. With a word of thanks, she took a few sips with her perfect, red lips and sighed with relief. The ice cubes tinkled against the surface of the glass. Del could smell the actress's perspiration beneath her perfume.

Setting the glass aside, she furrowed her brow, pursing her lips as she sized him up.

"How old are you, young man?"

"Eighteen, ma'am."

"Eighteen! Why, you're but a child!" she replied with a voice that bubbled. Closing her eyes, she went limp, as though she had escaped into her own private wonderland. "Oh, to be so young." Her eyes shot open. "Not that I'm an old maid. Thirty isn't exactly ancient!"

"Of course not," Del ventured, measuring his words, cautious not to overstep his bounds and incur wrath from an actress who could get him fired if he inched out of line. Still new to his job, he'd made it his policy to keep his ears open and his mouth shut as much as possible. "You have happy memories of your childhood, I'd imagine."

At first, she didn't respond, and Del detected something askew in her silence. Her countenance lost its sparkle. Had he said something wrong? What would happen if they fired him in London? He couldn't afford a plane ticket across the Atlantic.

"Happy memories? Oh, I had a few of those, I suppose…"

Narrowing her eyes, Marilyn scrutinized him again, to the point that Del felt self-conscious.

"Your accent—you don't sound like a boy from the west coast," she noted at last.

"No, ma'am. I'm from Nebraska. I grew up on a farm near a small town."

"Nebraska! Well, how's that for a coincidence!" she blurted. The upper register of her voice possessed the playful tone of a child's. "I have a half sister who grew up in Kentucky. What do you know! You two were practically neighbors!"

Del tried to estimate how many hundreds of miles lay between Nebraska and Kentucky, then brushed the comment aside. Both smitten and awestruck, he would have agreed with anything this screen icon said. The fact that she seemed to treat him like a human being of equal stature made him lightheaded. If he were to pinch himself, he wouldn't be surprised to discover this was a dream.

But it wasn't. Marilyn Monroe was conversing with him like an old friend. Though wary and unsure, Del began to feel at home in her company. Why would a starlet like her want to chat with an errand boy like him?

"You live in Los Angeles, though?" she asked. "You moved there permanently?"

"Yes, ma'am."

"All by yourself? All alone?" A flamboyant snap of her fingers. "Just like that?"

"Yes, ma'am. Just like that."

"Why would a boy from a Nebraska farm town do that?"

Del blushed. His dreams outsized his status quo by a substantial margin. At this point, he couldn't even see beyond the horizon of his menial errands. All he knew was that a fire burned in his heart.

"Well, ma'am...I'd like to be famous one day. An actor," he said. "A film star, like you."

"How grand! A future leading man!" Marilyn's face lit up again. The overhead lights caused her eyes to twinkle. She reached out and, with the wisp of a feather, touched his hand with her fingertips, which felt creamy on Del's flesh. Hand lotion, perhaps. "That's what I shall call you: my bright star. What's your name?"

"Delbert, ma'am. But everyone calls me Del. Del Corwyn."

"Young man!" A shout. A female voice with what Del pegged as a New York accent.

Del turned to find a woman in her forties, slender with dark hair twisted into a bun the size of a cinnamon roll, scurrying in his direction. Not only had Paula Strasberg, Marilyn Monroe's acting coach, joined her student on the film set, but from what Del heard, the woman made more money than everyone except Marilyn and Olivier. The woman seldom left the actress's side, and crew members referred to her—in hushed tones, of course—as a nuisance. Upon meeting Strasberg, the first qualities Del had noticed were her sharp, intimidating eyes and her perpetual frown. Even when she smiled—another rare occurrence on the set—her teeth remained hidden, for she kept her lips sealed shut, like a tomb filled with centuries of tension. The crew attributed her prima-donna air to her former life as a stage actress. A handful of members in the lighting crew had secretly nicknamed her *Bun Bitch*.

Strasberg struck Del as possessive toward Marilyn, as though Strasberg were an authority figure, not a hired hand. And now she marched up beside her pupil, who stood several inches taller than the middle-aged coach, and glared at Del as if he were a mouse.

"Young man, leave Ms. Monroe alone! Can't you see she must focus? She must remain in character between takes." Sweeping her hand behind her, she added, "These people have already made the production a nightmare for her!" Then, with a dramatic pivot toward Marilyn, Strasberg jabbed a finger at her pupil. "Honey, you practice your lines and let Paula handle this."

Del retreated a step to escape the harsh woman's wrath. "I'm sorry, Ms. Strasberg," he squeaked, "but I—"

"Oh, leave him alone, Paula," interrupted Marilyn, who lifted her hand with panache. "Can't you see you're speaking of a future leading man?" Then, turning to him with a smile that reminded Del of the Pacific waters shimmering beneath the sun, she winked. "Del Corwyn, my shining star."

# PART ONE

## AS YOUNG AS YOU FEEL

# CHAPTER 1

**LOS ANGELES, SIXTY YEARS LATER**

DELBERT "DEL" CORWYN AWOKE with the sunrise. Every day, he allowed his body clock to respond to the pink light of dawn that seeped through his window and painted his bedroom wall with its electric glow.

For twenty years he'd started his day like this.

And more often than not, Del had woken up alone.

Not that he had any complaints. He savored his life as an eligible bachelor.

Alone? Yes.

Lonely? Not on your life.

He'd shared his bed with numerous ladies over the years. Young starlets with big dreams. Some had arrived in Hollywood mere months earlier; others had watched doors of opportunity open that suggested a miracle awaited around the corner. Still others, particularly in the days of his prime, were household names—modern legends, even. Kids listened to their exuberant voices on their headphones. Parents watched their films on the sofa. Little did they know, while they discussed those lush women over their meatloaf dinners, one of those young beauties had her mouth around Del's cock. For reasons not even Del could explain, they found in him the allure of a classic leading man.

And they grew up faster today. Oh, the tricks they taught *him* in bed!

Twelve inches of memory foam hugged Del's body as he arched his back and stretched. A grin crept across his face as he tossed back the down comforter and stepped to the floor.

Facing the glass door to his bedroom balcony, he placed his hands against the small of his back, eased himself into a straight posture, then gave himself a careful twist at the waist to work the cricks from his lower back. Part of his daily routine. He felt something snap and, once again, felt as young as he did when he was in his twenties.

Seventy-eight years old? Fuck that. Del's cheeks remained as smooth as a young Cary Grant's ass.

The speed at which the sun rose and the sky deepened to blue never ceased to mesmerize him. Del glanced at the glass door, where he kept his window curtains open overnight. From beside his bed, he saw nothing but azure, which drew him closer.

Even in Malibu, which he'd called home since hitting it big, January temperatures were crisp at this time of day. But that first blast of morning air invigorated his body. So according to his daily routine, he shuffled across the room, threw open the door, then stepped out to the balcony. Del slept in the buff, and he could already feel the tingle of the chilly California air nip at his bare skin. Nobody could see him from here. He'd spent many nights stargazing naked from this balcony.

He closed his eyes and absorbed the sound of Pacific breakers. From his perch high upon a mountain and far away from the individuals who lived in their little houses along the Pacific Coast Highway—their homes reminded him of the tool shed his father had built in their Nebraska backyard during Del's childhood—Del marveled at the ocean, a sliver of which glistened beneath the rising sun. As he peered down the mountainside, he admired its rocky surface covered in wild, rugged green growth and acknowledged, yet again, why he considered this state his land of milk and honey.

A sharp gust rushed in from the Pacific and caused goose bumps to prickle across his arms and legs. Del scurried back inside.

He padded down the hallway, descended a curving staircase, and cut across the living room into his kitchen, where the aroma of double-strength coffee made his stomach grumble. With his coffeemaker programmed to brew at seven o'clock, a fresh pot of Jamaican blue-mountain roast awaited him. He poured himself a cup, added a splash of soy milk, then closed his eyes to savor the first taste. Del focused on its warmth as it raced down his gullet and across his stomach lining. Yes, he'd enjoyed countless cups of coffee in the morning, just past daybreak, and while his evenings might not have been carbon copies of each other, his mornings were identical. The mornings he woke up alone, that is.

Strolling into his library, Del gazed at shelf after shelf of literature. He'd collected rare editions of classics, those editions printed a century ago by America's earliest publishers, although he had a particular love for Tolstoy and would have invested a chunk of his own fortune for one of the first copies printed this side of the Atlantic. But he loved to read modern fiction, from literary greats like Steinbeck to suspense by John Grisham to romance by Nora Roberts. Del devoured books, visualizing himself portraying the male protagonists, on a quest for his perfect comeback role.

He'd entertained many guests in the living room. Once, he'd opened a fine, aged bourbon while swapping industry war stories with John Wayne. A month after purchasing his home, he and Kim Novak had sipped a smooth, Bordeaux merlot as a Miles Davis record played on the phonograph. And, of course, Marilyn Monroe had visited on many occasions, though a romantic encounter had never occurred between them here. But numerous romantic encounters *had* taken place in this living room, on every piece of furniture and in every nook and cranny imaginable. Oh, the stories his shag carpet could have told if he hadn't remodeled the room several times since he'd shagged upon it! Today, the room possessed a retro charm, a return to the decade in which he'd first arrived in Hollywood. Rich mahogany details surrounded leather furniture as soft as butter.

Invigorated, Del downed a final gulp of coffee, curious to see how life would surprise him before bedtime came around.

———

Donning a track suit with reflective stripes along its sides, Del left the house for his five-mile run through the winding streets of his neighborhood, past homes once unseen by the general public, but now viewable from the sky through satellite photos on the Internet.

Del's street resembled a cul-de-sac turned inside out, where people could see each others' homes in the near distance but only saw one another when entering or leaving the private road. Del passed the driveway of one neighbor, a music producer, and curved his way to the next street.

Del inhaled as the first bead of perspiration dripped from his brow. Amid his routines, he regained his footing in life and sensed he was on the verge of a dawning point in his career.

Del selected his acting projects with care and precision. He'd acquired a reputation for being a true artist at heart, but this was show business, and much of show business could be a mirage, a fabrication derived from image and spin. Sure, the public perceived him as choosy and elusive—but Del certainly hadn't chosen that arrangement.

The truth was, Del Corwyn's talent hadn't been in de-mand for forty years. Not since an Academy Award eluded him at the height of his career.

After a string of box-office hits, critics called Del Corwyn a commercial success but an artistic lightweight. Determined to prove them wrong, he won the coveted role as a Mafia hit man who suffered a life-threatening injury on the streets of New Jersey, where an impoverished family found him and treated his wounds. After returning to health, the Mafia man underwent a personal renaissance, shedding copious tears and dedicating his life to helping children plant gardens in urban neighborhoods. Unfortunately, Del's character was murdered in a quaint little herb garden because, as conventional wisdom warns, nobody leaves the mob.

Del's performance brought critics and audiences to tears. The Oscar was considered his to lose—until he lost to Richard Dreyfuss, who, as of 1978, became the youngest man to win the Best Actor statue for *The Goodbye Girl*.

*Silly Del,* mused Del's detractors in their perfect 20/20 hindsight. *He should have worked with Neil Simon.*

That Oscar loss cost Del his career.

Yet once the Oscar nomination enhanced his status, Del's fans assumed he had morphed into an artist with discerning taste. He was a man who took rare roles, only as a featured player with the special "and" billing beneath the film title, or cameo roles on television during sweep weeks, which caused viewership to skyrocket.

Industry insiders knew, however, his public persona didn't match his private reality. Shunned by peers, they seldom took Del's calls.

At least the general public thought he was a winner, even if he knew better.

His mouth dry, Del swallowed and gained traction up an incline. Wiping perspiration from his face with the underside of his forearm, he focused on maintaining a steady breathing pattern. He hated running but refused to sacrifice his trim figure.

He examined the veins along the underside of his arm and swore they appeared more prominent, a darker shade of purple, than when he was young. Yet another telltale sign of aging which he preferred to ignore.

Del craved a comeback. A return to glory. A breakthrough role that would earn him that elusive Oscar win and seal his career. Del Corwyn would die a legend!

Returning home, he showered and fixed himself a smoothie filled with organic milk and Greek yogurt, protein powder, flax seed, honey, and a trio of berries. Firing up his laptop, which he kept on his kitchen table for the sake of convenience, he logged into his Twitter account and typed the first thing that popped into his mind.

**Finished daily run. Homemade smoothie. Ready 4 the day. #success**

He punctuated it with a thumbs-up emoji and posted his status update. With a click to his profile, he eyed his count, which stood at 547,000 followers. Thousands of people who wanted to hear what he was having for breakfast! When he'd first heard young actors speak of tweeting and followers and such on the late-night talk shows, the concept had made little sense to him. What a surprise to discover the speed at which he could follow the latest trends in social media and learn how to use the tools of the trade! Then again, he had plenty of time on his hands.

Technology these days! With one click, he could broadcast his status across a personal kingdom of social media accounts!

After taking a cursory look at the news, he hopped over to a website which consolidated the latest updates in the entertainment industry and the deals that had closed in the last twenty-four hours. While he respected a portion of the emerging talent, he considered much of young Hollywood soulless, lacking substance, eager for fifteen minutes of notoriety. Fame seemed to carry a shorter shelf life these days. Granted, directors no longer pounded on Del's door, but after half a century in this business, at least people still knew who he was. Twenty years from now, Kesha could only hope for that.

Del felt a grin, tight and self-satisfied, ease across his face as he closed the browser.

He hadn't lost this battle.

His day would come.

# CHAPTER 2

ORIGINALLY AN EXCLUSIVE evening club for top celebrities, Morocco Night first opened for business during Hollywood's golden era. From what Del heard, W.C. Fields enjoyed getting hammered here. By the early seventies, it was no longer the hot spot, but old Hollywood still frequented the place to relive their glory days. The dress code required men to wear a suit and tie, and the exorbitant menu prices helped ensure that patrons from undesired echelons would not invade the ranks of the clientele. Del loved the cuisine at Morocco Night. Its chefs drew upon influences from all corners of the world. But some nights, he stopped by for an expensive drink in the lounge. He had carried on countless conversations here with David Niven and Eli Wallach, before the actors passed away.

Each time he walked through the intricate, wood-carved doors of Morocco Night, Del surged to life. The club imported its furniture from the mother country. Patrons had their choice of various dining lounges, each decorated in a unique flavor.

Veering left, he made his way to his favorite room, which featured four-chair clusters around small coffee tables. He took a seat at an empty table, which wasn't difficult to find. Tonight the club was near desolate, as was often the case during the workweek nowadays. With a furtive glance around the room, he found it speckled with a few patrons, none of whom were regulars, except a former producer whose demeanor Del had always found irritating. Del planned to ignore him.

"Good evening, Mr. Corwyn. What may I bring you tonight?" asked Franklin, an aging waiter donned in a tuxedo and starched white shirt, as Del took a seat at a small coffee table. The man had worked at Morocco Night for as long as Del could remember. Del had watched his parted hair transition from Italian black to salt-and-pepper to smooth silver.

"Hello, Franklin. A Manhattan, please."

"Very good, sir," replied the waiter with a slight bow. "I trust your evening is going well?"

Del nodded in response. When the waiter departed, Del eased back in the chair and dreamed of the taste of strong, expensive bourbon that would soon wash over his palette.

Bright orange walls contrasted with splashes of turquoise and gold in the draperies. Turquoise pottery accented the environment. Del found the room dim yet inviting. In lieu of overhead lights, tiny lamps sat atop the tables and throughout the room. The tables and chairs were sculpted in blond wood and possessed the comfortable charm of a home in Africa, while royal-blue seat cushions ignited the lounge with the magnetic pull of the exotic. Tony Bennett's voice crooned from Bose speakers hidden among the decor.

When his drink arrived, Del sipped the honey-colored delight and savored the sensation as it raced toward his veins.

That was when he recognized her.

The median age at Morocco Night had to be eighty-five, though if you were to believe the face lifts and half of its patrons' claims, you might downgrade that average to seventy-four.

Either way, the young actress didn't belong here.

He'd caught several of her films. And Del never missed an issue of *Variety*. He knew for a fact she was only twenty-five. So why was she sitting in this retirement home of Hollywood's golden elite?

Yet there she was. And she sat alone.

In general, Del preferred not to date anyone under age twenty-six. Blame it on his scruples. Yet something about this young actress fit. Draped in a midnight-blue dress that hugged her form, she possessed an understated sex appeal that would have personified Morocco Night during its heyday. Without a second thought, Del eased from the chair, gave his body a subtle twist at the waist to chase the minor stiffness from his back, then strolled across the room to her table.

"Pardon me," he said, "but I hate to see a woman drink alone."

# CHAPTER 3

NORA JUMELLE PEERED up from her whiskey sour. Her hair was raven, its gloss youthful, as though God had stroked it with baby oil.

Her eyes, a steely gray, enraptured him. He'd heard of gray eyes but had never seen them firsthand. He felt his libido stir but stifled the thought. He appreciated women but wasn't a dirty old man.

She set her drink on the table and appraised him through wary eyes. Younger women always sized him up this way when he approached them. Del would fool nobody by dying his hair or attempting to hide his age, so he allowed its dark silver to emerge in all its glory. And though, at first glance, these ladies knew he was an older man, Del knew their second glances ushered in a hint of his irresistibility, which was his strong suit. Nobody was coldhearted enough to tell a silver-haired man to fuck off, which always improved the chances of their *giving* him that second glance. How had he gotten so lucky?

Nora leaned forward, which betrayed her curiosity.

"You're Nora Jumelle?" Del offered a winning smile.

She crossed her legs away from him but continued to appraise him.

"I didn't expect anyone to recognize me *here,* of all places."

"Del Corwyn," he said as he reached out for her right hand. He'd held his drink high with his left hand so she would notice the absence of a wedding band.

She allowed him to plant a light kiss on her fingers but her eyes widened, as though he had caught her off guard. Maybe she was too stunned to stop him. She gave him a quizzical look.

"Del who?" she said.

"Del Corwyn," he repeated with a smirk, then waited for the recognition to sink in.

Nora's eyes narrowed as she attempted to place his name. After a few moments of silence, she tilted her chin upward. Her countenance remained unchanged.

"I'm embarrassed to say this, but I can't place the name. Have we met...*Del?*" she replied, adding emphasis to his name in afterthought, the way you would when you wanted to let someone know their name hadn't escaped your memory already.

This was awkward. Granted, he'd stayed out of the spotlight for many years, but he'd received an Academy Award nomination! Was she too young to recognize him? Del's greatest fear was to fade into the abyss of irrelevance, where nobody remembered who you were—or cared why they should remember in the first place.

Guarding his composure, he decided to forge ahead, his confidence intact. "No, we haven't met. I've been around the industry, but I'm afraid we've never had the privilege of working together."

Her eyes brightened. "Oh! You're a director?"

*Hmm.* "An actor. I was nominated for an Oscar in 1978, actually."

"Oh," she murmured, lifting her glass for another sip. As her gaze lingered, the narrowness dissolved from her eyes. Del could tell he was back in the game, even if she didn't know who the hell he was. Her softening countenance indicated she hadn't ruled him out.

"May I join you?"

She offered a lighthearted chuckle in response, as though unsure how to respond to this older man, yet her eyes never left his. Nora continued to appraise him. With her forearms on the arms of her chair, she gestured to an empty chairs. "Be my guest."

Nora had an alluring smile, a contagious grin that brought a gleam to her face. Del slipped into the chair beside her. Because the chairs were the size you might find in a living room, the proximity didn't strike him as an invasion of her personal space.

"So you were a nominee?" she asked.

"Best Supporting Actor. Dreyfuss won that year."

"Is it true what they say, that it's an honor just to be nominated?"

"As I recall, you came quite close to finding the answer yourself. Your performance was brilliant in *Faces*. To portray a character in such a riveting way in your debut role is impressive. You should have been nominated that year." Just a few short years ago.

"I doubt I'll win one of those," she replied.

Del dismissed the notion with a wave of his hand. "I beg to disagree. Besides, the public adores you. You've had nothing but commercial success ever since."

"Why do you think that is, Del?"

Del felt his pupils widen as a connection formed between them. "Probably because you're gorgeous."

She smirked. "And you're relentless."

"Too forward?"

Bashful, Nora replied, "Don't worry, it's cool. I'll take it as a compliment."

With a glance around the room, Del returned his attention to the striking young woman beside him, with the raven hair and those stunning gray eyes. "So what is a beautiful woman like you doing in a geezer place like this?"

Another smirk as she lodged her tongue against the inside of her cheek. "Why do you ask? Am I in imminent danger? Are you here to rescue me?"

"You never know what might happen in a crowd like this," he snickered. Eyeing the near-empty room again, he spotted a frosty-haired couple who had come in and occupied a corner table. Del leaned toward Nora and nodded toward the couple. "You see those two over there?"

Nora leaned closer to him, her movements now silky. "What about them?"

"Former talent scouts," Del replied with a wink. "They founded gangsta rap."

Nora burst forth with laughter, a verbal gunshot which shattered the subdued atmosphere. Her hand flew to her mouth to stifle the noise. Her eyes widened as she realized she'd disturbed the tranquility. On the other side of the room, the older couple glanced in Nora's direction, then resumed their conversation.

"You're a charmer, aren't you?" she said to Del.

"I aim to please."

Nora studied her drink and ran her index finger around the rim of the glass. "To answer your question, I've come here a few times. I enjoy the peace." She paused. "When I sit here, I feel like I'm part of something bigger. Part of a continuum, like people started a tradition in this city, and I'm part of the club. I don't mean a popularity contest, but a respectable club: Clark Gable, Ginger Rogers, Cary Grant, Marilyn Monroe. All the greats, the ones who made an imprint."

"You wouldn't know it nowadays, but in another era, Morocco Night was quite the hot spot. All those people you mentioned? They frequented this lounge."

"Did you know them back then?"

"Sure. Clark and Ginger were older. But when I was old enough to drink, Cary and Marilyn were in their prime. My career had just begun at that point." He paused. "I knew Marilyn quite well."

"So you're part of the continuum."

"As an artist, a part of you wants to find acceptance with the people who surround you and the people who see your work. You want them to know there's a real you deep down inside."

"Or maybe it's just daddy issues." She shot him a wink over her whiskey sour.

"Maybe so," he chuckled, lifting his drink to her as if in a toast. When he swallowed, he noticed a longing in the way Nora surveyed him. He could tell he intrigued her: Her eyes focused on one aspect of him, which she studied before shifting her focus to another quality and repeating the process. She peered at the corners of his eyes, where crow's-feet were at a minimum, then moved on to his cheeks. Women always noticed Del's perpetual tan, which he credited to his early morning jogs as much as to his mother's Mediterranean genes.

Nora's gaze lingered upon his large hands. His left hand, of course, lacked a wedding band—which, if Del's plan had worked, Nora had already noticed when he'd lifted his drink.

"You're not married, I take it?" she remarked, as if on cue.

"No, I'm not. Does that surprise you?"

"I never know what to think. Some men try to hide it, but you don't even have a tan line where a wedding band would be."

"No, I've never have been married."

"How does a charmer like you remain a lifelong bachelor?"

He pondered her question. Oftentimes he asked himself why he felt so content without a spouse, but he had never arrived at an answer. "I suppose I've never met my soul mate." Once again, his mind wandered to the fact that Nora Jumelle sat alone among the aging patronage of Morocco Night. "I could ask you a similar question. Why aren't *you* involved with anyone? A significant other, I believe they're calling it these days."

"Oh, that," she said with a shrug. "Relationships take time. They're messy. Besides, I don't know if I want to get married." She tapped her glass with her fingernail, which responded with a slight ping. "I guess I don't know what I want in life."

"Not many people do." Del grinned. "It's what keeps Dr. Phil in syndication."

"I'm open to the options, though. I like to take chances, learn by experience."

"Meaning?"

To Del's surprise, Nora moved her hand forward and allowed her fingers to make contact with his. "The fact that I don't know what I want in life doesn't mean I don't recognize a magnetic soul when it crosses my path."

And with that, she tickled his forearms with her fingernails. The alcohol lent an airy feature to her eyes.

"Let's talk somewhere else," Nora said.

# CHAPTER 4

THEY SAT ON Del's living room floor, angled toward the fireplace, yet facing each other as they chatted. Though the January evening was cool, turning on the heat wasn't necessary. Nora's shoulders were bare amid her strapless dress, so she had wrapped herself in a fleece throw. Del had turned off the lights and so they could watch the flames flicker. He admired how the firelight brought a golden glow to Nora's skin.

Since they left Morocco Night after their first drink, Del had mixed each of them another one when they arrived at his house.

"Do you always bring strange women home with you?" Nora teased.

"You mean to my *crib?*" he jested in return.

With a delightful laugh, Nora tilted her head and leaned toward Del. Her white teeth gleamed beneath a muted shade of lipstick, which had all but worn off as the evening progressed. Their faces were inches apart. "Yes, your *crib.*"

"Not always. Only the ones willing to humor me."

Another staccato laugh from the young woman who searched his eyes with a combination of desire and enthrallment.

Although Del enjoyed her attention and found her riveting, he couldn't ignore the signals his conscience sent to his heart. Damn honesty. He never admitted his age, especially not when entertaining someone this much younger than he, but

Del detected a special quality about Nora Jumelle. Besides, he never took advantage of women. He didn't want to feel shitty in the morning.

Del broke his gaze and grimaced. "You realize you're twenty-five years old and I'm...*not*, right?"

With a shrug, Nora laid her drink on the hearth. She reclined upon her elbows. "I like to try new things."

Reading between the lines, Del grinned and sipped his drink, wondering how he'd gotten so lucky tonight. This young woman was more than stunning. She was intelligent. Witty. Someone who analyzed her options before making a move—which was why Del was fascinated to find her in his living room, inviting him to make the next move.

Finally, she said, "You don't need to feel like you're robbing the cradle, Del. I date men of all ages."

"You do?"

"Sure. Guys my age are enjoyable. They bring a sense of adventure. But older men intrigue me."

"How so?"

"Remember when we talked earlier about the continuum?" When Del nodded, Nora added, "I haven't found many men my age who think on that level. Yes, they have their careers and interests, but I come across very few who live beyond the here and now, who seek to fit into a bigger picture. It's not that they don't want to; it hasn't occurred to many of them yet. But life is so much bigger than the big screen and its silver surface. Don't you agree?"

"Of course, but everything comes with a price." Glass in hand, he gestured around the room. "I'd be a liar if I said I didn't enjoy the good things in life."

Nora paused and gave his features another once-over. Squinting her eyes, she murmured, "You're a very attractive man."

Del felt his confidence blaze. "You're—"

As he attempted to reply, Nora eased toward him, feathered his bottom lip with her own. Before he knew it, their lips were locked, their breathing had grown heavier, and Nora began to stroke his biceps with her thumbs. The throw slipped from her shoulders and pooled on the floor.

Holy shit. Was *she* seducing *him?*

He couldn't resist her advances. Del felt himself stir below the waist. He'd never had a need for Viagra.

Nora slipped her fingers between his shirt buttons and massaged his chest with her fingertips. Del glided his lips to his right, planting kisses behind Nora's earlobe and making his way down her neckline. Her shoulders smelled like citrus and honey.

"You haven't lost your touch," she whispered.

# CHAPTER 5

A FAINT BREEZE, though chilly, tickled Nora's senses and kept her alert. From the darkness of Del's balcony, beneath the light of a crescent moon, she saw nothing but inky blackness in the distance. On the other side of the glass door, Del was sound asleep.

With her eyes halfway open, she focused downward, toward her chin. Although it had taken several minutes for her to release the tautness in her back as she kept her posture straight, she perceived, at last, tension melting from her muscles. She kept her mouth closed and inhaled through her nose.

Slow.

Deep.

Searching for the fire she hoped was still within her.

Cross-legged, Nora held her right hand in her left, the tips of her thumbs in contact, in front of her belly. A trace of breeze tickled her flesh as it wove between her elbows and the sides of her abdomen.

How long had she maintained lotus position? An hour? Two? She had lost track of time, but it didn't matter anyway. Sleep eluded her tonight, as it often did.

She listened to waves that crashed somewhere in the abyss of ink before her. Aside from that, Nora heard nothing but the silence of time as her life ticked along, second by second, inch by inch. Alone on this balcony, engulfed in an atmospheric shroud, with oxygen swirling in her lungs and coursing through her veins, Nora controlled her destiny. For this limited spectrum of time, when all held still, nothing could unearth her. Colors sprang to life upon the canvas of her mind. She could feel them, smell them. She could detect everything around her, including whatever might approach. Amid the calm, she knew what to expect to come her way.

Nothing.

A tear materialized from the melancholy in her soul. It pooled in the corner of her eye with a feverish heat and snaked down the middle of her cheek.

# CHAPTER 6

SUNRISE.

Del awoke on his side, so he plopped onto his back, too exhausted to open his eyes until another moment passed. As he recalled his companion from the prior evening, he grinned and reached out this hand, running his palm across the other side of the bed.

He found the sheet cool to the touch.

Curious, he sat up and opened his eyes, then noticed the cover and blanket turned halfway down the bed. He cocked his ear in the direction of the bathroom but heard nothing. No water running through the faucet. No swishing of a toothbrush. Nothing.

She was gone.

And judging from the temperature of the sheet on her side of the bed, she had slipped out long ago.

Del swung his feet onto the floor. With a twist at the waist, he scanned the bedroom again. At the foot of the bed, he noticed Nora's clothes scattered on the floor. Maybe she hadn't left after all. A glance through the glass door to the balcony told him she wasn't out there, either. Had she roamed his house?

Assuming Nora was in the vicinity, he headed to the bathroom to grab his favorite bathrobe but couldn't find it. He was sure he'd left it there. Then again, he hadn't worn it in a week, so his memory might have failed him. Instead, he pulled on a T-shirt and pajama bottoms, then wandered down the hallway, toward the staircase. When he reached the bottom of the stairs, the scent of freshly brewed coffee jolted him and swept the heaviness from his eyelids.

The aroma lured him to the kitchen, where he found Nora leaning her hip against his counter, sipping coffee as she stared at a decorative window near the kitchen table. Apparently, she'd searched the cupboard farthest from the sink—the one where he kept random items he rarely needed or sought—and had selected a mug he'd purchased at an airport in Zurich. German script flowed across a watercolor rendition of the Swiss Alps. With her face turned in the opposite direction, she didn't see Del approach her.

A thick, royal-blue robe—*his* robe—swallowed her frame. Since Del was several inches taller than Nora, it covered the full length of her body and brushed against the floor. Her shoulder-length hair, half of which hung over the collar of the robe, appeared tousled in the perfect spots. Nora Jumelle possessed a sexuality understated yet undeniable. When she crossed one leg over the other, the lower half of her leg, that porcelain flesh of hers, peeked through the opening of the robe, her toes curling upon the floor. Her toenails were painted cherry red.

Del's joint cracked behind his knee—many women had quipped that he couldn't sneak up on them if he tried—and Nora turned. Most of her makeup had worn away; her lipstick was gone, and her eye shadow was a mere remnant of the prior evening's incarnation.

"I made myself at home," Nora remarked. "Hope you don't mind."

"Not at all." Del wondered if she noticed the way his pectoral muscles shaped the sleeves of his T-shirt, even at his age. He still visited the gym each week.

"Would you care for some coffee?" she asked.

She'd found his red, plastic tub of Folgers. Del hadn't

31

bought into the gourmet coffee fad, whose product tasted like mud to him. He retrieved a mug from his collection of rarities, filled it from the pot, and stirred in a splash of soy milk. When the coffee hit his taste buds, he tried not to wince. The scent was familiar; the taste was not. Nora must have recognized this wasn't a fancy dark roast and tripled the dosage. He hoped this stuff didn't set his bowels in motion and send him scurrying to the bathroom.

"Delicious," he fibbed.

"Coffee's my specialty," she replied with a wink and lifted the mug to her lips with both hands. She'd painted her fingernails the same shade of red as her toes.

"Do you work today?" asked Del.

"I'm between projects. We don't start shooting until April due to schedule conflicts. Do you work today?"

"I'm between projects myself." Eager to deter her from digging into the details, he added, "You really are a fine actress."

"Some would disagree." Nora shot him a crafty glare. "I'm sure you've read what the critics say: 'She's box-office gold but not an artist.'"

"I don't understand why they would write that. Your latest performance was brilliant. Whether the critics agreed or not, the public loved it."

She shrugged.

Del marveled at her nonchalance. Not that she didn't care; rather, she'd managed to maintain a semblance of naïveté. He remembered how it felt for his career to skyrocket and couldn't help but be thrilled for Nora. If she played her cards right, he estimated, she had the talent to build a career that would last until she chose to retire—*if* she chose to retire. Del saw in Nora an enduring presence, the next Diane Keaton or Meryl Streep. She was the type of actress who could reinvent herself in each stage of her life.

"I hear a lot of Oscar buzz," he said. "You appear to be the frontrunner."

"Surprise, surprise," she chuckled. "I'm not banking on that one."

"They say it's a virtual lock for you."

"All the more reason not to get my hopes up. Life has a way of kissing you on the mouth and shitting on your feet."

He fought to keep a straight face. "That's one way to put it."

She stared at him. Her gray eyes reminded Del of winters in Nebraska: bleak and impenetrable. As a child, after months of stale winter temperatures and an absence of sunshine, what he wouldn't have given to open a window and inhale fresh, balmy air.

Nora ran her index finger along the rim of her coffee mug, studied its path, tapped the porcelain surface with her shiny, painted fingernail.

"Do you know where I was five years ago?" she murmured in a skeptical tone.

Del furrowed his brow. As far as he could recall, her breakthrough role had arrived only three years ago. "Can't say I do."

"I was working in the butcher section at a grocery store."

"You're kidding."

"Nope. I learned every cut of steak. Veal, pork, sausage—you name it, these hands touched it." She wiggled her fingers with her free hand.

"I'd imagine that knowledge comes in handy…somehow."

"I'm a vegetarian now. I learned I can't stand the sight of blood."

Why had she mentioned steak? Now Del craved a filet mignon.

"I'd moved to the City of Angels a few weeks earlier, had no job. This guy in the apartment downstairs got me a job at the store. They asked me if working with raw meat bothered me, and I figured, *How bad could it be?*" She shook her head and snickered. "I spent the first week feeling nauseous and the next three weeks feeling numb. Sometimes the money comes in handy and you think you can handle anything, but then you look around at the carnage and you say to yourself, *What the hell am I doing here?*" She tossed one hand on her hip. "Have you ever asked yourself that? *What the hell am I doing here?*"

*Tell me about it.* "How long did you keep that job?"

"Two months. I had to escape. After that, I went to work as your stereotypical cocktail waitress while I worked on indie film shorts. That breakthrough project, *Faces,* the one that got rave reviews? It was a full-length indie film that nobody should've noticed, but we gained a following at Cannes. Next thing you know, it opens on two hundred screens in the U.S. and sells out. They expand to a thousand screens and it cracks the top five at the box office that weekend. Suddenly, they're dubbing me 'Jennifer Lawrence 2.0' or some nonsense like that. Is that how it was back in your day?"

The speed at which decades could roll along, each one faster than the last, astonished Del. People Nora's age spoke of fifty and sixty years ago as if teenagers hand-jived to Beethoven on *American Bandstand* back then. Granted, he could remember Michael Jackson as a kid with an afro in a perfect sphere, but that didn't make Del *old.* Nora didn't seem to understand what golden career coins she held in her hands. To be able to pick her projects! These days, the only roles Del turned down were of the Hallmark or Lifetime channel variety. Not even the indie people called him. Not that he would have said yes to a project like that, but nonetheless…

"Options are a good thing," Del noted. "Look at how it turned out for you: no more butchers or blood. And you have the option of turning down any roles that come your way."

Nora poured herself another cup of coffee, stirring in

plenty of soy milk and sugar.

"Sometimes I wonder why they would want me," she said. "I'm not extraordinary. Is it fate? Luck of the draw? I mean, a girl I worked with, another waitress, tried to make it as an actress, too. We covered each other's shifts whenever one of us had an audition. Why would they chase after me and not her? What makes *me* so special?

"Would you believe I was *happier* during that indie season?" Nora held his gaze a moment before shaking her head. "That must sound silly. Maybe I'm just not cut out for this."

Del reached out and stroked her shoulder which, beneath the far-too-big robe, felt bulky to the touch. "Don't worry, I went through the same thing. You chase after that elusive opportunity and can't make it happen. Then, one day, you wake up and discover you've entered another world. That project you worked on—the one that felt like all the others, the one where you showed up and did your job like any other day—that project turns out to be a rocket that propels you into another stratosphere. Everything changes. You can never go back to the way you were." He chuckled. "Trust me, you don't *want* to return to the way you were, living paycheck to paycheck."

Nora watched him as he spoke, lifting the coffee mug to her lips without appearing to realize it. When Del paused, she responded with a slow blink, a single flutter of her eyes, the speed of a dying butterfly giving its wings yet another flap as it lay helpless on the ground.

"I'm being ridiculous, aren't I?" she said.

"Not ridiculous. You've entered a new world and you're trying to find your place."

At that, Nora drained her coffee, rinsed the mug, and placed it in the dishwasher. She turned to Del and bunched the edges of the robe closer together, concealing the milky porcelain of her chest. With a subdued smile, she rose on her tiptoes and kissed his cheek.

"I'd better get dressed. Thanks for the coffee." She winked. "And the robe."

"My pleasure," Del replied, sipping his now-lukewarm coffee and peering out the window.

When Nora reached the entry threshold, she paused and turned. "Thank you for listening, Del."

Del caught a glimpse of a smile at the corner of Nora's lips, the wisp of an afterthought. And with a lingering glance, as if she were giving him a second consideration, she turned and left the kitchen, still wrapped in his robe.

# CHAPTER 7

THE LAST FEW YEARS, Del had come to dread his meetings with Grant Pevely, his accountant. Yes, Del hired the guy to keep his books intact, but Pevely interpreted it as getting paid to worry. Del appreciated his efforts, but his accountant approached life from the opposite end of the positive-negative spectrum. He could picture Pevely as a teenager in the backseat of his car, a girl melting beneath a romantic, full moon, waiting for his hands to cup her breasts. Pevely, ever the pessimist, would sit there and list a host of reasons why the moon didn't look as bright as it would if it hung lower in the sky. Meanwhile, the girl was pulling her top back down. His point was accurate but he'd squandered life's latest opportunity.

Every day, without exception, Pevely wore a suit and tie to the office. He wore his tie in the same double-thick knot he'd worn years ago—the same plaid ties, too, if Del wasn't mistaken—and a black pin-striped suit. Balding in the back, the accountant maintained an otherwise-full head of gray hair and, to this day, spent countless hours at his desk. His eyes appeared dark and heavy, droopy like a bulldog's, and his jowls had grown more prominent. The man always looked one week away from a heart attack. He was a gem, though. They had done business together since Del's heyday and had, over the course of time, developed a semblance of friendship. Or trust.

The accountant spoke in an even tone that dripped with

rationality. "Del, I've been going through your books, preparing for tax season…"

*Here we go again.* The annual spiel. At the other side of Pevely's desk, Del sank back in the visitor's chair, the cushions of which felt like foam infused with newspaper scraps. Del shielded his eyes with one hand and began to massage his temples with the thumb and middle finger of his other hand.

"Do we have tax issues?" Del interrupted.

"No, you're in good shape in terms of taxes, the legality side. Being selective with the roles you choose has limited your employment income. One benefit that brings is to reduce your adjusted gross income, but—"

"It's not a bad thing to owe less in taxes, Pevely."

"—*but,* that benefit is a technicality."

"Meaning?"

"Meaning you can't consider it a permanent fixture in your life, Del."

"I've survived this way for thirty years. The money's there."

"Unfortunately, it's not there to the same extent it was thirty years ago—"

"The bills are getting paid."

"Yes, but the question is, how long can you afford to pay them?"

"We have this conversation every year, Pevely."

"I wouldn't be doing my job if I didn't make you aware of this."

"And your expertise is duly noted," Del volleyed in return. "Hollywood is a cutthroat business, but I'm a survivor."

"I understand that, and I certainly respect where you're coming from." Pevely pinched the bridge of his nose before putting on his reading glasses, the half-height type that allowed him to peer over the top of their black frames as he spoke. He removed some paperwork from a manila folder and gave a few pages another perusal. Then he laced together his fingers atop his desk and looked up at his client. His forehead creased.

Del saw hesitation in the man's eyes. That *wasn't* typical.

"Del, do you know what other people your age are doing right now?"

"Where?"

"Anywhere."

"Give me a place, Pevely."

The accountant sighed. "Rapid City," he offered with a halfhearted wave of one hand.

"South Dakota?"

"Yeah, sure."

"So these are normal people."

"Yes. Average, everyday people. Do you know what they're doing right now?"

"Playing shuffleboard at a retirement home?"

"I'd imagine some are doing that, if it makes them happy. But many others are taking advantage of each year, living life to the fullest. They're cruising around the Caribbean, traveling to Europe, venturing state to state to explore wineries. These are happy people, Del. And they don't have financial concerns. At least, not beyond the norm. These people worked regular jobs in an office or business their entire careers, yet they live their lives in a way they never could while they were working. They maintain the same standard of living to which they'd grown accustomed before they retired. And do you know how they can afford to do that?"

"Beats the hell out of me. Investments? Good advice from an accountant, I suppose."

"Yes, and that accountant advised them to plan ahead— not simply the next few years, but for the decades to come. On a gradual basis, they conserved funds, made wise investments, spent less so their nest egg would last the rest of their lives."

"Look, I understand what—"

Pevely lifted a hand. "Just hear me out. Please, Del. As you know, I've recommended a similar strategy for you since you were sixty-five years old. Steps you could take that would allow you to maintain a standard of living to which you've grown accustomed. But Del, you're no longer sixty-five. You're seventy-eight years of age. And you're in terrific health, which means we can expect you to look forward to many happy years ahead—but you need finances intact to do so."

"The royalty checks haven't stopped coming in."

"True, but those films are older now, and less in demand. The royalty checks have continued, but the dollar amounts have decreased. Inflation, meanwhile, continues to rise, which increases your cost of living. If this trend continues, royalties alone won't be sufficient down the road."

"That's why we made all those investments—real estate, for example."

"Yes, but as you might recall, we had a couple of recessions the last twenty years. And the recession of 2008 continued for many years. Some would argue we still hadn't recovered eight years later, despite the White House's spin. When the housing bubble burst, it didn't just affect home values and families. People spent less. Businesses contracted, they stopped hiring, stopped expanding. They weren't renting or buying as much property. Remember, you chose to sell many of those real estate investments at a loss—against my recommendation—in order to obtain an inflow of cash to last you for the foreseeable future, rather than accept those project offers from Hallmark."

Perspiration broke out along Del's upper lip.

Pevely paged through more paperwork. "You also liquidated a large percentage of your savings, which was built primarily upon your royalties, which is the reason you don't have as much to fall back on today."

"So what are you telling me, Pevely?"

"You need to cut back," his accountant replied, emphasizing each word. "Significantly."

40

Del felt heartburn settle in. His neck felt feverish. "Look, Pevely, you and I both know the entertainment business is unpredictable. People have comebacks."

"And I don't disagree, but you can't count—"

"These roles come unexpectedly, and circumstances turn around for the better with the right film. It happens in a heartbeat—"

"Del." Pevely's voice remained steady, but Del noticed something unusual in its force: resolve. Severity, perhaps?

Del stopped talking and watched his accountant like a hawk.

Pevely removed his reading glasses and folded them. He glanced down at the paperwork once again, tapped it with the edge of his frames, then focused his attention on Del. Pevely looked exhausted.

"Del, how long have you and I have known each other?"

"Forty-something years. Why?"

"And in all that time, I've met you halfway. Even when you opted against my advice, we found a way to make it work. But I've always been honest with you."

"Of course you have."

Pevely leaned forward and pursed his lips. "I'm telling you this as a friend, Del." He placed his palms flat on the desk, which was Pevely's typical gesture whenever he was adamant about something. It was Del's signal to listen up. The accountant kept his voice reserved yet firm. "You need to cut back. Drastically. Not next year. Not tomorrow. Now."

# CHAPTER 8

DEL SHIFTED in his seat. The conversation was beginning to scare the hell out of him. "And this sudden turn of events is because…" he prompted.

"It's not a sudden turn of events. Unfortunately, it's the byproduct of disregarding your accountant's advice year after year. And each time you chose not to listen, I warned you. *Pleaded* with you. I told you, 'These issues will augment over time, and they will result in catastrophe.' Do you remember me telling you that?"

"Of course I do, but accountants are paid to say that, aren't they?"

"I wish I had better news, Del, but I don't."

This couldn't be happening. Fear spiked through Del's veins. He began a desperate mental search for a detail Pevely might have overlooked, or better yet, evidence that this discussion was nothing more than a bad dream.

He was Del Corwyn, after all. An Academy Award-nominated actor with a reputation to protect.

Sure, people went broke—or whatever Pevely claimed he was tracking toward—but that occurred at the *bottom* of the entertainment food chain, didn't it? These hassles happened to the Gary Colemans of the world, who rose to stardom as kids, before they plotted strategies or established artistic visions. But Del Corwyn?

Then Del froze.

Oh, shit—the media would smell blood. His face would show up on the tabloids at the supermarket. He'd look like a seventy-eight-year-old fool.

"Maybe I should get a second opinion," he mumbled.

"They'll tell you the same thing. This isn't good. You're in dire shape, Del. If you don't make changes now, you will run the risk of declaring bankruptcy before you die. Is that something you want?"

Del's accountant had slugged him in the groin. Del exhaled but couldn't seem to breathe in again. A cold sweat burst through the surface of his scalp. He removed a handkerchief from his pocket and patted his brow.

He hadn't faced defeat since he was in his late twenties. Not total annihilation, anyway. When bad news hit, he could spin it to a degree that rivaled the greatest publicist.

But not today. This time, his good looks, wit and charm failed him.

When he spoke, the words escaped one notch higher than a murmur.

"What do I need to do, Pevely?"

"Downsize. ASAP."

"As in?"

"Your home, for starters. It's an immediate way to liquidate some assets and will free up significant resources for the future."

"Leave Malibu? I've lived in that house for—"

"I'm not talking about downgrading to a condo, Del. You can live in a large home and remain in the Los Angeles vicinity. If you expand your radius to include—"

"I'm not moving to fucking Corona!"

"Corona is a very nice option. Plenty of people like yourself have made their homes there."

Deflated, Del sank back in his chair like a kid sitting in the principal's office. His accountant wasn't doing his standard tap dance. No doubt about it: Del was in trouble.

Big trouble.

"Look, if I stay in town, everyone will know what happened. But I need to be available for work. That perfect role might be around the corner."

"Air travel is always an option. Many people live outside of California. You can find even better home values elsewhere."

*Hold on.* If Del stayed in town, he would face the humiliation of admitting defeat—and possibly forfeit his chance at a comeback. No A-list filmmaker wants to hire a desperate loser. He had to spin this. Find a way to make this look like *he's* the one in control.

Air travel. Maybe Pevely had a point.

Then it hit him.

"Florida," Del said.

"Florida's nice."

"If I buy a home in Florida, I can keep the upper hand. I can make it look like I'm escaping the rat race of Hollywood and reaping the rewards of a solid career."

"Desmond Child lived in Florida."

"The music producer?"

"Even while he was in high demand," Pevely nodded. "Some people want the climate and culture, but also the breathing room. Their own space to be creative."

Still discouraged, Del stroked the stubble on his chin as he pondered that idea. The notion of selling his Malibu house sickened him. It was his home, after all. He adored California and never wanted to leave. Grief settled into his soul.

But if the other option was to die penniless…

"Fine," Del sighed. "I'll do it."

# CHAPTER 9

TRISTAN ALBRECHT ZIPPED ALONG a busy suburban street in Oxnard in his Chevy Impala. At thirty-three years old, he could convince anyone he was ten years younger. He bobbed his head to an odd track of Mexican rap music that blared from his stereo by way of Bluetooth and a playlist on his phone. A market existed for every desire. Give them what they want.

The midmorning California sun radiated upon his arm as he hung his elbow out the window. He held the steering wheel in a loose grip with his right hand. From behind his sunglasses, he watched the traffic light turn red at the intersection ahead, eased to a stop, and sipped his café Americano. He pinched the flesh above his waist. Although he'd managed to keep his waistline trim, early signs of a muffin top horrified him.

Once the light turned green again, he made a sharp left and veered into his neighborhood, tires screeching into a parking spot in front of his first-floor apartment. He cut the ignition, hopped out, and headed inside. His next-door neighbor sat cross-legged and shirtless on a yoga mat in the grass, wearing sunglasses and shorts that exposed far too much thigh for Tristan's heterosexual taste. Tristan gestured hello with his coffee cup to the schmuck who had his hands at his sides, each thumb and forefinger connected. The dude offered no response, so he must have had his eyes shut, too busy drifting between Mars and Venus or wherever those people traveled. Tristan enjoyed slamming his car door shut to see if the guy flinched. He never did.

Heading into his apartment, Tristan shoved his keys into the pocket of his jeans, kicked off his flip-flops, grabbed his laptop from the coffee table, and shuffled to a small patio outside his living room. Another pull from his Americano as he logged into his email and changed his identity to Russell Merritt.

Russell Merritt, wellness coach.

When you're online and faceless, you can become anybody you wish. A market existed for every desire.

In the case of his latest email message, the desire resided within a lonely housewife in Beverly Hills. The woman had interacted with him for the last few years, a sporadic client who, Tristan suspected, contacted him whenever her hormones got out of whack. But he was no doctor, so who was he to judge?

According to her email, she'd followed his advice and continued her steady use of herbs and traditional supplements—little tidbits he'd discovered online when he first started this venture. Tristan hadn't noticed changes when he himself had tried them and didn't believe they made a difference, but he'd noticed when his clients popped them, they could convince themselves a positive change had occurred in their bodies, which gave them a renewed sense of self-control. Feeling stressed? Try some chamomile tea and take a magnesium tablet before bed.

The woman claimed her name was Jennifer. When it came to a go-to name like that, Tristan suspected it represented a higher proportion among his faceless clients compared to the general population. Last time they chatted, this particular Jennifer had sought help finding a therapeutic hobby. According to the notes he'd saved under her client ID in his makeshift database, she'd expressed an interest in colors and perspective. *Why not try painting?* Tristan—that is, Russell

Merritt—had suggested. Jennifer soon reported newfound freedom after picking up some basic supplies at the store and channeling her emotions onto a canvas. According to her latest email, however, she'd hit a snag and wanted to know if he had time to contact her.

He knew she lived on her cell phone and would have it with her, so Tristan (Russell Merritt) opened his instant messaging application.

> **RMerritt44:** Hi Jennifer. Are you available?

A pause as he sipped his Americano and Bluetoothed some more rap music through his stereo with the volume down. His laptop pinged.

> **Jen99288:** You were right about painting. It's the perfect outlet. I think I've found my calling.
> **RMerritt44:** Have you researched a particular method?
> **Jen99288:** My method is to put on paper what I feel at the moment. I think it's helped me cleanse my soul.
> **RMerritt44:** I understand. Excellent thinking on your part. You can't underestimate the importance of your soul. Inner well-being is as important as, if not more so than, your outer well-being.

That line seemed to be a winner with his clients. Tristan had used it more times than he could count. Inner well-being could mean whatever each client wanted it to mean; he didn't care, as long as he got paid. But he had to admit, it made him sound pretty damn intelligent.

> **Jen99288:** I showed one of my paintings to my girlfriend Gillian, who said she believes they could appear in a gallery.
> **RMerritt44:** That is wonderful! You sounded doubtful in your last email.

**Jen99288:** Yes, it's my husband. He hasn't been so supportive. I don't think he understands how important painting is to my soul.

Tristan pushed aside his brown hair, which had flopped over one eye, and made a mental note to get a haircut. He maintained a shaggy cut in the current trend of careless cool. He shaved every other day.

**RMerritt44:** Do you recall what I have told you about his opinion?
**Jen99288:** Yes, you're right. You said it takes time for greatness to become appreciated. My opinion is what matters, and I should search for my own inner happiness.
**RMerritt44:** I believe you have made much progress. Next time you paint, try to find the colors to express inner peace. I believe that will help you.

Tristan could help himself. Even *he* had to chuckle at *that* line of bullshit.

**Jen99288:** Thank you, Russ. I always feel better after my sessions with you.
**RMerritt44:** My pleasure. And tell you what, I won't charge you for this session. We'll consider it a follow-up appointment.
**Jen99288:** Talk later.

Tristan hadn't planned on becoming a wellness coach. Hell, he'd never even sought training in it.

Fifteen years ago, upon graduating high school, Tristan skipped town and migrated to Los Angeles. An idealistic teenager, he'd had one plan: to become famous. After all, he considered himself a decent-looking guy with aqua-blue eyes, a hot tub into which females couldn't help but wade.

Tristan didn't become famous. He never stumbled across an acting gig. However, within six months of his arrival, he'd become the most popular server at his neighborhood Denny's.

The Internet had come into its prime. People had grown more comfortable purchasing merchandise, making donations, and conducting business online. Everyone he knew had acquired an email address. Within a few short years, websites had advanced enough to handle more complex content.

Around that time, Tristan had wandered to an outdoor shopping mall and, peering down from the second floor, he noticed a kiosk, around which a handful of individuals sat on barstools. He'd caught sight of one of the patrons, a young woman with a blond ponytail and sunglasses. Once his lust subsided, Tristan watched with curiosity as the woman lifted something to her nose and inhaled it. He couldn't shake how odd the sight appeared. After purchasing a shirt at a clothing store, he jogged downstairs to see what the kiosk sold—and discovered it was a scent bar.

*A scent bar!*

Those suckers had paid to sniff air freshener!

At that moment, Tristan realized people would hand over money for anything.

Serving tables for pocket-change tips? Sucks to that. He knew he could do better. And that was when the idea hit him.

Tristan had tinkered with web design in high school and grown adept at it, so he created a few pages, designed a rudimentary database, and wrote some JavaScript to make them interact. *Voila!* Tristan was a wellness coach. He would charge people for bullshit advice. He'd conduct his business by email and the occasional online chat. That way, he could control his own schedule and work around his hours as a server. And by working online, clients didn't need to visit an office or endure the awkwardness of looking someone in the eye as they admitted their problems. They could remain anonymous with him—and, more importantly, they would never see how young he was. He'd lied in his original online bio, but once he grew his business, his conscience got the better of him. So he revamped his bio to focus on his years of experience as a wellness coach to many satisfied clients, which was true.

When he started his business, Tristan had hoped to give the finger to his restaurant job, maybe even sleep late in the mornings.

He'd posted flyers on public bulletin boards and left stacks in restaurants and salons. He'd even sneaked a few onto the corner of that mall kiosk to attract those gullible scent-bar schmucks.

And you know what? They bought it! The suckers paid him like he was some badass psychotherapist! His website took off. Soon he raised his prices and, in time, overshadowed what he earned at the restaurant. As it turned out, his advice, though fabricated as needed, proved adequate. Satisfied clients talked to their friends, and as word of mouth multiplied, so did demand for his advice. Clients ranged from young wannabes to wealthy wives in Beverly Hills, like Jennifer. When demand surged, he bloated his prices further.

To increase demand and come across as personable, he'd wanted to include a photo of himself on his website. But why would middle-aged career people seek advice from a guy who, when he first set up shop, was still a teenager? So he spent forty bucks on a stock photo of a respectable-looking man whose dark hair had started to gray along the temples. The man wore trendy eyeglasses and possessed an undercurrent of sex appeal, the kind of professional Tristan could picture women dreaming about behind closed doors.

And Tristan adopted the alias Russell Merrick.

Russell Merrick, online wellness coach.

Within a year, he had quit his job and given the finger to the diner.

# CHAPTER 10

THEY CLINKED wine glasses at a table at Morocco Night. More patrons populated the room than on the night they'd met, but it still offered the privacy Nora sought. Del couldn't help but grin as she licked her red lips and swayed to the voice of Billie Holiday in a manner that reminded him of the playful innocence Marilyn Monroe brought to the screen in *The Seven-Year Itch*. Nora's husky voice, however, shattered that image with a point-blank gunshot.

"Of all the people you worked with, did you have a favorite?" she asked.

Del gazed around the room and discovered new comfort in the furnishings of yesteryear. He sunk the toes of his shoes into the rug, which felt an inch thick. "So many, I've lost track of them all. Doris Day would be in my top ten."

"Doris who?"

Del caught himself before his mouth fell agape. "Doris Day."

"And she was an actress?"

What the hell? "Yes, from the sixties. She did all kinds of work, from comedies to Hitchcock. Eventually, she had her own television show."

"I've never seen that show, I guess."

"It was before your time."

"I have to admit, I'm not well versed in *all* the legends of

Hollywood. I know the big names."

"But not Doris Day?"

"Nobody's perfect."

"In that case, you'll have to forgive me if I relive my own era," Del chuckled, "I grew up on *Howdy Doody.*"

Nora's brow wrinkled. *"Howdy Doody?* Is that how you told people hello when you were a kid?"

"It was a TV show. A children's program."

"Kind of like *Sesame Street?* That's the show I grew up with." She paused for a moment, looking perplexed. "Did Bert and Ernie ever get married?"

Del shook his head at how things had changed. Then again, after all those years watching *Howdy Doody,* he never did figure out if Clarabell the Clown was male or female, so maybe every generation grew up with its share of gender speculation.

Del studied Nora further as she sipped her pinot noir and scratched at the fabric on her chair. "Where did you grow up, Nora?"

"Philadelphia. Where are you from?"

"Nebraska."

"That sounds quaint. You don't strike me as Nebraskan."

"I haven't been there in years."

"Not even to see family?"

"Well, my parents passed away twenty-seven years ago, so…"

"Did you get along well with them?"

"Oh, sure." He reminisced for a moment, then added, "Except when I got caught sticking chewing gum under my desk at school. Teacher sent me straight to the principal's office. My dad tanned my hide for that one."

A quizzical expression overtook Nora's face. "For gum? Did the police arrest you for *that?*" she chuckled.

"The police?"

"Didn't you have a police officer monitoring your school?"

She looked serious. Del didn't know how to respond. "No, I can't say that we did. Did the police monitor *your* school?"

"Of course."

"What for?"

Nora shrugged. "Drugs, alcohol, whatever. Or in case some kid decided to pack a gun and go on a rampage."

"Is that what went through your mind as a kid?"

"Sometimes. I mean, if it could happen in Arkansas or Colorado, it could happen anywhere, right?"

No wonder he didn't date women this young. Lingo alone would produce a gulf between them if Del didn't keep track of the latest idioms.

Such a shame, too. Nora possessed an enigmatic beauty.

And true to form, she beat him to the punch.

"We're a romantic mismatch, aren't we?" Her words came across as an acknowledgment of fact rather than a question.

"As much as I hate to say so," Del winced. "That said, the other night was nice."

"Yes, it was." She leaned forward, her eyes squinting as she examined him, then added, "Too bad. You're a very sexy man."

"I'll take that as a compliment, my dear."

"You should." Her countenance glowed in the light of the small table lamp.

"Friends?" Del offered.

"Friends."

And they shook on it. Her idea. She reached out, gave his hand a firm pump, then giggled at the gesture. Del couldn't help but snicker in response.

Nora settled back into her cushioned chair and rubbed her pinky along the stem of her glass, peering into the pool of magenta inside.

"I'm a mess anyway," she mumbled in afterthought. "You wouldn't want to get involved with me."

"A mess? I find that difficult to believe."

"It's the honest truth." She paused to ponder her admission. "I'm not as confident as I come across on screen, not the way people try to portray me. Insecurity torments me."

"That's part of being an artist, though, wouldn't you say?"

"I suppose. But it's more than just being an artist Being in the spotlight—it's all so...*new.*

"I've fought to get to where I am," she continued. "Maybe you get so used to fighting, it becomes your norm. Then one day, you wake up. You've got what you've been seeking; meanwhile, everything around you has changed. Your comfort zone has vanished. You look for stability, for something to remind you that however shaky you feel, life goes on and you'll find a way to breathe.

"Then you start to wonder if you truly *want* what you've sought all along. At first, it looked like a dream; but when it crosses your path, it turns out to be the foothill of another mountain to climb, a bigger one, but this new one isn't a mountain you *chose* to climb. You're forced to climb this new mountain blind, and that scares the hell out of you."

She shook her head, as though clearing pixie dust from her vision, and looked at Del with childlike eyes, innocent and confused.

"Am I even making sense?" she asked. "How ridiculous to feel that way. I must sound like a crazy person."

With a sympathetic sigh, Del reached across the table and stroked her hand.

"You're not crazy," he replied, then refilled their glasses from the wine bottle they shared. "We all have insecurities, fears we bury in our souls, hoping no one will unearth," he murmured, half to himself. "Things we hide from the world around us—maybe even hide from ourselves."

Nora responded with a smile that gleamed from one corner to the other. She had perfect teeth, whiter than milk.

"Older and wiser," she observed.

Del hated hearing references to his age. Nora must have noticed a shift in his demeanor, because she startled, her smile contracting into an O shape of concern.

"I'm sorry," she said. "I didn't mean 'older' in a negative way."

"I'll admit I'm not a spring chicken."

Twisting her mouth into a wry grin, she reached out and touched his arm. "You're the most youthful mature man I've ever met."

He couldn't help but laugh to himself.

"Seriously!" she exclaimed. "I wouldn't have wound up at your house the other night if you weren't. Do you realize how many older men have tried to lure me into bed? When I said older and wiser, I meant you've been through this change of life before, the spotlight thing, and you've survived. So have all the other people that this Morocco place represents." Nora examined him further, her eyes flicking from one part of his face to another. "Maybe that's why I feel comfortable with you and why I feel comfortable here."

"Perhaps you're an old soul," Del observed.

"Maybe."

Del's heart went out to her. Such a strong young woman, yet so vulnerable here, where nobody could see. Now he regretted their spending the night together. Del enjoyed the company of women but never took advantage of them, and he hoped he hadn't overstepped a boundary with Nora. Fortunately, they had moved beyond that night and enjoyed each other's company. He felt drawn to her, not for her appearance or reputation, but for the woman he'd begun to discover beneath the surface. Honest. Intense.

The club's music switched to an instrumental. "The Stripper," by David Rose and his Orchestra. A fleeting pain pricked Del's heart. He seldom heard this song, but for Del, it ushered forth painful memories of Marilyn Monroe's death.

The song was in the top ten the week she passed.

He decided to change the subject to something more pleasant.

"Nora Jumelle," he said, lending a lush accent to his pronunciation. "It has an intriguing ring to it."

"It's French."

"That can't be your birth name."

Her eyes narrowed and her platonic flirtation returned. "What makes you so sure about that?"

"It's too perfect. Too mysterious."

"Not all enigmas evolve. Some were created that way."

Del grinned. "You're a special woman, but I think there's a girl-next-door tucked beneath the façade."

Nora brushed a drop of wine from her lip and rolled her eyes. "Tasmyn."

"Come again?"

"That's my birth name: Nora Tasmyn."

"It's not exactly boring. Why did you change it?"

With a shrug, she replied, "It's part of the continuum, I guess. I chose the name when I was thirteen. Jumelle sounded bigger, more sweeping, more glamorous. *Tasmyn* is so abrupt, you know?" Spreading her fingers into claws. *"Tasmyn.* It's like you reach the last syllable and come to a screeching halt. But *Jumelle*—" Her face lit up. "Can you hear it? The last syllable lingers. Listen to how that sounds: *Nora Jumelle.* Doesn't it flow from your tongue? It's passionate, infused with mystery."

This girl was no dummy. Even at thirteen years old, she'd known what she wanted and had the instincts to get there. Maybe she *was* born an enigma.

Del wasn't used to profound chats like this, but to his surprise, he rather enjoyed it.

"How about you, Del Corwyn? Is that your real name?"

"I'm afraid so. *Delbert Corwyn,*" he said with a mock French accent that ignited a giggle in Nora. "I can't say I was creative with it. Delbert Corwyn, simple as that," he shrugged. "I'm just Del."

Setting her glass on the table, Nora eased her elbows onto her knees, interlaced her fingers, and rested her chin atop them. "I like 'just Del,'" she murmured.

Her timeless smile returned.

Del sipped his wine, a young man once again.

# CHAPTER 11

WHEN DEL WANTED to relive the classic era in films, he'd grab lunch at a deli near Hollywood Boulevard. He wore short sleeves today, and the sunlight felt balmy against his tanned arms. Dodging locals and tourists, he strolled along the sidewalk and visited his friends, now immortalized through stars implanted along the pavement.

Several blocks from Mann's Chinese Theatre, he slid away from the pedestrian traffic and toward the curb, where he stared at a specific star, the one he sought during each visit.

His star.

Delbert "Del" Corwyn, with a movie camera icon beneath it.

He'd received it during a ceremony in 1986. Although his star—that is, the star of his career—had diminished years earlier, he'd hoped the ceremony would revive it somehow.

It didn't.

The event spawned news clips, twenty seconds long, around the country, little blurbs on entertainment segments of local noon newscasts. By the next day, he'd faded into the abyss of the public's memory.

Del removed his sunglasses, tucked them above the buttons in the V of his polo shirt, and watched the other pedestrians weave along without giving him a second glimpse. He shook his head in disbelief. Here he stood on Hollywood

Boulevard, a celebrity hovering over a star *named after him,* for crying out loud, and everyone around him was clueless. Not a soul recognized him! They walked right past him, as though he were no longer newsworthy, some poor schlub selling incense in a hippie shop!

Del glanced half a block behind him and caught sight of a television news van as it approached the intersection and slowed for a yellow light. Its two occupants chatted with each other in the front seats. Del recognized the woman in the passenger seat from the evening news. She didn't notice him, either.

Then again, why should he expect attention? Nobody wouldn't expect to find him here, would they?

He turned on his heels and started the trek back toward his car. He gazed out at the street, where the traffic light turned green.

Del jolted at a sudden outburst from a nearby store.

"Stop!" shouted an angry, middle-aged voice. "Somebody stop that little bastard!"

# CHAPTER 12

DEL SPUN his attention toward the shops. As soon as he did, a young man who looked no older than sixteen slammed against Del's shoulder as he flashed past him. Beyond the scent of cheap cigarette smoke, nothing registered in Del's mind until the intruder had passed.

The young man tried to dodge another pedestrian, a female, but his impact with Del's shoulder had caused him to lose his balance. After a few wobbly steps, he stumbled and fell, face first, onto Del Corwyn's star. On his way down, the kid stuck out his palms, scraping his hands but protecting his nose, though Del swore he heard a crack when the kid's knee hit the pavement. Had the little bastard gotten blood on his star?

Too stunned to move, Del gawked at the kid, who now grabbed one knee and writhed on the ground, his face twisted in a combination of frustration and pain. A group of tourists stood in the middle of the sidewalk, gawking at the sight. Locals detoured around the kid the way they would avoid an orange construction cone.

Del felt the clap of a hand against his shoulder.

"Thanks, buddy," said a bulky man with thinning hair, whose voice matched the outburst of anger, as he rushed past Del and hovered over the kid, hands on his hips and muttering something. Del assumed the older guy was the store manager.

"My knee!" hollered the kid, still thrashing in pain, his

voice filled with resentment. "I broke my fucking knee! You dumb bastard, I'm gonna fucking sue your ass!"

Yet the manager continued to stand guard over the kid, one hand on his hip and the other hand on a cell phone he'd grabbed from his back pocket. Probably dialing 911.

At that point, the circumstance dawned on Del: The kid must be a shoplifter, and Del had, albeit inadvertently, become a hero! But of course, nobody else knew this except the store manager, who was too busy guarding the kid until the police arrived. The kid continued to roll on the ground, his elbow scuffed, grunting in pain as he cradled his knee.

"Excuse me, did you witness what happened?" shouted a female voice.

Del spun on his heels and discovered the news van had parked at the side of the road. The female reporter came running up, microphone in hand, a cameraman attempting to keep pace as he lugged his equipment.

As Del prepared to answer the reporter's question, she rushed past him and stopped beside a woman. She was the next pedestrian the kid had attempted to dodge after he'd rammed into Del, before the kid had hit the pavement. The cameraman lifted his camera to his shoulder and began to shoot footage.

*She's interviewing someone else!*

The woman faced the reporter as she answered her questions, which prevented Del from getting a good look at his competition. He tried to hear what the female bystander said, but she must have kept her voice under control, because her answers were beyond his earshot. Amid the commotion, Del hadn't noticed the woman earlier and hadn't seen her face, but now he examined her from the rear. Her graying brown hair ended in curves halfway down her neckline. She wore a casual top and pants, a conservative mix, yet one that revealed she was in respectable physical shape. A decent ass. By Del's estimation, this woman was pushing age fifty and was in no particular hurry to get there.

She accented her answers with an occasional hand gesture, just two females having a conversation. She appeared neither fazed nor honored to be the center of attention. She didn't seem to care that she was on camera.

One little nugget of attention was all Del needed to remind people he was still alive, still available. A reluctant hero who'd stopped a crime, albeit without realizing it at the time. A man of destiny.

*She's stealing my spotlight!*

He couldn't buy a twist of fate like this. A publicist couldn't have arranged it. This opportunity had dropped into his hands, then slipped between his fingers like water.

*He* was the one who'd gotten rammed in the shoulder! The scent of the kid's cheap cigarettes still lingered on his shirt. The kid reeked of them, and now Del did, too. And all for naught!

Before he knew it, the reporter concluded the interview.

"Thank you for your time anyway, ma'am." The reporter turned to her partner and nodded toward their van. "This is just a petty theft, nothing big here. Let's go." And they trodded in Del's direction.

When the kid, still clutching his knee, heard this, his mouth fell open, his eyes wide in aghast.

"What the fuck?!" the kid screamed at the reporter. "What do you mean, 'nothing big'? My fucking knee's broken!"

Either the reporter didn't hear his bellows or ignored them. She didn't even bother to look back. Even the store manager scratched his head, as though confused because nobody had asked him to give his side of the story. As the reporter passed Del, he caught her eye. She offered him a confident smirk but didn't slow her pace.

Several blocks away, sirens wailed, which Del assumed were police vehicles. The news van departed before they arrived.

The woman who had given the interview turned around

and tucked her hair behind her ear. She studied the thief, as though indecisive about whether to tend to him, then bit her lower lip and peered at the approaching police vehicles and their twirling emergency lights. She must have decided the professionals would take care of the kid's needs, because she headed in Del's direction, scratching her brow furrowed as she tried to make sense of what had unfolded in the last five minutes.

She was quite attractive, he had to admit, even if she did steal his spotlight—and all for nothing. But on a positive note, at least neither he nor she would get dragged into a police investigation. Technically, neither of them had witnessed a crime. Just a kid on the run, even if it didn't take a genius to determine what had occurred.

Whether he made a conscious decision to do so or just reacted, Del didn't know, but he offered the woman a grin when she crossed his path.

"A lot of excitement, eh?" he said.

She paused midstride. "Apparently. I didn't really see what happened—"

Their eyes locked, and Del felt his pupils dilate, a reaction that appeared mutual in the first split second he looked into her brown eyes.

From a closer vantage point, Del noticed subtle age spots on her cheeks. Now he estimated she was in her sixties. Quite a bit older than he preferred in a female companion, but she looked damn good for her age. She possessed a classic, understated beauty.

In the aftermath of the confusion, the woman pursed her lips, peering this way and that. Del was glad the kid, who now shook his cuffed hands and wailed in protest, hadn't collided with her and hurt her.

"Are you okay?" Del asked.

The woman moved a strand of hair from her face with her

left hand. No wedding band.

"I'm fine, thank you."

They exchanged glances again. Del hesitated. He couldn't believe he was doing this.

"Can I buy you a cup of coffee?"

At first, she didn't reply. She chewed her thumbnail a moment, no doubt sizing him up and determining whether he seemed safe. When she caught herself chewing her nail, she grimaced and dropped her hand, the way one would when smothering the remnant of a habit broken but not forgotten.

Judging from the way her glance lingered, Del could tell she found him attractive. His heartbeat quickened.

"I'm sorry, I'm a little shaken at the moment," she replied.

Del felt blood rush to the surface of his flesh. He hoped he wasn't blushing. He'd better provide cover for himself.

"I didn't mean to make a big deal out of the offer. It's just a cup of coffee—"

She grinned as she held up a hand to stop him. "It's okay, I meant my brain is a bit preoccupied after—" She nodded behind her, then a worried expression overcame her face. "Oh, I forgot about that young guy. Normally, I wouldn't have walked away and ignored him, but everything erupted so fast." She turned and noticed two paramedics had arrived to assess the damage. The kid had hobbled to his feet. "I'm sure they have it covered, though. And it looks like he might've exaggerated about his knee."

Del grinned. "It appears he turned a minor scuff into a mortal wound."

She returned her attention to Del, her face now solid with satisfaction. "Yes, a cup of coffee sounds nice, thank you. I don't think my nerves will handle anything beyond decaf, though."

Relief rushed through him. To face rejection within reach of his own star on the Hollywood Walk of Fame? How pathetic that would have been!

"I'm Del," he said, reaching out his hand.

As the woman smiled, fresh life filled her eyes. She tilted her head to one side. Del felt magnetic attraction drawing them together.

"Felicia," she replied with a handshake, feminine yet confident. "Nice to meet you, Del."

# CHAPTER 13

WITHIN A FEW MINUTES of settling into two well-stuffed chairs in a coffee shop around the corner—to Del's surprise and, he suspected, to hers as well—Del and Felicia had each other laughing.

"So what does Felicia do for a living?" Del asked.

"Felicia is a minister," she replied.

Del felt his mouth drop open. "A lady minister?"

"We do exist."

"What would bring a minister to Hollywood Boulevard?"

"I have a meeting in the area this afternoon, so I decided to come early. I was on my way to lunch."

"You must be starving by now. Let me buy you something to eat."

"Given the course of events earlier, I managed to lose my appetite." She shrugged. "I could stand to lose a few pounds, anyway."

"You? No, you look perfect." When she shot him a curious look, Del cleared his throat and sought to backtrack his remarks. "I apologize for my reaction to your career. When I picture a minister, a man always comes to mind. Apparently, I'm not immune to stereotypes."

Felicia waved off his comment. "You're not alone, believe me."

"You've seen worse?"

"I've been looked down upon by people in other churches. Then there are others who, when they learn I'm a minister, show a degree of respect for the office but don't take me seriously. Some don't believe women should be allowed to preach or teach."

"Yet you soldier on?"

"Life is too short to worry about the naysayers. Too many people need help." Dressed in black pants, she crossed her legs and lifted the coffee to her lips. She drank it black. "Not that people's opinions have ever bothered me. I've always been something of a free spirit."

"How so?"

"Let's just say you and I grew up in similar eras."

"I refuse to ask your age," he said.

"I'm sixty-eight."

"You look terrific for sixty-eight."

"Thank you." She set her coffee cup on the end table they shared.

Del inhaled the aroma of coffee beans and noticed he no longer detected the scent of the petty thief's cigarettes on his shirt. Smooth jazz music played overhead, which complemented the coffeehouse's organic shades of autumn.

"You have to admit, a free spirit does defy the stereotype of a minister," Del said.

"What can I say? I'm a child of the sixties."

"The sixties? You were barely out of the cradle," Del winked.

"And you're good," Felicia replied with a staccato laugh Del found endearing. "I was fifteen years old in 1969. One of the last of the hippies."

"How'd you wind up in that situation?"

"I have two older siblings who were involved in the whole counterculture thing, so I followed suit. Obviously, I didn't find it satisfying. I no longer wear love beads."

"Good riddance to bad rubbish, as they say."

"I wore Janis Joplin sunglasses. Long, frizzy hair. It was pretty bad." Felicia shook her head as she reminisced and took another drink of her coffee. "But here we are in the twenty-first century, and people haven't changed. I understand how it feels to search for meaning in life. It's the classic pursuit, as old as human history. Eras change, people exchange love beads for tattoos, but the search remains the same. The need is intrinsic. Everybody seeks to explain the inexplicable, to reach for something higher than themselves, to know they fit into a bigger picture. Everyone yearns for significance."

"And you help them find their way?"

"The best I can," she replied. "I'm not a perfect individual. Not by any means. I don't have all the answers, but I can offer one overarching answer."

"The God thing?" Del said. "I grew up with religion. Back home in Nebraska."

"Imagine that."

"It was a long time ago."

"But not today?"

Del shrugged. "I'm not opposed to it. I suppose I've found fulfillment in other ways." He tapped the handle of his cup. It was green, the color of a sour apple. "The minister at our little country church was always kind to me."

Felicia regarded him for a beat. "You never mentioned what you do for a living. Unless you're enjoying retirement."

"I'll never retire. I'm not made for that," he said with a chuckle. "I'm an actor."

"That's impressive. Anything I'd know?"

"Sure, a whole list of them. But I'll always consider *The Changing Tides* my best work."

"That's one I haven't seen in a few years. A classic, though. You must have had a plum role in that one if you consider it your best work."

Del couldn't hide his amusement. "I'm beginning to think you're serious."

Felicia wrinkled her eyebrows, as though accepting a punch line existed but unsure what it was. "Did I say something wrong?"

"No, it's just—you don't know who I am, do you?" Del marveled.

"I'm sorry, should I?"

"I received an Oscar nomination for *The Changing Tides.*"

Felicia rested her hand on her palm. "Really? Let me try to picture you..."

"I was fairly young back then."

"Let me see...*The Changing Tides*...a guy named Del..." Felicia squinted her eyes as she concentrated on him. No words passed between them for a while. Then she tossed him a look of skepticism. "You're kidding me. Del Corwyn? You're *that* Del?"

"The one and only."

"My, my. This *is* an honor," she teased. "You'll have to excuse me. I tend not to run into many actors in my line of work, and I don't seek them out."

"After all, what would a minister find attractive in a guy like me, right?"

"Don't sell yourself short. I'm a minister, but I'm still female."

With each passing moment, Del found this woman more beautiful, yet he found himself drawn to Felicia for a reason *unrelated* to her beauty. Was it the confidence that oozed through her pores? Or perhaps it was her contentment. Whatever it was, he felt at ease with her. He'd always used his career to draw attention from the opposite sex, but today, he was astonished at the refreshment he discovered in capturing a woman's interest because of who he was on the inside. This was new.

Del wanted the afternoon to linger.

Felicia checked her watch, then gasped as she slammed her cup on the table. Coffee splashed on the napkin beneath the cup.

"My meeting! I need to be there in ten minutes!" She shot up from her chair, grabbed her purse, and sighed. "I lost track of time. I hate to abandon you, Del, but I do need to go."

Del's reflexes kicked in. He jumped from his seat. He couldn't let her disappear from his life just like that.

*Say something! Anything!*

"I'd love to see you again, Felicia."

She stopped. Gazed into his eyes. Time slowed.

She responded with a delightful smile. Del remembered to breathe again.

"That sounds nice."

Del fished in his pocket for a pen, then handed it to her, along with an unused napkin. "Write down your number and I'll give you a call later."

She nodded. In a flurry, she jotted her name and number on the napkin, then spun around and darted for the door. From halfway across the room, she peered over her shoulder and waved good-bye.

Del felt like a teenager as he looked at her handwriting. She curved the corners and embellished her fours when she wrote. The free spirit in her had manifested once again.

He lifted her coffee cup and, with a grin, admired the lipstick imprints she'd left behind.

For the first time, Del indulged in the notion that perhaps, years from now, those markings could become an everyday occurrence in his life.

# CHAPTER 14

THAT EVENING, he dialed her number. She answered on the third ring.

"Felicia?"

"Del, you called! I wasn't sure whether I'd hear from you."

"I don't suppose a minister enjoys a glass of wine now and again?"

"Some do. This one does. Why do you ask?"

"Would you like to stop by for a glass of chardonnay on my patio? I have a hunch you would love the view."

"At your home?" She hesitated a beat. "Del, I—"

"No ulterior motives, I promise." And he meant it.

He heard her exhale on the other end of the phone. "I suppose that would be fine."

What was it about this woman that made his heart race?

# CHAPTER 15

THEY CLINKED glasses. He'd opened a bottle of French chardonnay, one he'd reserved in his wine cellar for a special occasion. Del couldn't pinpoint why his heart had moved within him to open it with his present guest, but he had followed his hunch. Aromatic and rich, the wine proved an ideal companion to the coastal breeze as Del and Felicia overlooked the Pacific shore from on high.

"Wow," she remarked as she took her first taste.

"A good reaction, I hope."

"You're looking at a woman on a budget. Most of my wine comes in the form of a box."

Unpretentious—that's how he would describe her. And, by his own admission, his polar opposite in that regard. What were the two of them doing together, still laughing and enjoying each other's company a day after they met? A minister, of all people! What did she see in him? He knew it wasn't the fame factor since she hadn't even recognized him when they met.

He watched as Felicia closed her eyes and breathed deep. Breeze tousled her hair. Why did he find her so captivating?

"Johnny Angel," the 1962 song by Shelley Fabares, interrupted Del's thoughts. His ringtone.

Felicia grabbed her purse and sifted inside. "Yours or mine?"

"Looks like mine." Del waved his phone in the air but

continued to gaze at her.

Incredulous, she nodded at his phone, which continued to ring. "Don't you want to get that?"

To be honest, he didn't want to. He wanted to cradle this snapshot in time. But old habits are hard to break.

"Excuse me a moment." He remained in his seat and tapped his phone to answer it. Before he could utter a greeting, a scream pierced his eardrum.

# CHAPTER 16

"DEL! The nomination! I got it!"

"The Oscar?"

"Yes! They contacted me this morning and I've been in PR mode ever since. But I couldn't end the day without telling you!"

Nora's youthful buzz was contagious. Del recalled his own excitement at hearing such news.

"Congratulations! I told you that you were all but a lock for it. You gave a powerful performance and deserve this. Enjoy every minute of it."

"Del, I have to go, but let's do lunch this week, okay?"

"Sounds like a plan." He paused. The news was bittersweet for him, a reminder of his own shortcomings since his own nomination, yet his happiness for Nora was genuine. "I'm so proud of you."

Another scream. Del cringed at the high pitch, then smirked at the idea of this young woman—this old soul who kept her emotions under lock and key—who suddenly couldn't contain her elation.

He eyed Felicia. "Okay, then, don't party too hard."

When he ended the call, Felicia studied him over the rim of her wineglass. "That sounded exciting."

"A friend of mine. She just received an Oscar nomination and called to share the news. Have you heard of Nora Jumelle?"

"I think so. Dark hair, right? Young?" she replied, nonchalant. "I assume you two are close?"

"We're friends."

"Friends, eh?" she said with a sip, implication heavy in her tone, but in a teasing manner.

Del rolled his eyes. "Maybe more than friends. Once." He paused, then gave Felicia a second glance. "Look, Felicia, I'm not a perfect man, if that's what you think. If I was, I'd be a minister."

She relaxed her shoulders and set her glass on the table. "Ministers aren't perfect either, believe me. Besides, I have enough events tucked away in my hippie phase to fill a book."

"So what changed?"

She paused to consider his question. Her demeanor, though steady, grew matter-of-fact. "I hit emotional rock bottom. Then I found my faith, and that tends to alter things."

He could respect that. Del nodded but didn't pry further.

Then a thought occurred to him.

"What did you mean by 'Yours or mine?'"

"Excuse me?"

"Earlier, when my phone rang. Why did you think it was *your* cell phone ringing?"

"'Johnny Angel' started playing, and I—" Stopping midsentence, she shook her head and chuckled, her eyes narrowing in suspicion, as though Del could have arranged this coincidence. "You're kidding me. We have the same ringtone? I can't say I would've pegged you for that."

Del shrugged. "It's a bit out of character, but 1962 was…well, it was a pivotal year for me."

"How so?"

He thought of Marilyn Monroe. It was one of the final memories he had of her. He had seen a side of her most others hadn't and, to this day, missed her. She had loved that song, and they had sung it together in the car many times in 1962.

That was the year she died.

"It reminds me of a friend who passed away," he replied.

After an awkward silence, Felicia's minister instincts must have prompted her to change the subject.

"So, that's exciting news for your friend Nora."

Del shook himself free from Marilyn's ghost and stepped back into the present.

"Absolutely," he said, though he had a hard time infusing his remark with more than halfhearted enthusiasm.

Felicia cocked her head. "You don't sound as excited for her as she is." When Del responded with a questioning glance, she added with a wink, "I heard her scream from where I'm sitting." And when Del offered no indication of humor, she asked, "Is everything okay?"

Del shifted in his seat. He came from the Baby Boomer generation and preferred not to communicate too many of his feelings. Besides, he wasn't used to confiding in the opposite sex. His relationships with females never tended to progress that far.

So why did a piece of his heart want to open up to *this* woman? That made him nervous. It gave him a sense of yielding control over his own life. Was it because Felicia was close in age and he wasn't accustomed to equal ground? And if he'd gone this long without admitting this particular facet about himself, why do so at the age of seventy-eight?

Then again, was there a reason *not* to?

*Oh crap, I'll give it a shot...*

"You're a preacher, so if I admit something, you'll take to the grave, right?"

She made a tentative reach for her glass. "Of course."

He grimaced. "I'd say there's a side of me that...perhaps...resents—" He stopped himself and decided to hedge his words. "Well, maybe not *resent*—that's a strong word. But when I watch other people succeed in my field, it's difficult to find, shall we say, *enthusiasm* to share in the whole celebration. Don't get me wrong. I *want* to be thrilled for them. Not that it's absent—it's there, I just need to dig for it."

"Why do you think that's the case?"

With a shrug, Del replied, "I'm not exactly a psychologist here. But I didn't always feel that way."

"So what changed?"

Why was he putting himself through this? How ridiculous.

But the sincerity in her brown, teddy-bear eyes invited him to keep talking.

"I mentioned *The Changing Tides*…"

"And your award nomination."

What sweet memories. A glow emerged in Del's inner being, its embers stoked and its flame rekindled. "When that nomination happened, everyone—myself included—expected my career to skyrocket. I received script offers by the dozens, some better than others. The one thing I wanted to *avoid* was making a film that would discredit me as a serious actor. I had an aura now, a professional with the potential for a legendary future, and though I didn't *win* the award that year, the nomination put me on the short list for future ceremonies. So I made a smart choice—what *I* believed was wise, at least—and opted for a project that could replicate my success. Try to win *next* year's statue. So I signed on to a film with a prominent director, one whose projects were daring yet refined. He was like the Alejandro Iñrritu of the late seventies."

"What was the name of the film?"

*"Gardens of Chile."*

Felicia's brow wrinkled. "I don't remember that one."

Del snorted, a mournful little grunt. "No one does. The film plummeted at the box office. We released it in October, while the Hollywood folks were starting to hone in on potential nominees. But the film got such a poor reception, few people bothered to consider it for an award. The only attention it garnered was the director's and my bad decision in making it. I got devoured by the press for that."

Felicia set down her glass. Her clothing swished as she leaned forward, elbows on the arms of her chair, and rested her temple against her forefinger. Del switched his posture and eased the stiffness from his back. In the distance, a seagull screeched. Breakers added a bass line to nature's symphony.

"A month later, the nominees were announced. Our film wasn't on the list—for anything. Not even editing or costume design. I wasn't even mentioned in the press speculation as a possible *contender* in the months leading up to the final selections.

"That spring, a new circle of winners received their awards. And by that point, people had forgotten all about Del Corwyn. The script offers dried up. I lived in the shadows of the next round of actors who made savvier choices for their follow-up projects. Granted, people know my name, they recall a few of my films, but that year, their focus shifted from the future to the past."

Felicia scooted her chair closer. So close, Del picked up traces of pear and plum on her breath.

He took a generous swallow from his glass. Yes, he felt a tad resentful toward those who had leapfrogged over him, but he refused to put any bitterness on public display. He had his pride, after all.

Del shook his head. To this day, he remained awestruck at the speed at which his career had vanished.

"It's ironic, isn't it?" he mused aloud. "That Oscar nomination looked like a door that would open to more greatness, abundant opportunities—but it turned out to be the death knell of a thriving career." He turned to Felicia. "People see the glitz and glamour, but the truth is, we're working people like everyone else. We have bills to pay. We have dreams and desires, the sense that you can accomplish much more than you have already. So my life has been a series of what-ifs ever since."

As Felicia listened, Del found compassion in her stare.

"You want your life to matter," she said at last. "That's not a bad thing, Del."

"One week, early in my career, I had a small role on *This is the Life*. Remember that television show? The religious one? That counts as a good deed, right?"

Felicia grinned at his sad attempt at humor.

In this moment of honesty, Del couldn't hide his embarrassment. "I *look* like I'm a guy who matters—or *mattered* at one point. But the truth is, I'm not so sure how relevant I am anymore. And the what-if that frightens me is the notion that I'll reach the end of my life, and on my gravestone, etched in letters that'll withstand wind and rain and corrosion, you'll find a memory of something that happened in 1978, as if I hadn't been alive all those years since. One inch shy of invisible."

Felicia took his hand in hers, examined his aging fingers, then gazed into his eyes.

"Sometimes we matter in ways we can't begin to fathom, Del."

Del responded with a lifeless chortle. "I appreciate the kind gesture, I really do. But I've seen people spend their whole lives searching for relevancy."

His mind flickered to his "Johnny Angel" duet in the car with Marilyn back in 1962.

"Some people's lives have ended without resolution," he said. "What a tragedy."

He peered down at his hand in hers, both hands speckled with faint age spots, his more numerous than hers. He, however, had tried to hide his own beneath a perpetual tan.

When their eyes met again, he wondered how far she could see into his soul.

Del exhaled.

"And that, my dear, is what scares the hell out of me most in life."

# CHAPTER 17

THE REALTOR WAS all business.

Del couldn't recall the day he'd bought this home, but he knew he'd never forget the day he put it back on the market. Though he hated to admit it, Pevely had gotten through to him. He didn't want to trim down, but he had no job prospects in the pipeline, and who knew when he would? He needed to downsize. He also needed to search for a new home and find one fast. Not that he couldn't fit it into his schedule. These days, if he had one resource in abundance, it was spare time.

All he had to do was sign on the line at the bottom of the agreement he held in his hands. Once he did, his home would be on the market.

His gut wrenched.

He held the pen an inch above the paperwork, but his hand wavered. He couldn't bring himself to sign his name. Del glared at the realtor.

"Only serious buyers," Del stressed. "I don't want people traipsing through my house on a celebrity tour."

"Absolutely. That goes without saying," replied the man in a red tie and blazer, his tone either reassuring or patronizing. Del couldn't pinpoint which. "Don't fret, Mr. Corwyn. I've listed and sold many homes with sellers of your caliber."

"Yes, you came highly recommended."

"I believe your home will sell quickly."

Del winced.

This whole process broke his heart, but he resolved to maintain a firm veneer and the upper hand—even though he felt like he'd lost a battle in life. Like a World War II soldier he'd portrayed as a young man, a fighter who'd suffered a mortal wound in Normandy while his compatriots pressed on toward victory.

What a mess. His life wasn't supposed to turn out this way.

Del's hand shook as he procrastinated. He stretched to work a crick out of his neck.

And forced himself to sign his name.

# CHAPTER 18

THAT NIGHT, Del poured himself a stiff drink. Something to take his mind off of leaving his memories behind.

He marveled at his own deftness. For so long, he'd outmaneuvered reality, convincing himself that he lived in a fantasy realm of his own making. But today, reality had slapped him in the face with a wet towel.

As he licked a remnant of liquor from his lips, Del wandered through rooms and hallways. He recalled parties he'd hosted here, with acquaintances like Burt Lancaster, Sonny and Cher, Natalie Wood. And who could forget the famous Jacks: Lemmon. Nicholson. Palance. All right here.

He lived in a small mansion and, truth be told, seldom stepped foot into some of the rooms farthest from his bedroom. After all, he was a bachelor. He didn't need to spend time in them, and he no longer entertained guests the way he had in the past. Ridiculous as it might sound, as the years rolled along, he'd *forgotten* to step foot all the way over there.

Rocking the drink in his hand, he listened to the ice rattle and took another gulp. When he reached the far end of his house, his eyes fell upon a door to the left. A storage room. Talk about the old days—he hadn't gone inside there since...when? Wow, the drink had started to make his mind fuzzy.

Upon opening the door and flipping the light switch, he

entered a large storage room filled with boxes stacked in rows. Del had stashed all of his old memorabilia in here, tokens he'd kept from various sets on which he'd worked, along with other miscellaneous items he couldn't recall if he tried. Not that he was a hoarder. On the contrary, these belongings had come into his possession so fast, he'd needed to put them *somewhere.* At least they were already in boxes. Less packing required when he moved.

Walking several feet into the room, he brushed his finger along the boxes he passed. Traces of dust lay upon the tops of each row, but they were minimal. Nobody entered to stir things up.

Lifting one box lid, he found scripts from the early seventies, projects he'd considered but declined. Some had entered production; others hadn't. Why had he kept them? Maybe he *was* a pack rat after all. But perhaps they were worth something nowadays.

Setting that box on the floor, he opened the next one in the stack. Here he found old letters—with four-cent postage stamps! Many were from friends who had lived in Manhattan, plus family members, long since deceased, with whom he'd kept in touch.

From the bottom of the box, he retrieved a thick manila envelope. On its face, someone had scrawled his name in feminine handwriting. Turning it over, he unwound the red string of the envelope's clasp and pulled out a screenplay bound with brass fasteners along the sides. Protected in the envelope, the brass had lost its sheen around the edges but remained in solid condition. The white paper had discolored with age and, Del swore, felt heavier with the passage of time.

True to its era, someone had constructed the screenplay on a typewriter, then sandwiched it between two sheets of manila card stock. In the lower corner of each page, Del found a small, handwritten box with a fingerprint inside, large enough to resemble a thumb. Whoever made the print had used black ink, the type of ink pad one would have used with a rubber stamp.

Clipped to the card stock, Del found a cover letter, which its writer appeared to have constructed on the same typewriter. He pulled his reading glasses from his shirt pocket and put them on.

The letter was dated March 12, 1962. The same thumbprint appeared in its lower corner. Its signature block contained a name scrawled by hand in faded blue ink:

### *Marilyn Monroe*

Del gasped. He remembered this! He'd forgotten about it as the decades elapsed, but now that he read her letter again, its familiarity returned:

My Dearest Del,

After filming *The Prince and the Showgirl,* I felt exhausted. As you know, I went on hiatus for nearly two years after making that film. Arthur and I had an opportunity to bond, to travel, to enjoy each other's company, to escape the spotlight if only for a short time. As you can imagine, I couldn't bear to escape for long! I sought to mature as an actress, to become an artist who would be taken seriously. Working with Laurence Olivier had left me feeling morose. I felt inadequate, childish and whimsical, rather than an equal, the woman who had produced that film with him.

A hiatus of that nature also allows much time for searching one's soul, for exploring new endeavors. And it was during this season of relaxation that I tried my hand at something new: pouring my soul into the written word. Perhaps it would help me make sense of this turmoil inside me. As it turns out, the endeavor accomplished exactly that, but I fear what I have written.

Del, you have been a true friend to me, one of the few people I trust in this confusing world, especially after some of those I trusted locked me up in that mental institution. I almost didn't escape. What would stop them from betraying me again? If they read what I have written, they might send me back to that damned place.

Yet I have a lingering fear that something imminent is about to occur, so I shall put this script into your hands. Should I no longer be able to make my own decisions, you shall have authority to do with this script as you see fit, and to reveal it in its proper time.

People will, no doubt, wonder about the authenticity of this script. Many will refuse to believe I had the intelligence to write such a thing. Therefore, I have placed my thumbprint on each and every page. When they read my words and see the precaution I've taken to prove its authenticity, everyone will know I wasn't the silly, dumb blond I played in pictures.

This world hurts, darling. You've been my compass through life's dark, confusing maze. This letter explains much, but words could never express how much you mean to me.

With love,

Marilyn Monroe

Del took another gulp and laid down his glass. Taking a seat upon a box, he began to page through the screenplay. Given the pace of his career at the time she'd given it to him, he hadn't had a chance to read her words. But as he read them tonight, the mental fog cleared and he remembered the day she placed this piece of work into his hands.

———

"You wrote a screenplay?"

Wide-eyed, Del ran his fingers across the crisp, white paper, a stack of sheets bound together by brass fasteners along its left margin. He was in his early twenties.

"Don't look so surprised," Marilyn Monroe replied with a staccato laugh. "I'm a woman of many wonderful traits." Though thirty-six years old, she took childlike pleasure in his reaction. Innocent. She had exquisite diction, a byproduct of training with Natasha Lytess, her first acting coach.

"When did you write this?"

"During my hiatus, the one I took after we wrapped up production on *The Prince and the Showgirl*. Arthur and I split our time between New York and Connecticut, and he helped me as I wrote," she replied, her countenance now matter-of-fact, her voice sultry yet airy. "I believe it was an outlet for him, too. He was so frustrated by that time, wondering about his own future. He believed in me, and I think it helped him believe in himself. So as I wrote the scenes, he gave me advice on how to make the characters richer, more alive."

They sat together in the living room of her home in Brentwood. "Johnny Angel" played on her phonograph. They were alone in the house.

"This must have taken a long time to write."

"I had eighteen months before I returned to Hollywood to shoot *Some Like It Hot*," she replied. Her gaze fell to the floor, and her voice grew softer. "I'd been through so much by that point. Trying to make my second marriage work. The pain of losing a child…"

As her words drifted, young Del noticed she had waded into the territory of the forlorn. For the past year, she had seemed more prone toward that tendency, and pain filled Del's heart whenever he watched it emerge. He tried to return her attention to the script, which seemed to make her happy. It was an obvious source of pride for her.

"You never mentioned you're a writer. Why doesn't anybody know?"

Her countenance brightened again, and Del felt relieved. She shot him a cunning glare.

"There's more to me than the reporters know about," she replied with a wink, wagging a red-polished fingernail at him, ever the mentor. "Here's an important tip for you: *Never tell them everything.* Always keep a little secret or two for yourself, something to hold in your heart. Something *you* can control in this crazy world."

Del fanned the pages, opening the document at random points to scan snippets of dialogue. What a sense of accomplishment she must have felt! He admired its professional layout, which looked identical to the scripts he'd used on the sets. Del wondered if Marilyn had typed this on the manual typewriter he'd seen Arthur Miller use in their home.

"Is this any good?" Del asked. "I mean, have you shown it to anyone?"

"Only to Arthur, back when we were married." She giggled in her typical Marilyn manner. "Can you imagine? The great Arthur Miller coaches Marilyn Monroe in literature," she punctuated with a male reporter's voice, underscoring it with faux solemnity. "You do know he rewrote the script for *Let's Make Love,* don't you? He said the original was a catastrophe and he wanted to protect me. Wasn't that sweet? Many people don't know that. He wrote the script for *The Misfits,* too. The man certainly knows what he's doing, if you ask me. Look at *Death of a Salesman*. Pure genius! Regardless of how our marriage worked out, the man was a brilliant writer."

Young Del ran his hand across Marilyn's screenplay again, eager to read it from beginning to end. Maybe they could perform in it together!

Yet he couldn't ignore a chill that raced up his spine. Why here? Why now?

"Why are you giving this to me?" he asked.

Marilyn regarded him a moment. Her somberness returned. Biting the inside of her cheek, she looked toward her left, which struck Del as nothing more than an attempt to procrastinate before giving him an answer. When she met his stare again, Del saw the vulnerability of a young girl. Was it a plea?

"We're friends, aren't we?" she whispered.

"Of course we are."

"I need you to keep this safe for me."

She returned it to its large envelope, along with a letter, which Del hadn't read.

"I don't understand. Why can't you keep it here at home? Why won't you show it to anybody?"

She enveloped herself in her arms, as though to comfort herself with her own embrace. Her next words sounded measured.

"Do you ever get goose bumps, Del?"

"Yes."

She nodded. "I've gotten goose bumps a lot as of late. It scares me."

"Why?"

"Because I fear something is about to happen."

Del's pulse surged. "Don't you feel safe? What's going to happen?"

Her pupils shrank in what appeared to Del a blend of

confusion and fear.

"It's just a feeling I get," she said. "Bobby and Jack—a lot of people follow them around. People who *watch* me. They whisper into little microphones and show up at nearby tables in restaurants when they think I don't notice them."

"Bobby and Jack *Kennedy?*" he exclaimed. "The Attorney General and the President?"

"It's not just them," she replied. "Joe McCarthy tried to target me as an enemy of the state, remember? And others even say I'm a danger to myself."

Del noticed she still hadn't answered his question: *What's going to happen?*

"Should something happen to me, you'll know what to do with this evidence."

"Evidence?"

"They'll use it against me. To try to say I'm crazy. And I'm *not* crazy, Del." She paused, a woman in mourning. She had lost much in the last ten years. For that matter, Del wondered if she'd *ever* known genuine joy. "When the time is right, I'll retrieve it from you. But for now, I can't keep it in this house. No one can see this. I'm frightened, Del."

"That's silly. What do you have to be afraid of?"

"I don't want them to send me back to that horrid place."

"What place?"

"That institution. The mental one." She closed her eyes. Wincing, she added, "I hated that place."

When she opened her eyes, Del found them covered with a film of tears. At that point, he realized the memories she hid in the corners of her soul must haunt her. Every day.

Her jaw firmed. She blinked back her tears. Fury filled her eyes.

"They'll never lock me up like a criminal again. People have tried to lock me up all my life."

"Marilyn—"

JOHN HERRICK

"They have, Del. They locked me in an orphanage when I was a girl. They locked me in that horrible institution when I was an adult. I begged them not to, but that's what happens when they believe you're weak. When they think they can have their way with you. I'll *never* let them do that to me again."

"But if you're scared of that, why did you take the risk by writing this?"

"I needed to get the torment out of me somehow. The anger. The pain. The pressure. The confusion—I grew up so fast. I married so young. And when I was a little girl—" Her eyes sealed shut again. She took a labored breath, regained her composure, and changed course, perhaps to escape a memory that held particular pain. "I was desperate, Del. So I poured it all into these pages. Perhaps they can lock up my body, but they can't lock up my soul." Tapping the envelope, she added, "This darkness is part of me. I can't help it. This is who I am."

Del watched as her eyes turned sullen, pleading, once again.

She placed her hand upon his. "But if they read this script—if they see what has gone through my mind—'She's a threat to herself,' they'll say. 'She has a violent temperament. She's sexually disturbed.' And you know what will happen next? My independence will disappear. They'll send me back to that horrible place. And this time, I may not escape. I almost didn't make it out the first time." She focused on him, the plea in her eyes growing. "Please, Del. Please take care of this. Will you promise me?"

90

# CHAPTER 19

AS HE RELIVED that memory, Del shook his head. Marilyn had a reputation for being difficult on the set, for forgetting her lines, for showing up late. She was world-renowned by that time. An enigma to some; a hassle to others.

But no one had *immortalized* her yet.

And so, when she had handed Del her screenplay, it was nothing more than a side project from a friend, handed to him for safekeeping. He'd had no way of knowing he held a piece of history at the time.

That wouldn't be the case today.

Del had never told a soul of its existence. He had tucked it away and, ashamed as he felt to admit, forgotten about it. In the weeks and months following Marilyn's death, he'd wanted to open the script and read its pages but wondered if he could bring himself to do so. As much as he missed her, reading her words would have invoked a measure of grief.

He reminisced how the public had adored her. Del also recalled how many of her peers had scoffed at her and discounted her talent.

Yet it appeared Marilyn might, after all these years, have the last laugh.

Del finished his drink.

He considered stuffing the package into a small vault embedded in the wall of his study, secured with two layers of combination locks and hidden behind a painting, then decided against it. Too predictable in the event of a burglary.

He would put this package in his safe deposit box tomorrow.

# CHAPTER 20

AS DEL LAY in bed that night, sleep evaded him. He'd begin to doze, catch himself, then shudder awake again. He couldn't help it; energy buzzed through him.

His mind returned to the treasure he'd extracted from his personal collection that evening and deliberated on what to do with it.

An original screenplay written by Marilyn Monroe!

He could picture the reaction among industry executives. After all her films and as much as people thought they knew about her, not even a rumor had arisen that she was a writer, too. They would eat this news for lunch and spit out the seeds.

Had she sought a last laugh against her detractors and tasked Del as the guy who would arrange her chess pawns on the board?

After dwelling in obscurity, would Del Corwyn emerge as a kingmaker?

Still, his moral compass tugged at him. Del considered his motives and couldn't deny he stood to gain much from this scenario. To most people, Marilyn Monroe was an icon, but not to him. Suppose he shopped her screenplay among producers. Would that honor her memory? Or would it betray their friendship?

This discovery, if revealed to the public, could also mark his final comeback, and that struck Del as self-serving. If he used her iconic status for his own gain, would he be any better than those who had used her in the past? He didn't want to do that. No, some things in life are sacred.

Then again, she had placed the script in his care so he could make the best decision on her behalf, not necessarily because she wanted it hidden. Wasn't that the wish expressed in her letter? For Del to do with the screenplay as he saw fit? To reveal it in its proper time?

After all, she had longed for her peers to take her seriously as an artist, beyond the sex appeal and publicity that hounded her. She was a shrewd businesswoman and had even obtained a production deal as part of her contract. Marilyn Monroe Productions had produced *The Prince and the Showgirl.* And how could Del forget the acting coaches Marilyn toted with her to every film set? Del remembered how controlling others had considered Natasha Lytess and Paula Strasberg.

No, Del concluded, Marilyn wouldn't want her hard work hidden. Knowing her, if she had invested the time writing for the public, she would have intended to share it.

To this day, fascination and speculation continued to swirl around the actress. And now she had given her friends and fans the opportunity to see another side of her.

Unable to resist the temptation, Del had decided to read the first pages of her screenplay before going to bed. Within a few minutes, he couldn't stop. He'd torn through the pages. True to her word, what she had written would lure the public into the most intimate regions—and the darkest psychological corners—of her mind and heart.

And they would discover that the Marilyn Monroe they thought they knew was, in fact, a mere fraction of who she was.

Indeed, even Del had found some of the content disturbing. He could understand why she feared showing it to anyone while she was alive. Del often wondered if the time she had spent in the psychological ward, locked away against her will, had damaged her rather than healed her. He had doubted her suspicions that she might have wound up imprisoned there again—this time permanently—if they had read her words and discovered this side of her personality. After reading her words, however, Del couldn't say those suspicions weren't warranted.

When it came to this endeavor, the woman was ahead of her time. Even today, it would prove controversial, testing the borders of what mainstream society was willing to accept on film. Yet, wasn't that what she'd sought during her career, to forge a path for herself that no one else could duplicate?

Perhaps now she would receive the recognition she deserved, even if it arrived posthumously.

Del's eyelids felt raw along their edges. He needed sleep.

He turned on the lamp beside his bed. Reaching for his phone, he hit speed dial and awaited his agent's voicemail greeting.

"Arnie, this is Del. We need to meet tomorrow, probably in the afternoon. I have a couple of errands to run beforehand. This is urgent. Trust me, you'll want to *make* room for this."

# CHAPTER 21

NORA COULDN'T SHAKE the heaviness.

News of her Oscar nomination had brought a wave of elation. So why did she feel so despondent this morning?

She'd gotten minimal sleep last night, and unfortunately, that wasn't an isolated case. She had fought insomnia for weeks. Though she'd tried sleeping pills on the worst nights, she hesitated at the idea of pumping barbiturates into her body. She wasn't a fan of laboratory chemicals and had heard horror stories of addiction.

She'd avoided a pill last night. And so, on top of her glum emotional state, she felt exhausted.

Random chatter surrounded her as other customers waited in line to place their orders. One customer carried away a cheddar-jalapeno bagel, crisp from the toaster oven, the tang of its charred edges enticing her. India.Arie's "A Beautiful Day" played overhead. Nora wished her heart could take hold of the song.

Same coffee shop. Having maintained her anonymity for a longer stretch of time, she wanted to believe she'd grown more agile at it. As long as she kept herself hidden, no one recognized her here. Given time, she knew that would change, which would force her to move on, to find another shop where she could bide her time and try to make sense of her life.

In the meantime, however, she enjoyed this semblance of

freedom.

She'd entered the coffee shop dressed in a baseball cap, sunglasses and a track suit, as though she had come from a gym. She hoped, by dressing like she didn't care about her appearance, it would decrease the likelihood that anyone would recognize her or even give her a second glance.

Nora placed her order, then wandered away from the counter. The shop possessed the air of a gourmet gift shop, somewhere between urban and rural, and smelled like cinnamon sticks. The tables and chairs were the color of walnuts, and interspersed among them sat quaint shelves of products for sale—bags of coffee beans, boxes of loose-leaf tea, mugs and thermoses imprinted with a corporate logo and a clever quip. The cacophony of voices, a coffee grinder, and drink equipment ushered liveliness into an otherwise laid-back environment.

She wandered to one corner and browsed a community bulletin board while she awaited her drink. She scanned the advertised events and services: a dentist and chiropractor, an upcoming trivia night to benefit a local animal shelter, piano lessons.

Then she noticed a business card with a tagline printed in green letters across the top:

### FIND YOUR HAPPINESS. REGAIN YOUR LIFE.

Beneath the tagline, the remaining text was printed in black. It looked like a normal business card. No picture; then again, she wouldn't have expected one. She perused its next lines.

### RUSSELL MERRITT, WELLNESS COACH
*Online guidance to accommodate your schedule and needs.*

A wellness coach? She'd heard of them but always wondered who sought their advice.

Nora had battled waves of depression ever since fame arrived in her life, yet she hadn't confided in anyone about it. She didn't want rumors to travel. Plus, she felt a tinge of shame, along with a measure of embarrassment: Why should she feel down? Millions of people would give their life's savings to switch places with her.

Another inspection of Russell Merritt's card.

Nora glanced around the room and, to her relief, found nobody paying attention to her. Lifting the pushpin, she removed the card from the bulletin board and slid it into her pocket. As soon as she removed her hand, a shout startled her.

"Venti skinny hazelnut latte with soy milk for Shelly!"

Shelly. Was that the alias Nora had given the cashier? She'd already forgotten. It was the drink she'd ordered, though.

She found a cozy chair at the far end of the dining area, angled away from most customers and beyond their immediate view, just in case someone happened to study her and figure out who she was. People in Los Angeles were accustomed to celebrities in their midst. They didn't make a spectacle when they spotted one. Even so, she could sense their tactful stares. If someone recognized her today, she decided, she would bolt. She didn't feel like being the center of attention, not when she felt like shedding tears.

Settling into the chair, she removed her smart phone from her purse and posted an update to her social media accounts.

The latte burned her throat as it descended. She remembered the business card she'd hidden in her pocket, pulled it out, and gave it another once-over. What could it hurt to visit the guy's website? Nora rolled her eyes at how ridiculous she felt entering the site address.

Russell Merritt had a pristine, organized website. When she opened his bio page, Nora found a photo of a polished, professional man in a tie and modern eyeglasses. Judging from the hints of gray above his ears, Nora estimated he was in his late forties. She gave him a second perusal. Was it considered unacceptable to find your wellness coach sexy? He looked like a man who had his life together and savored every moment, regardless of how banal or significant it was. Behind the eyeglass frames, his eyes appeared gentle. Understanding.

According to his bio, he had spent the last fifteen years coaching satisfied clients from all walks of life. And sure enough, when she read his coaching policy, she confirmed their interaction would occur online only. They would never need to meet face-to-face.

"This offers many clients the privacy and anonymity they seek," Nora read.

The first appointment was free, which allowed prospective clients to determine whether the arrangement worked for them before they pursued the relationship further.

Nora was intrigued.

Total anonymity? She had nothing to lose. She could create an alias for herself. This guy would never deduce her true identity. And unlike visiting a psychologist, Nora wouldn't have to endure the awkwardness of looking this man in the eye, admitting private details to someone who had seen images of her ten feet tall.

Russell Merritt required neither contract nor commitment. If his advice didn't help, she could move on, no strings attached.

Maybe he would have answers. Stranger things had happened to her.

Following the directions on the website, she created a user account. It didn't require her to enter a name for the trial session, just an email address, for which she entered the account she used for junk mail. Then she submitted an initial message expressing nothing more than a desire to chat.

She wondered how long she would have to wait for a reply. She assumed it would take twenty-four hours.

# CHAPTER 22

UPON RETURNING HOME from her coffee run, Nora grabbed her tablet and fell onto the sofa in her living room. She checked her email for any scripts of interest which her agent might have passed along. Finding none, she opened her Internet browser, surfed a bit, and landed on a website about Eastern religions and philosophies.

She marveled at people who found higher meaning in their lives. Nora wondered if she would ever unlock that type of contentment in her own life, though she kept her search casual, reading material in spare moments like this. Maybe, one day, she would stumble upon a way to escape the sense of isolation that nagged her in the midst of her success.

A notification popped up on her screen. Russell Merritt had responded to her request. According to his message, she could reply to schedule an appointment to chat online, or they could interact by email.

Or, if she was available in the next thirty minutes, they could conduct a live chat immediately. He provided instructions on how to log into his website's chat program.

Nora checked the clock. It was worth a try.

**CAGirl202:** Are you there, Mr. Merritt?

She curled her legs beneath her and leaned against the arm of the sofa. Less than a minute later, she heard a chime and, sure enough, his reply appeared.

**RMerritt44:** Please feel free to call me Russell. Would you prefer me to call you by name?

Nora stopped. She didn't want to use her real name, but calling her by username seemed silly. Cali Girl? Hold on...

**CAGirl202:** Call me Callie. I'm the one who emailed you an hour ago.

**RMerritt44:** Hi Callie. Thanks for reaching out. You didn't mention any specifics.

**CAGirl202:** I've never contacted a coach before. How discreet is this?

**RMerritt44:** That's the primary benefit of this online environment. You can remain as anonymous as you wish. I keep everything confidential, as long as you don't mention anything illegal.

**CAGirl202:** Of course not. I just meant I need to stay discreet.

**RMerritt44:** Understood. I have several clients in that situation.

**CAGirl202:** So how does this work? Do I spill my guts and you take it from there?

**RMerritt44:** Some clients consider me a good sounding board. Others seek ways to advance their careers or general well-being. Do you have a particular goal?

**CAGirl202:** Honestly? I'm not sure why I contacted you. I have a great life. My career is on track. In fact, you could say it's on a fast track. I have every reason to be happy.

**RMerritt44:** But you're not?

Nora squirmed in her seat. *Was* she happy? Logic told her she should be.

**CAGirl202:** Do you know how it feels to know you *should* be happy, but you can't quite get there?

**RMerritt44:** So you seek contentment?

**CAGirl202:** Maybe.

**RMerritt44:** And perhaps a larger perspective on the meaning of life?

Nora found herself growing more comfortable with him.

**CAGirl202:** I have this yearning inside me that nobody else can see. I don't like not having answers. It makes me feel like I don't have control of my own life, and I'm used to being in control.
**RMerritt44:** What do you do for a living?

She bit her lip. With a groan, she hedged her answer.

**CAGirl202:** I can't go into much detail. Let's say I'm in the public eye. Will that suffice?
**RMerritt44:** It makes much more sense. Not only do you face your own internal pressure, but you have expectations placed on you by those around you. For most people, it's a handful of others placing those expectations on them. You, however, are trying to please thousands of people?
**CAGirl202:** At least.
**RMerritt44:** Yet you yearn to remain true to yourself. Perhaps this public image arose before you had a chance to figure out who "yourself" is.

What a relief! He understood her predicament without knowing the details. This might be the outlet that would help.

**CAGirl202:** My career shot ahead so fast, I'm trying to figure out how to live in a new world.
**RMerritt44:** And that can feel quite lonely.
**CAGirl202:** Yes, it can. I've never admitted that to anyone.
**RMerritt44:** You reached out to me. That marks a first step.
**CAGirl202:** I don't know what I need to figure out, but I could see this coaching relationship being helpful. I'd like to continue chatting with you. How does that work?

**RMerritt44:** You can always try to reach me instantly if it's urgent. However, in most cases, we schedule an appointment time and then message each other, the way we did today.

**CAGirl202:** And how do you get paid?

**RMerritt44:** You'll find a link on my website. Like most online vendors, the transaction occurs via a secure third party.

**CAGirl202:** I figured that might be the case.

**RMerritt44:** And because of that, you maintain as much anonymity as you wish. I don't keep any personal information or credit card numbers online. Not even your name.

Nora grinned.

*Perfect.*

# CHAPTER 23

THE REALTOR WAS right. It didn't take long for Del's home to sell.

Del's mind stirred as he considered the possibilities surrounding his discovery of Marilyn's script. Granted, no guarantees existed in Hollywood, but this was a lock if he ever saw one. The question was how to handle it. Who knew how long it might take to negotiate the details and see this project through production?

In the meantime, reality loomed large.

While en route to his agent's office, Del's phone rang. He'd established a Bluetooth connection to his car stereo speaker and wore an earpiece. If the cops caught him holding his phone while driving in California, they'd nail his ass. He didn't need bad publicity.

"I have a buyer for you, Mr. Corwyn," the realtor said, his voice breaking across the phone connection. "And he's agreed to your asking price."

Del swerved his car. The driver beside him slammed on her horn. Del couldn't believe his ears.

"That never happens! Not from what I've heard."

"And he's willing to buy it sight unseen."

"Is he nuts?"

The realtor's chuckle sounded tinny through Del's phone. Del wished Felicia were sitting beside him to listen in.

It was the fourth time she'd crossed his mind that day.

"No," the realtor replied, "he's a businessman from Belgium, the CEO for a worldwide corporation. The man has an enormous ego and a penchant for American pop culture. He's enamored with the idea of purchasing a celebrity's home. Bragging rights, you might say."

"Sounds like he has more money than sense."

"Nevertheless, Mr. Corwyn, you have an offer. As you might imagine, the likelihood of any future offers coming in at the asking price is rather slim."

Del was shell-shocked at the news. He hadn't expected an offer so soon, and certainly not at the list price. His realtor was right. This wouldn't happen again, and he needed to sell. The Marilyn script would bring a windfall, but he didn't know if it would provide enough to maintain his current lifestyle for the duration of his life.

He would need to hurry and find a home in Florida.

"This happened so fast," Del said. "I haven't begun searching for a new house. You said the buyer is in Europe?"

"Yes, he plans to reside in the United States part-time, whenever he conducts business here. That, and it's a vacation home for him."

"So he isn't relocating? He isn't in a rush?"

"I didn't get that impression."

"Could we negotiate into the contract that I could continue to live in this home—with rent, of course—for three months after closing? It would give me time to search."

"I believe the buyer would be willing to work with you on that."

He needed to take advantage of the opportunity while he could. Del eased to a red light and sighed.

"Tell him I accept his offer."

# CHAPTER 24

"THIS IS URGENT, you said?"

Arnie Clemmons, Del's agent, shut the door and settled into his leather chair, which had cracked along the seams. The window blinds were open and exposed a view of the parking lot from the office's second-story roost.

Arnie had managed to salvage his hair along the bottom half of his head, but his bald dome looked waxy as sunlight glinted upon it. A man in his late fifties, Arnie's roster featured a variety of former A-list talent that had fallen from their perches but whose reputations remained respectable around town.

"I have an intriguing prospect for a new film," Del replied as he took a seat. He tapped the manila envelope tucked under his arm, which contained Marilyn's script.

He could've sworn he caught Arnie in the onset of an eye roll brought to a sudden halt.

"What kind of project?"

"A pop-culture type of thing. You could say it has a retro feel to it."

Arnie sighed. "Del, I realize you like to relive the past—"

"This is a winner, Arnie. I guarantee it."

"And what does this winning project involve?"

"Marilyn Monroe. It's a screenplay."

"With all due respect, isn't that a bit clichéd? This would

need to be an angle no one else has covered. Many people have done films about Marilyn Monroe, not to mention books and memorabilia and everything else under the sun."

"You don't understand. This isn't *about* Marilyn Monroe." Del felt a surge of adrenaline and couldn't contain himself. He leaned forward and, with great pomp, planted the thick package on Arnie's desk. It landed with a thump. "It's *by* Marilyn Monroe."

Arnie sat open-mouthed as he tried to follow along. His eyes widened in perplexity. "*By* Marilyn Monroe," he repeated.

"That's right."

"Del, what the hell are you talking about?"

With a lighthearted laugh, Del eased back into the chair. "Last night, I rummaged through some boxes I'd stored away long ago. Hadn't looked through them in years. Relics from my heyday. Things I'd forgotten I'd saved. And at the bottom of one of those boxes, I found this."

He patted the envelope, which crinkled at his touch.

"It's a script, given to me in 1962." Del caught Arnie's eye to make sure the man paid full attention. "Written by Marilyn Monroe."

# CHAPTER 25

ARNIE SHOT HIM a skeptical glare, then leaned back in his leather chair. The chair squeaked under his medium-size ass. "And somehow, you have possession of it? Something she wrote?"

"We were close friends."

"I've never heard a word about her writing a screenplay. Not even a rumor."

"She kept it a secret, but she considered herself a true artist. She was shrewd, and had growing ambitions. Remember her film contract, the one that included a provision for films to be produced under her own company, Marilyn Monroe Productions?"

"Marilyn wasn't a writer."

"But she was married to one. Arthur Miller, remember? He influenced her."

Del handed the envelope to Arnie, who grimaced as he took it in hand.

Arnie waved the package with an attitude of indifference. Skepticism continued to fill his glare. "And this is the script?"

"Yes."

*"Marilyn's* script?"

"Yes, Arnie."

With a sigh, Arnie stared at the envelope, then unsealed it, removed the brass-fastened screenplay, and stared at it as if it were a bowl of cauliflower.

Arnie read the title aloud. *"Beautiful Mess."*

Del watched his every move as he scanned the document's title page and flipped through the first few pages.

"This is a photocopy."

"I put the original in a safe-deposit box. I made one photocopy for you, one for me."

"Unfortunately, we can't prove this isn't a hoax, can we? You *say* it came from her, but how could we prove it? That's the first question anyone would ask." Arnie furrowed his brow and held the script closer. "And what are these little boxes in the corners? The ones with smudges in them?"

"Those are the proof it's a Marilyn Monroe original: her thumbprints."

"The quality doesn't look too good."

"It's just a photocopy. They're crisp on the original. Ink from a stamp pad."

"And these thumbprints are here for what reason?"

"She wrote me this letter in 1962." Del pulled a photocopy of Marilyn's letter from the breast pocket of his blazer, unfolded it, and slid it across the desk. "It explains how the thumbprints prove the original came from her."

Arnie scanned the letter, then examined the script closer. He raised an eyebrow.

"And her thumbprint is the only fingerprint that exists inside these boxes?"

"I assume so. I was careful not to touch them. And according to Marilyn, she was afraid to show the document to anyone else. That would prevent any other prints from interfering with hers."

Arnie rapped his knuckle upon the desk and shot Del a tentative gaze. Del watched the man's skepticism subside as he reread the letter's body.

"Smart move on her part," he said. "She certainly covered

her bases."

Del nodded. "She wasn't the dumb blond that she played on the silver screen. Consider how well she constructed her public persona. The woman knew how to strategize and think ahead."

Del caught the first hint of a grin at the corner of Arnie's mouth and knew his agent was on board.

"My only question," Del said, "is how we could verify her fingerprints."

"That shouldn't be a problem," Arnie shrugged. "I'm sure they have her prints on file from the autopsy. Given the circumstances surrounding her death and who she was, they would have wanted official confirmation of her identity to eliminate the possibility of foul play. For the record, if nothing else. And her death predated all that HIPAA crap, so the prints are probably floating all over God's green earth. We'd just need to hire someone credible who can verify that it's an authentic match. At that point, we hold all the bargaining chips when it comes to making a deal."

Arnie's cheeks turned rosy as he grinned at Del. A wide, toothy grin. The discoloration of enamel betrayed a long-entrenched penchant for red wine. He rolled the script and slapped it against his palm.

"Do you realize how many people would dry-hump a flagpole to get their hands on this?" exclaimed the agent. "We're talking history here! Hollywood's best-kept secret!"

Del felt a bittersweet quiver in his gut but suppressed it. His life was about to become interesting again.

Arnie paged through the screenplay further, scanning the dialogue. Several minutes ticked past. Del savored the silence which, in this case, was the sound of power.

"Have you read this, Del?"

"I have."

"Pretty deep shit in here. *Dark* shit, the kind that scares the hell out of you." Arnie skipped to the screenplay's midpoint and read some more. "And talk about explicit. The profanity, the sexual content, everything."

"She made herself vulnerable, no doubt."

"Damn, Del. This woman must've been more fucked up than we thought."

Del winced. "Arnie, cut it out."

"Sorry, I forgot you two were pals." The agent shook his head in an absentminded manner, his mouth hanging open as he read further. "No wonder she didn't show this to anybody else. Can you imagine how people would have reacted to this in 1962? The film would've been X-rated—if ratings had existed back then—and gotten banned from theaters. People would've protested outside. This script would've ruined Marilyn Monroe's career."

"But today—"

"—it'll *resurrect* it."

The men stared at each other for a moment, sizing each other up.

"But why you?" Arnie asked at last. "You said you two were buddies, but she knew tons of people. For all intent and purposes, she bequeathed it to you without realizing it. One of her final acts before she died. Why did she put this into *your* hands?"

Del shrugged. "I never betrayed her."

He made his way toward a mini-fridge Arnie kept behind a bureau door and helped himself to a bottled water. He took a swig and began to pace the room, piecing the puzzle together with each stride.

"Many people aren't aware of this," Del said, "but her emotional state took such a dive, she was forced into a mental institution against her will for a brief period. That event left a permanent scar. Toward the end of her life, she didn't trust many people, especially since people she trusted betrayed her and sent her to that place. Once she escaped, she feared the day would come when they'd lock her up again.

"This script exposed some of the inner workings and torments of her mind. What if authorities used it as evidence of a dangerous mental condition and sent her back to the one place she feared most? It was Joe DiMaggio, another ex-husband, who worked to get her out of there—and she barely made it out. If they had recommitted her, she would have lost her freedom forever."

"But something must have prompted her to give this script to you, Del. If she was so paranoid, why did she risk giving the script to anyone? Why didn't she keep it to herself?"

"She mentioned possible trouble ahead but didn't go into detail."

"You're telling me Marilyn Monroe was a psychic?"

"Of course not. More like intuition. A sense that something was about to happen." Del returned to his seat and crossed one leg over the other. He interlinked his fingers across his knee. "And she was right. A few months later, she died from a barbiturate overdose. Some speculated it was accidental, but the amount of drugs in her system were so high, it was hard to believe it was anything but suicide."

Arnie tapped a pen against a legal pad. Del's heart stirred. The memory of her death threatened to bring tears to the resilient man's eyes.

Del leaned forward and locked eyes with his agent.

"For Marilyn, this script wasn't about business. It wasn't about fame." Solemn, Del added, "This script is my chance to bring Marilyn Monroe back to life, one more time—on her own terms. To position her as a serious artist, the way she craved people to view her."

"Your sentiment is honorable. That said, this revelation will set in motion a feeding frenzy." Arnie paused, and Del caught a glint in his eye. "And I know you, Del. You like the cameras, the adoring fans. You want a career comeback—and this is the best ticket you'll ever get."

"Arnie—"

"All I'm saying is this: I don't doubt your motive to honor Marilyn Monroe's memory, but once we set this in motion, you'll get caught up in the whirlwind. I'm warning you now because I don't want to have to dig you out of a guilt complex later."

"I'll be fine, Arnie. Trust me."

His agent regarded him for a moment, then nodded in resignation. "In that case, we need to set a plan in motion. How do we release the news of this discovery? How do we consider contenders? Where do we set the minimum bar for a deal? We get to call the shots here. They'll need to play by our rules, and this script needs to be on strict lockdown."

"Agreed."

"In that case, the first thing we need to do is establish its authenticity. I'll get the proof lined up and we'll keep it in our back pockets. Next, we'll hold a press conference to announce the existence of the screenplay—but let the press *speculate* about whether it's authentic. We'll hem and haw for a while, tease them a bit, make them think they have us cornered."

Del didn't want to look like a fool in public, regardless of how temporary or intentional, but he was willing to hear the rest of the idea. He stroked his chin and clasped his hands upon his chest. "And what happens next?"

"Then, when attention is at its peak, we release the evidence. It'll be good for another round of marketing. So instead of releasing the evidence at the first news conference, we'll get twice the bang for our buck."

"Makes sense to me." Del felt much more at ease. He exhaled and took a swig of water. The bottle's thin plastic crackled in his grip.

"We'll need some time to strategize this while the thumbprints are verified. I know a guy who can get it done under the radar. Meanwhile—and I'm sure you know this, but I'll stress it anyway—don't breathe a word of this until the day of our big announcement. Not to the media, the studio people, producers—not even to the chef at your sushi restaurant. The element of surprise will strengthen our bargaining position. Agreed?"

"Agreed."

Arnie exhaled, as though in relief, and scratched his bald head. His fingers left behind red streaks. "This is big, Del."

Del's pulse increased with anticipation, yet he maintained his composure. He finished his water and crumpled the bottle.

'Big' didn't do it justice.

This wasn't just Marilyn's final chance.

It was Del Corwyn's, too.

# PART TWO

## GENTLEMEN PREFER BLONDES

# CHAPTER 26

NORA HAD HOPED a wellness coach would be helpful, but she hadn't expected to look forward to their next appointment the way she did.

Russell Merritt had proven easy to talk to, especially given the luxury of anonymity. Nora had forgotten how wonderful such freedom could be.

> **RMerritt44:** You mentioned a successful career, but that you also lack joy in your life. Why do you think that's the case?
>
> **CAGirl202:** Isn't that why I'm paying you? To tell me?
>
> **RMerritt44:** Humor me. I'm gathering background. Sometimes difficulty finding happiness has deeper roots. Did you have a happy childhood?

Nora snorted. *Yeah, right.*

> **CAGirl202:** My childhood was fucked up.
>
> **RMerritt44:** Your parents? Siblings? Socioeconomics? Would any of those come into play?
>
> **CAGirl202:** Parent.
>
> **RMerritt44:** I beg your pardon?
>
> **CAGirl202:** One parent. I never knew my father. He was a deadbeat dad, skipped out on us before I was old enough to remember. Never paid child support. Never kept in touch.
>
> **RMerritt44:** And your mother?

Nora hesitated. Did she want to go into detail on this? Did it matter? She never talked about this stuff. Then again, maybe that was one of her issues. Wasn't that why she contacted Russell Merritt in the first place? To find answers?

She tugged at her ear lobe, then decided to throw caution to the wind. Anonymous, right? She put her fingers to the keyboard.

> **CAGirl202:** My mother was in bad shape. A drug addict. Sometimes she was present in mind, other days she wasn't. Let's just say when I grew up in Colorado, I had issues.
>
> **RMerritt44:** Someone else must have taken care of you. Is that correct?
>
> **CAGirl202:** I had an aunt who stepped in. Mom's sister. She became a role model for me.
>
> **RMerritt44:** That doesn't sound like an easy life, by any means.

Second thoughts settled in. Should she disconnect their session right now? On one hand, it felt awkward admitting personal details to a stranger. Yet, on the other hand, she could picture a cleansing on the horizon, albeit no more than a glimmer. Part of her wanted to talk to someone, but she didn't have many options in her life. She knew a lot of people, but she'd never been one to confide in others. Now that her career had exploded full-force and she existed on everybody's radar, she didn't know who she could trust.

She decided to press forward and set her red fingernails in motion.

> **CAGirl202:** I've always wondered what a normal family was. I used to look at my friends, the way their families interacted, and I wanted to be part of something like that.

A pause. Then she heard the familiar *ping* that indicated Russell's response had arrived.

**RMerritt44:** And you feel your lack of contentment, or happiness as you call it, might have its roots in that aspect of your childhood? A lack of family?

**CAGirl202:** I guess. Maybe. Who knows.

**RMerritt44:** Sometimes you can find family where you least expect it. A surrogate of sorts, but it can help fill that void. Consider the relationships in your life. Are those relationships moving you forward?

**CAGirl202:** I wish it were that simple. I'm in a complicated situation.

**RMerritt44:** I understand. But keep your eyes open for opportunities to trust. Little ones.

**CAGirl202:** I suppose. But my other fear is failure. I guess I think back on my childhood, consider the way things were and the lack of direction, the way things spiraled out of control with my mother's addiction. It didn't happen fast. It was gradual. But the scary thing was the silence.

**RMerritt44:** What sort of silence?

**CAGirl202:** The way things went unspoken. We knew there were issues, but we didn't confront them until it was too late and Mom's addiction had taken over control of her life and decisions. So much pain. But nobody outside of those four walls knew the extent of it because we never talked about it. One day, Mom died of an overdose. Part of me suspects she turned to drugs to mask her own pain in life.

**RMerritt44:** That's quite possible.

**CAGirl202:** Even today, that silence scares me. I fear the silence of unspoken words, unspoken pains, unspoken struggles. The idea that you can look so good on the outside but hide such torment in your soul. I don't want to die in silence.

A pause. The cursor blinked on the screen. And a shroud returned to Nora's heart, the familiar veil of depression.

The silence.

**RMerritt44:** You've taken one step forward, though. Haven't you?

Nora tried to smile, but her effort felt shallow. Numb.

# CHAPTER 27

THE DRIVE FROM Del's home to the Malibu shore took five minutes, most of that time spent winding through his neighborhood and down the mountain. With Felicia in the passenger seat, Del guided his silver convertible along a two-lane road. Splotches of greenery dotted the mountain's surface, the kind of growth that, from a distance, resembled a scouring pad. Large homes speckled the hillside in strategic positions, to allow for privacy without obscuring stellar views of the Pacific.

When they reached the shoreline, Del parked his car on the side of the Pacific Coast Highway, where they removed their shoes and made their way toward the ocean. Early on this January evening, they were the only souls walking the beach.

Del had never outgrown his fascination with the Pacific Coast Highway. Los Angeles was the second-largest city in America. People flocked here from all over the world. And yet, this stretch of road, squeezed between water and mountain, felt like slice of rural America. Or, at least, the California version of it.

He took Felicia's hand in his and they strolled along the shoreline, though tonight, neither dared dip their toes in the cold water. Fine grains of sand rubbed between their toes. The incessant motion of breakers spoke to Del's soul.

So did the touch of the woman who ambled beside him. What drew him to her? Was it possible to find contentment with someone so close to his own age?

"Were you ever a surfer?" Felicia asked.

"I tried a couple of times. It was never my thing. I moved to L.A. while I was young enough to enjoy the ocean, but kept so busy, I never allowed myself time for it." Del eyed Felicia with faux suspicion. "Don't tell me you were a surfer."

She laughed. "Not at all. Most of the time, I was preoccupied with the whole counterculture thing. Besides, even if I'd wanted to, half the time I was too stoned to balance myself on a surfboard."

Del loved to hear her laugh. It sounded lighthearted, carefree, yet tinged with wisdom acquired through years of both joy and disappointment along the way.

He gazed into her eyes, where he found notes of tranquility. They soothed his soul even more than the waves, which now seemed to dance rather than roar.

"You've never told me much about yourself," Del said.

She teased him with a soft bump, shoulder to shoulder. "You don't ask."

The gleam in her eyes confirmed her attraction toward Del was genuine. This woman wasn't star-struck. She didn't seem impressed with his past achievements. Del wasn't accustomed to that.

"Does it count if I start asking you now?" he asked.

"No time like the present, as they say."

Del peered down at her hand, absent of a wedding band, a sight he'd noticed many times prior. "Were you ever married?"

He wasn't sure, but he thought he noticed a twitch of her eye. Felicia's posture grew rigid. She held silent for a moment, staring at the vast horizon. Her calmness remained intact.

"Once, long ago. We were young." She took a deep breath of resignation. "We all make mistakes. That was mine."

"I'm sorry to hear that. We don't need to talk about it."

"No, it's a part of me. I don't mind. I've shared it with

many people. I'm a minister; it goes with the territory."

Del's heart longed to know her better, but he endeavored to tread with care. He didn't want to cause her heartache. "How long were you married? I hope the divorce wasn't complicated."

"Actually, it was quite simple."

"How so?"

Felicia stopped walking. When she turned toward him, Del observed the aura of a young, vulnerable girl in this mature woman's eyes.

"He walked out on me."

# CHAPTER 28

THE REVELATION CAUGHT Del off guard. With a marriage component absent along his own life's journey, he lacked an appropriate response. But as he looked into Felicia's eyes, his heart softened. He didn't know whether to continue holding her hand, but before he could stop himself, he'd allowed it to fall from his.

"I'm sorry to hear that."

"It's not a big deal anymore." Although she waved off the memory, Del noticed an ember of pain lingered in her eyes. "But as I look back, I can't say I'm surprised. We had eloped. A couple of hippies who lived in a commune in northern California for a year. I was sixteen years old. Far too young to get hitched."

"You never mentioned any children."

"The marriage ended before that could happen. Which, in my opinion, was the best thing. No child should have to grow up without a father."

"Did your ex-husband ever try to get back in touch with you?"

"I haven't heard a word from him since he walked out."

Del was dumbfounded. He found this woman striking. How could anyone abandon her?

"What kind of man walks out on a woman like you?"

A puckered smile emerged on Felicia's face, which told Del

he might have succeeded in relieving her surface-level pain. To a small degree, at least.

"A boy with a dream." She gazed out at the ocean. Strands of her hair fluttered in the breeze. The speckled flesh on the front of her neck hinted at her age.

She ran her hand through her hair once, and Del thought she looked stunning.

"I hope the dream was worth it to him," he said.

"He'd been a drummer in a small-time band. They wanted to be the Allman Brothers. One day, he came home and told me he'd run into a former bandmate at the grocery store. They were trekking to L.A. in a VW bus and asked if he wanted to rejoin the band." Felicia returned her attention to Del, a knowing look in her eyes, a combination of struggle and maturity in hindsight. "He hit the road and never came back."

"Classy guy."

"It was another era. Things were different."

"Some things should never change."

Although Del had neither married nor ventured as far as a proposal, he had engaged in too many romantic relationships to count. He wondered if he had scarred any women the way Felicia's ex-husband had scarred her. A shadow of guilt lurked at the corner of his conscience.

"And today?" he asked.

"Today?" Felicia smirked. "Today...let's say I'm no longer sixteen."

Del could relate to that. Once again, he reached for her hand, and she allowed him to take it in his as they resumed strolling. The sun had set, and shades of indigo began to settle in their midst. Without warmth from the sunshine, the sand felt cool against their flesh. A lone seagull squawked in the distance.

They had known each other for such a short time. He couldn't have started falling in love with her, could he? Yet, in the moments they spent apart, he discovered he missed her.

Even now, his heart seemed to yearn for her. He'd never experienced that sensation with a woman.

"So what were *your* younger years like, Del Corwyn?"

Del grinned at the pleasant memories. "I started working when I was eighteen years old and never stopped. We're talking the late fifties, early sixties. I consider those years the final breaths of Hollywood's golden era. I did a lot of film work, met a lot of famous folks."

"I do remember watching you when I was younger. You worked with your share of memorable individuals."

"Of course. Katherine Hepburn, Marlon Brando, Marilyn Monroe—"

"You worked with Marilyn Monroe? I saw many of her movies, but I don't remember seeing you."

"Early in my career. Nothing impressive, I assure you. Before I spoke a word on camera, the studio assigned me to her as an errand boy on the set of *The Prince and the Showgirl.*" Del shrugged. "I was a kid. She and I became friends, though."

"You're kidding!"

"Close friends, as a matter of fact."

Felicia lodged her tongue against the inside of her cheek and shot him an astute look. "For some reason, I can't picture that about you—a close friendship with Marilyn Monroe, I mean."

Del responded to her teasing by feigning shock. "And why is that?"

"Don't take this the wrong way, but you strike me as a man who tends to keep intimacy at bay. That's not to say you aren't the romantic type…"

"But?"

"But you also have a reputation for being a lifelong bachelor by choice. I tend to wonder if the desire for commitment exists at all beneath those layers."

"Maybe I just haven't found the right woman," Del hinted.

"Maybe so." Moments of silence passed before Felicia spoke again. "Such a sad situation."

"My love life?"

"Marilyn Monroe. It breaks my heart to hear of troubled souls who can't find hope, who can't find a way out of whatever predicament they're in."

Del considered the remark. "She was well known, yet truly *known* by only a few."

"A deep person?"

He nodded. "And plagued with insecurity. She craved for her peers to accept her as a serious artist. Imagine the paradox she dwelt in: an entire persona built around her sexuality. But she was a savvy marketer. She constructed that image and knew how to perpetuate it. Yet, at the same time, she longed for people to look *past* that facade, to know her as the *opposite* of the persona she had boxed herself into."

"The secrets people hide inside."

"She was smarter than anyone realized. And more talented than anyone was aware of."

"How so?"

Could he trust Felicia? Despite his love for publicity, but he wasn't one to show his hand. Still, a part of him wanted to share this moment with her.

"Can you keep a secret?"

# CHAPTER 29

"WHAT KIND of secret?"

"A good secret. One that will come to light in due time, but for now, you can't utter a syllable about it."

"I'm a minister. If I do one thing well, it's to take someone's confidence to the grave."

Del pivoted toward her, took her other hand in his, and their eyes locked.

"I'm about to make history, Felicia."

"More than you have already?"

"Marilyn Monroe wrote a screenplay."

"That's one piece of trivia I've never heard."

"*No one* has heard about it. But it's true. She wrote a screenplay, never told a soul about it, and put it into my care in 1962—five months before she died. She asked me to reveal it in due time. It was the last favor she ever asked of me."

Felicia's eyes grew wide in astonishment. She appeared as if she wanted to say something but couldn't locate the words. Finally, she found her voice.

"You've kept this secret for more than half a century, Del!"

"I'd forgotten about it until a few days ago. As you know, I'm selling my house, and I was feeling sentimental. I went through some old boxes I hadn't opened in who knows how long, and there it was. A script written by Marilyn Monroe, attached to a letter she'd signed by her own hand. I didn't give it much thought when she gave it to me. After all, she was still alive. She was an icon, but not immortalized. Just another popular actress at the time. When she passed away, I was heartbroken, couldn't even think about that script. After a few years, I'd forgotten I had possession of it."

"And she gave you authority to take the next step with it?"

"In full."

Felicia pondered for a moment. "Her script would reignite *your* career, as well."

"Yes, it would"

"Would you welcome that chance?"

Del hesitated to answer. He had grown so accustomed to keeping his guard up. But something about Felicia made him want to relax his defenses.

"I've dreamed of a comeback. You see, it isn't just a career or fame to me; it's something special. I've known so many others who have faded or, even worse, died too soon. *Marilyn* died too soon. But she always cared for me, took me under her wing." Del shook his head in what would have been disbelief had he not known better. "Even after her death, she's looking out for me."

"How so?"

"She had low points in her career like all of us. Maybe one reason she put her script in my care was because she knew *I'd* hit a point where I'd need a trump card."

Felicia stopped walking. "A trump card?"

"Absolutely. Like you said, it would reignite my career. Can you imagine how much attention this will draw?" When he noticed Felicia furrow her brow, he added, "Don't misunderstand me. I would rather have my friend alive. But if Marilyn had the opportunity for a career resurgence, she would seize it. She would want me to take that opportunity, too."

"And this is how you need to accomplish it?"

"At my age, opportunities are few and far between."

Felicia pursed her lips and studied him. When puzzlement didn't drain from her expression, Del grew concerned. Granted, he didn't have the most stellar level of integrity she could find in a man. Del had his shortcomings. But for a reason he couldn't ascertain, he didn't want to look at Felicia and find disappointment in her eyes.

"It's a game, Felicia. I didn't write the rules of this industry; I play by them," Del explained. "You're looking at me like I stole sunflower seeds from a bird feeder and snacked on them myself."

Felicia appeared perplexed. In spite of the reservations she seemed to harbor, though, she hadn't released his hand. Del took that as a promising sign.

They continued to meander in silence, listening to the tides recede and saltwater fizzle upon the shore. As twilight deepened, they reversed course and headed back in the direction of Del's car.

Del's mind wandered to the weeks that lay ahead. Arnie had arranged for an expert to verify Marilyn's thumbprints and would have the proof in hand soon. At that point, the momentum would augment. The longer the wheels remained in motion, the harder it would be for Del—or anybody else—to stop them. Marilyn had crowned him a kingmaker.

Felicia's voice startled him.

"What if it doesn't work out?"

"What do you mean?"

"Your comeback. What if it doesn't happen the way you expect it to?"

"Why wouldn't it?"

Felicia shrugged and cast her stare at their feet as she pondered. "Things happen. *Life* happens. People change."

"Thanks for your vote of confidence," Del volleyed with a smirk.

"I'm sorry, Del, I didn't mean it that way. Yes, it could pan out the precise way you envision it, and no one would be more thrilled for you than I. But you have a *Plan B*, right?"

"A *Plan B?*"

"Life seldom unfolds, verbatim, the way we expect it to. You've alluded to that yourself," Felicia replied. "Have you thought about how you might adapt if life takes you along a different course?"

"That won't happen."

"But suppose it does. What would you do?" She gave him a playful nudge. "Humor me."

Del tried to imagine a scenario in which his prospects could fail or wind up short. His mind retreated to the recent years of his life, month after month, maintaining his own image of relevance and having precious little to show for it. He hated the thought of enduring the rest of his life in such an empty way.

"I'd keep pressing on, figure something out," he answered, though he felt ridiculous with his naked response. "I've never been one to concoct a *Plan B*, as you call it. Isn't *Plan B* a clever way to anticipate defeat?"

"It doesn't need to be. It resides in your perspective. A *Plan B* can offer its share of fulfillment, though at first glance, it might not look as shiny or exciting." She turned her head toward him. "Sometimes *Plan B* turns out ten times better than your original desire."

"Spoken from experience?"

"I've thanked God many times that He gave me my *Plan B* instead." She rested her head upon his shoulder. "In hindsight, that is."

Moonlight cast a milky glow upon Felicia's silhouette and piqued Del's fascination. The woman was gorgeous.

As they walked, the scent of honeycomb from her hair intermingled with the salty aroma of the Pacific. Goose bumps rippled along Del's arms, and he wondered if Felicia felt the same way. He wrapped his arm around her waist and, to his delight, she melted into him.

Del nuzzled his cheek against the top of her head and they walked in silence.

When had he last enjoyed such simplicity?

# CHAPTER 30

TRISTAN BELIEVED a drive-thru window would add efficiency to the process of the coffee shop around the corner and wondered why they didn't add one. Then again, plenty of folks appeared willing to park their cars and wait several minutes in line to place their orders.

He couldn't help the critique. He saw opportunities everywhere. And if he had the means to take advantage of a few, he would. Why not increase revenue when opportunity stood in front of you waiting to order a café Americano with soy milk?

He tucked the arm of his sunglasses into his shirt and waited. Most days, Tristan grabbed his drink and ran. But today, maybe he would linger and soak up the ambience.

When his coffee was ready, he picked it up at the far end of the counter and wandered to one corner of the dining area, where a couple of cozy chairs were arranged.

A young woman occupied one chair. Dressed in a baseball cap with a raven ponytail sticking through the back, she kept to herself as she sipped her drink, staring straight ahead.

As Tristan set his cup on the coffee table and backed himself into the seat, the chair rubbed against the tile floor and rendered a sudden, loud squeak, which startled the young woman. Wherever her thoughts were, her focus must have been intense.

"Sorry to startle you," Tristan said. "Is this seat taken?"

She gave him a quick glance, then returned to her focus to her cup. She seemed nervous to have someone—anyone—nearby, but perhaps it was Tristan's imagination.

"Feel free to take it," she replied. "I'm getting ready to leave anyway."

She possessed a natural beauty, the kind you don't notice at first glimpse, one which grows on you and overtakes you.

Tristan didn't want her to leave.

"Please don't head out on my account."

She gave him another peek, longer this time, and her features softened. "Well, I wasn't ready to leave *quite* yet."

Why did it seem as though Tristan had met her in the past? She looked familiar.

"Have I seen you here before?" he asked.

"Probably not. I don't come here often."

He gave her another sideways perusal. Maybe she was in film or television, a B-lister from years ago. It wasn't unusual to run into those people here and there. He never made a big deal of it.

Based on how she kept to herself, Tristan figured she preferred her privacy, so he grabbed his coffee and rose from his seat. "I barged into your quiet corner here. I'll let you have your space."

As he turned, he felt a tug upon his shirt tail. When he spun around, Nora blushed, which told Tristan she had reacted before thinking. After attempting to avoid his eyes once more, she peered into them, her gaze darting from left to right, perhaps sizing up whether she could trust him. Her shoulders relaxed.

"Please stay," she said. "I don't mind."

Tristan hesitated. He almost felt guilty. "Are you sure?"

"I could use some company."

And with that, Tristan settled into the chair once again.

He was between romantic relationships and didn't spot a wedding band on this woman's finger.

There! She did it again! It struck him as self-conscious, the way she sneaked peeks over her shoulder to see if anyone noticed them speaking. Should he worry? Tristan didn't detect any vibes that concerned him, yet this quirk of hers seemed odd. Borderline obsessive—nervous, as if the FBI had waltzed through the door five minutes earlier and handcuffed a guy.

"I'm Tristan." He held out his hand.

She offered a curious smile, which caused him to wonder if his initial attraction to her might be mutual. Her lips curled into a twist; she appeared to find the handshake cute.

She hesitated, as though to weigh her simple response, then took his hand and replied, "Nora."

"Nora? I don't hear that name much. One of those classics."

"It was my grandmother's name." She sipped her coffee and continued to size him up. Her arms and shoulders relaxed. "What do you do for a living, Tristan?"

"I'm an entrepreneur." Indeed, he considered himself such. He'd invented his own style of wellness coaching. And to his knowledge, he was the first in the area to accomplish this as an online-exclusive endeavor.

His answer appeared to pique her curiosity. She leaned forward and furrowed her brow. "Shouldn't you be in an office somewhere instead of hanging around a coffee shop in the middle of the morning?"

"I conduct all my work online, so my time is flexible. All hours of day or night."

"And you enjoy it?"

"Pays the bills," Tristan shrugged. He didn't view it beyond making a living, though it seemed to help people improve their lives, which, to him, affirmed it as an honest career. Did he have all the answers? No. Then again, he didn't need to.

People will do what they're going to do; he helped them cut through the crap on the way to their destination.

They spoke in hushed tones. Tristan couldn't figure why, but he followed her lead, and their conversation felt natural nonetheless.

"What type of business is it?"

"You could call it online sales."

"What do you sell?"

Tristan tapped the lid on his coffee cup. He'd had this conversation on countless occasions. "Whatever the customer needs. People need a particular improvement, and I provide the service that gets them the information they need to make that adjustment."

All true. Whenever anyone asked about Tristan's profession, he kept the description vague. Not to hide what he did, but to protect his alias. The flipside of conducting coaching online was that he didn't know who was on the other side. What if a client was a psychopath who would hunt him down if he phrased something wrong? Time to change the subject.

"What do you do, Nora?"

There! She did that weird self-conscious thing again, glancing over her shoulder! She looked like she wanted to trust him but needed to overcome an obstacle first.

Then he recognized her.

# CHAPTER 31

"HOLD ON." Before he could stop himself, he whispered, "You're Nora Jumelle, aren't you!"

The tentative way she stroked her ponytail and avoided his stare told him everything he needed to know. He wished he hadn't blurted it out. Celebrities didn't matter much to him. They were ordinary people. At least he'd spoken at a volume only the two of them could hear.

"You probably don't get many chances to be yourself," he noted.

"I've had surprising success in this shop. From time to time, I hit on a quiet, normal place like this. Most people are cool, but on occasion, somebody will recognize me and start to get pushy. If it gets out of hand, I have to move on and find someplace else. I keep a mental checklist." She said with a shrug and offered him a trusting smile. Her shoulders eased. "This place is a bit of a drive for me, but it's worth it."

"Don't worry, your secret's safe with me," Tristan winked. He tried to imagine the suffocation you must experience when your privacy vanishes. Does it feel like the walls of life are closing in around you? "When was the last time you could go to a public place without being recognized?" he asked.

"A couple of years ago. Nobody knew who I was until *Faces* became a hit. At that point, my world changed overnight."

"Was it difficult to adapt?"

Nora weighed her answer. "I'm *still* adapting. Every day."

"Fame isn't a natural fit for you?"

"I thought it would be. Then it emerged in my life."

"Don't you enjoy it?"

"Fame and I have a love-hate relationship," she replied with a smoky chuckle, swirling her beverage. "You're easy to talk to. Your demeanor—you have a way of putting a woman at ease."

"Call it a job requirement in my field. Besides, celebrities aren't a big deal to me. You're an individual, right? Not an object."

"'Not an object.' That concept comes in short supply these days."

Tristan's heart went out to her. And she seemed to need someone around with whom she could be herself. Though he tried to convince himself otherwise, he sensed loneliness about her.

So he decided to take a chance.

"Nora, I realize we just met, so feel free to decline…"

Did he catch a flicker of hope in her eyes? Was this happening?

He pressed forward. "Would you like to go to dinner sometime?"

She pursed her lips as she studied him. She had exquisite gray eyes that enraptured him.

Then she responded with a genuine smile.

"Dinner would be nice."

# CHAPTER 32

LATE THAT NIGHT, Nora lay in bed and listened to the quiet hum of a ceiling fan. She'd considered getting a small dog, or perhaps a cat, something to provide companionship, but with her odd work schedule, owning a pet would prove cumbersome. When a film was in production, she would work all hours of the day or night. She could envision the hassle of trying to accommodate an animal.

Her eyes felt raw. Turning onto her side, she reached for her alarm clock to see how long she'd been lying awake.

Two hours.

That evening, the darkness of depression had clinched her in a vise and hadn't let go. Maybe tomorrow would improve. If only she could fall asleep in the meantime.

With a huff, she shoved the covers from her body, then padded to the bathroom, where she grabbed a package of sleeping pills from her medicine cabinet. Not wanting to stimulate her vision, she kept the lights off and fumbled with the package until she'd squeezed a pill through the layer of foil. After chasing down the pill with a swig of water, she returned to bed, one phase shy of a walking mummy.

Nora pulled the covers over her face and waited for nothingness to overcome her.

# CHAPTER 33

*THIS* WAS WHERE she lived?

On Thursday evening, Tristan parked his car on the street in front of Nora's house. For an actress who had seen such recent success, he'd expected Nora Jumelle to live in a mansion. Instead, she resided in a standard-size home in the Valley, albeit on a semi-isolated cul-de-sac. Nora had few neighbors.

Peering at his rearview mirror, he noticed the silhouette of a hefty man sitting behind him in an ordinary Chevy. Security, he assumed. She must have kept someone there around the clock.

Sure enough, as Tristan climbed out of his car, he heard the Chevy's door slam shut and footsteps approach him.

"Help you with something?"

"I'm here to see Nora."

"Name?"

"Tristan Albrecht. She's expecting me." Though tempted to try to engage the man in a verbal joust of wit for fun, Tristan noticed the man packed heat. He decided to play nice instead.

The man had a bushy mustache and huge hands, each one large enough to grip Tristan by the balls and, if provoked, squeeze them till he squealed for mercy. With a nod, the guy gestured toward the driveway, then ambled back toward his car. Leaning against his vehicle, his glare glued to Tristan, as he muttered something into his cell phone. Even when Tristan turned his back, he could sense the dude's eyes piercing him. Daring him to flinch.

Before Tristan made it to the front door, it opened, and out walked Nora. With a wave to the security guy, she met Tristan on the front porch.

At just past dinnertime—they had decided to avoid attention if possible—twilight had already set in.

Tristan held out a red rose. He'd intended to hide it behind his back and surprise her with it, but when he saw the security guy, he'd decided to keep his hands visible at all times. He wouldn't put it past the dude to tackle him and kick his ass, right there on Nora's lawn, before their first date.

"It's beautiful," Nora purred as she took the rose, lifted it to her nose, and inhaled. "Thank you."

Tristan nodded toward the Chevy. "Is your friend coming along?"

"No, I'll be fine, as long as we go someplace subdued."

They climbed into Tristan's car, and he steered through some local streets until they wound up on the State Route 118.

"You're full of surprises," Tristan said.

"How so?"

"The security guard didn't shock me, but the house did."

"You anticipated something bigger?"

"Can you blame me?"

She chuckled. "I rented the place when the roles began to look steady. Three roommates at first, and one of them had a dog. The roommates and dog are long gone, but I never got around to finding another place."

"You got busy faster than you expected?"

"This month is the first breather I've had since *Faces* was released."

"Doesn't the paparazzi track you down?"

"I've developed a talent for disappearing into obscurity."

As they passed streetlights on the freeway, their beams

added a subtle glow to Nora's gray eyes. They looked like smoldering ashes.

They opted for a Mongolian barbecue restaurant, a tiny dive which had emptied of patrons by this hour during the workweek. They agreed she wouldn't attract attention here. Tristan felt like an undercover agent trying to duck a handful of foreign spies. Fun for him, but he wondered how long it had taken Nora to feel trapped. At times, she must have felt like a convict on the run, yet she'd done nothing wrong. Her sin? She had excelled.

He inhaled the savory aroma of his pork entrée, and once Nora had taken her first bite, he started on his own. Sweet, spicy flavors tingled on his tongue. Nora had opted for a vegetarian meal, which didn't appeal to Tristan at all, but she appeared to enjoy it.

With nobody else in the restaurant except the married couple who owned the joint and spoke broken English, Nora looked at ease and chatted at a normal volume. No one would overhear their conversation and turn their heads at the first detail that intrigued them.

"So why aren't you working on a movie right now?" Tristan asked.

"I needed a break. The next shoot starts in April. In the meantime, I've been reading scripts."

"Anything good?"

She laid down her fork, her eyes on her bowl. "Would you mind if we talk about something else?"

"Sure. What did you have in mind?"

"Anything. It's not that I don't enjoy my work, it's just that sometimes…"

"You need a break from it?"

"Something like that."

"Not the aspect of the career you dreamed about as a kid, huh?"

142

Nora regarded him a moment, then swallowed her bite. "Fatigue wasn't part of my childhood dream."

"And her mysterious side emerges." He grinned at her, and the way she caught his eye in response swept away all doubt that she was interested in him. "So tell me, what *was* your childhood dream?"

"You first."

"Fine," Tristan said with a shrug. "I wanted to be Sammy Sosa."

"The baseball player?"

"Don't judge. What kid doesn't want to be a superstar?"

"Fair enough."

"What about you? Wait, that's a stupid question. You always wanted to be an actress, didn't you!"

With a roll of her eyes, Nora giggled and covered her face with one hand. Was she blushing?

"You don't want to know," she said.

"When you put it that way, I do!"

"It's silly."

"Come on," Tristan teased, reaching over to nudge her arm.

"Fine," she sighed. Peeking through the opening between her index finger and middle finger, she cringed. "I wanted to be an archaeologist."

"You're kidding."

"I told you it was silly."

"Not silly, just unexpected."

Nora removed her hand and poked at her entrée with her fork. "I always did well in science. Plus, other cultures fascinate me."

"So, why archaeology?"

"Structures captivate me. It wasn't so much the architecture, but the logic that went into *why* they chose to build a particular type of architecture. The physical representation of the philosophies that guided them."

"And the scientific part of it?"

"I'd love to dig an artifact out of the ground, something that looks thousands of years old, and determine its age using history and chemical testing."

"Chemicals? You're starting to sound dangerous," Tristan winked.

"I set fire to the chemistry lab in high school once."

Tristan almost choked on his beer. "Remind me not to let you play with matches."

Nora laughed, and Tristan could tell she had grown comfortable around him. He enjoyed her company and, for a few minutes, had forgotten about her fame.

"What can I say?" she said. "I have a tendency to push things to their limits. If one drop of a chemical turns a blue liquid clear, what would *five* drops do?"

"Hypothetical question: If I were to run to the restroom, would my food be safe to eat when I return? Or would I need to poke around it first to see if it starts to glow?"

"Very funny. I'm not that bad."

"You admitted to causing a fire in the chemistry lab."

She spread her arms in a defensive gesture which Tristan found endearing.

"It was an accident! Besides, that's what fire extinguishers are for," she quipped. "It was just a spark."

"You said it was a fire."

"Yeah, yeah." She chuckled under her breath, a smoky rasp.

Nora's simplicity grew on you. She wore minimal makeup and had no need for it. Her skin resembled porcelain. Stunning, in Tristan's opinion.

This must be the true Nora, he figured. The Nora you get when she can be herself. When she doesn't need to look over her shoulder or protect her privacy.

144

The gleam in her gray eyes drew him in, and they locked gazes. He reduced his voice to a murmur.

"You're full of surprises indeed, Nora Jumelle."

She pursed her lips into a cunning little rosebud, then shot him a wink.

"And that's with my clothes *on.*"

Tristan rearranged the napkin on his lap to hide his arousal.

# CHAPTER 34

DEL RETURNED from his morning jog, hopped into the shower, then made himself a smoothie, tossing in an extra dash of spinach.

As usual, he scanned his Twitter feed, posted a random comment, then moved on to a national news website. And there it was, smack dab on the home page, in big, bold letters:

## MARILYN SPEAKS FROM BEYOND!

When he clicked to open the article, he found a brief blurb with a red teaser across the top: *DEVELOPING STORY.* Beside the text was a shot of Marilyn Monroe from one of her films. According to the article, a screenplay had surfaced which, allegedly, she had written. No word on the subject matter or who controlled the rights. A half-page in length, the article contained precious few details, focusing instead on filler material about Marilyn's iconic career and infamous death. More than anything, it struck Del as an excuse to justify the front-page headline.

He surfed a few more sites and found the same news phrased in different ways. Word had swept in like a siege of locusts and spread overnight, courtesy of the Associated Press. It was all over the place.

*How could they have heard about this?*

Del's mind shot to Felicia. He couldn't imagine she had breathed a word about this. She was a minister, after all.

Besides, he sensed she was trustworthy. He felt confident she'd kept her promise to him.

No, another explanation had to exist.

He grabbed his cell phone and hit speed dial. Arnie answered on the third ring.

"Have you seen the big news?" Del asked, giving his tone a curt edge for extra measure.

A pause, then Arnie replied.

"Swing by my office as soon as you can."

# CHAPTER 35

DEL BURST into Arnie's office and slammed the door.

Arnie didn't jump at the intrusion. Instead, he fixed his eyes on his client. Before Del could utter a word, Arnie held up his hand to stem an onslaught of fury.

"I leaked the news to the press," Arnie said. "Anonymously, of course."

"What the hell were you thinking, Arnie?!" Del gritted his teeth and planted his palms on the desk with as much noise as possible. He hovered over Arnie and leered at him, Del's blood in a boil and his heart beating to the rhythm of *La Cucaracha*. "We didn't agree to that! You never said a word to me, you never got my permission—"

"Hold on, Del. Calm down."

"One shot, Arnie! We have *one shot* at this, and you're gonna fuck it up!"

At this point, Arnie splayed his fingers and extended both palms in self-defense. "Hear me out, Del. Please."

Del plopped into a chair and crossed his arms over his chest. "This better be good."

"We needed a preview of coming attractions."

"We don't have our ducks in a row yet. You haven't even lined up the proof we need that this isn't a hoax."

"Don't worry, I've got it covered. I know a guy who knows a guy. I've already talked to him. He can get the prints verified and confirm her signature isn't a forgery."

"And what if he opens *his* mouth along the way? You know how delicate this is."

"He signed a confidentiality agreement with a strict provision to keep his mouth shut."

"But why tease the press so early? They're gonna speculate, Arnie. We haven't unveiled who possesses legal guardianship of this script yet. We risk someone stealing our thunder before we can steer the situation. Suppose some schmuck who lives in his parents' basement spends the next three days pounding out a script about a secret Marilyn Monroe project, then sells the rights to *his own* script. Did you consider that?"

"Yes, I considered it, but this current route works more in our favor. Think about it: Better to get the word out now and verify early, while the speculation is underway. Otherwise, if we wait—if we set up the verification process *after* we announce—can you imagine the circus that will follow? They'll track down my guy and hound him until he spills what he knows, confidentiality agreement be damned. He'll fold, and it'll happen before we line up any power players to read the script. *Poof!* The whole aura of mystery—gone!" Arnie punctuated his remark with a snap of his fingers. "That would dilute our position of strength and decrease the price of the script. Is that what you want?"

Del calmed as he rolled the strategy around in his brain. "Of course not."

"This way, *we* maintain control of the process. By the time the media could begin to suspect you own the rights—which they won't—we'll already have the verification in hand. We'll call a press conference to announce you as guardian, but we won't share our proof of authenticity yet. We'll lie low with that for a few more days before going public."

Del shook his head. "But if we already have our proof in hand the day we announce who owns the legal rights to the script, why should we sit on it? It's the first question the press is gonna toss at us."

"We'll double our media coverage this way, build some momentum. Let *the media* ask the question. Let them challenge us. That way, they feel like *they're* in control because we're playing by *their* rules. If we play by their rules, we can anticipate their reactions—which means *we* control *them.*"

Del clucked his tongue as he sorted through the logistics. He had to admit, Arnie had made an excellent point. The more hype they could engineer, the stronger their position of negotiation.

"That makes sense," Del said. "But next time, clear your strategy with me first."

"Done."

Arnie extended his hand and the gentlemen shook on it.

The agent scratched the top of his waxy head and eyed Del. A tentative tone hung upon his next words.

"You realize, don't you, that if we can't verify the script's authenticity, we're in deep shit?"

"Don't worry, Arnie. It's real."

# CHAPTER 36

TRISTAN—RUSSELL MERRITT—KEPT his eye on the television while interacting with a client, though the programming had dissolved to background noise. When the noon newscast started, the station's music trumpeted that an urgent announcement would follow. An attractive African-American anchorwoman spoke with precision, her voice severe.

"Good afternoon. Breaking news today: Hollywood is buzzing at the alleged discovery of a screenplay written by film legend Marilyn Monroe, mere months before her death."

Tristan dropped his hands from the keyboard, grabbed the remote control, and stepped closer to the television, increasing the volume on his way.

"Few details are known, including the big question: *Who owns the rights to the script?* The firm representing Monroe's estate has denied the existence of such a script. Yet news of its existence first broke through a reporter with the Associated Press, who received the tip from a highly credible source, a source who requested anonymity because he did not have official permission to speak on the matter."

Tristan couldn't believe what he'd heard. He'd never watched any of Marilyn Monroe's movies. They were too old for his taste. Who wouldn't recognize her name, though? Even with his own limited knowledge, he could picture the iconic images of her leaning toward the camera with her red lips parted just so. Or standing on a subway grate in Manhattan, her white dress fluttering wild in the rush of a passing train.

"Speculation abounds regarding the content of the screenplay, including whether it was inspired by a possible reignited relationship with Joe DiMaggio, a former spouse with whom Monroe was in touch toward the end of her life."

Awestruck, Tristan shook his head at what he'd heard.

Lucky bastard who owns the rights to *that* thing.

# CHAPTER 37

"HELLO, Nora."

"Excuse me?"

"You *are* Nora Tasmyn, aren't you?"

"Have we met before?"

"You don't remember me?"

Now that he mentioned it, maybe he did look familiar. Dirty-blond hair. An inch-long scar beside his right eye. A face that looked older than the man's voice suggested. He must have lived a rough life.

Nora shook her head. "I'm sorry, I meet a lot of people."

"Poor little dear, you must be confused. You must be *so* confused."

"I am." Nora quivered at her honesty. "It's the light. Do you see the spotlight over there?"

"I do."

"It's so bright. I can't see, I—I can't find my way."

"Take my hand," said the man. "I'll show you the way"

"Can I trust you?"

"Of course you can."

Nora hesitated. A detail about this man seemed off-kilter, but what was it? Nervousness began to bubble within her gut.

"Take my hand, Nora."

"I don't think so." A hint of trepidation. Her legs, weak as a wishbone in carbonated water, quivered before her mind had a chance to respond. "I'm sorry, I need to leave."

"I'll come with you."

"No. Don't. Please leave me alone."

She began to run.

The man followed. She could hear his footsteps, his filthy leather shoes scratching the pavement.

Nora sprinted faster and dared to look over her shoulder. She'd had a head start, which had broadened the distance between them. The man ran, too, yet he appeared to do so with halfhearted effort. A jog. At any moment, she sensed, he could accelerate and overtake her. Was he teasing her? Did he know something she didn't?

Terror struck her. Nora tried to run faster. Before long, she gasped for breath. Why hadn't she given up those cigarettes long ago? Now she regretted her decision to continue smoking. Her body would be in much better condition today.

Nora approached a lawn and continued running toward a forest on the other side, one that reminded her of a park in Colorado where she and her high school friends had hiked on weekends.

Seconds later, the man's footsteps stopped scratching and began to swish.

He had reached the grass.

Sooner than she'd expected.

Nora glanced at the forest ahead. Could she find a place to hide?

No, she thought, the man was too close. Wherever she turned, he would see her. And once she reached the trees, dodging them would slow her momentum.

Her lungs were on fire. Muscles burned in her legs. Her breaths came quick and shallow in her fright.

Nora veered left. She had almost reached the edge of the forest. What was on the other side of it, she had no idea.

*Keep running, Nora. Don't let him catch you.*

Finally, she reached the forest. Nora stumbled over dead foliage and wound between trees. As she knocked branches out of her way, they swung back and scratched her face, cut her arms. She couldn't keep her footsteps steady on the cracked, uneven ground. If she twisted her ankle, she knew she was as good as dead.

She heard the whipping of tree branches behind her. The stranger had entered the forest, too.

Aside from Nora and her pursuer, the forest was deserted. Nobody to see or hear her scream as she died. Treetops loomed overhead, blocking the daylight, obscuring her view further.

Tears stung her eyes and dribbled down her face. When she peered over her shoulder again, she discovered the stranger had closed the distance between them by half.

*Somebody help me!*

She mouthed the words but couldn't locate her voice. A squeak grated against her vocal cords, which were raspy from those cigarettes. She felt her energy start to dissipate, which caused her to stumble as she ran. But she couldn't let herself stop. He would kill her.

One more glance over her shoulder. The man had donned a black ski mask. Nora's blood turned to ice.

When Nora reached the other side of the forest, she stopped short. Her heart jumped in terror at what she saw: a swimming pool, aqua blue, the shape of a jelly bean. The water's surface appeared pale beneath the leaden sky.

Then it happened. Her greatest terror.

Arms locked around her belly and squeezed. The man wore black gloves. She detected the pungent scent of oil, the kind used to maintain a shotgun. The smell of his polyester ski mask sickened her. His breathing pattern, though heavy, remained collected and determined.

Soon he overpowered her. Nora feared what he might do to her *before* he killed her.

"Don't hurt me!" Nora pleaded. "Please don't hurt me!"

The man didn't reply. He grabbed her by the hair and pulled her to the concrete surface beside the pool. Nora tried to fight, swinging her fists in a frenzy, but the man responded with a throaty laugh as he dragged her across the concrete like a wounded deer. Her legs scraped against the prickly surface and she knew it had broken her skin. She was bleeding, though not much. It was only her leg. Right now, anyway.

Her voice returned. She screamed.

Nobody answered. Who owned this pool? A crow, poking along the side of the water, squawked and took flight.

"Please don't!"

"I know who you are. You're Nora Tasmyn, a frightened little creature," the man grunted. "I'm here to help you. To end your fear."

"Please!" she whimpered as the man dragged her closer to the water. She gasped for breath. To her horror, she discovered her legs had become deadweight. She couldn't move them. "I'm begging you! Please don't hurt me!"

"This will end soon."

The man twisted her hair tighter. As he did so, his fist moved closer to her scalp and the pain decreased.

But her face inched closer to the water as he forced her head forward. Nora flailed her arms.

"No! Please! No!"

When her face hit the water's surface, she held her breath.

*Fight, Nora! Fight!*

If she didn't escape, she would die underwater. Somebody had to help her. Anybody.

She opened her mouth to scream—and realized her mistake immediately.

Water filled her lungs and Nora felt a burning sensation. She flailed faster. Water splashed around her.

The man shoved her head down farther.

With her last remnant of breath, Nora screamed, but the water muted the sound. Large bubbles spewed from her mouth as the final trace of oxygen departed her lungs.

Total darkness.

Sweat had drenched her body and dripped from her hair. Nora bolted upright.

The clock read 1:48 a.m.

Her heart palpitated. She sucked deep breaths through her mouth. Panting, she willed her hands to slow their tremble. A shiver overtook her, so she laid her head against the pillow and drew the ivory sheet closer to her chin, then pulled it over her head completely.

Thirty minutes later, she realized sleep would elude her for the remainder of the night. Nora climbed out of bed and slid her feet into a pair of slippers she kept at her bedside.

She thought back to when she had roommates. If they still lived here, her roommate's dog, a Corgi, would have followed her through the hallway, its claws tapping along the hardwood floor. When she stopped to turn on a light, she would have found the animal staring up at her, its head cocked, waiting to see what she would do next. On nights like these, she missed that dog's company.

Nora padded into the kitchen, fished through a cupboard, and settled on a box of chamomile tea. When the kettle whistled, she tossed a teabag into a mug and poured the boiling water into it. A few squirts of honey and lemon juice, then she stirred the concoction and breathed in the aroma. Steam warmed her nose and cheeks.

Allowing the teabag to steep, she wrapped her fingers around the mug's hot surface and made her way to the living room, where she nestled on a sofa, crossed her legs, and tucked her feet underneath them.

Tonight marked the fourth consecutive night she'd experienced insomnia, but the issue had plagued her over the course of two months. As for the nightmare, she hoped it was a one-time occurrence.

She covered herself in a fleece throw and sipped her tea. The liquid soothed her throat, which she had worn raw in the midst of her intense screams. Listening to the swirl of a ceiling fan and the soothing noise of the water heater in the garage, she tried to snooze, careful not to drop her mug. Yes, she wished her roommate's dog were here to hop onto her lap and nuzzle against her.

Every day, she fought a lingering impulse to cry. It wasn't always a heavy, emotional feeling; sometimes it felt like a light burden, a shadow upon her soul, winter frost upon glass.

Nora refused to take another sleeping pill tonight. It was too late for that option anyway. For that matter, she wondered if tonight's nightmare was a side effect from putting those chemicals in her body in the first place. She had popped them with growing frequency. Already Nora sensed herself treading along the verge of dependency and feared the cliff.

So here she was. Sleepless, scared and sullen.

She retrieved her cell phone from its charger—she hadn't browsed the Internet all day—and visited a news site. She scanned a few world news stories, then navigated to the entertainment section, where she noticed her name in big, bold letters.

That wasn't unusual, so she didn't react—until she read the rest of the headline.

## NORA JUMELLE SHOCKER
### *SEXTING PHOTO LEAKED!*

It wasn't the top headline, but it appeared above the fold. Nora gasped.

She clicked to read the article, and when the page opened, she found a large, unflattering photo of herself just below the headline. A full-frontal shot, with black bars censoring the Rrated areas.

Nora's eyes darted to the article's posting time. Just after midnight. A couple of hours ago.

*Fuck,* Nora muttered.

She felt too humiliated to cry.

# CHAPTER 38

FROM THE CORNER of his eye, Del noted the time as the doorbell rang again.

3:17 a.m.

Rubbing the sleep out of his eyeballs, he opened the front door and, as expected, found Nora standing on his front porch. A light drizzle fell, which had moistened her hair.

"Sorry to bother you," she said, "I didn't know who else I could trust."

"That's okay," Del replied with a yawn, his voice groggy. "Come in. I've got a pot of coffee brewing."

Nora had called thirty minutes earlier and asked if she could stop by his house. She didn't mention why, only that she needed to talk to someone before the world awoke that morning.

The last time Nora had visited his kitchen was—well, that one night and the morning that followed. To his credit, he remembered how she liked her coffee. Del poured two cups and they sat at the kitchen table. Nora shivered, wrapping her hands around her mug for warmth.

"A cold rain has started outside," she said.

"Just a spot shower. They haven't predicted anything bigger."

Del eyed Nora. Based on how she bit her bottom lip and tapped the cup with her fingernail, he figured he should let her begin the conversation. If she'd called him in the middle of the night, it couldn't be good.

"Do you know why I'm here?" she asked.

"No, can't say I do."

As he took further note of her, she didn't strike him as nervous. Instead, she looked troubled, perhaps scared. Come to think of it, her voice had sounded off-kilter on the phone. Had he noted a tremor in it?

Nora stared at the dark liquid. Del perceived it as an attempt to avoid eye contact. Then her shoulders slumped.

"There are some pictures," she said at last, her voice restrained. "Some not-good pictures. Online."

Del had a hunch where this topic would lead. "Pictures of you?"

"Yes." A confession, as though he were her priest. "I met a guy at a frat party while I was in college." Nora met his eyes. "I was on my own for the first time, eighteen years old, free to be myself. And a bit of a wild child back then."

Del nodded. He detected nuances of shame in the way she spoke and hesitation in her demeanor.

"As you can imagine, we did a lot of drinking at that party. He was a gorgeous guy, and I made the mistake of giving him my phone number while I was still half-sober. A few hours later, we were both drunk and started texting back and forth. One thing led to another..." Her voice drifted. She waved a hand in defeat.

"And?"

"And...the words became photos." Nora took a deep breath and sighed. "I deleted the photos he sent me."

"But he didn't return the favor."

"No, it doesn't look that way." She'd returned her eyes to her coffee and sipped. "I'd forgotten all about that night until now."

Del felt bad for Nora, who looked numb.

He sympathized with Nora. Del, of all people, understood indiscretions. He had engaged in his share of them. Fancying himself an expert on the female form, he had explored dozens—make that hundreds—of nude women over the years. But Del Corwyn had never left a woman humiliated or scared. Some called his lifestyle selfish, and perhaps it was, yet he had always respected a woman's dignity.

"These photos have hit the news in the midst of all the Oscar publicity. The timing would have been bad no matter when it happened, but lately, people are paying closer attention." She gasped with fresh realization and her hand flew to her mouth. "Oh shit, that photo's gonna go viral. Already has, probably!"

Del eyed her but said nothing. She leaned forward, her face full of sincerity.

"Photos like this—I would never do this type of thing, Del. Not anymore."

"I know you wouldn't," he whispered, giving her a pat on the hand. His response seemed trite, but it was all he could think to do. He wanted to embrace her, to comfort her in her distress, but felt unprepared for this.

Nora shook her head, her movement ever so slight, which Del assumed was a reaction to the mental bombardment that must have roiled inside her. The anger. The resentment.

The regret.

Finally, Nora peered at him again, her face exhausted. An air of resignation hung heavy upon her.

"This must seem so strange to you," she said. "None of this social media existed when you became a public figure."

If Del had come of age in Nora's era, he admitted, he might have made the same error in judgment. But she was right, social media had changed things. When he was a teenager, sexual experimentation occurred live, in person, on Friday nights in the back seat of a car at the drive-in. Once the moment passed, the evidence vanished.

Things were so different today. The evidence never disappears.

In truth, Del did understand Nora's dilemma. He had seen it before.

To this day, he could recall Marilyn's reaction when her nude image appeared in print without her permission. She had agreed to the photo shoot as a starving artist, long before her fame, back when she was known as Norma Jeane Mortenson. She'd needed the quick cash. At first, her photo was included in a little-seen, dirty calendar. But when the photo rights were sold, she'd felt like a prize horse, sold to the highest bidder at a state fair. People made millions of dollars from that photo and, by Marilyn's account, not a single person had bothered to thank her for making them wealthy.

She had sought recognition as an artist, yet the public had seen her as a commodity for trade.

According to Marilyn, she had received fifty bucks for the photo shoot. Years later, it cost her a fortune.

She had felt hurt, betrayed, as if she no were no longer allowed to control her own life.

Yes, Del understood. This online picture was Nora's calendar shoot.

Del rose from the table, then eased behind Nora and wrapped his arms around her. He hoped she wouldn't consider it awkward.

She didn't.

Nora closed her eyes. Del watched as a tear pooled along her eyelid and tricked down her cheek.

And he held her closer.

# CHAPTER 39

THEY SCHEDULED the press conference a few days after Arnie received confirmation and written documents proving the authenticity of Marilyn's thumbprints and signature.

Because speculation had fueled such widespread buzz, Del and Arnie expected an enormous crowd. To accommodate such interest—and to project an image of power—Del booked a conference room in a four-star hotel. He had sought a room large enough to contain plenty of media players, yet limited enough to give the impression that one room couldn't contain this once-in-a-lifetime event. At first, the hotel staff balked at such short notice, but when Del mentioned the subject matter and the ensuing publicity the hotel would receive, they changed their tune. Amazing, the influence you could wield when power was in your hand.

He and Arnie wore suits and ties—a power red tie for Arnie, while Del opted for royal blue.

Del observed from behind a curtain as the room filled to capacity, attendees donning credentials. Reporters from national and local news sources filled the seats, pens, paper and mobile devices in hand, while a slew of videographers set up shop along the sidelines. Photographers lingered near the podium, ready to duck and shoot once the action started. As Del had hoped, the rumors had attracted an overflow crowd. Many reporters, unable to find a seat, assembled toward the rear of the room, while late arrivals spilled into the hotel corridor and elbowed each other for a peek inside the room. A cacophony of chatter filled the conference room.

Del's energy surged. Soon he and Arnie would become the center of attention. He'd received precious little media hype since the year of his Oscar nomination, and today's ambience fired him up. As far as Del knew, Arnie hadn't received this much attention in his whole career.

When the press conference commenced, he and Arnie made their way to the podium. Per their earlier agreement, Arnie would do the talking, while Del, as possessor of the rights, would project an image of authority by standing silent until a reporter directed a question to his attention.

"Good morning, ladies and gentlemen of the press." Arnie cleared his throat. "My name is Arnie Clemmons. As you are aware, rumors have circulated regarding the existence of an original screenplay written by the late Marilyn Monroe."

Arnie gave his remarks a dramatic pause.

Del watched the crowd, which sat rapt under his agent's spell. Cameras flashed. Videographers zoomed in.

Arms crossed at the wrists in front of his waist like an executive in waiting, Del savored his command of the moment, inhaled the scent of hot lights upon him. The fragrance of fame. A sweat began to break upon his brow.

A glorious occasion! Relevance felt so good.

"This morning," Arnie continued, "I stand before you to confirm that this information is *not* a rumor. It is true."

A gasp among the press. More flashes popped. The top of Arnie's head gleamed amid the lights.

"In a letter dated March 12, 1962—five months before her passing—Ms. Monroe, of her own free will and volition, placed the screenplay in the possession of her close friend, Mr. Delbert Corwyn, and conferred upon him full rights. I will now read Ms. Monroe's letter, the text of which we will also make publicly available." Without further ado, Arnie removed an envelope from the breast pocket of his suit, unfolded the letter, and read its text, including Marilyn's explanation of her thumbprints on the script pages.

In truth, the letter Arnie held was a photocopy of his photocopy, which Arnie had folded and stuffed into a blank envelope, then creased twice for good measure. The original still sat in Del's safe deposit box at an unnamed bank in Beverly Hills.

When Arnie reached the end of the letter, he added, "We will consider all interested parties and offers worthy of the project at hand. As you might imagine, we anticipate a deluge of interest in turning Ms. Monroe's vision into reality, so we will only be able to consider studios and production partners of a minimum caliber, the standard of which Mr. Corwyn will apply at his discretion. As the agent who represents Mr. Corwyn, appointments will be arranged through my office. We have provided that contact information in your press packets, which we will also provide to parties we deem strong contenders for this opportunity." Arnie paused, scanning the crowd. "At this time, we will take a few questions."

A flurry of activity ensued, hands shooting into the air and reporters calling Arnie's name. Arnie acknowledged a brunette female in the second row, who rose to her feet.

"Mr. Clemmons, does the script have a title?"

"Yes, Ms. Monroe named it, *Beautiful Mess.*"

"And how will you distribute copies of the script to interested parties?"

"Excellent question. The script is on complete lockdown. No copies will be provided at any time prior to signing a deal. Interested parties must schedule an appointment with my office and view the script in person." Arnie maintained a confident, no-nonsense demeanor. "Next question?"

More shouts and raising of hands as the first reporter sat

down. Arnie called upon another.

"You mentioned the script is on lockdown. What measures have you taken ensure control?"

"We have discussed the matter with our attorneys. All parties will be required to sign a confidentiality agreement prior to viewing Ms. Monroe's screenplay. No photocopies or photographs of any portion of the script will be allowed, nor will parties be allowed to take notes. All writing utensils and electronic devices must be stored away during the duration of the read. I will be present the entire time to ensure the integrity of our needs are honored."

"Isn't that rather unusual?"

"Given the circumstances, I think we can agree extra security is warranted. If we discover an individual has violated our trust, they will be removed from our list of contenders. No exceptions."

"Can you reveal the premise of the script?"

"Absolutely not." Arnie raised an eyebrow. "What I *can* tell you is that the screenplay reveals a side to Ms. Monroe that will challenge the public's assumptions about her and finally establish, albeit postmortem, the full respect Ms. Monroe sought as an artist. Next question?"

A man with graying temples asked, "Can you provide concrete proof that this screenplay and its accompanying letter belonged to Marilyn Monroe?"

"The letter and thumbprints provide her identification."

"Yes, but assuming the print on the letter matches the prints on the screenplay, can you prove their authenticity?

Del smirked. *Let the reporters think the question was their idea.*

"Yes, the fingerprints were verified as those of Marilyn Monroe. Her prints are on file as a result of her autopsy in 1962. A match was confirmed by experts in the field. In addition, we acquired the services of handwriting experts, who verified her signature is not a forgery. The analyses were conducted by three independent contractors each. The analysts documented their procedures, findings, cases and conclusions in writing, which are also included in the press packets."

More bulbs flashed. And with that, Arnie wrapped up the press conference, dramatic tension hanging in the air, reporters still waving and begging for attention. If Arnie allowed it to continue, the press would ask questions until sunset. But as he and Del had agreed prior to the event, they planned to leave most questions unanswered so speculation would continue to swirl.

Del salivated at the future. His hunger to return to prominence in the industry had gone unfed for so long.

# CHAPTER 40

AS SOON AS TRISTAN REPLIED to his client by email and started to close his laptop, a chime interrupted him. A chat window popped open. He had hoped to head out for an early evening break, but he eyed the clock and, with a grunt, decided to make himself available.

Checking the username, he recognized it as a client who had started working with him in the last couple of weeks. The public figure, whoever she was. He hoped she didn't make a habit of using these live chats. He didn't mind them on occasion and felt they made a great first impression, but they prevented him from prioritizing his responses.

**CAGirl202:** Hi Russell, it's Callie. Are you available to chat?

Well, as long as he'd already stopped what he was up to, maybe he could tackle this one right away. She wasn't one of his more difficult clients.

**RMerritt44:** Hi Callie, I'm here.
**CAGirl202:** Are these live chats OK?
**RMerritt44:** Yes, but if I don't respond, please know I'm simply assisting another client.
**CAGirl202:** I understand. It helps to talk to a live person. I don't have many of those. Not many I can confide in, anyway.
**RMerritt44:** So what's on your mind?

A pause. Was she putting together her thoughts? Tristan eyed the clock again. He'd promised some friends he'd meet them at a karaoke bar for appetizers and hang time in an hour or so.

At last, another chime.

**CAGirl202:** It's been a rough day.
**RMerritt44:** How so?
**CAGirl202:** I've done some thinking.
**RMerritt44:** About?
**CAGirl202:** My career. My life.
**RMerritt44:** What spurred your sudden evaluation?
**CAGirl202:** Something happened. Something not good.
**RMerritt44:** Can you share more?
**CAGirl202:** No, it's too humiliating. It's the worst thing that could happen to me at this point.
**RMerritt44:** These things tend to pass, don't they? You mentioned you're a public figure. Surely you've endured challenges before.
**CAGirl202:** Not like this. This is—it couldn't get much worse. It's funny, fame looked so enticing before I had it. But now, it's like I don't belong to myself anymore. Everyone feels entitled to a piece of me.
**RMerritt44:** Everyone?
**CAGirl202:** Not everyone. But I don't know who those exceptions are. I don't know who I can trust.
**RMerritt44:** Can you take a sabbatical?
**CAGirl202:** It's not that easy. This thing that happened, it's not project-related and it won't go away. The pressure is building. It was always there, but it's tripled with this latest incident.
**RMerritt44:** Is a mental vacation what's needed?
**CAGirl202:** No. In my career, the only way I can avoid these things is to totally walk away. End the whole thing.

Tristan considered how many people ended one career and began a new one. How many said they found more contentment in the next chapter of their lives than in the previous one?

> **RMerritt44:** Sometimes you do just need to walk away from everything. Something better might be on the other side.
> **CAGirl202:** But what if the other side is darkness?
> **RMerritt44:** Risk is part of the equation.
> **CAGirl202:** I'm so tired. Maybe the pressure isn't worth it.

Why did she keep talking that way?

> **RMerritt44:** Callie, are you OK?
> **CAGirl202:** I think I need some time to myself. Maybe this chat was a mistake. I'm wasting your time.

Tristan straightened in his seat. Something wasn't right, but he couldn't put his finger on it.

> **RMerritt44:** You're not wasting my time, Callie.

He waited, but no response arrived.
Shit. What had he done?

> **RMerritt44:** Callie, are you there?

A longer pause. Tristan jiggled his knee.
A reply never arrived.
His stomach went sour. Now he was nervous. Would he hear from her again? Ever?
Tristan had dealt with an array of clients. He'd grown accustomed to people complaining about their lives. After all, the primary reason most contacted him was because they were dissatisfied and sought improvement.
But Callie was different. As he reflected on that afternoon's odd chat, apprehension mounted. This sounded more serious than what he was used to, and Tristan wondered if he'd gotten in over his head. He was just a guy making a living. He never intended to make anyone's life worse.
So what the fuck just happened? Where was she?

Another chime. Tristan gasped and looked at the screen, then a hammerhead sunk in his gut. She had signed out.

All he had was her username. He didn't know her real name, her address, or her billing information. He couldn't track her down. And by her own admission, she had decided not to offer any clues about her predicament.

Yes, this was more serious than he'd realized at first.

Tristan tensed his jaw and slammed his hand on the arm of his chair, kicking himself for not paying closer attention, for trying to breeze through their conversation.

Suddenly, he wasn't in the mood for karaoke.

With a sigh he grabbed his keys and headed out to grab coffee. Might as well. His work was finished here.

# CHAPTER 41

NORA CLOSED her chat window.

Maybe it was a mistake after all. This wellness coach had never been in her situation. How was he supposed to guide her? She couldn't offer him any specifics about her life: Considering the photos had just leaked, Russell wouldn't need a degree in rocket science to make the connection and figure out his client was Nora Jumelle.

Granted, countless other celebrities had fallen victim to her predicament. But that didn't make this any less personal for her. And she refused to engage in nude scenes, so this latest development invaded her privacy in a new way.

She could have strangled the frat guy who leaked her photo. She couldn't even remember his name.

Was this worth it? Why did people feel entitled to a piece of her?

Nora had dressed in her comfort clothes, casual jeans and a flannel shirt with the sleeves rolled up, her go-to wardrobe whenever she felt down. Though Alanis Morissette had reinvented herself in a similar stripped-down version around the time Nora was born, Nora had discovered the musician's *Jagged Little Pill* album in her mother's music stash and had grown up listening to it. She related to the artist—her simplicity, her understated sexuality, her yearning to be taken seriously as a creative force.

Curled on a loveseat in her living room, she browsed the latest Oscar buzz online, fingering the cozy fabric that covered her arm. Soon she stumbled upon a website that cited the Vegas odds on the current Oscar race. *People bet on* that, *too?*

According to the website, odds had increased in her favor this past week. She remained the favorite. For that matter, Nora Jumelle looked more and more like a sure thing.

Though she wanted to deny it, exhilaration mounted within her as the race continued. She had dreamed of this before she arrived in L.A.

So why couldn't she shake the sadness that haunted her? It peeved her. Why couldn't she feel normal? She ran through this emotional cycle day after day.

Nora slammed her laptop shot.

Fuck it.

Fuck the sadness. Nora Jumelle was gonna go have some fun.

# CHAPTER 42

STILL PROTECTIVE of her privacy on her home turf, Nora hopped in her car and ventured twenty minutes away, near the coffee shop that had become her refuge. The air felt balmy and brought a tingle to her skin. A perfect day to sit outside.

When she turned a corner, she spotted a Mexican restaurant hosting a happy hour. Taking advantage of the unusual warmth on this winter day, a crowd of patrons mingled outside on the patio, a closed-in area with a bar at one end and gaps at the corners to allow customers to come and go. The place was a beehive of activity. A salsa beat thumped from a pair of gigantic speakers. Individuals laughed and conversed at a handful of high-top tables along the periphery, but otherwise, people swarmed within the patio and spilled out to the parking lot. Hovering overhead was a sign featuring the restaurant's trademark character, a laughing jalapeno, its comic-strip arms extended: *Welcome to the fun, folks!*

Perfect. She could interact with a few people, yet maintain a degree of anonymity among the crowd. Nobody would notice her unless she chose to allow them to. No one would hear her over the blasting music unless she chose to talk to them.

She squirmed through the crowd toward the bar, ordered a Grey Goose martini dirty, then worked her way into the middle of the crowd. She had no destination here, and it felt good. She'd float along, a cork in the ocean, and see where she landed.

A man with a five-o'clock shadow turned around. Tall, dark and handsome, dressed in a sport shirt and khaki pants, he looked as though he'd arrived from an office that allowed business-casual attire. In one hand he held a bottle of Corona with a lemon wedge floating inside. Before Nora had a chance to divert her gaze, the man laid eyes on her, and their glances locked. Measuring at least six feet tall, he had to lean down to interact with her.

"Did you come from work?" the man shouted over the music.

Nora still had to cock her ear toward him to decipher his words. "No, I had the day off."

"What do you do?"

"I'm an actress."

"In that case, you fit right in! Half the women here are actresses!" The man chuckled. "Name's Ben."

"Nora." She raised the martini glass to her lips.

"You been in anything I'd know?"

"A few."

The man nodded, then inspected her closer. His upper eyelids twitched as if her reply registered with him.

"Hold on! *Nora,* you said? Are you Nora Jumelle?"

"You bet."

She loved this. Individuals engaged in conversation and laughter all around her. Nobody else could hear a word she said. The sense of control ushered in a feeling a triumph. Once again, she had defeated the odds, wandered into a public place, and managed to maintain her anonymity except with whom she chose to reveal herself. Her confidence revived.

"What would Nora Jumelle be doing here?"

"I came on a whim. Decided to grab a drink."

"Yeah, I've had a few myself." Ben lifted the bottle and took a quick pull from the longneck. "Been here an hour. This is my fourth."

She nodded, then scanned the crowd for someone else with whom to mingle. If Ben was on his fourth drink, he wouldn't be as much fun as she'd hoped. Intelligent conversation wouldn't be an option.

Nora felt a man's touch on her arm, and she pivoted. Ben had laid his fingers on her, though he had kept it light and respectful. As respectful, she supposed, as you can keep things with a stranger. But the fact he'd made contact within two minutes of meeting her—after tossing several beers into his system—put her on alert. At first, she'd found him attractive; but on second thought, she decided to keep her distance and wade to the other side of the crowd.

Standing a few feet from one stereo speaker, the beat started to sound like chaos.

"I'm going to head the other way," Nora said. "It was nice meeting you, Ben."

His hand dropped. "Why don't I come with you? We can talk."

"That's nice, thank you. But I'm gonna go it alone."

A grin emerged on Ben's face. Whether out of kindness or desperation, Nora didn't know, but goose bumps prickled along her arms.

And now he'd put his hand on her again.

"Come on, I'll buy you another drink."

"I'm good. Thank you."

"But you came to mingle, didn't you?"

"Yes, so I'd better start working my way through the crowd."

"What's the matter? Nora Jumelle can't talk to a regular guy?"

Shit. Why wouldn't he leave her alone? And now his hand bordered on gripping her.

She pierced his eyes with hers. "I'm sorry, but I said no."

"Come on, just one drink. What've you got to lose?"

Nora squirmed in an attempt to free herself. Ben tightened his clutch. If she hadn't shifted her drink to her other hand, she might have spilled it.

"I said *no, Ben.*"

"You've known me five minutes, and you're judging me already? The great Nora Jumelle is judging an average guy?"

Nora couldn't wriggle loose. Now Ben scared her. This was a mistake. She needed to get away from him. Somehow.

She shook her arm. "I said no!"

The salsa beats intensified.

"Come on, Nora, give a chan—"

Call it survival instinct, but she tossed her drink in his face and, in the process, splattered several patrons around him. Wondering what had happened, they ceased chatting and spun around. Ben dropped his hand to his side—and, by accident, dropped his beer bottle. The glass shattered when it hit the concrete.

One man, a burly sort who looked as though he'd stopped for a drink on his way home from a day of hard labor at the gym, tensed his shoulders when Nora's drink splashed him. He inspected the woman with whom he'd been having a conversation, wiped martini drops from her shoulder, then turned in a single step. Nora guessed he was in his mid-twenties and consumed protein shakes by the liter.

Assessing the situation, the man took note of the jagged glass at Ben's feet and eyed Nora's empty martini glass. He gave Nora a protective perusal, then glared at Ben, who tried to mop his face with his shirt sleeve. Alcohol dripped from Ben's hair onto his temples.

Mr. Protein's eyes narrowed, and Nora could tell he'd started to size up Ben already. The man's face flushed plum purple.

"What the hell, man? You got my girlfriend wet. The

fuck's the matter with you?"

Ben tried to hold his ground, but from the way his pupils shrank, Nora could tell he wanted to recoil in terror. His eyes flicked toward Protein Guy's biceps, then returned to the guy's fuming glare.

"Nothing's wrong," he replied. "We're good."

"Your face is all wet, dude."

"I'm cool, man. Let it go, okay?"

Still stunned at what she'd done, Nora stood frozen. The man turned at the waist toward her and jabbed a stubby thumb in Ben's direction. "This guy bothering you?"

Before Nora could answer, Ben spoke up. "She's fine. Why don't you mind your own business? Okay, pal?"

Bad idea.

Now the man planted his feet so he could stare Ben down, face-to-face. He crossed his arms, muscles bulging beneath his T-shirt, a dagger tattoo peeking past one sleeve. Still gripping a longneck in one hand, he appeared ready to smash it across the back of Ben's skull. Nora cringed.

"You need a beating, *pal?*" A thick vein popped to attention and snaked along Protein's neck.

"We're fine," said Ben, who looked frustrated by the man's refusal to move on. He held out one hand and added, "We were just leaving."

When Ben nudged Nora with his fingertips, she jerked away. Protein Guy noticed this and must have smelled trouble.

"I don't think she wants to go with you, *pal.*" And with that, he swiped Ben's hand away from Nora.

Ben's jaw line flexed.

People swarmed around them. Nora angled her face toward the ground and hoped nobody else recognized her. She sought a way to escape without anyone noticing, but unfortunately, courtesy of Ben, now she was the center of attention. From her five-feet-eight perspective, she couldn't see above many onlookers' shoulders, beyond the occasional gap that occurred as people shifted. Although tempted to escape, she didn't want to see Ben beaten bloody, despite his aggression. The guy had had too many beers, that was all. Then again, she wondered if she should get out of there while she could. She eyed a route to the parking lot.

But when she heard the first shriek from the crowd, she returned her attention to the antagonist and her knight in T-shirted armor. Protein Guy had grabbed Ben by the neck, and Nora tried—too late—to intercede. Ben must have made another smart comment or two while she wasn't paying attention, because Protein Guy suddenly landed a meaty fist into Ben's face.

Ben stumbled backwards, hands flailing. The crowd gasped and herded closer to watch the fight ensue. Someone's shoulder knocked the martini glass from Nora's grasp. She tried to catch it, but the mass of bodies had engulfed it. Two seconds later, she heard the glass shatter on the ground.

She tried to squirm away from the throng but couldn't budge against the bodies packed together, who appeared to relish the spontaneous entertainment.

She was trapped in a mob.

# CHAPTER 43

PULLING OUT of the coffee shop's parking lot, Tristan turned a corner and spotted a mob to his left, outside a Mexican restaurant, the one with the laughing jalapeno character. When a red light trapped him at the intersection, he rubbernecked to try to ascertain what was happening. At first, he assumed it was a special event, but on second glance, it almost appeared violent.

In a flash, he caught sight of a young woman with raven hair and porcelain skin before the crowd engulfed her again.

It couldn't be...could it?

She mentioned she frequented the coffee shop here, but not the Mexican restaurant.

Nonetheless, his gut tugged him toward the mob.

When the light turned green, Tristan veered to his left in the middle of the intersection, which triggered the blaring of a car horn behind him. He waved an apology and hoped a cop wasn't sitting nearby. Courtesy of a green arrow giving full right of way to those making a left turn, he didn't face oncoming traffic. His tires squealed on the asphalt as he accelerated into the parking lot.

Tristan eased his car parallel to the restaurant's patio, riding the brake so he could better scrutinize the scene.

There she was again—the raven-haired woman he thought he'd seen! Sure enough, it was Nora.

*What is she doing? Why hasn't she gotten out of there?*

Never mind the answer. Without further thought, Tristan put his car into park beside a yellow no-parking stripe, left the engine running, and hopped out. Having laid eyes on her a moment ago, he knew where to fight through the chaos. As packed together as people were, she couldn't have moved far.

Latin beats thumped from two large speakers, oblivious to the fact they now provided the soundtrack to a ruckus.

People faced the center of the patio, bobbing to see over one another. A few half-drunk guys whooped and hollered, the way kids would at a fistfight in a schoolyard. Other people looked on with their mouths agape or covered with hands in shock.

Tristan slid his arm between two individuals and shouted, "Excuse me! Coming through!"

He wedged himself between them without waiting for accommodation. Poking his head between two more sweaty bodies, he caught sight of Nora again. Despite pressing his chest against those in front of him, he couldn't budge forward. Nora must have been the center of attention. He wondered if someone had recognized her and started trouble. He couldn't imagine it occurring here, but he needed to isolate her before she got hurt and before the police—or worse, a news van—showed up. People already had their cell phones out, shooting videos. When he caught sight of her again, he ducked low. Perhaps he could pull her through and avoid getting her face within view of the phone cameras.

By sucking in his breath to narrow his stomach, he managed to gain an extra inch. Not much, but enough to lurch forward and grab her by the hand.

A frightened Nora screamed. When she couldn't retrieve her hand from his grip, she ducked, peered through the bodies to see who had seized her, and recognized Tristan.

Tristan figured he couldn't accelerate the situation by

adding force, so on the count of three, he shoved one guy out of the way and pulled Nora through. This sent part of the crowed into a domino effect, causing the last person to stumble into one speaker, which sent it crashing to the floor. By that time, however, Nora and Tristan had pushed their way out of the patio enclosure.

Tristan stopped, grabbed her by the shoulders. She appeared shaken.

"Nora, are you okay?"

At the sight of Tristan, a tear formed in her eye. Dumbfounded, she shook her head, not in answer to his question, but as if confused about what had happened.

He didn't know where her car was, but she seemed too shaken to drive. He decided to get her out of there before more trouble erupted for her. As it was, she'd started the day with problems: Tristan had seen her picture online, the one somebody had leaked earlier that morning.

"Come on, I'll drive you home," he said. "We'll swing by here later tonight and get your car."

Guiding her into the passenger seat, he shut the door, climbed behind the wheel, and sped away.

# CHAPTER 44

HALF AN HOUR LATER, Nora and Tristan sat on her loveseat, her living room windows cracked open, listening to the distant swish of trees. Twilight had settled in. To help herself relax, Nora had lit candles throughout the room. Candles reminded her of her aunt's home while Nora was a child. They helped her maintain a sense of balance in her life.

She felt calm in Tristan's presence. He inspired in her a sense of security, and as she sneaked glances at those blue eyes, her heart told her he was a guy with romantic potential.

At the moment, however, he looked unsure about being in her home. Although he tried to appear comfortable, he cracked his knuckles.

Nora almost reached for his hand, then gave it a second thought.

"Some happy hour *that* turned out to be," she said instead. "Thanks for getting me out of that place. You had more sense than I did."

"No big deal," he shrugged. "What happened over there?"

"A stupid misunderstanding." She rubbed the arms of her flannel shirt, which amplified her feeling of comfort.

"Why did you go there?"

Good question. Nora hadn't considered the rationale behind it. She's simply lunged into it.

"I don't know why," she said. "Maybe I reacted to the pressure these days."

Tristan shifted in the seat. Distance appeared in his gaze. Hesitation.

"I saw what happened this morning," he said. "I mean, you know...the photo thing."

She felt her face blush and mustered a chortle, which turned out weak. "Oh yeah. That."

Tristan crossed his arms and gave her an appraising stare. "It's hard for a regular guy to imagine how that must feel. It happens, but when everyone knows who you are, it puts a different spin on things."

"It's become my new normal, I suppose. Maybe one day, if I hang in there, I'll get used to it." When she glanced his way, she found him focused on her, listening with full attention. His brow was knit with concern. Maybe she could trust him. "Have you ever felt like you don't control your own life?"

"You mean in a celebrity kind of way?"

"Any kind of way."

Tristan considered her question, then replied, "If you think about it, nobody has complete control. No one has all the answers. Life is a lot about running blind, isn't it? Taking chances? Hoping to heaven you're right?"

Yeah. That was how she felt.

Why was her heart drawn to him?

Tristan appeared lost in thought.

Nora considered what she was about to do, then decided to move ahead with it, hoping he would understand. She scooted closer and cuddled against him. To her relief, he wrapped his arm around her, his hand resting upon her upper arm, the way she enjoyed being held. She sank into him further.

Tristan rested his cheek on her forehead as Nora listened to him breathe.

They said nothing.

They didn't need to.

Nora had found a friend.

# CHAPTER 45

AS HEALTHY AS HE PREFERRED to eat, Del had his limits. He never found the scent of veggie burgers as appetizing pure Angus beef. You can't duplicate what's genuine; you can only come so close. He'd observed that in Hollywood.

He couldn't remember the last time he'd grilled, but Felicia proved herself adept at it on his patio as she flipped several patties. The flames kissed them and brought them to a sizzle.

This woman was full of pleasant surprises.

He felt awkward. Del was accustomed to entertaining his guests, not the other way around. Besides, call him old-fashioned, but he wondered if the man should be the one playing with fire.

"You shouldn't be doing all the work," he said.

"I don't mind," she replied. "Besides, I'm used to it. It goes with the territory in my profession. I tend to be the one who fills in holes here and there."

"Do I have your permission to slice the onions?"

She shot him a wink. "You may."

With a playful salute, Del sliced off both ends of a red onion and shaved the remainder into rings. A smoky aroma emanated from the grill, teasing his hunger.

A few minutes later, his doorbell chimed. Del wiped his hands and set down the knife. Sneaking behind Felicia, he planted kiss on the nape of her neck, which she had started allowing him to do.

On the second ring, he trotted to the front door, then waved Nora and her guest inside.

Nora offered Del a quick hug and held out a bottle of wine. "I hope red is okay."

"Beggars can't be choosers."

"Del, this is Tristan."

"Nice to meet you, Del."

A firm handshake. Not bad. Somebody had trained the young guy well.

Nora's friend looked like a stereotypical southern Californian, his brown hair carefree as a surfer's. And even though Del realized it was the current style, he still found it shaggy. Kids.

"Let's head out back," Del said. "Felicia's on the patio."

Del led them through the house and out to the patio, where he introduced each of them to Felicia, who transferred the final patty to a plate and turned off the gas grill. With a pop of the cork, Del poured four glasses of Nora's wine. Conversation unfolded smoother than he'd anticipated, given the diverse backgrounds the four individuals brought to the table. Within a few minutes, Tristan ignited the first round of laughter, and the foursome interacted as if they had met ages ago.

Del shook his head and marveled at how a wide span in generations could blend with such ease. Maybe he should've had kids. On second thought, he grinned at the images of a teenaged Nora and Tristan lashing out at their parents, then decided he'd made a suitable choice after all.

After filling their plates with burgers, redskin potato salad, and vinegar-based coleslaw, they took their seats around the table. They were about to begin eating when Del watched Felicia pause and have a private moment to herself before picking up her fork. His memory retreated to his childhood in Nebraska, to the old minister who had always treated him with kindness.

"Everyone hold on," he blurted.

Nora halted, looking at him as though he was about to unveil breaking news. "Is something wrong?"

"It occurred to me that we have a woman of the cloth present." Turning to Felicia, he took her hand beneath the table. "Don't you usually do a blessing or something before meals?"

Felicia responded with a delightful chuckle. "I'd be glad to." And with that, she bowed her head and offered a quick prayer of thanks. Nobody objected. Nora and Tristan bowed their heads in respect. In fact, they looked like they enjoyed the diversion. Afterward, they resumed eating.

With a sip of his wine, Tristan glanced at Felicia, who sat on his left. "So, you're a preacher?"

"That's what they tell me."

"You don't look like one," he said, then rolled his eyes. "Sorry, what I mean is, aren't you supposed to wear one of those white rings around your neck so people know to keep their language G-rated?"

Felicia grinned. "Yes, I have a couple of those collars. I save them for worship services, hospital visits, that sort of thing."

"I'll bet you've seen your share of crazy stuff."

"I've been around the block. But the people are worth it."

"How do you mean?"

"I try to take the long view," she replied. "We all make mistakes. We all try to navigate through life. So I focus on the long-term potential in people, view them in light of eternity rather than the here and now." Felicia sampled the coleslaw, which Del had watched her make from scratch. An old parish recipe, she'd told him. "And what do you do for a living, Tristan?"

"I'm an entrepreneur," he replied. "I run an online business."

"That's interesting. What kind of business?"

"Long story, but you could say I connect people with solutions," he said. "They have questions, and I provide answers." He regarded her for a moment, then added, "Kind of like what you do, right? Give or take eternity."

She grinned at that. "I suppose so."

As Del looked on, amused by the exchange, he realized he wasn't the center of attention this evening.

And to his surprise, he discovered he had no complaints.

# CHAPTER 46

ONCE DINNER ENDED, the rounds of banter and laughter subsided, and the foursome grew quiet. Nora, her face sincere, placed a hand on Del's wrist.

"Del, I have a favor to ask you. I hope you don't mind."

Curious, Del couldn't imagine what *he* could do for *her.* "Okay, shoot."

"Will you be my date at the Oscars? Even though it's as friends?"

Del was shocked. He hadn't seen this one coming. The media coverage arose in his mind's eye. "Won't I look like your grandfather?"

"Don't be ridiculous. We'll look like one of those classic couples. Like Cary Grant and Dyan Cannon."

*Cary Grant and Dyan Cannon?* "I thought you weren't very familiar with old Hollywood."

"I've been studying up," she replied with a twinkle.

Del tried to find words. Was he speechless? Finally, he shrugged and said, "If it would make you happy, I'd be honored to do that."

Nora beamed. "Good, then it's a done deal."

When the subject changed, Felicia leaned against him. "I think it's sweet," she whispered in his ear. "She sees you as a father figure. That's a compliment."

When did *that* happen? He hadn't even tried!

Nora rose from the table and gathered the empty plates. "I'll bring these to the kitchen."

"Don't do that, please." Del shot up from his chair. "I'll take care of those."

"I don't mind. Honest."

Del relented. "I'll help you, then. I've been standing around in my own house with nothing to contribute all day," he said, giving Felicia's shoulder a playful squeeze.

Del and Nora gathered two stacks of plates and silverware. She followed him into the kitchen, giving him a lighthearted jab with her elbow on the way.

With Del on rinsing duty, he handed each item to Nora, who arranged them all in the dishwasher.

"Tristan comes across as a pleasant individual. How'd you meet him?"

"Pure chance. We crossed paths at this coffee place we both go to. He didn't know who I was until after we started chatting."

"Are you sure about that?"

"I can read people by now."

Del nodded, his due diligence as her self-appointed guardian done. "Long-term possibilities with him, perhaps?"

"It's still early." Nora turned to him, pursed her lips, the hint of a grin forming as she narrowed her eyes. "Del Corwyn, are you looking out for me?"

"Somebody needs to." He raised his hands in innocent surrender. "Besides, you named me your Oscar date. I have certain duties."

"You're adorable. Thank you." And with that, she gave him a peck on the cheek. "As long as we're prying into each other's lives, Felicia seems nice."

Sunshine burst in his chest. "We get along."

From the way she planted her hands on her hips, he could tell Nora didn't buy his casual response. "Oh, please! You invited me to meet her. You must be interested in her beyond the—" Her jaw dropped. Nora gasped. "You're *falling in love* with her, aren't you!"

"Shh!" Del darted his attention to the kitchen entrance to make sure no one had walked in.

Nora lodged her tongue against her cheek and savored her victory as a sleuth. "That happened fast. How many times have you taken her out?"

"I don't know if you'd call them dates, per se."

"Fine," Nora said, altering her voice to a joshing tone. "How long have you two been *'per se-ing'* each other?"

"A while, here and there."

"Uh-huh."

Del decided to change the subject before she got him to admit anything he'd regret. Nora was smart. He didn't want her to figure out anything else before he had a chance to do it himself.

"I've been following the buzz on your nomination," he said. "It sounds good."

Nora turned toward the sink. Whatever humor she had shown in the last few minutes evaporated. Was it something he said?

"You're right about that. Lots of attention."

"And you're no longer thrilled with that achievement?"

"Winning would be a dream come true," she said. "It all comes with a price, though. Doesn't it?"

"Everything worth its weight in gold comes with a price to pay, including those little golden statues. It's worth it though, wouldn't you say?"

Del noticed hesitation in her response.

"I'm still thinking about that photo," she replied.

So that was what bothered her. Not that he could blame her. "Online? The one you mentioned the other night?"

"I don't even remember the guy's name," Nora snorted,

her humiliation obvious. "Isn't that absurd?"

"We've all made our share of missteps. You can't see into the future, but you do the best you can."

Nora gestured toward the patio. "Does Felicia know about the picture?"

"Yes, I think she does."

With a laugh, Nora covered her face with one hand. "A minister. Lovely. I'm sure that made a great first impression."

"I don't think she judges you, Nora. If she judged people by every action they've taken in their lives, do you think she'd be having dinner at my house?"

"I suppose you're right." She exhaled long and slow, rubbing her thumb along the clear polish she'd applied to her fingernails. "This type of thing didn't happen when you were my age, did it?"

"On the contrary, it happened to someone I knew. A photo resurfaced, a regret that lay hidden in her past—or so she thought."

Nora furrowed her eyebrows. "Are you talking about Marilyn Monroe?"

"Yeah."

Nora nodded in resignation. "So at least I'm in good company, right?"

"Not that it erases your regrets."

"No, it doesn't." She stared into his eyes, a sad, pleading look. "Tell me this will go away, Del."

"It'll blow over. Give it time. It's part of the game, albeit an ugly part. You and I love what we do, but it's not always the life of champagne some people believe it to be."

Del regarded her again. Why did he get the sense the viral photo wasn't the only thing that tormented her? He suspected something else lurked beneath Nora's melancholy. He wanted to ask but couldn't find an appropriate opening.

Del's mind bounced back to Tristan's description of his

career. It struck him as rather vague. "So this new guy, Tristan—he's an entrepreneur online? What does that involve?"

"Could be anything."

"He didn't go into detail?"

"No. Then again, I haven't asked much about it. As long as it isn't online porn, I think I'm okay with it."

Del made a mental note to prod Tristan for more details.

Nora turned off the faucet and shook the water from her hands. Del must not have hidden his curiosity well, because she examined him as if she found humor in his questions.

"Lots of people start businesses online these days, Del. Even wellness coaches."

"Wellness coaches?"

"Yeah, who knew, right?"

"Where did *that* come from?"

Nora bit her lower lip, as though tentative on whether she should say more. "Don't breathe a word about this, okay? I've been talking to a wellness coach. Anonymously."

"Why?"

"Just to get some things off my chest."

"But how do you manage to stay anonymous?"

"It's entirely online."

"You've never laid eyes on this coach in person?"

"Nope, and he's never laid eyes on me, either."

"You're kidding."

"I figured it couldn't hurt."

"I didn't realize wellness coaches could conduct business exclusively online."

"Apparently, this one does. And it's helping."

She couldn't be serious. Del held his tongue, not wanting to make the young woman feel bad. But who the hell can give quality advice to someone they've never met? Then again, Dear Abby made a career out of it.

Nora crossed her arms. "You're suspicious."

"I wouldn't say *that*... "

She burst forth with a staccato laugh. "You're *totally* suspicious! Tell you what..." With a roll of her eyes, she pulled her phone from her pocket. Her thumbs went into motion.

"What are you doing now?" Del's phone vibrated in his pocket.

"I texted you a link to the guy's website. One day, maybe it'll come in handy for you, too."

Yeah, right.

# CHAPTER 47

LATER THAT EVENING, Del led Felicia to his front porch. For a moment, they lingered in the breeze, peering into each other's eyes. A full moon glowed overhead, its light lending an angelic luster to Felicia's skin.

With his forefinger, he swiped a strand of hair from her face, to which she responded by leaning toward him. The depths of her eyes invited him to meet her halfway. So, with the softest kiss he could muster, Del bid her goodnight.

The moment ended on the same subdued note on which it began. Before Del knew it—and, in his opinion, all too soon—their lips parted.

As Felicia searched her purse for her keys, a pang pricked Del's heart. He reached out and touched her shoulder.

"Wait," he murmured. "Please, Felicia."

Call it romance, call it the full moon, but he felt giddy. He felt young again.

"What's wrong?"

"Please don't go. I don't want you to go."

She chuckled. "I've already overstayed my welcome."

"That would be impossible," he whispered, drawing her near, placing another delicate kiss on her upper lip. From the way she peered into his eyes, he knew the romantic mood still lingered for them both. "Please stay."

She uttered a sympathetic groan. "Del—"

"Spend the night with me, Felicia."

She shook her head. Her keys jingled in her hand, but she kept her eyes on his.

With a shrug, she replied, "I can't."

"Don't you want to?"

"It's not a matter of desire. It's just—I'm a minister, Del."

"Ministers don't long for company?"

"Of course they do."

He let forth a soft, sexy chortle and embraced her. "Then stay."

"That's not who I am, Del."

"But we find each other attractive, don't we? On the inside *and* the outside."

"Yes, we do, but—"

"We're both carefree individuals. You can't tell me there wasn't a time when you would have allowed yourself one night with a man you found attractive."

Felicia searched his face, and in her stare, Del noticed an expression halfway between pity and desire. Compassion, perhaps?

"That was so long ago, Del. I've changed since I was young."

He paused a beat. Then his heart sank.

"So the answer is truly no? I can't change your mind?"

Her eyelids fluttered once and she teased his lower lip with her forefinger. "I'm sorry."

Del nodded. Granted, he'd hoped for a different outcome, but he realized this wasn't rejection. Her boundaries were different than his. He could accept that. He could even appreciate it.

"You'll need to excuse me, Felicia. I didn't intend the invite as disrespectful."

She smiled. "I know you didn't."

"I'm an old man stuck in his ways."

She responded with a laugh.

"You're the youngest man I know." Then, with a little peck to his cheek, she added, "Change isn't a *bad* thing, you know."

"It's difficult." He sighed, teasing her with a pitiful look. "I'm not accustomed to being told no, you know."

"You might find gratification exists when you meet somebody halfway," she winked. "Goodnight, Del."

"Goodnight," he whispered, giving her upper arms a playful squeeze.

And with that, she turned and meandered to her car, the full moon casting a glow upon the driveway to illuminate her path. Another moment passed, and she stepped outside the light of the moon, her body a silhouette treading upon shadows. An angel in the night.

Del felt as though he were in high school again, discovering love for the first time.

Then again, maybe he was.

# CHAPTER 48

WHEN FELICIA WOUND her car out of his driveway, Del retreated into his house, his youth intact, but tired nonetheless. Tonight, he'd added to his collection of cherished memories in this home.

Upon reaching the top of the staircase, he padded down the hallway and into his bedroom. On his way to the master bathroom to brush his teeth, he stopped. Opening a dresser drawer filled with T-shirts, he reached in, dug beneath one stack, and retrieved Marilyn's screenplay, the photocopy he kept at home. He breathed in its scent. It still smelled like fresh toner. Unlike the original, this duplicate was crisp, as if Marilyn had handed it to him that week, though the reproduction made the typed text appear blotted and fuzzy.

Del ran his fingertips across the title on the cover page, then returned the treasure to the drawer, a hiding place discreet yet accessible. Much simpler than punching in a security code on his safe downstairs. Why he felt the need to hide the script in his own home, he had no idea, but one could never be too careful with these things.

As he brushed his teeth, he thought back to one afternoon in 1962. Late January in Los Angeles, a day much like today. Del was in his early twenties, not much younger than Nora. Marilyn was thirty-five years old—not even middle age, yet by that point, she had endured so much. Far more than many individuals bear in their entire lives. She seldom talked to him of her childhood, but on that particular day, she had felt drawn to Del and opened up about facets of it.

Marilyn Monroe's insecurities lay not just in her fame and the challenges that accompanied it, but more than that, in her unsettled childhood.

She never met her father. In fact, though theories abounded, his identity remained a mystery to her. According to her birth certificate, her father was Edward Mortenson, her mother's second husband. However, because the spouses separated shortly after Marilyn was conceived, circumstances called the man's paternity into question. Marilyn even had a half-sister, a relative of whom Marilyn was unaware until Marilyn herself turned twelve years old.

Marilyn's mother, Gladys, cut negatives at Columbia Pictures and suffered from paranoid schizophrenia.

On that afternoon in 1962, Marilyn confided in Del the troubles Gladys had endured. She also spoke well of Albert and Ida Bolender, her first foster parents, who cared for Marilyn during her earliest years. The Bolenders, who were evangelical Christians, also planted seeds of spirituality in the young girl's life.

After several years, Grace Goddard, who was like an aunt and had taken Marilyn under her wing, became her legal guardian. They lived together off and on, as Marilyn bounced between stints at Grace's home and the local orphanage. She and Grace lived in places where other lodgers lived.

One of those lodgers, according to Marilyn, sexually abused her when she was eight years old.

To this day, Del couldn't help but shake his head in dismay.

Not knowing her father. Prolonged absences from, and minimal contact with, her mother. No place she could dare call home, because she never knew how long her residence would last.

What pain and emptiness, Del wondered, had such insta-
bility and rejection wrought in the little girl's life?

———————

"I've found my Jesus," she said.

The remark took young Del off guard. "You've gone to
church?"

She giggled. "No, silly. I'm talking about Dr. Greenson.
He's my psychiatrist, and I adore him. I call him my Jesus."

"Why?"

"Because he gives me what I need. He listens to me and
helps me. He affirms that I'm worthy. I tell him my concerns,
and he reassures me that everything will be all right. I feel so
much better after I've spent time with him. So that's what he is
to me: my Jesus. He's my savior, who helps me not to be
afraid."

"Why do you need a psychiatrist?"

She peered at him in a maternal manner, a mother indulg-
ing a child's questions.

"It's not a bad thing, is it? We're all a bit messy, wouldn't
you say?"

Del didn't reply. She had confided in him about her
childhood. From her description, Del knew they had come of
age in two different worlds. She had seen so much more than
he. Compared to Marilyn, Del *was* a mere child.

Marilyn regarded him. "You don't have a motive, do you?"
she said, an observation rather than a question.

"A motive?"

"You know—when people believe they can get something
out of you." She paused, examined his eyes, and gave his
expression a deep, probing stare. "No, you're an innocent
young man. A *kind* young man. There's so little kindness in the
world, wouldn't you say?" She looked away, the pain evident in

the way she wrapped her arms around herself in an embrace. "People can be so cruel sometimes. But *you*—I can trust *you*, can't I?"

"Of course you can." Young Del sat awestruck by this stunning beauty, a woman he'd grown to love.

Marilyn smiled, an intimate grin. She placed a soft kiss upon her fingertips, then placed them upon Del's lips. He buzzed with delight.

"There now, that's better," she said with satisfaction. "Something for my handsome young man. My handsome, *genuine* young man."

# CHAPTER 49

SEVENTEEN YEARS HAD PASSED since Del received his last invitation to a party following a film premiere. But tonight, the powers-that-be had requested his presence in celebration of Clint Eastwood's latest film.

What a difference one week in the news can make.

Last month, he could stroll along Hollywood Boulevard and not a single soul recognized him. Tonight, however, as soon as he entered the soiree, actors, actresses and studio executives of all ages recognized him at first sight.

Del Corwyn was, once again, a hot property in Hollywood.

Music from an R & B artist lent the party a chic tone. As a server passed, Del lifted a glass of champagne from his tray, took an initial sip, and savored the bubbles that tickled his throat. The film's leading man hosted this party at his home, so compared to the industry's larger events, this evening's gathering had turned out intimate. And like a dumbass, Del had worn his tuxedo, while everyone else had dressed in a manner much less conventional. Perhaps formalities had shifted since his heyday, as well. Yet no one seemed to notice his error. In fact, Del swore his attire fed into his classic Hollywood image, the same aura that enshrouded his current ticket to prominence, the Marilyn Monroe script.

From the corner of his eye, he spotted two young actresses

sipping drinks and casting gazes of intrigue in his direction. They looked barely old enough to drink. Del sensed they were checking him out, which reinforced his belief that he had aged at a pace worthy of Dick Clark. Del raised his glass toward the young starlets to indicate hello, then sauntered in the opposite direction.

"Del Corwyn! My guy!"

A rugged, raspy voice, followed by a hearty pat on the shoulder. Del turned to find Clint Eastwood reaching forward to shake his hand. The legend's countenance communicated confidence. His gray hair crackled and a fiery glint fueled his badass grin. Del admired the man's stamina. Not only did Clint possess the Midas touch, turning everything he directed to gold, but he had a reputation as one of the kindest gentlemen in Hollywood.

"Clint, it's been a long time since we've seen each other."

"Not since—oh, you'll have to forgive me," the legend said with a gruff chuckle, "I lose track of these things."

Del could understand. Besides, the man had earned the right to forget a detail here and there.

Clint lifted his glass of bourbon, which he'd ordered from the open bar. "Hey, I was talking to someone and couldn't remember: What was the project we worked on together long ago? We figured it out at one point."

"*A Fistful of Dollars,*" Del replied. "I had a bit part. Early in my career."

"That's right," said Clint, shooting Del with a pistol he formed with his free hand. "A few years after Marilyn died."

"Yes."

"A damn shame, Marilyn Monroe. I always wanted to work with that one. Never got the chance." Clint, deep in thought now, examined his bourbon. "That screenplay of hers—the suspense is killing me. What's it about?"

"I'm sorry, Clint, but I can't say. It's on total lockdown.

You understand how that goes."

"Can't argue with you there." Peering over the rim of his glass, Clint scanned the crowd, downed the remainder of his bourbon, and punctuated it with a hearty exhale. *Badass!* "I'd like to take a look at it, consider the rights. Maybe direct it, too."

Given the mystery surrounding the project, the director's response shouldn't have come as a surprise, yet he couldn't help but marvel that a legend had his sights on something within Del's control. That said, Del knew *all* the major players smelled a hit and he needed to aim high.

"To be honest, Clint, we're looking to sell the rights to one of the studios so all the marketing and distribution aspects will be covered in one swoop."

"I'd still like to take a look at it, though. My production company has an ongoing development deal with one of them."

Del nodded. "You can contact my agent. He'll set up the appointment."

"What's his name again?"

"Arnie Clemmons."

"Who?"

"Arnie Clemmons. It's in the press release."

Clint's eyebrows furled. The agent's name didn't ring a bell. Then again, why would an A-lister like Eastwood recognize it? Del felt a tad sheepish, but at this point, what could he do?

"All right, I'll check it out." With another clap on the back, Clint sealed their conversation with another grin. *Badass!* "Stay in touch, Del. I need to find my wife. She's mingling somewhere."

And with that, the cowboy strode away, planting his glass on a drink tray as he passed. Del, who could hear the coyote-sounding whistle from *The Good, the Bad, and the Ugly,* watched in admiration.

"Hello, Del." Another husky voice, this one female. Enter Faye Dunaway.

"Faye! You're a sight for sore eyes!"

"You could have seen me much sooner if you'd behaved yourself. You never called after our first date."

How long did women remember these things? He couldn't remember not calling her, but then again, he'd scattered many stupid mistakes along his life's path, like a dog marking its territory. He and Faye had worked together decades ago, and he might've taken her out. Del struggled to find a quick response. "I apologize, Faye. My intention would never have been to—"

A full-throated chortle. "Del, you're adorable! I was only kidding you."

Del, attempting to save face, laughed along with her, relieved to hear he hadn't treated her the way she'd described. It *sounded* like something he might have done in a prior era.

The soiree's music transitioned to a silky ballad.

"You look stunning, Faye. Beautiful, as always." And wow, did she ever! Adorned in a sparkling white gown, the woman possessed an ageless grace. She kept her hair long, but tonight, she wore it up in a classic style. To this day, he couldn't resist those high cheekbones.

"You look good yourself, Del."

"And your performance was delightful," he added. In the film, Faye had played a vivacious grandmother who found herself attracted to her granddaughter's landlord.

"The crazy grandma figure." Faye rolled her eyes. "There's not much of a place for individuals like us, Del."

"Can't say I disagree. The industry has changed. We're like strangers, aren't we?"

"What do the kids call watching our films? 'Kicking it old-school?'"

"I think even *that* expression might be passé already. Of course, I'd imagine Mickey Rooney once felt the same way about you and me." Del sipped his champagne and considered the attendees who surrounded him tonight. While a handful were his age, he doubted half were even born when he began his career. "A time for everything, as they say."

*"You're* the man of the hour, though. With that little discovery of yours, I mean."

In spite of her encouraging remark, Del, upon closer examination, detected a combination of joy and pain in her countenance, despite her confident veneer. He wasn't the only one who had struggled in his career. Like Del, she had experienced her share of successes and dry spells.

Del dropped his guard, loosened the chain he wrapped daily around his heart, and opted for honesty.

"When you're in our shoes," he noted, "you take what you can get, and you promote it as a special event." He couldn't stifle the wryness in his grin. "We've all learned how to spin bullshit, haven't we?"

She laughed. Tension disappeared from her shoulders. "Where have you been all these years? I haven't heard much from you."

"Getting ready to relocate."

"From your home? You've lived there forever! Where are you headed?"

"Figured I'd try Florida for a change."

She furrowed her eyebrows. A quizzical expression emerged on her face. "Florida? Why?"

*Exactly.* Del still detested the notion. "The change of scenery might be nice."

*Talk about spinning the facts.*

"Isn't it a busy time for you to move?"

"It was in progress before Marilyn's script appeared. As a matter of fact, that's how I rediscovered it: while sorting through some boxes at home."

If only he'd waited a few more weeks to set the house sale

in motion. He could have changed his mind.

A man in his late fifties, with a professional smile and hair dyed the perfect shade of brown, strolled up to them. Del recognized him in an instant: Bernard Schulman, the head guy at one of the major film studios, one which had amassed a string of hits the last five years and now dominated the industry in both profits and power. The studio had released tonight's film. Del almost salivated.

"I apologize for interrupting," Schulman said, "but I wanted to say hello. Faye, a gripping performance, as always." Schulman and Faye exchanged kisses on the cheeks.

"Thank you, Bernie. Will you excuse me, please? I'm going to get another glass of champagne."

As she wandered away, Schulman turned to Del. "Del, good to see you tonight."

"Bernie. Always a pleasure."

The studio chief looked amused. "So, I finally got to read the script today. You made me sign a *confidentiality agreement?* Come on, Del, you know I'm a straight shooter." At that, Schulman raised his glass, wrinkled his brow, and sipped his drink. "You're taking this seriously. I had to read it on-site at your agent's office. No copies, no notes, nothing."

"I trust you understand the rationale."

"Well, you've done an excellent job keeping it under wraps, I'll give you that much. I seem to be the only one at this party who knows its premise. The script was nothing like I anticipated, by the way. I'd expected a romantic comedy from Marilyn Monroe, but *this?* The woman must've been pretty fucked up."

Del winced at the remark. It seemed, to an extent, sacrilegious. She had written that script from a place of pain.

Del bit his lip and decided to hold his tongue. "She was deeper than many of us give her credit for."

"How many others have read it?"

"A few." *Many.*

"And have you entertained any offers?"

"A few." *Many.*

Schulman regarded Del in what the actor hoped was an attempt to decode his poker face. Then the chief lifted his glass to his mouth and took in another view of the industry professionals around him, servants in his fiefdom. "Any clues on what they've offered? Off the record, of course."

Del savored this. In his past life, he'd loved to play coy and jerk the collars of the bigwigs. He could get used to this again.

"Let's just say the offers have been quite generous."

For the next second, Del didn't remove his attention from Schulman. He wanted to see if the guy twitched in reaction, which he didn't. A poker face in return. No surprise. Schulman was royalty and played it cool, but Del sensed an undercurrent of envy. Behind closed doors, this guy salivated for a deal.

For once in his life, Del Corwyn was the kingmaker in this town.

Schulman nodded. "I'll be in touch with Arnie about an offer," he said, followed by one final smirk as he knocked back the last of his drink. "I think you'll find we can be the most generous studio on the block."

"We look forward to receiving it."

"I'd like to see a deal happen between us, Del."

Del had to marvel at what had unfolded before his eyes.

Bernard Schulman, one of the most powerful insiders in Hollywood.

And Del was in position to crush the guy's balls with his bare hands if he had the notion.

# CHAPTER 50

NORA SAT facing Tristan on her sofa, each individual bent at the knees, their toes resting against each other's. Tristan tapped away on his laptop, working on business. Nora didn't ask him for details on his work—she considered it none of her business—and he didn't inquire about hers.

As she paged through a script her agent had sent for her consideration, she paid nominal attention to a cable news station, which Tristan had turned on. The station had a reputation for mixing soft news and entertainment with world events, which Nora found comical. The anchors bantered back and forth during the day, inserting commentary into their reports, which gave the station's programming an Oprah Winfrey-meets-the-news feel. Eventually, their commentary dwindled down to gossip, which rendered down the show to nothing more than a glorified tabloid, minus the space-alien pregnancies.

At the top of the hour, introductory music sounded, the breaking-news variety, and the co-anchors, Greg Gelman and Virginia Wheeler, both middle aged, looked all-business.

"New details today about the recently discovered screenplay written by Hollywood legend Marilyn Monroe," Virginia began, her voice firm.

Both Nora and Tristan looked up from their work.

Virginia continued, "Although trustee Del Corwyn has

kept the screenplay sealed and copies have not been made publicly available, industry insiders have read the screenplay and made offers for a production deal. One source has estimated offers in the eight-figure range, a figure Corwyn and his agent will not confirm."

Nora dropped her script and absorbed herself in the program. Tristan seemed intrigued, as well.

"Although insiders are required to sign a confidentiality agreement prior to reading the script, vague details have leaked concerning its content, with one insider saying, 'This is not the Marilyn Monroe you saw on screen.' In fact, that same source, who asks to remain anonymous for fear of being blacklisted from consideration, tells us he believes the script parallels the mental and emotional drama Monroe battled in the final years of her life."

Greg Gelman initiated their commentary banter. "That's right, Virginia. This insider describes the script as a disturbing psychological drama with graphic violence and sexually explicit content. And when you consider Monroe wrote this in the early sixties, it's no wonder the pages never saw the light of day. I mean, rumor has it that whoever ends up making this film will have a challenge on their hands. There's serious talk of, 'How will the director keep the script's integrity intact and still squeak by with an R-rating?' Sources confirm it's *that* explicit— and yet, if done well, it's already considered a strong contender for Best Picture."

"And what if they can't get the R-rating and need to go NC-17?" Virginia asked. "We haven't seen a Best Picture contender of that nature since *Midnight Cowboy*. It just doesn't happen. So this could be history in the making—and Del Corwyn has emerged as the power broker at the center of it all."

Tristan turned to Nora. "Has Del said anything to you about this?"

"He mentioned the screenplay, but no specifics. All I know

about it is what I've heard on the news."

They returned their attention to the program, where Virginia continued the banter.

"As of right now, Arnie Clemmons, Corwyn's agent, tells us only top-tier studio executives and high-level producers have been privy to Monroe's project. But according to the buzz, many industry insiders believe the female protagonist is a role best suited for actress Nora Jumelle, who herself is an Oscar contender this year."

Nora felt her jaw drop. She couldn't peel her attention from the program. Her mind raced to her leaked photo, the one which had gone viral not long ago. Was that the reason the powers-that-be were tossing her name around?

"Holy shit!" blurted Tristan. "I take it you didn't know about *that,* either!"

"I hadn't heard a word."

"Maybe you should talk to Del."

Once the initial shock fizzled, Nora pondered what she'd just heard. Call it instinct, but she had a hunch she would identify with this female protagonist, whoever she was and whatever her dilemma.

Greg Gelman wrapped up the story and said, "We'll share more as details become available. Lots of speculation out there."

*You're telling me,* Nora thought.

# CHAPTER 51

DEL SAT in his home office, perusing a proposal he'd received from one studio. He wasn't happy with it.

The rumors were accurate. Production offers had, indeed, snowballed to eight figures, fueled by Arnie's covert attempts to prune the grapevine. But this particular studio had low-balled its offer. And not only that, he envisioned much greater marketing potential than this studio proposed. After all, he was talking Marilyn Monroe, not Donna Reed.

He considered the demand for this project. Sure, he'd expected it to become the hottest item around. And it was big news for the Baby Boomers, those who grew up watching the actress's films in theaters. But the themes into which her script delved were ahead of her time. Del harbored no doubts this film would resonate with Gen-Xers and Millennials, too. If he could get those kids to double their attention to it on social media, it might drive up demand for the product—and the selling price of the rights.

But it needed to happen under the radar. The fire needed to burn at the grassroots level. If he hired a publicist to handle it, word would leak to the studios that he'd manufactured a mirage of demand.

Who might know the right channels to maneuver this in a subtle way? Who was more adept at social media than Del?

He scratched the stubble on his chin. The answer was so

close, he could mouth the name, if only he could locate the syllables to fill the gap. He clenched his fists. *Think, Del, think!* His instincts told him he knew someone in his circle of acquaintances who—

Nora's new friend! Or boyfriend, or whatever he was. What was his name again?

Tristan!

Didn't he run some sort of business online? He would know how to stimulate demand and cause it to multiply!

Del grabbed his cell phone. He'd entered Tristan's contact information the evening they met. Mere habit. Del never expected to contact the kid, but he'd learned long ago never to discard a contact. The world was too small for that.

Tristan answered on the third ring.

"Del?"

"Tristan, my man! Long time, no talk!"

Silence. Confusion. "Okay...how's it going?"

"Listen, I have a conundrum here, and I could use your expertise, if you're willing to help."

A pause, followed by a voice of hesitation. "Me? How?"

"You're familiar with all this social media stuff, aren't you?"

"Sure."

"Much more familiar than I am. You know all the outlets I'd never fathom, and you probably have social circles I don't. I need to get word to trickle out in a way that's effective, but shall we say...discreet."

"Is this about the script?"

"Indeed. And since you mentioned you run your business online, I figured you might know all those little marketing tricks that create demand."

Tristan sniffed on the other end, then said, "I'd love to help you, Del, but the work I do—I don't run *that* kind of business. If I did a ton of marketing, I'd have more demand

than I could handle. I've got a heavy load as it is."

Whoever heard of tempering demand for a product? How did the kid pay his bills with *that* kind of logic?

"Surely you'd have an idea or two, though. What kind of merchandise do you sell?"

"I don't sell merchandise, Del. I sell a service. And I handle the whole workload myself."

"What kind of service?"

"I'm a wellness coach, and I do it all online."

Had Del heard correctly? He shook his phone, then turned up the volume a notch.

"Did you say you're a wellness coach?"

"Yup."

"And you're how old?"

"Thirty-three."

Del wanted to burst forth in laughter but, dumbfounded as he was, he couldn't bring himself to the precipice.

"Don't take this the wrong way, but what does a thirty-three-year-old know about the fullness of life's answers?"

"I don't need to know the *answers*, Del. I just need to say the right things to make people feel better about themselves."

Del could hear the shrug in Tristan's voice. Did this seem ordinary to the kid? Just your average, everyday way to make a living? He was a professional bullshitter! Either that, or he was a genius.

"And people *pay* you for that?"

"I make a decent living."

"Are they other people your age?"

"Most are older. You'd be surprised."

"And they tell you their secrets? Their private stuff?"

"It's anonymous, from beginning to end, including their online payments. Totally faceless. So they feel like they can drop their guard. They use fake names if they want to. I just give them practical advice, reassurance. I'm their motivator, like a personal trainer for the mind or whatever."

"I realize so much occurs online these days, but aren't people skeptical of an online wellness coach they've never met?"

"As long as there are enough people who *aren't* skeptical and the dollars roll in, it doesn't matter. Frankly, I don't care how it *looks*—I'm the one with the killer income."

Del thought he'd heard it all. Then *today* happened. Frustrated, he scratched his head.

"And you got certified in this?"

"You don't need certifications. You just open up shop."

"Isn't that illegal?"

"Of course not." Tristan snickered. "You sound shocked, Del."

"So you don't really have the answers," Del said.

"Hey, man, does *anybody* have the answers? No. So I'm not gonna bust *my* balls over it."

"I don't understand," Del said. "Don't you feel weird taking people's money for advice without having any actual qualifications to give it?

"Look, people are gonna spend their money on *something*. Many of them want somebody to tell them what to do. I just give them what they want."

"Which is?"

"Well, everyone's different. Most of my lady clients want a gentle listener, so I give them that. If a dude needs a set of balls, then for a few hundred bucks, I'll strap a pair of brass ones to his crotch. Figuratively speaking, of course."

"And your advice works?"

"Clients tell me it does."

"But if it doesn't, won't you lose a client? Shouldn't that concern you?"

"Listen, man, I have more clients than I know what to do with. Suppose I lose one, or ten, or a *hundred*. What are they gonna do, tell their friends not to contact me? That's how many prospects nixed per rejection? Ten? Meanwhile, people find me on search engines by the *thousands*. I don't need to lift a finger to advertise anymore."

Unbelievable. And all these years, Del had fancied *himself* the clever one. "And it's a random assortment of clients?"

"They run the gamut of backgrounds. Businesspeople, graduate students who don't want to leave academia, bored housewives. Anywhere from Boston to Boise. I even have some sort of celebrity these days—sounds like an actress or something. A sad situation, really. She's under a lot of pressure."

*Uh-oh.*

Tristan's words felt like a crescent wrench sinking to the bottom of Del's gut. He tried to recall the details of his recent conversation with Nora. She had mentioned talking to a wellness coach. And she'd said he was online. Exclusively.

"A celebrity?" Del hedged. "Who?"

"I can't tell you that. Besides, she uses a fake name. She must be huge if she won't even tell me her *first* name."

"What's she looking for advice about?"

"Come on, Del. Please don't ask me for details. I need to respect the whole coach-and-client confidentiality thing."

*Sure.* Now *he makes the case for professional standards.*

"How'd she hear about you?"

"She stumbled across a business card. I leave them lying around. Said she never tried a coach before, figured she'd give it a shot.

Del couldn't blame Tristan for playing the game to make a living. After all, Del himself played the game in his own professional sphere. Yet his suspicion that Nora was Tristan's client concerned him. If not for Del's chat with her and its timing, he would have discounted the coincidence as unlikely.

Tristan wasn't a bad guy, but Nora was in a delicate position these days. After Del's experience with Marilyn, he didn't want to lose another friend before her time. And if she happened to get advice from Tristan under the impression he was someone else, and it ended up hurting her…

Del would need to keep his eyes open.

"Well, I suppose everyone needs to make a living."

"Exactly. It's not like my motives are sleazy, Del. I'm not living on the government dole. I'm earning an honest living."

"True," Del conceded. "So you don't have any social-media advice for my little project?"

"I don't think you need to stimulate anything," Tristan replied, his tone revealing a knowing smirk had taken up residence at the other end of the phone connection. "I have a hunch this wildfire is bigger than you could hope to control. Big bucks for you, huh?"

"Yeah," Del replied, his mind elsewhere. "Something like that."

He clicked to end the call.

Del couldn't move. He locked his jaw as he tried to convince himself he'd stumbled upon a coincidence and nothing more.

# CHAPTER 52

DEL PARKED his car in the studio lot, the zone to which Bernie Schulman's assistant had directed him. Getting out of the car, he noted the office building the assistant had described—not that he needed to be told—and found it would require a small trek across the parking lot. Best parking spot he'd ever had on this lot, though.

Bernie Schulman had asked Del to come alone, without Arnie. He wouldn't make an offer here, Schulman had promised, but some things were best kept hush-hush while talking possibilities.

Schulman had called Del personally. After so many years without anyone stroking his ego this way, Del had fallen for it. And with gusto.

Upon entering Schulman's office suite and checking in with his assistant, he took a seat. Schulman kept him waiting for a few minutes. Then again, should Del have expected anything less? This was the head guy, after all. He was eager to negotiate but wanted to maintain whatever impression of an upper hand he could. Smart move. Del could respect that.

When Schulman emerged, he welcomed Del with a hearty pat on the back, instructed his assistant to hold his calls, and led his new best friend into his office. The scent of leather furniture filled the room.

"Please, have a seat." Schulman waved to a small group of

chairs around a coffee table, which sat at one end of his office, far away from that formal, unnecessary desk that makes things so complicated. Just a casual chat between two power brokers.

Del took the seat closest to himself. Behind him, at the rear of the room, he spotted one of those little putting greens, the kind by which filmmakers have stereotyped CEO offices, with a golf club and three orange golf balls resting upon it.

Schulman settled into the seat beside Del's. "Would you like some coffee? Water?"

"No thanks, Bernie."

"It was good to see you at the little soiree the other night. Always a pleasure."

Del crossed his leg, his heel facing away from his host. "Congratulations on the film. It looks like it will be another success for the studio."

"Yeah, we've had a solid string of hits for several years now." Schulman brushed an invisible piece of lint from his knee. "We're the winning team in town, Del. *We're* the ones people want to work with when they want a blockbuster."

"I've kept abreast of your track record at the helm. Quite impressive."

Schulman nodded. "You're a smart guy, Del, so I'll cut to the chase."

"I appreciate that."

"I would like to partner with you on this script of yours—of hers, that is. You and Marilyn were friends, as I understand?"

"We were."

"So this is personal for you. You have an opportunity to honor her memory."

"You're observant, Bernie."

"Can I be blunt with you, Del? In the wrong hands, this film will plummet. It will fail from the launch—poor quality, poor vision, poor marketing, whatever the case. And this project is a gem, Del. It's a rarity. We can't let failure happen, can we?"

"Should I remind you that you said you wouldn't present an offer here?"

"And I won't. This meeting is my attempt to set forth a vision. The project is delicate, and we want to keep it all in-house. I've talked to corporate. The studio and its parent company are interested in sweeping rights—and as the dominant force in town, we have the muscle to make it happen. We want to sink a *lot* of cash into this."

Smothering Del with sincerity, Schulman continued his pitch by counting off details, one by one, on his fingers. He was one of those guys who started with his thumb.

"I'm talking screenplay rights; production from start to finish; theatrical and video distribution rights, both foreign and domestic. Soundtrack rights for our sister company's record label. Vertical marketing from top to bottom: the studio, the music arm, plus all the TV and radio stations, Internet outlets, publications, and restaurant chains our parent company owns. Director and principal approvals for you. We'll even name you as a producer. And get this, Del: Our company has a partial interest in a vineyard in Northern California. We'll cultivate an exclusive *wine* in honor of Marilyn Monroe and this film for our upper-brow audiences. Can you imagine! A smooth, luscious red wine—something dark and sexy, just like this script."

Del fought to maintain a straight face, but he felt his jaw go slack. Moisture evaporated from his tongue. He wished he'd accepted Schulman's offer for that bottled water.

"This is history in the making, Del, and public response will be stratospheric. Normally, we'd spread the risk by incorporating other studios at partners, but not this time. We're willing to bet huge on this. No selling partial rights to try to recoup our costs, no allowing some other studio to come in and fuck it up—and you can put that in the contract."

221

"Is that the phrase you plan to put in the contract? 'No fuck-ups?'"

Schulman responded with a hearty power laugh. "What can I say, Del? I'm a straight shooter. Neither of us is one to mince words, am I right?"

Del switched legs and tried not to drool at the fortune, the clout, within his reach. What could be behind door number *two*? "I don't know what to say. I do need to take extra care with this."

Schulman held out his hands to communicate his willingness to back off and respect Del's space. "I understand," he nodded. "Like I said, this is special, and we want to handle the entire thing—vertical, horizontal, and all the way around—to protect its integrity. We owe that to Ms. Monroe's legacy, am I right?"

"Absolutely." Del almost felt guilty, but he pressed on. Would he ever receive another opportunity *this* good? *Poker face, Del. Keep your poker face.* "You've made a compelling case, but Arnie is handling the negotiations. Don't get me wrong, I appreciate the reach, but why call *me* all the way over here to discuss the details without him?"

Schulman's eyes narrowed, and Del could have sworn he caught a twinkle in one of them. The studio chief grinned.

"You're a savvy guy, Del, so I won't play games." Schulman leaned forward and interlaced his fingers, speaking in a hushed tone as if they were portraying spies in a World War II film and the director had called, *Action!* "I did have one more idea for this film, but I wanted to gauge your interest—under the radar—without getting agents or other delegates involved. You know how people misinterpret things."

Whatever would come next, Del couldn't imagine, but it sounded like the mother lode.

Del remained carved granite. He didn't flinch, didn't utter a word—and didn't take his eyes off of Bernie Schulman.

"I want to cast you in the major supporting role." Schulman took a dramatic pause, while his words sank into Del's mind. "You've read the script, Del. You know which character I'm referring to. We're talking a plum role—the type of role *comebacks* are made of." Schulman pierced Del's eyes. "And it can be yours."

His dream. Set before him on a silver platter.

*Say something, Del! Say something!*

"I, uh, don't know what to say, Bernie."

Schulman leaned back into his seat, then crossed his leg to match Del's, their feet facing each other.

"We know this film will be a commercial success," the studio chief said, "but the script itself is golden. I don't know where Marilyn Monroe found the words or the concept, but apparently, the woman had more raw, biting talent than anybody was aware of. We're talking an Academy Award contender here, from top to bottom, and it's anchored in the script."

When Del tried to glance down at his hands, Schulman tilted his head, caught his attention, and made sure their eye contact Del remained locked.

"And Del, that means a real chance for you—not just for a career resurgence, but for a golden statue that has eluded you since 1978."

Del had never considered *that.*

"Bernie, I'm a bit skeptical about—"

Schulman flattened his hand and waved it to cut off Del's speech. One slice.

"Think about it, Del: Henry Fonda was nominated in 1940 and lost. He wasn't nominated again for more than forty years—but he *won* with that second nomination. *On Golden Pond,* remember? The guy was what, seventy-five years old?"

He had a point. The acidic feeling, that niggling sense of guilt, continued to dance in his heart; at the same time, however, Del's imagination tangoed to its rhythm. He caught himself strategizing several steps ahead.

"What about the lead role?" Del asked. "It would require a strong female. Any thoughts on that?"

"As a matter of fact, I think the chatter is dead-on. I'd want Nora Jumelle in the role. Have you ever met her?"

"We've crossed paths once or twice."

Del's mind retreated to the night he had invited Nora, Tristan and Felicia to his house for dinner. He replayed his conversation with Nora in his kitchen, when something about her demeanor didn't settle well with him. He sensed darkness about her, emotional vulnerability that stretched beyond the leaked nude photo. Something else disturbed her.

Before Del could wade deeper into his thought process, Schulman's voice lured him back to reality.

"So you tell me, Del." Bernie Schulman smirked, his tongue poking against the inside of his cheek. "Am I on the right track?"

# CHAPTER 53

DEL AND FELICIA CLINKED miniature porcelain cups at a Japanese restaurant in West Hollywood. Sizzles and pops surrounded them as grills filled the room with the aroma of fresh meat and vegetables cooking. In the middle of the restaurant was a rectangular area similar to a bar, its perimeter enclosed by a high counter and elevated chairs. In the center of it, a chef in a crisp, white uniform and a tall, white hat prepared entrées in a made-to-order fashion.

Throughout the dining room, patrons sipped sake as another chef rolled a small cooking station to each table and prepared meals from scratch. Aside from the crackling grills, the clink of cooking utensils, and the murmur of private conversations, the room was tranquil.

As usual, nobody recognized Del. He had re-entered the public's consciousness mere weeks ago. That would soon change, he knew; but for now, at least in subdued environments like this, he and Felicia still had their privacy.

The classic Japanese music playing overhead reminded Del of a James Clavell novel he'd read once. Del adored Far Eastern cultures. He could picture himself sitting in a quaint restaurant buried in the Pacific Rim, where calligraphy accented the décor, watching candlelight dance upon the face of this intriguing minister, a woman whose smile disarmed and inspired him.

Del updated Felicia on the details of his meeting with

Bernie Schulman and the other producers and executives with whom he and Arnie had met that week. He felt refreshed, like a teenager with a new car and newfound freedom. Freedom to roam. Freedom to dream again. His whole countenance felt alight.

"I'm happy for you," Felicia said. "You've waited a long time for this."

"After I sign the deal, I'm going to take you to Bora Bora, just for fun!"

Felicia rolled her eyes. "Just the two of us? I'm a minister, Del! How would *that* look?"

With a merry heart, Del grabbed the sake flask and poured Felicia another serving. "Fine, we'll get separate rooms."

Felicia laughed at that.

Each moment Del spent with her, he grew fonder of her company. He was serious about Bora Bora. And he didn't want to stop there. He wanted to show her the world.

Madrid! Tokyo! Rio!

He took her hand and cradled it in his.

"Once this deal happens, we'll be set for life. You and me. I'll work when I want to. We can do whatever we want, Felicia," he promised. "You'll never need to think about money again."

Something changed in the way she looked at him. A distance in her eyes, as though they had shrunken back and she'd begun to erect a wall of caution. Her glance darted to her plate.

Del stopped short.

"Whoa, what happened?" he asked, her hand still in his. "Aren't you excited about this?"

"I'm thrilled for you, Del."

"Did I say something wrong?"

"No, it's just…" Her voice trailed off.

"Talk to me. You should be excited! I want to take you

along for this ride!"

Felicia shrugged and seemed a tad shy. "The whole wealth and fame thing, material stuff...I don't know, I've never considered those things important, I guess."

"And I love that about you," Del said, his heart sincere. Her genuine nature had always drawn him to her. "But you have to admit, material possessions are nice. I don't see anything wrong with that. Do you?"

"I don't disagree. At the same time, though, it's all so..."

He leaned toward her. "Yes?"

"Temporary."

Her gaze dropped to her lap. Had she grown uncomfortable?

"Temporary?" prompted Del.

"In terms of the bigger picture. Eternity. The fame and money—you can't take it with you when this life ends, right? I think of those Egyptian mummies, buried amid all that wealth—and what did it do for them? It stayed behind when they died. So wealth isn't really a factor to me."

"But it's not a bad thing to have."

"Of course it isn't. But it also isn't a source of joy."

The chef's arrival interrupted them. He confirmed their orders and prepared their meals.

Del lifted his cup and sipped his drink. The sake went down smooth and warm. He pondered what Felicia had said. Of course he couldn't take anything with him when he died. He knew that. But he didn't feel as though she had judged him; rather, when she spoke, she widened Del's perspectives on life. He loved that about her. Del had lived a life of luxury; Felicia hadn't. And yet, Felicia seemed more content than he was. It was one reason he wanted to know her more.

When the chef departed, Del invited Felicia to speak a blessing over their meal, then they began to partake. Del added a dash of soy sauce and savored each bite. He could live on Japanese cuisine alone.

"Speaking of the script deal," Del said, "people seem to have their sights on Nora as the lead."

"And how do *you* feel about that?"

Del's mind returned to his lingering nervousness about the young actress, then remembered his conversation with Tristan, and the career coincidence that seemed too close for comfort.

He tried to wrap words around his thoughts in a way that wouldn't come across as overbearing.

"They're right," Del replied, his hesitancy intact. "The part is ideal for her. But…"

Felicia squinted. Del recognized that look. She had entered scrutiny mode.

"But what?" she coaxed.

"I don't know," Del hedged, "maybe this project isn't right for her. Not at this time, anyway."

Felicia laid down her chopsticks and gave him her sole focus. "What do you mean, 'at this time?'"

Should he say more? What if he was paranoid? He had no evidence to suggest Nora was in trouble. At this point, it was pure speculation.

"You know I've never been much of a religious guy. I'm not opposed to it, but my background—it hasn't been part of my life since childhood. So I don't know much about it. But you're a minister, so you know about giving guidance and advice, right?"

"Here and there, the best I can."

Wincing, Del sighed, still feeling foolish. "She told me she's talking to a wellness coach. But I think there could be more to it than needing advice."

"Such as?"

"Well, this is nothing more than guesswork, but do you ever get a sense that somebody is in trouble, even though, on the surface, all appears normal?"

"Sometimes. And you're saying you sense that about

Nora?"

"Perhaps."

"Why do you think that is?"

"I'm not sure…" Del didn't want to raise an alarm for no reason and didn't want to make Nora look bad. But the past had planted in him seeds of fear about the future when it came to those rare individuals he treasured in his heart, and for whatever reason, Nora had captured a piece of his heart. "It's a strange feeling I get about something she said."

"What did she say? Are you allowed to talk about it?"

"I don't think she would mind," Del replied. "She mentioned the pressure she's facing with all the media attention. That's normal; we all go through it." He paused. "It wasn't so much what she said, but the—I guess you could call it melancholy—that I picked up *underneath* what she said. It's nagged at me ever since."

Felicia nodded. "Has she done anything unusual?"

"I haven't known her long, so I don't know what's usual or unusual. The melancholy, though—"

"Yes?"

"It reminds me of Marilyn Monroe's final months before her death. You could sense in her demeanor that something was off, but you couldn't put your finger on what it was. You don't know how to mention it, other than to ask if everything is okay. And of course they'll tell you all is fine," he explained. "But what concerns me further is that she's talking anonymously to a wellness coach who doesn't know what's going on with her. What kind of advice could he be giving her? What if he steers her wrong?"

"Nora's a smart woman. Do you think she would follow bad advice?"

"Perhaps not," Del replied. "But there's more to my suspicions about this coach."

"Have you checked him out?"

"Yes, and he appears legitimate. As far as you can determine from a website, anyway."

Felicia's eyes narrowed. "But you suspect there's more to the story?"

Grimacing, Del surrendered. "I think her coach is Tristan."

"Her friend? The one we met at your house?"

"Yes."

"Del—"

"Hear me out," he said. "How long has she known the guy?"

"She said they met at a coffee shop a while back. Two months, maybe?"

"So there's a lot she doesn't know about him."

"Tristan says he's an entrepreneur. He runs an online business."

"Entirely online," hinted Del. "I asked him about his business the other day, and he shed more light on it. Get this: He's a wellness coach."

"What!"

"I kid you not. When I asked him more about it, he described the same approach Nora described, down to the detail." Del leaned forward, willing her to believe him. "And he mentioned one of his most recent clients is a celebrity who keeps herself anonymous. Around the same time Nora mentions the whole thing on *her* side."

Felicia's countenance softened, and Del knew she'd begun to give merit to his suspicions.

"But the Internet is worldwide, Del. This coach could be anywhere."

"His website says he's based in L.A. It shows a picture of some guy who claims to be this coach, but for all we know, it could be a catalog photo. And as far as I'm aware, neither Tristan nor Nora has mentioned the coaching thing to each other. So think about it: She keeps it quiet because she's embarrassed; meanwhile, he keeps his client interactions confidential, so he never talks about his business."

"Nonetheless, it would be a substantial coincidence."

"The world is much smaller than we tend to think."

"And you haven't mentioned this to either of them?"

He shook his head. "Tristan himself might even not suspect Nora is his client. Like I said, they probably haven't talked about it. After all, they haven't been friends long." Del paused. "Tristan's a nice kid, but would you want to take advice from him?"

"Where does he get his answers?"

"He says he doesn't need any. It's all a matter of affirmation or reaffirmation or whatever he considered it. Telling people what they want to hear and letting them believe they've taken a step forward. He looks at it as meeting a demand. I don't think he intends to take advantage of anyone; if anything, he strikes me as naïve."

Felicia shook her head. From the way she pursed her lips, Del read not only that she agreed with his suspicions, but now she felt the same awkwardness he did: the helpless feeling of sensing truth but possessing no proof.

"Maybe you should mention something to him, Del. Keep it casual. No need to confront him."

"I agree."

They returned to their meal, which, by now, had cooled to lukewarm. Nevertheless, Del held no regrets about focusing on the discussion at hand. Whether his misgivings were accurate or faulty, at least he had company.

"How's the home search coming along?" Felicia asked.

"Ugh, I haven't had a chance to research. Things got busy, as you know. At least we wrote the extra months into the contract for me to rent the house in the meantime." What he wouldn't have given to take back his decision to move. He finally heeds his accountant's advice, and now *this* happens. Of all the times for a home to sell with lightning speed! "This script deal would have enabled me to keep my home for the rest of my life. I wish I hadn't sold it."

"Has the sale closed yet?"

"Not yet."

Felicia regarded him a moment, then said, "Would the buyer be willing to reconsider?"

Del hadn't thought of that. It was worth a try.

# CHAPTER 54

EARLY THE NEXT MORNING, Del retrieved his real estate file from the desk drawer in his study. The buyer, in an apparent attempt to stroke his own ego, had passed along his personal contact information in case celebrity Del Corwyn ever wanted to chat.

And today, Del Corwyn wanted to indulge him.

Jonas Fricke.

The guy's business card was in English, but it contained an address in Switzerland. Del checked the clock. How many hours ahead would that be? Ten or eleven? It should be late afternoon over there. And the man had handwritten his personal cell phone number.

Skipping his morning jog, which Del hated to do, he dialed the number. Considering the significant distance between continents, the call took longer than usual to connect and Del noticed a slight difference in the sound quality as it rang. He increased the volume a notch and waited.

"Jonas Fricke." A distinct German accent.

"Mr. Fricke!" he began. Perhaps formality would stroke the man's ego. Small price to pay for Del to get his home back. "Del Corwyn here. You gave me your phone number. Hope I didn't catch you at a bad time."

"No, Mr. Corwyn. Is something wrong with the house?" For a second language, Jonas Fricke spoke excellent English.

Then again, he conducted business around the world.

Del offered a hearty chortle in response. "No, no. All is fine. In fact, I have excellent news regarding the home."

"Excellent news?"

"You're about to make an immediate profit on your new home, sir! Quite an investment."

Silence, followed by curiosity in Fricke's voice. "A profit? How so?"

"You're a businessman, Mr. Fricke, so I'll cut to the chase. This will sound strange, but I'd like to buy back my home."

"You—come again, please?"

"And I'll offer you ten percent more than what you paid for it." Del could sign a script deal tomorrow if necessary.

Fricke hesitated. "Ten percent?"

Wasn't that sufficient? "Fine, make it twenty."

"Why this offer, Mr. Corwyn?"

"I've had a change of heart. The truth is, I never wanted to move in the first place, so I gave it some additional thought."

"According to what I've read, *you* had some excellent news of your own recently, too."

"Yes, that's correct. So you can understand why a relocation wouldn't be feasible at this time."

"But you built extra months into the contract to rent the home. I am willing to extend that agreement, if you wish. I will not need to make use of the home immediately."

Del clucked his tongue and wondered how straightforward he should be. He was willing to bargain, and he wanted his home back, but he didn't want to be a chump.

"That's generous of you, Mr. Fricke. But as reality has settled in, I've realized—well, Los Angeles is my home, and—"

"There are plenty of homes in that city, Mr. Corwyn. I'm sure you could find one at the price you're willing to pay."

"Yes, but—" Del grunted to himself. This wasn't working. He needed to change tactics. Lay down his pride and be honest.

"It's my home, Mr. Fricke. You can understand that, as one human being to another." Del paused. Then, to his own dismay, he softened his voice to what sounded like a prayer. "Please, Mr. Fricke."

Del heard nothing on the other end of the line and, for a moment, wondered if their connection had dropped. The silence brought ripples of anxiety. Then Jonas Fricke answered.

"I can appreciate your predicament, Mr. Corwyn—"

A wave of relief. "I'd hoped you might."

"—but I cannot sell your home to you."

*No, no, NO!*

"Surely you can understand where I'm coming from, Mr. Fricke."

"Indeed I can, Mr. Corwyn. But, you see, selling the home at this time would not be a wise step."

"Not to be presumptuous, but may I ask why not? If you don't mind, that is."

"As it turns out, I have made a choice investment, albeit an accidental one. Your house, Mr. Corwyn, is now worth much more than it was when I purchased it. I keep track of the news in America. Your home was where the script by Marilyn Monroe was discovered. That means your home—my home— is now historic. A collector's item, if you will. You wouldn't sell a rare coin before its time, would you?"

"No, of course not, but…"

"This home is now, shall we say, a rare coin."

Of course. The bragging rights. The man had bought a celebrity's home as a status symbol—and had stumbled upon an even greater status than he could have dreamed.

Jonas Fricke had acquired another tale to share over cocktails. Meanwhile, Del's home—and the memories he cherished within in—was slipping from his grasp. It wasn't over, though. Not yet. Del still had one fingernail embedded in it.

A tear formed in his eye, but he refused to let Fricke hear

him weep. Not a chance. Nevertheless, Del's voice caught when he spoke again.

"Please, Mr. Fricke. I'm—" He sucked in his breath and cast aside his caution. "I'm begging you."

A pause. Del had reached the man's heart.

Or so he thought.

"I'm sorry, Mr. Corwyn."

Del ended the call in a gracious manner, then slammed the cell phone onto the sale contract.

With his elbows on the table, he planted his face in his hands. The tear he'd felt earlier pooled and trickled from the corner of his eye.

# CHAPTER 55

ONE O'CLOCK in the morning.

Once again, sleep eluded her.

Nora scrolled through her Twitter feed. The Academy Awards ceremony was two weeks away and, though she hadn't thought it possible, she looked like an even tighter lock to win the trophy. At least she had *that* going for her. To her astonishment, the buzz about her had increased further.

So had the buzz about her notorious photo. The respectable outlets, like the one on which she'd first discovered the photo, continued to censor it. Other outlets bore all. Nora was humiliated.

One mistake. One drunken night in college, and now this fraternity prick—whoever he was—felt entitled to her, along with the rest of the world.

All she'd wanted was acceptance.

Setting her phone aside, Nora rubbed her eyes, which felt heavy and raw. She couldn't tolerate another night without sleep. Although she began each night attempting to doze off without the aid of medication, she'd given up the fight a week ago.

Disheartened at the idea of putting sleeping pills into her body on a regular basis, she padded to the bathroom and retrieved the familiar package from the medicine cabinet.

Only a few left. She'd need to stop by the drugstore.

In the meantime, she took a tablet and washed it down with a glass of water.

Then she crawled into bed, pulled a sheet over her head, and hoped to escape the torment of her heart for the next several hours.

# CHAPTER 56

ONCE REALITY, in the embodiment of Jonas Fricke, slapped Del in the face, he knew he'd never keep his home. Though he wouldn't need to evacuate the premises for several months, he'd begun packing possessions in boxes, those treasured memories on which he'd want to keep a close eye. The movers would pack the rest.

Not that he'd found a home to move *into*.

Del browsed a list of houses on the market along the southeastern coast of Florida, narrowing his search to Jupiter Island, Golden Beach, and other high-end areas. The houses were impressive, but he didn't want to live in them. His heart resided *here*.

As he searched, he listened to an old David Rose album, despite the bittersweet memories it brought. He had set the album to repeat, and its title track, "The Stripper," began again. A tune about a working woman in the midst of a tease. What a precise embodiment of Marilyn Monroe. While she had viewed herself in an artistic light, countless others saw nothing more than her body.

When his cell phone chirped, Del reduced the volume of the music and answered.

"Del! Max Yeager here."

Another legendary director. No doubt about it: Del Corwyn was the man of the hour. Even interest in his old films had skyrocketed, both in sales and on-demand streaming. Directors and producers had begun to pursue him with projects. Minor parts, but stepping stones nonetheless. He needed to wade with caution.

"Listen, Del, I'm lining up a film that you'd be great for. A small role, but a choice one. We've scheduled production for early next year. I'd be thrilled if you'd consider."

Del was flattered. "Of course, Max. Send me the script and I'll take a look."

"Good deal. Oh, hey, while I have you on the phone, what's the latest on the Marilyn project? How close are you to a deal?"

"We're still considering offers. Regardless of how it turns out, though, I'm interested in your film role."

A pause on the other end of the line. "Yeah…sure, Del. Let's see how the Marilyn project goes, then we can talk. How's that sound?"

Del's instinct reverted to skepticism. He decided to save face for himself.

"Sounds good, Max. We'll talk soon, okay?"

"Yeah. Keep me updated on the status."

"Will do, Ma—"

Del heard his phone beep, as though the director couldn't wait to end the call. Motionless, Del stared at the phone in his hand.

The hesitation in Max Yeager's responses lingered in Del's gut. That familiar pause. It made Del nervous. Come to think of it, whenever conversations veered toward a potential resurgence for Del's career, he had noticed a pattern: the uncomfortable pause, followed by evasion and noncommittal.

Del's mind continued to churn. The whole purpose behind a deal should be to honor his friend's memory. He considered the screenplay's content, and all it revealed about her. It ran contrary to how most people perceived her—in that respect, the buzz was accurate. According to her letter to Del, when she put the script into his care, she sought protection from others. Was it possible she sought, in fact, protection from *herself?* Was it possible that, by putting the script into Del's hands, it would prevent Marilyn Monroe from allowing her personal torment to become an event for individuals to salivate over? To prohibit audiences from munching on hot-buttered popcorn and watching as her heart rent before them on the silver screen?

Would selling this piece of her honor her memory, or had the prospect become all about Del Corwyn? Would the sale enhance her memory or damage it?

Del's mind churned faster. He replayed his phone conversation with Jonas Fricke. Even the sale of Del's home had morphed into intrigue about the starlet. Someone she'd *never met* schemed to profit from her life—or, rather, her death—all these years later.

As Del considered these things, a realization hit him.

Del Corwyn wasn't on the verge of a career comeback.

And he never would be.

All this media attention, all the pandering, all the ego strokes—they didn't want Del Corwyn. They wanted something in Del Corwyn's possession, and they needed to go through him to get it.

Del felt like a battered suitcase. Bang him around, drag him along the street, as long as it didn't affect the money generator.

Was this how Marilyn Monroe had felt?

Once this script deal occurred, these people would relegate Del to obscurity once again. No doubt, he could line up a role for himself in the Marilyn project as a contractual provision when he sold the rights, but after that, he would fade from the spotlight as quickly as he'd re-emerged into it. And afterward, he would *never* resurface again.

Nobody gets a *third* comeback.

These people had no use for a guy of his nature, no matter how young he felt, regardless of how he carried himself. No rationalization, no fitness level, no activity on Twitter, no young woman would alter that truth.

Suppose he portrayed a role in the Marilyn film. Suppose Bernard Schulman was correct and Del won an Oscar. What was next for a guy who was almost eighty? A string of roles as a leading man?

Del Corwyn, the hottest property in Hollywood.

These people didn't want Del. They wanted something only he could deliver. They would use him until they had what they wanted, then they would disappear. His phone would quit ringing. His contacts would hide in alleged meetings like they did a few months ago. Del's calls would go unanswered and unreturned.

Then again, what if he was wrong? What if he defied the odds and became a legend in his own right?

Sure, he needed them. But they needed *him,* too.

And he couldn't let go. Not now.

Del caught himself rotating his cell phone in his hand, around and around, as he contemplated.

Then he laid the phone on his desk and closed his eyes.

# CHAPTER 57

FELICIA'S OFFICE WASN'T DESIGNED to impress. It was smaller than any room in Del Corwyn's house, with the exception of his bathrooms—and even those were close to it in size. A far cry from the offices and buildings that had opened to him over the course of his career. And yet, Del felt at peace here.

Her desk sat beside a small window at one end of the room, its surface tidy with a couple of open books and a computer that hummed. At the other end of the room, he noticed a small coffee table with a sofa and two living room chairs, which Del assumed she used for counseling. Potted plants rounded out the décor. On the wall hung a replicated painting that depicted Jesus as a shepherd, as well as two other historical paintings which, to Del, appeared religious in nature. A tasteful, decorative cross hung behind her desk.

The church itself was small and tucked away like a piece of yesteryear. Del guessed it had been built in the 1950s, if not earlier.

Maple bookshelves lined the walls. Upon arriving here, Del had scanned the shelves and found them filled with theological books and various copies of the Bible, some translations commonplace, others more obscure. As a child, he'd memorized the books of the Bible during Sunday school classes, and recognized their names as he'd browsed centuries' worth of commentary on Felicia's shelves. She seemed to have at least three volumes of commentary for each book of the Bible.

"Did you have a conversation with the home buyer?" she asked.

Sitting across from her at the desk now, Del crossed one leg over the other and sucked air. "I did."

"And?"

"No dice. It seems the buyer is *thrilled* to own the home where a piece of Hollywood history was uncovered."

Felicia regarded him a moment, and Del could see in her eyes that her heart reached out toward his.

"I'm sorry, Del. I know how much you wanted to remain there."

"It was worth a try, right? Anyway, it means I need to kick my home search into high gear." Del clasped his hands around his knee. "It's not like I couldn't buy another home in California, but I can't buy the memories of the people who have come and gone. And those memories live in my home." He hesitated, sensing his vulnerability on the rise, then sighed. "It's all I have, Felicia. My home—it's all I have."

"It sounds as if Del Corwyn has done some soul searching."

Is that what it was? "The last month has been a rollercoaster."

"I think your sensitive side is sweet."

"Yeah, well…"

"Maybe it's an opportunity for a fresh start, a change in environment. A chance to make *new* memories."

No, Del intuited, this sale wasn't the sole reason he lacked happiness.

"It's not just the house, though," he said.

"You mean your career? Making all things new?"

"Here I am, with my pick of deals. And believe me, they are exquisite. One in particular—have you heard of Bernard Schulman? He offered me a plum role in the film, too." Del marveled at the thought, which grew more tantalizing by the day. "It's better than I would have imagined."

244

Felicia tilted her head, nodded.

"Have you ever faced something extraordinary," Del continued, "something you've waited decades for, and when it finally comes, it's…flat?"

Felicia compressed her lips. "Flat?"

"As if your heart isn't in it. Or perhaps not your whole heart," he said. "Why am I not enjoying this as much as I thought I would? Everyone wants a piece of me these days."

"I can empathize, Del. For most people you're talking to, this is part of their news cycle, something that could make a historic mark on the industry in which they work. But for you, it's greater than that. This holds a sentimental aspect for you."

"Sentimental. Maybe that's it." He scratched the stubble on his chin. As Del allowed his mind to stroll along that course of thought, another sinking feeling emerged in his heart. "Have you ever thought you had everything you could ever want, then discovered you have nothing? Not in a literal sense, but you take another look around your life with new perspective, and suddenly, much of it strikes you as meaningless?"

"And this is how you feel?"

This was difficult. Del wasn't accustomed to talking to anybody this way, and especially not a woman of romantic interest. But he found Felicia refreshing, a trustworthy soul. He wanted to confide in her his latest realization that his cohorts in Hollywood sought him for the treasure in his hands, not for who he was as an artist. But he wasn't ready to admit that to anybody else.

"I'm not sure how I feel about it," Del replied. "On second thought, my comment was ridiculous. Forget I mentioned it, okay? Please."

Felicia appraised him, then relaxed in her chair and appeared resigned to what she would say next. "What if this isn't about signing paperwork for this particular project? Have you considered that possibility?"

"What do you mean?"

"Maybe you fear what will come *after* you strike a deal."
She paused. "Or maybe you fear what *won't* come next."

Dammit, how did she do that? The woman could shoot an
arrow at his doubts and hit the bulls-eye, the place he felt most
susceptible, and pierce it.

When Del didn't reply, Felicia gave him a tentative glance,
then asked, "Have you ever considered how brief this life is, and
what happens when this life is over?"

"You mean eternity?"

"Eternity is the biggest part of it. But also the impact you
make today, which will echo after your life ends."

"I can't say I've thought much about after I'm gone. Isn't
life as we know it enough of a treadmill?" It seemed that way to
Del. All the stress, the worry, the strict adherence to his health
habits. On occasion, Del wondered if those efforts were
nothing more than subconscious attempts to prolong his life.
And when his life needed to end, he didn't want friends and
acquaintances showing up at his funeral, speaking flattering
words about his career while knowing, in reality, Del Corwyn
had ended up a disappointment.

Felicia tapped her fingernails on the desk, three decisive
raps to punctuate her thoughts, then arose from her chair.
Grabbing her purse from the bottom drawer, she made her way
to the door. A confused Del followed her with his eyes.

"Come with me," she said.

"Now? Where are we going?"

"Trust me. You'll see."

Caught off guard, Del didn't move, unsure of what he was
about to step into.

"What's the matter, Del?" Felicia winked at him. "Did you
have something more critical on your calendar than sitting here
in my office, shooting the breeze?"

# CHAPTER 58

UPON STEPPING OUT of the elevator, Felicia mouthed hello to a staff member as she and Del walked past a nurses' station. Felicia seemed to know her way around the maze of color-coded, alphanumeric wings. In fact, many people who worked here, from nurses to maintenance workers to cafeteria employees, knew her by name.

Del counted patient rooms as he followed her down a corridor.

Once he discovered she had driven him to a hospital—and recovered from the false notion that she was luring him to a psychiatrist's office there—wariness settled in. Now Del felt claustrophobic, careful not to touch any surfaces. He could envision himself lying sick in bed tomorrow. He caught himself trying to cover his nose and mouth, and, as a safety precaution, was on the lookout for hand sanitizer. Selfish as it sounded, he hated being around sick people. Perhaps it went back to the few films he'd shot overseas, where he'd feared developing an infection and getting stuck in a foreign hospital, where a third-world doctor would slice him open and start poking around his organs, on the search for solutions.

White institutional walls scared the hell out of him. And he *detested* hospitals. The pungency of disinfectant reminded him of death. Too many friends and acquaintances had ended up in places like this, more recently due to age issues, but long ago, due to drug overdoses and other tragedies.

Felicia must have visited this patient before. When she found the room number she was looking for, she gave a respectful knock before entering the room. The door was open.

The first thing Del noticed were the closed blinds and the darkness which enshrouded the patient's room, as if when he walked past the threshold, he'd entered an alternate universe. He pictured the place receiving visits from death each night at the stroke of midnight. A grinning skeleton, cloaked in black and ax in hand, would tiptoe inside, scope out the room, and plan its eventual smothering of whoever lay inside. The vision brought goose bumps to Del's whole body.

When he and Felicia reached the bed, Del discovered a bony man. He might have been asleep, but Del wasn't positive. As far as Del could tell, they were the same age, but the man in the bed appeared frail and weak, his breaths labored, his flesh hoary and sick. Tubes everywhere—face, arms, you name it. Wires. A machine monitoring his pulse. And the plastic bag against which Del almost brushed his arm—was that *urine* inside? This patient looked like death personified. Del wanted to haul ass out of there.

But then, he took another look at the man and felt pity.

Del had portrayed a dying character once, in a scene much like this, but it couldn't have equipped him for what he saw today. Though he'd done due diligence to prepare for that part, as he looked at this patient before him, Del doubted he had done the role justice. He felt guilty for not doubling his research efforts back then, if only out of respect.

Leaning over the patient's shoulder, Felicia whispered into his ear. "Mr. Carter, are you awake? It's Pastor Whitby."

The man's eyes fluttered open. He wasn't asleep after all, just worn down to the bone. He sat up, alert, but quite weak. Del got the impression even a short conversation would exhaust him.

Felicia offered a compassionate smile and patted the man's arm. A mother's touch. "How do you feel, Mr. Carter?"

He nodded, mouthed something but couldn't muster the words. Del saw one corner of the man's mouth expand a smidgen—an attempt at a smile—and witnessed a fresh dose of life rush into his eyes. Did this man receive many visitors? How many years of heartache had he faced?

"You're not giving those nurses too much trouble, are you?" Felicia teased.

Another wisp of a smile. He responded with a labored, near imperceptible, shake of his head, his eyes glued to hers.

"Good. I'm glad to hear you're behaving yourself," she added with a wink. Then she turned to Del. "I've brought a visitor. This is a friend of mine, Del Corwyn."

With what looked like much effort, the man angled his head toward Del, a quizzical expression on his face, followed by a labored smile when the fullness of Del's identity registered in his mind.

"Mr. Carter is a member of my congregation." Felicia shot Del a knowing grin. "He once told me *The Changing Tides* is his favorite film of all time."

Suddenly, Del felt uncomfortable, though he couldn't explain why. It wasn't a privacy concern; rather, his fame felt inappropriate for this moment, a mismatch, unworthy to enter the hospital room of what appeared to be a dying man.

The man managed to lift his hand, albeit a mere inch from the bed. An intentional movement nonetheless. Del wondered why, and then realized it was an effort at a handshake. Easing closer to the bed, Del gave the man's hand a gentle pump. When he caught sight of the underside of the man's arm, he noticed thick, purple veins beneath the pasty skin.

Del hesitated. What did Felicia expect him to say next?

"It's always nice to meet someone who enjoyed that film," he offered. Was he handling this the right way? With a tentative glance at Felicia, Del asked the man, "What do you do for a living?"

Felicia gave the patient a tender pat on the shoulder and answered on his behalf. "Mr. Carter taught advanced mathematics at several universities across the country. He retired from UCLA a few years ago. You saw a lot of change in the culture over the years, didn't you, Mr. Carter?"

The man attempted to nod. As he warmed up to Del, Del could have sworn a dim radiance spread across the man's face.

Del tried to picture himself ten years from now and grew anxious at the thought. Lying in a hospital bed wasn't on his bucket list. Then again, he doubted it was on Mr. Carter's, either.

Del wasn't heartless, but he couldn't wait to wrap up this visit and escape the room.

A man Del's own age, disintegrating in a hospital bed, where any given breath could be his last. Del fought to maintain a straight face, but within his soul, he panicked.

# CHAPTER 59

DEL STARTLED at the electronic tone announcing the elevator had arrived. At the parting of the doors, he and Felicia entered the empty compartment. A push of the button for the lobby and they began their descent. Felicia's smile had faded as soon as they departed the patient's room, her brow now knit in concentration.

Del couldn't shake the image of the man in the bed. Or the realization that Del himself could end up in a bed like that any one of these days. Is that how it happens? In one moment, a screw comes loose, you break down, and life as you know it drains from your hands?

He struggled to locate his voice which, at first, sounded raw. He cleared his throat.

"What's the matter with that man in the hospital room?" As soon as he asked, he felt a prick in his heart. *That man has a name, Del.* "Mr. Carter, that is. He didn't look good. Will he recover?"

"The doctors have given him six weeks."

"Six weeks to recover?"

"Six weeks to *live*, Del."

He was hoping his initial prognosis had been incorrect, but to his dismay, he'd proven spot-on. Del couldn't fathom living his life knowing that, in six weeks' time, it would come to an end.

The elevator jolted to a stop and the doors parted. He and Felicia entered an atrium, where greenery surrounded a fountain. Del listened to the splashes of water as it landed on the surface of the small reservoir. Whenever he passed a fountain, he wondered what caused the familiar tang in its scent. Algae, perhaps?

On the other side of the fountain, tables and benches dotted the area around a small café cart, where individuals dined on boxed lunches, snacks, and gourmet coffee drinks. Sunlight gleamed through the skylight overhead.

Del glimpsed Felicia from the corner of his eye.

"How did Mr. Carter find out he was ill?"

Felicia stared straight ahead, past the atrium and into the small lobby on the other side, en route to the parking lot.

"He's a widower and loves to garden," she replied. "Two weeks ago, while he was manicuring his plants, he fainted. Never sensed anything wrong before that. A neighbor found him unconscious in his backyard. When she let her dog out, she heard an unusual amount of barking and headed outside to see what was wrong. If the paramedics hadn't arrived when they did, he might not be alive today."

"But the doctor gave him six weeks."

"Yes."

"And that was two weeks ago. So they estimate only four weeks left?"

"That's correct," she said. "It happened two weeks ago Monday, in the morning."

Del tried to recall where he was on that date. He knew he'd reversed his jogging route, and…that's right, he and Arnie met with a couple of producers who didn't seem a good match for the project.

A regular day. He'd awoken and felt so healthy.

Apparently, so had that Carter man.

As Del compared his Monday's events to those of Mr.

Carter's, Del's seemed superficial by comparison. As it turned out, Del had precious little to worry about in his life.

His throat went dry. He swallowed, which was so loud, he could hear it.

With one stealth movement, careful not to let Felicia see, Del wiped a tear from the corner of his eye. He couldn't help it. Why did that patient's predicament tug at him?

He tried to smother the emotion and move forward. Keep walking.

"Sick or not, the guy appears to be hanging in there," Del said, if for no other reason than to shift his attention away from his own discomfort.

Felicia nodded, deep in thought. "Mr. Carter has hope."

"He does?" Curious, Del hoped Felicia knew a detail about the man's situation that wasn't apparent.

"He looks forward to heaven," Felicia said. "He looks forward to walking on streets of gold, transparent as glass. He looks forward to touching gates of pearl, walls of jasper and amethyst and sapphire."

"Isn't he disappointed his life is about to end?"

"It's an adjustment for him, but a natural one. He's talked about heaven for many years. Granted, the suddenness of his circumstances have come as a shock. Good-byes are never easy with people you love. But he looks forward to a reunion with his wife and other loved ones." Felicia gazed ahead as if she were peering into the future, and it brought a smile to her face. She appeared lost in thought.

As they approached the hospital entrance, she turned to Del.

"Most of all," she continued, "he looks forward to being held in the embrace of God Himself."

The automatic glass doors parted before them, and they entered the parking lot. After the chilliness of the hospital lobby, Del welcomed the warmth that the California sunlight brought to his arms and neck. Yet he found the sensation difficult to enjoy as he considered the pain that dwelt on the other side of those hospital doors.

# CHAPTER 60

BY THE TIME FELICIA PULLED into the church parking lot, Del's mind had gone into a full stream of consciousness. It had begun with the man lying in the hospital bed, transitioned to Felicia's description of heaven, and morphed into the realization of how short life was. That notion, the brevity of life, had brought Del full-circle to the present. Not only did some aspects of his life feel empty—an uncomfortable struggle, though he hadn't mentioned a word about it to Felicia—but he had caused an unintentional consequence regarding the memory of a friend. Under his care, people had begun to use Marilyn Monroe all over again, a fresh wave after her death.

And Del had contributed to that treatment. Heaviness filled his heart.

"You're deep in thought," Felicia said. "You've hardly uttered a word since we left the hospital."

When Del turned his head, he found Felicia searching him for clues about what traveled through his mind. And he wasn't ready to tell her.

He hated when life's circumstances screwed with his plans. Yet he couldn't bring himself to let Felicia see what roiled inside him. He had a difficult time trusting people. Chalk it up to pride, habit maybe, but Del Corwyn had lived on his own far too long for that. He had settled into a mode of independence and self-sufficiency. Change wasn't in the cards for him.

Or was it?

"I'm fine," he replied. "Just thinking."

Felicia turned off the engine. Neither individual moved. She must have been deep in thought, too. Or praying. Although she never made a show of her prayer life, Del had a hunch she did more of it than she let on. He suspected she'd said a few prayers for him, too, which he didn't mind. God knew, he needed all the help he could get.

Del unfastened his seatbelt and gazed into Felicia's eyes. She was beautiful, indeed, yet he couldn't drop his defenses. He couldn't help but feel uncomfortable around her. Not because of anything negative, and he knew she wouldn't judge him. But she challenged him in a way no other woman had. Del Corwyn wasn't accustomed to that.

His life wasn't perfect; he didn't have answers to the larger questions she posed, but at least he had felt *comfortable* before Felicia emerged in his life. He couldn't reconcile the conflict inside him. And Del didn't like it when he didn't have the upper hand.

For a moment, he lingered, drank in the depths of Felicia's soulful brown eyes. He stroked her cheek with his thumb.

"You are beautiful, do you know that?"

Felicia blushed. With a chuckle, she waved off his comment. "It's been a long time since anyone told me *that.*"

"It's true nonetheless."

She eyed him as though he hid an ulterior motive. "Is everything okay, Del?"

"Why do you ask?"

"I don't know, you seem…I don't want to say *unhappy,* but—"

"Unhappy?"

"That's not the right word, but—"

"Everything's great," Del lied. Before he knew it, his defensive instincts kicked into action. "Life is good. They *love* me right now."

Felicia, facing forward once again, rested one wrist on the steering wheel. "They *love* you?" Judging from her facial expression, she found his response droll. Had she mimicked him?

"Do I sense derision in your tone?"

"No, Del. Your choice of words was interesting, that's all."

He didn't follow. "How so?"

"I suppose it's a matter of how you define love," she replied with a shrug.

She was challenging him again. She intended no harm, but Del wasn't in the mood. She wasn't exactly flawless, after all. They each had their pasts.

"A matter of definition? As in…" He held out his hand to prompt her for more.

"Love is *outbound*, Del. It's a matter of valuing the other person for who they are, not for what they can do to benefit you."

"Are you suggesting that's what's happening? I'm being *used*? Like a pawn?"

She turned toward him again. "Let me ask you this: Did those people 'love' you a year ago, before you found that script in your home?"

"Everyone has an angle," he shrugged.

"And that doesn't concern you?"

"Isn't it a bit naïve to believe someone could love someone else without an ulterior motive?" He lent an edge to his tone to let her know he'd taken a passive-aggressive jab at her words. He reacted that way when somebody scraped his ego.

Her eyes hinted the next move was his, as though he were supposed to solve a riddle she'd laid at his feet. "Surely *someone* out there could love you for you."

"Yeah, right," Del chuckled, hardening his heart. "And my Botox treatments are for the pure pleasure of getting stabbed in the forehead with a needle."

Felicia reached out and stroked his hand. *"I love you for you, Del."*

That remark made him nervous, but he didn't know why. Fear of getting himself tied down to a commitment? And sure enough, his mouth went into action before his brain had a chance to catch up.

"Surely my persona comes in handy for you, too," he said.

"That's not true, Del."

He feigned nonchalance. "Not that it's a bad thing. People just do it. I've grown accustomed to it. Like you said, they derive a benefit from me."

She pursed her lips, glaring at him through squinted eyes. Her voice remained steady, soft-spoken. "I've *never* used you, Del."

He snorted. "Of course not."

His passive-aggressive jabs didn't go unnoticed. Felicia's jaw grew rigid. Still strapped beneath her seatbelt, she didn't peel her sight from him.

"All right, I'll play along. *How* did I use you?" she asked, crossing her arms. "I'd love to know."

"You need an example?" Del's damned pride wouldn't allow him to back down. "How about the hospital visit today?"

Was he *angry* at her for drawing closer to him? Was he trying to push her away? Granted, over the course of dating her, he'd grown aware of a hole that existed in his life, a vacuum begging for someone or something to fill it. But Del Corwyn was a fighter. He couldn't accept the notion that somebody else might pinpoint weak spot in his life before he did. He wasn't one to let the other person believe they'd won.

"Del, that man is in the final weeks of his life. He'd mentioned your film in the past. I thought meeting you would bring him a few minutes of joy amid his pain. I never considered that *using* you. Besides, if you recall, I didn't plan that visit. It was a spur-of-the-moment decision."

"And that makes it look better? If it was spontaneous, doesn't that indicate you're taking me for granted?"

*Stop, Del, before you regret this.*

Felicia made an unsuccessful attempt to disguise her disgust at his latest comment. "You know full well that's not what it was. Can't you see I don't care about that part of your life? Those achievements of yours—I celebrate them because they're important to you, but they don't define you."

"Surely you can understand why it might appear otherwise. How many others know about your fabulous boyfriend, or significant other, or whatever they call us at our age?"

"I haven't told a soul we're dating, and you know that. I've respected you from day one. I didn't even *recognize* you on day one!"

"Like hell you didn't." But even Del knew what she'd said was true.

Shaking her head, Felicia sealed her lips tight and refused to face him. She stared at the dashboard instead. Del watched her eyes glisten. It pricked his heart.

The couple sat in silence for a minute. Del heard Felicia swallow, the tangled kind that occurs when someone tries to contain their throbbing pain.

She still wouldn't look at him.

"Maybe I overestimated you, Del." Del detected the hurt that resided in her whisper. And a timbre of finality, which didn't bode well for the two of them.

"Maybe so." His jaw tightened. He refused to back down.

At last, she turned to him again. Beyond the plea in her eyes, her face remained stone, a cross between pain and anger.

"I love you, Del. I love you for who you are," she said, her voice still soft. Soft and wounded. "But I can't do this. Not with someone who doesn't trust me."

And with that, she fixed her sight straight ahead, staring

through the windshield. Her eyes had turned raw. Del could tell it took every inch of her will to resist shedding tears.

Del didn't know much in life, but he'd always known he was fucked up. And he'd been happy that way, until he met the woman who sat beside him. The woman he was afraid to love.

He felt ashamed but didn't know what to say. He'd never found himself in a predicament like this. He'd never fallen in love until now. And that left him confused.

When Felicia spoke again, an edge emerged in her voice. "Do you have anything else to say?"

He didn't have a clue what to say.

"No, I don't."

"Then I think maybe you should go home, Del."

He started to reach for her, but she remained rigid and wouldn't allow their eyes to meet. She glanced at him from the corner of her eye, then returned her focus to the church building ahead and squinted. She'd planted her hands on the steering wheel, her knuckles white as she gripped it.

When Del pulled the door handle, it sounded twice its normal volume.

Without a word, Del climbed out of the car and closed the door with care.

With one last glance through the passenger window, he caught sight of the only woman he'd loved.

The woman he'd managed to cut. Just by being himself.

Felicia. Marilyn. Himself.

How many more lives could Del Corwyn disrupt before spring ended?

Yet why couldn't he let go? Why did fame feel like an addiction to him?

He climbed into his car, stuck his key into the ignition, then halted.

On second thought…

He retrieved his cell phone. Sadness, frustration—whatever

he felt, he planned to defy it. Del Corwyn would not be a pushover.

"Arnie, it's Del," he said when his agent answered. "Call Bernie Schulman. Tell him we've got a deal." Film rights, soundtrack rights, distribution rights, a plum comeback role for Del. Hands down, the best offer.

Arnie, no doubt, had calculated all the deal's perks and realized, when it came to commission, he would strike the biggest payday of his career. A grin was evident in his voice.

"Del Corwyn," he replied, "you're my hero."

# PART THREE

## THE MISFITS

# CHAPTER 61

CAMERA BULBS flashed. The area was packed with women in designer gowns and men in tuxedos. Video cameras and reporters holding microphones dotted the crowd.

To Del, the evening's energy was palpable. He hadn't experienced this in more than forty years. As if that weren't enough to get people buzzing, he and his date would, without a doubt, be the most talked-about couple at this year's Academy Awards.

When their limousine door opened, Nora stepped out first and waved to fans who cheered from the sidelines. Dressed in a green, unconventional Armani gown that shimmered in the sunlight, she had attempted to straddle the line between glamour and her own striking personality. She wore her raven hair up, which exposed her elegant, creamy white neck, around which she'd adorned a long, silky scarf.

Little did she know, the following day, critics would balk at her attire and label her the ceremony's worst-dressed attendee. Del thought she looked gorgeous.

But more than Nora's attire, critics would chatter about that night's unexpected May-December pairing with Del Corwyn, setting the grapevine afire with speculation.

Emerging from the limo, Del stood beside his date on the red carpet, where he rested his hand upon the small of Nora's back. Her muscles felt tight.

Oh, the spotlight felt so warm on his face. Del Corwyn couldn't contain his grin if he tried.

———

Halfway through the ceremony, murmurs of conversation filled the auditorium during a commercial break. As a Best Actress nominee and the expected winner, program planners had assigned Nora Jumelle an aisle seat in the third row, a spot accessible to roving cameramen, who had taken several reaction shots of her applauding already. Del sat to her left, within the scope of those camera shots, too.

Del leaned over to Nora and whispered into her ear. "Looks like your category is next. Your big moment. Are you ready?"

Though she responded with a nod, Nora couldn't stifle the queasiness in her stomach. She had rehearsed her acceptance speech too many times to count and still wasn't satisfied with it. But she couldn't do anything about that now.

The anticipation had gotten to her, but in a positive way. The distinction overwhelmed her. Gratitude filled her heart. And although she wouldn't admit it to anybody, she had bought into the frenzy. This acceptance from her peers meant everything to her.

A place to fit. Nora Jumelle—Nora Tasmyn—had longed for that her entire life. To know she mattered. Tonight, she would matter to someone.

Within a few minutes, the commercial break ended, and the attendees applauded as the host welcomed the prior year's Best Actor winner to the stage. Nora's gut flipped. She gripped the armrests of her seat and took a deep breath. She tried to visualize herself at peace, sitting in the lotus position on a beach in Antigua.

The actor starting announcing the nominees in alphabetical order. Nora was third on the list. When he announced her name, she fought to retain her composure and offered a smile amid the applause. Like all nominees who preceded her, Nora pretended not to notice a video cameraman standing in the aisle, shooting live footage of her face as she awaited the actor at the podium to break the seal and announce the winner's name. She began to perspire, which she hoped the camera shot didn't reveal.

Del gave her hand a squeeze. That helped calm her nerves.

When the actor finished reading from the teleprompter, he lifted the mystery envelope.

"And the Oscar goes to..."

With that, he unsealed the envelope and removed a solitary card. Nora's destiny was engraved on that stiff, oversized piece of cardboard. Although the winner of this category was considered a shoo-in, the actor turned astute, teasing the audience with a twist of his lips as he prolonged, for a few ticks of the clock, his status as the only individual in the room who knew the winner's identity officially.

Nora fought to breathe, her stomach unsettled, an emotional shroud upon her heart despite the joyous occasion.

The actor swept the crowd into his gaze.

"...Charlize Theron!"

The dark-horse nominee.

Stunned, Nora's limbs morphed into a state of paralysis. Then, remembering the broadcast would capture the immediate reactions of all five nominees in a split screen until the winner rose from her seat, Nora summoned her most gracious smile and applauded the winner. But the rejection sliced through the center of her heart. Not disappointment over the loss of an award, but the pain of the little girl she thought was no longer alive inside her. As it turned out, Nora Tasmyn had attended the Academy Awards, after all.

Once the cameraman moved on—which took him an eternity—Nora closed her eyes. Darkness settled into her soul.

Del rested his forehead against hers.

"I'm sorry," he whispered into her ear. Rather, it would have been a whisper, but he needed to shout for her to hear him over the applause that erupted throughout the auditorium at the unexpected development.

Nora didn't reply. Instead, she masked the pain with the façade she'd fashioned so well. She glanced at Del and allowed the Hollywood gleam she'd perfected to overtake her countenance, hoping the overhead lights didn't reveal the sheen upon the moist surface of her eyes.

# CHAPTER 62

WHEN DEL AWOKE the next morning, he simmered. The events of recent days had converged in a pot of anger.

Anger at how he had treated Felicia the day they parted ways. Anger at letting her go, forfeiting the chance to win her back. Anger regarding the sale of his home.

Anger at the worthlessness Nora must have felt after her loss.

He knew that feeling all too well after his own loss and humiliation in 1976. After last night's ceremony, Nora had chosen to drown the numbness in alcohol, and Del had allowed her to do so, doing his best to monitor her intake, making sure she arrived home in one piece. After all, who was he to judge her? And what was he supposed to do, offer insight or provide the answers? He'd managed to damage his own life by losing the only woman with whom he had ever fallen in love.

Then Del's mind pivoted to Tristan. Nora would turn to him—or his alter ego—wouldn't she? And that kid had no more answers than the local bartender. Another point of anger for Del before he climbed out of bed. In fact, fair or not, Tristan now emerged as the prime target of Del's fury.

When Del returned from his morning jog and his irritation hadn't subsided, he resolved to take action. He'd intended to take the reins in this situation for a while.

Grabbing his cell phone from the kitchen counter, he

opened his text-messaging app, scrolled through his contacts, clicked Tristan's name, and set his index finger in motion.

**I need you to stop by my house.**

Impatient, tapping the phone in his palm, Del waited as the message beamed through space. One minute later, the device vibrated in his grip. He read Tristan's reply.

**Now???**

**Yes. Right now. My house.**

Another minute passed, then came Tristan's reply.

**Be there in 30.**

Del tossed the phone onto the kitchen counter and headed upstairs for a quick shower before his visitor showed up.

# CHAPTER 63

WHEN TRISTAN ARRIVED, Del led him to the patio, where their foursome had eaten dinner a while back. The two men settled into the patio furniture and eyed each other with curiosity. Del's thoughts scrambled in his brain, so he took a moment to weigh his words.

"Is everything okay, Del? You seem less chill today. Your text message was kinda freaky, but you look fine."

Del wasn't in the mood to fool around. He locked eyes with the wellness guru, who looked as if he'd stepped off of a yellow school bus five years ago.

"I don't know how to be tactful with this," Del said, "so I'll be blunt."

"Okay…"

"Your celebrity client? The one you mentioned when we talked last month?"

"Yeah? What about her?"

Del's heart hammered. "I know who she is. I *think* I do, at least."

Tristan snickered in doubt. "And who do you think it is?"

"It's Nora."

Tristan sighed. "Del—"

Del held out the palm of his hand to halt Tristan in midsentence. "Hold on. Hear me out."

The guru folded his arms across his chest. "I'm listening."

"Nora mentioned she's been talking to a wellness coach."

"Lots of people do that. Trust me. My bank account isn't hurting."

"She found the business card in a coffee shop she frequents."

Del caught a change in the way Tristan glared at him. Something in Tristan's eyes retreated, yet he tried to maintain a straight face.

"And you think it's me, huh?"

"Do you leave cards in coffee shops?"

"I leave cards everywhere."

"I visited the coach's website. The man looks like he could be a model," Del said. "The stock-photo variety."

Tristan shifted in his seat. As Del expected, this had begun to hit home.

Del set his hands flat upon the iron table's meshed surface and leaned in for the final blow. "You're Russell Merritt."

His mouth agape, Tristan slumped against the back of his chair, a clear indication he'd never fathomed his client's identity. Without a sound, his lips went into motion, as though he were trying calculate sales tax on the price of a washing machine. If the situation weren't serious, Del would have found the response comical.

"I take it this surprises you?"

"Shit, Del, how was I supposed to know?"

"You weren't, and that was Nora's intention. But now, you and I *both* know." Del let loose a decisive huff. "You need to put an end to it, Tristan. Tell her you're her coach."

Tristan, still in shock, shook his head. "Tell her? Are you crazy?"

"You're dating her, aren't you?"

"Yeah…"

"So if you care about her, and if you have any conscience at all, you owe it to her to come clean." Del leaned closer, tried to speak to him as one brother to another. "She's got a tender heart, Tristan. Beneath the confident exterior, she's trying to find her way through life, and she doesn't deserve to have one more person taking advantage of her."

"Hold on, Del. Who are you to lecture me? You've got a reputation yourself. With all the younger women you date, you're a player just like the rest of us. I mean, come on—like you haven't been taking advantage of your friendship with Marilyn Monroe to make a buck! Gimme a break."

"That's not what's going on with the script—"

"Like hell it's not! You know damn well that's what's going on with the script! So don't lecture me about taking the moral high ground."

Del smoldered. He wasn't used to anyone challenging him like this, and he sure didn't want to swallow it from someone half his age, who had half the life experience. "I'm preserving Marilyn's memory!"

"You're preserving your own ass, Del! Your career was drowning, and you found yourself a lifeline! Lucky break, huh?"

Del sealed his lips and counted to ten. He wanted to explode at Tristan and defend himself the best he could, but the script was a tangential issue. He needed to refocus this conversation.

"Look, Tristan, I'm not a perfect guy. I never claimed to be. But this isn't about a screenplay. This is about Nora, and I'm afraid she could be in a downward spiral. I'm trying to protect her."

Drawing his crossed arms even tighter against his chest, Tristan continued to fume. He shook his head.

Del toned down his volume and, forcing a calmer approach, implored Tristan.

"I don't believe you meant any harm. There's no way you could have known." Del believed that. He caught Tristan's eyes and wouldn't release contact. "Suppose a client described this situation to you, the one we're in right now. What would you tell that client to do?" Del paused for a beat, allowed the question to linger in Tristan's mind, then added, "For Nora's sake, Tristan."

Tristan bit the inside of his cheek and cast a wary glance at Del. Then, with a sigh, he rubbed his temples.

"Fine, fine. You're right," Tristan relented, his voice resigned. "I'll do it. But let me pick the time."

Relieved, Del settled back into his chair. "Good man."

"Whatever. Thanks to you, I'm becoming too fucking honest."

"I think she'd appreciate someone like that in her life."

"Yeah, I think so, too." With that, Tristan rose from the table, the iron legs of his chair scraping against the patio's brick surface. "And now, if you'll excuse me, I need to get back to my work," he said, a glint in his eye. "People to talk to, lives to improve."

# CHAPTER 64

TWO DAYS AFTER her Oscar loss, Nora still felt depressed. She wished she could say rejection didn't disturb her, but for Nora Jumelle—Nora Tasmyn—it personified the pieces of her life that rubbed her heart raw.

Her search would never end. Nora was a misfit in life and she knew it.

Childhood was so long ago. Why did she still allow people to screw with her head and emotions?

She should be happy with her success in life, but truth be told, Nora didn't have a clue whether she was happy or not.

She hadn't bothered to change out of her pajamas that day. Instead, she curled up on the floor against the leather sofa, her living room dim aside from the sunlight that brought a glow to the curtains. If anyone saw her in this state, she'd feel embarrassed.

No risk of that happening, though. She'd drawn the curtains and nobody else was in the house. This was one vision that *wouldn't* go viral.

The alcohol provided a pleasant buzz and soothed the ache.

At a few minutes past eleven o'clock, Nora lifted the coffee mug to her mouth and gulped her fourth helping of wine. Lunchtime approached and her empty stomach growled, but her motivation to eat had vanished.

She'd given her security guard a few days off. For once, she craved complete privacy.

She felt so exhausted. Nora longed to crawl back into bed and escape the weariness. Escape the sinking sensation. Escape the sense of losing control over her own life. She swore the bags under her eyes brought physical pressure to her face, yet she couldn't even fall asleep to rid herself of them. Her insomnia continued to intensify.

Then it occurred to her.

The sleeping pills.

She'd left them on her coffee table. She eyed the little packet.

Nora had taken one last night and fallen asleep on the floor in front of the television.

Drowsy from the alcohol, she thunked her mug on the table beside the near-empty bottle of Pinot Noir and reached for the pills. She took one in her hand, the sweat of her palm moistening it.

On second thought, she'd double the dosage. As of late, her body seemed to have built up a resistance to the medication. Nora didn't want any hiccups along the way to her escape. She deserved *something* to go right for her today, didn't she? Maybe tomorrow this cloud would dissipate.

Popping the extra dose into her mouth, she washed it down with the wine that remained in her mug, then wobbled over to the staircase. Dizzy from the effort, she paused to regain her bearings, then ascended the stairs, her footsteps heavy. She stumbled into her bedroom and collapsed onto her bed, where she curled on top of the comforter.

Nora breathed deep and allowed her muscles to go limp. Within a few minutes, magnificent wooziness settled in. She smiled with relief.

Then pictured herself lying on the beach in Monaco.

# CHAPTER 65

TRISTAN COULDN'T SHAKE Del's words from his mind.

Ever since their last conversation, each time Tristan interacted with a client, he thought of Nora and how they'd stumbled into their coincidence. Del was right. Tristan couldn't deny it, regardless of how he wanted to rationalize the situation. If Tristan wanted to dance around technicalities, he could point out that he didn't know with one-hundred-percent accuracy that Nora was his client. At the same time, however, he cared about her, and if she was open to the possibility, Tristan could envision a future together. Like Del suggested, maybe she was walking through a dark season and hadn't let on. Tristan didn't want to take advantage of her or, worse, put her at risk.

Come to think of it, Russell Merritt hadn't heard from his celebrity client in more than a week.

Wrapping up a message to someone else, Tristan grabbed his cell phone and speed-dialed Nora's number. After several rings, she picked up. He turned on his speakerphone and started talking before she had a chance to utter hello.

"Nora, it's me. I need to talk to you about something, if it's okay."

"Whooziss?"

Tristan detected a slur in her voice. She sounded tired. And why did she ask who had phoned her? Who doesn't read their caller ID?

"It's Tristan."

"Hi Triztannn…"

She sounded as though he'd awakened her in the middle of the night. Tristan checked the clock. Noon. She might have slept in.

Yet something didn't seem right.

"Nora, I need to admit something to you—" On second thought, this news should come in person. "Can I stop by in a while? You sound like you're just getting up, but how does an hour from now sound?"

"Mmmm."

He tried to decipher her reply. "Are you at home?"

"Mmm-hmmm." Faint. Eerie. Prolonged.

How was he supposed to reply to *that?* Tristan rubbed his eyes with the fingers of his free hand. "So it's okay to stop by?"

No reply.

"Nora? Hello?"

No reply.

Tristan looked at the screen on his phone. The connection was still intact. If she was listening, why wasn't she replying to him?

He heard a thunk. It sounded she had dropped her phone. On the carpeted floor, maybe?

His stomach muscles clenched. He held the phone closer.

"Nora? Are you there?" Now he caught himself jostling his knee. His jaw tensed. "Nora, talk to me. Please."

No response.

Tristan stared at his phone. She still hadn't disconnected. The call time, oblivious to whatever was happening, ticked off each second as if everything was normal—which, Tristan had grown convinced, everything was not.

Another attempt to gain her attention by saying her name. He shook his phone and willed her to reply, but heard nothing except the subdued buzz, which indicated the call remained in progress.

Tristan disconnected.

But he couldn't release the phone from his grip. Frustrated, he tapped it against one knee.

No doubt about it. Something was wrong.

Now both knees jostled. Whatever was going on with Nora, it scared the hell out of him. But what was he supposed to do about it? Call 911, tell them to knock on the door and demand to see an individual who had fallen asleep?

*Nine-one-one. What is your emergency?*

*I don't know if one exists...*

*Sir, this number is reserved for emergencies only.*

Who else could he call?

His brain felt cluttered. Why does your mind lose its focus when you need it most?

He massaged his temples. Why couldn't he think of a solution?

*Come on! Think, Tristan, think! You're a wellness coach, for fuck's sake!*

Several seconds passed. Desperation morphed into panic.

Then it hit him.

That friend of Del's, the one he'd met that night at Del's house! She was a minister. She would know how to handle these circumstances, wouldn't she? People must come to her about everything.

She'd given him her phone number in case he ever wanted to talk about life. He'd entered it into his cell phone out of habit, with no intention of calling. He wasn't a religious person.

What was her name? He'd recognized it, but it wasn't common. He sorted his contacts by first name. As he scrolled through the list, he muttered under his breath, trying to piece together the syllables of her name.

Delia? Francesca? Something along those lines. The first

letter was somewhere near the beginning of the alphabet.

Shit. The pressure mounted. Tristan felt time press in and suffocate him.

Fall…feel…fill… How did her name start?

He found it.

Felicia! That was it. Felicia Whitby.

As soon as she picked up, Tristan switched the phone to speaker mode and started putting on his sneakers.

"Felicia! It's Tristan, Nora Jumelle's friend, the one you met at Del's house."

"Of course! How are you?"

"Something's wrong with Nora. I don't have time to explain, but she sounded weird on the phone and then she stopped talking. I think she dropped the phone. I don't even know if she's conscious, so I'm heading over to her house to make sure she's okay. Can you meet me there? Bring Del too. He lives close by. Maybe she'll respond to him."

He bolted toward his front door and fingered through his keys. Removing the phone from speaker mode, he held it to his ear, just in case Felicia mentioned Nora's name and anyone was outside to hear it.

"Tristan, where does she live?"

"I don't know the street number, just the name; she was in the car with me the first time I drove there. I'll know it when I see it." Locking the door, he whispered her street name and added, "Del probably knows the address, and he'll know how to get there, too. I think he's been there before. Hurry! Please!"

He ended the call and raced toward the parking lot.

# CHAPTER 66

AS DEL LUGGED his suitcase into the garage, his mind remained on Felicia. He regretted the way he'd treated her, how he had managed to mess up the one relationship in his life that ever exhibited potential for permanence. Perhaps they could mend their rift, but even if that was possible, he knew today was too soon. Given the way he'd hurt her, Del was the last person from whom she would want to hear.

So he'd decided to get out of town. Spend a few days relaxing in Vegas. His life would heat up once he signed the paperwork with Schulman, though he had to admit, nowadays the thought of it had begun to make him nauseous. Perhaps the pressure of making a business decision while trying to honor someone's memory was the culprit. But no matter the cause, Vegas called today, and Del could use some fresh perspective.

He planned to surprise Nora and invite her along since she still had another week before production began on her next project. Maybe Vegas would cheer her up. The bright lights, live music, and pulsing activity always made him feel better—or, at least, distracted him for a few days. The city never slept.

As he shoved his suitcase into the car trunk, his cell phone buzzed. He checked the display and gulped at the name that appeared.

"Del, it's Felicia—"

"Felicia! I'm so glad you called! I've thought about you

ever since we parted ways. I'm on my way to Vegas to relax, but I can cancel if you—"

"Something's wrong with Nora."

Del felt a surge of anger. The protective kind. The kind you feel the moment your car slides on icy pavement, seizes control of your destiny, and glides you into a collision. "Where is she? What happened?"

"Tristan called me. She's at home, but he thinks she's in danger, maybe unconscious. Do you know her address? Can you meet us there? I can GPS it."

Del slammed the trunk shut.

"I'm on my way."

# CHAPTER 67

WHEN DEL ARRIVED at Nora's house, he found Tristan banging on the door, shouting her name at the top of his lungs. Felicia arrived five minutes later and joined them.

Del shielded his eyes from the sun and scanned the neighborhood street. "I thought she had a security guy out here."

"Who knows," Tristan said. "Usually, she does, but maybe she gave him the day off. Perfect day to do *that,* huh? I *told* you she didn't seem like herself when I called her."

Del placed his hands on his hips, surveyed the façade of the house. "You're sure she's inside?"

"I'm positive," replied Tristan. "She was in there when I called her thirty minutes ago, and I'm telling you, she sounded too spaced out to budge anytime soon."

To Del, the scenario felt all too familiar. It reminded him of August 5, 1962. He recognized the prickling along his skin, the same sensation that had occurred when he'd heard the world had lost Marilyn Monroe.

Felicia bit her lower lip. Del saw genuine concern in her eyes, as though she felt the pressure of time passing faster than they could afford. She scanned the house, too, probably hoping Nora had left a window cracked open. "Did you try calling her again?"

"A bunch of times. She won't pick up. That's why I started banging on the door."

"Maybe you should try calling her one more time."

Tristan nodded. Retrieving his phone from his back pocket, he made a couple of taps with his thumb and held the device to his ear. Although they couldn't have waited more than ten seconds, Del felt his stomach somersault.

Ten more seconds passed. Cursing under his breath, Tristan ended the call and shoved the phone into his pocket. "No answer."

"And you don't think her phone might be in another room?" Del suggested. "It's her cell phone, right? Maybe the battery ran down and she doesn't know it." But not even Del bought into those explanations. The foreboding sense sharpened.

"Something's got to be wrong," Tristan replied. "I'm sure she's inside. Even if her phone was dead, she would have heard me beating on her door. Nobody could've slept through that, not for as long as I pounded at it," Tristan replied. He angled his hands around his mouth to amplify his voice as he yelled for Nora once again.

Tristan glanced at Del and Felicia, his face drawn with worry. His hands fidgeted, as if they operated ten minutes into the future and had already gone into action. "I've gotta get in there," he muttered to himself.

The helpless trio stood in thoughtful silence.

Del and Felicia wandered around the side of the house in search of a back door Nora might have forgotten to lock. Del eyed the neighbors' homes, which appeared empty at midday, the homeowners at work, no doubt. If they were home, they would have wandered outside once Tristan started screaming like a madman.

"We'd better call 911," Felicia said, fumbling through her purse in search of her phone.

A sudden thud startled Del. It came from the front of the house. It must have stunned Felicia, as well, because she gaped at Del with her hand still in her purse. They hurried back around the house to find Tristan lunging, shoulder-first, at the front door.

"What are you doing?!" Del shouted as he scurried up the front porch steps.

"Trying to bust through the damn door, but it won't budge!" With a grunt, he battered the door once again, to no avail.

"Tristan, you can't just—"

"Are you gonna argue or help me out? I can't do this on my own!"

The three of them huddled together, with Tristan at the forefront, his shoulder angled forward.

"On the count of three!" Tristan shouted. "One...two..."

Del sucked a breath, then tightened his gut the way he did when he lifted a heavy box.

"Three!"

The trio heaved forward as one. The door remained in place, but they heard something split, maybe a hinge coming loose from the doorframe.

"I think something happened," Tristan said. "One more time."

On the count of three, they tried again. The door remained intact, but this time, Del could tell something had cracked. Even from his position as number two, he'd felt it.

Another count of three and the trio lunged. The momentum carried them through as the door fell forward and crashed, its hinges skidding across the foyer's hardwood floor. All three individuals stumbled to the floor. Del felt a muscle twinge in his back and wondered if, once he slept on it, he'd spend the next week paying the price. But he didn't care. He had to find Nora. Even if it meant hobbling through this house bent at the waist, he refused to give up.

# CHAPTER 68

THE SHRIEK OF A SECURITY ALARM PIERCED the stillness. It echoed in the foyer and throughout the house.

"Spread out!" Del shouted. To his relief, he was able to stand up straight, though he felt a tad sore. "We'll find her faster that way."

Without another word, they parted ways and sprang into action. Tristan darted toward the kitchen, Felicia took the bathroom, while Del aimed for the living room.

When he reached the living room, the scent of alcohol hit him. Wine, nothing heavy. A wine bottle on the coffee table caught his eye, and he rushed toward it. Picking it up, he found it almost empty. He also noticed a small pill packet, its foil lining punctured and twisted in several spots, sitting beside the wine. Call it intuition, but as soon as he'd entered the house, he'd expected to find pills of some variety. Reading the label, he discovered they were sleeping pills and cringed.

*Sleeping pills contain barbiturates,* he thought. *Barbiturates. Just like—*

Worry overtook him. Tears glossed over his eyes but he forced them back. He couldn't allow himself the luxury of emotions. Not now. Wherever Nora was, he had to find her. The room appeared empty, but he swore she had been here recently. The alcohol scent was stale, but not by much. He noticed a coffee mug and looked inside.

Wine.

When he tilted the mug, a bead of claret-colored liquid slid from one side of the surface to the other.

Still wet.

Tristan was right. She was in the house. And she had been in this room.

The sofa was empty, so Del scoured the room, searching for Nora's body on the floor but found nothing. Where was she? Had they arrived too late? The taste of bile tinted his palate. Del had no confidence that these circumstances would turn out well.

He raced toward the staircase and darted upstairs as fast as he could. He had only visited Nora's home once, but he had a vague memory of its upper-level layout. He veered left, toward the master bedroom.

When he reached the door, he halted and caught his breath. Nora was on the bed, curled in a fetal position, with one arm slumped over the side of the mattress. Though she had porcelain skin, even Del, from his vantage point, could see Nora's complexion was too pale.

He ducked his head into the hall and shouted over the alarm. "Tristan! Felicia! Master bedroom upstairs! Get in here!"

Del raced to the bed and lifted Nora's head.

"Nora!" She didn't respond. Her eyes were closed, her face slack. Panicked, Del gently slapped her cheek a few times to try to awaken her. Nothing. "Nora!"

Felicia and Tristan arrived at the door. Felicia turned to Tristan.

"Call 911!" she shouted. "The security company will have responded already, so they'll be on their way. But we need an ambulance too!"

With tears running down his face, Tristan grabbed his phone and ducked out of the room to talk outside, where it was quieter.

Del had fallen to his knees by this time, shaking Nora's whole body. Felicia shot over to the bathroom, and Del heard the faucet running. Felicia returned with a glass of cold water, which she splashed upon Nora's face, to no avail. Del slapped her cheek again to try to prompt a response after the drenching, but Nora looked dead.

Felicia eased beside him and placed her forefinger and middle finger on Nora's neck, beside her windpipe.

"She still has a pulse," Felicia said, her forehead perspiring, droplets of sweat falling onto Nora's shoulder.

The security alarm ceased. Del's ears continued to ring. He heard the faint sound of approaching police sirens.

"I found alcohol and sleeping pills in the living room. Recently used. The wine remnant hasn't completely dried in the mug she was drinking from."

"Then we definitely don't have much time, if it's not too late already." She moved her hair out of her face. "It'll take the ambulance a few minutes to get here. Move aside. I'll monitor her, and if she stops breathing, I'll be ready to take action. I know CPR." As she hovered over Nora's body and checked her pulse again, Felicia said, "Pray, Del."

Del stuttered. "I—I don't pray."

"This would be the perfect time to start."

Helpless, Del stared at what looked like a corpse on the bed—and feared he already knew how this would turn out.

His heart sank.

# CHAPTER 69

NONE OF THE THREE WANTED to leave the hospital. A staff member, upon recognizing Del and recalling he had attended the Oscars ceremony with Nora, had led them to a small, secluded room, where they could avoid unwanted attention from passersby. Del had thanked her but couldn't find words to express his true gratitude.

Hours passed without much chitchat as the trio awaited updates. Once, Felicia had offered to pray, which both Del and Tristan had welcomed. From time to time, Del glanced at Felicia, who sat in one corner of the room, staring out a window, her lips in motion. Though she didn't utter a sound, Del guessed she hadn't stopped praying all afternoon.

In an attempt at diversion, a restless Tristan had turned on a small television. He kept the volume low out of respect for the others, but nobody paid attention to the broadcasts. Not even Tristan himself.

The pain must have numbed Del's friends the way it had numbed Del himself.

Urgent music erupted. The evening newscast commenced and an anchorwoman's voice sailed over Del's head. As one might expect, Nora was among the top stories.

"Actress Nora Jumelle is recuperating this evening after suffering what authorities say was a near-lethal combination of sleeping pills and alcohol. Jumelle was rushed to the hospital after being found unconscious in her home by three acquaintances, including actor Del Corwyn…"

All eyes flicked toward the television.

Del shook his head with regret. When tragedies unfold, events that involve someone close to you, you wonder if you could have done something to prevent it, or if you should have recognized a warning sign and taken action on what you had seen.

"The incident occurred less than a week after Jumelle's Oscar loss surprised many. Physicians remain optimistic she will recover from the overdose, after receiving medical attention in sufficient time. We will report further details when they become available. The actress remains in critical condition."

Anxious, Del turned off the television. He couldn't handle more chatter. Thoughts of what could have happened tormented him.

Tristan must have felt the same way. He shook his head and meandered to the door, mumbling that he needed to get some fresh air. All Del could muster in reply was a sympathetic, halfhearted grunt.

As Del zoned out, he felt an arm slide around his shoulder and pull him close. He recognized the scent of Felicia's skin and covered her hand with his own. Settling onto his lap, she rested her cheek against his.

"Are you doing okay?" she whispered.

"What if we hadn't arrived in time?" Del murmured in reply. "That's the thought that churns in my mind."

"Thank God, we *did* find her in time." She rubbed his hand with her thumb.

Del shifted in his seat, sensing discomfort from a nerve he had pinched when they stumbled through Nora's front door. Now he pondered his surroundings, the hospital room dim despite sunshine peeking through the windows, and wished he could relive the last two months.

"Nothing was supposed to turn out this way," Del said. "I can't help but think I might have played a role in what happened to her."

Felicia removed her cheek from beside his. With a furrowed brow, she touched his shoulder.

"This isn't your fault, Del."

"The rational part of me understands that." His heart shuddered. "But the coincidence seems too obvious. All that's happened these last few months—the script nonsense and the media circus I created—Nora got dragged into it. She already faced enormous pressure in her life before this. Then the speculation started to swirl around her playing the lead role."

"Did you plant the seed of speculation, Del?"

"Of course not."

"Then this isn't your fault." She swiped a stray hair from Del's forehead. "It was just a coincidence, people doing what they do."

"The parallel, though—it replays in my mind."

"What parallel?"

He turned to her. "I've been through this before—or something like it. Think of who wrote the script, then look at Nora's career on the rise, just like that blond starlet of the early sixties. Both actresses misunderstood, both hiding their pain, both under enormous pressure they can't put into words. And both succumbing to it all in a similar way," he said. "Except one *didn't* die."

"That parallel would have existed regardless of the events in *your* life. You didn't cause this, Del."

"It's difficult to see it that way. It doesn't stop the taunting."

"Have you considered that maybe the script is the reason Nora is still alive?"

Del couldn't hide his stunned reaction. "In what way?"

"Consider when you discovered the screenplay and Marilyn's letter in your home," Felicia replied. "Think about the chain of events that followed. It refocused your memories on your long-lost friend and on her importance in your life. If your heart hadn't turned toward those memories at the right time, would it have been sensitized enough to recognize that Nora might be struggling?"

"Perhaps not."

"You put the pieces together regarding Tristan and convinced him to talk to Nora. Think about it, Del: That was the reason Tristan made the phone call when he did. And it ignited a chain reaction that led us to Nora's home in time to save her life."

"A lot of coincidences."

"I don't believe in coincidences."

Del gazed into her eyes and, as tired and red-rimmed as they appeared, he detected a glint in them. A fire that refused to die.

"So maybe the script's emergence played a key role," she added. "Rather than *causing* a tragedy, what if it prevented a *worse* one from occurring?"

She rubbed his hand, and Del enveloped her fingers in his.

"It was sunny, much like today," Del murmured. "Warmer that day, though."

"What day?"

"August 5," he replied. "Back in 1962. That was the day they found her in her home. Unconscious."

As he allowed himself to relax, the commotion of Nora's circumstances settled in, and the residual stress caused his vision to blur. He closed his eyes, and visions of the past flickered on the screen of his mind like a classic film, the film he had seen too many times to number.

"I heard about it on the news, like everyone else." Del clasped his hands in his lap and hunched forward. "It was a Sunday morning. I'd attended a party until the wee hours of the morning but, miracles of miracles, I'd avoided drinking too much and didn't have a hangover like I often did. I got into my car around eleven o'clock, about the same time Tristan called this morning, and I cruised north on the Pacific Coast Highway, watching the ocean glisten on my left and the mountains tower on my right. Not a care in the world.

"I turned on the radio and caught the final bars of that Neil Sedaka song 'Breaking Up is Hard to Do.' It was the number-one hit that week. When the song wrapped up, the station played one of those call-letter jingles, followed by 'The Stripper,' which was also in the top ten at the time. About halfway through the song, the deejay interrupted the broadcast and announced the latest details of Marilyn Monroe's death, which was the first I'd heard about it." Del trembled as he inhaled. "They'd found her at home in her bedroom. The police suspected suicide. Some people in the industry believed that report; others thought it was an accidental overdose. Still others suspected foul play, even government involvement. Bear in mind, Joe McCarthy had dragged her into the Red Scare, and she had been romantically involved with the Kennedy brothers. But whatever happened to her, it remains a mystery today." He paused. "All I know is, I wasn't there when she died. That's what haunts me most: I wasn't there to stop whatever agony she endured before she took her final breath."

Del peered up and found Felicia focused on every word he spoke. Listening.

People seldom listened to him anymore.

He closed his eyes again. The pain felt as fresh as it had in 1962, as though someone had stabbed him in the soul.

"Can you imagine? Interrupting 'The Stripper' to announce a woman's death—a woman people had taken advantage of? A woman who had been, dare I say, the victim of emotional abuse since childhood? The context of the announcement, coming in the midst of that particular song, seemed so disrespectful to me." Del shook his head and released a heavy sigh. "I drove several more yards until I rounded a bend and no traffic coming. Then I veered onto the shoulder and made a U-turn, as fast as I could on the narrow road, which didn't feel fast enough. She lived in Brentwood, so I sped southbound along the coast. Hard to believe I didn't get a ticket along the way.

"As soon as I reached her street, the reality of the news report hit me. That was the moment denial vanished and, in my heart, I knew she had died. Too many cars and too much foot traffic for it to be anything less. By the time I reached her cul-de-sac, it was chaos, with flashing police lights, press huddled together, a neighbor arguing with a police officer. It looked like a scene from a movie, but it was real. This wasn't a production. This wasn't a dream. This was reality." Del rubbed away the tears that had filled his eyes. "And reality broke my heart."

He opened his eyes. Stared at the cold nothingness on the television screen.

"I never took the opportunity to tell her I loved her. And suddenly, it was too late." He bit his lip as hot tears trickled down his face. His cheeks felt chapped. "Many celebrities wanted to attend the memorial gathering at her tomb, but Joe DiMaggio kept the invitations to a minimum. I think he wanted to ensure that her mourners attended only out of respect. Thankfully, he knew how close I was to her, and he invited me."

He sighed.

"I've never admitted this to anyone, but I've always felt partial responsibility for her death," Del whispered. "You see, she was a friend, a *close* friend. I look back on that day, and on the months that preceded it, and wonder if I missed some sort of clue. Was I so absorbed in my own life, my own career, that I failed to recognize a sign that she was in trouble? Did I miss a cry for help?"

He brushed aside another tear. Well, there it was: At long last, Felicia had seen him weep. Another first.

Felicia wrapped her arm around his shoulders and rested her head against his once again. The comfort Del felt in this woman's arms while sorrow enveloped his soul was a sensation he'd never experienced. Could he have had a relationship like this all along, had he trusted someone enough to allow it to develop?

Felicia cuddled closer to him and whispered in his ear.

"I'm sorry for your loss, Del. I realize you wish you could have saved a life in 1962." She paused, then added, "No, Marilyn Monroe didn't make it through her tragedy. But what if that isn't how her story ends? What if her legacy continues in a way the public *doesn't* know about, an aspect of her memory you get to preserve privately?" She massaged his shoulder with her thumb. "What if, all these years after her departure, she saved Nora's life?"

Dabbing his eyes with his sleeve, Del considered the wisdom in Felicia's words. He still wasn't comfortable letting Felicia see him this vulnerable, but he was getting there.

No, Del hadn't rescued Nora Jumelle. Not really. But another screen legend had.

Felicia was right. Del knew something else about the icon that few others did. Another treasure he would cherish in his heart.

# CHAPTER 70

THE NEXT DAY, before he departed for his morning jog, Del phoned his new friend.

"How are you holding up, Tristan?"

"Hanging in there. Concerned about Nora."

"At least they've stabilized her and she's out of Intensive Care."

"That's a plus." Tristan paused. "You hanging in there?"

Was he? Del didn't know how to respond. Once the prior day's events took their toll on him, his emotions had gone beige. "Unfortunately, I'd seen this type of thing happen over and over by the time you were born."

"I have a hunch it meant more to you this time, though."

Del felt his muscles surrender to the truth.. "Yes, it did."

"She talks about you a lot, you know."

"She does?"

"When we're together," Tristan replied. "She admires you. She says you two were cut from the same cloth."

"How so?"

"She says you both seek something deeper than fame can offer, and that's the reason you're both restless."

Del wasn't at a point where he could admit that. Fortunately, Tristan changed the subject for him.

"Are you headed to the hospital today?" Tristan asked.

"I can't think of anyplace more important to be," Del

replied.

Astonished, he tapped his finger on the arm of his chair.

Who would have thought a chance encounter with a charming young lady could introduce such a rich, new facet to his life?

# CHAPTER 71

HE KNOCKED on the door to the hospital room and peeked inside.

Nora sat up in bed, pillows arranged behind her back. She stared at raindrops which pattered against the window pane. The shower provided a welcome respite to months of drought.

"How's my girl doing?"

Nora gave Del an uninspired shrug and said, "I'm alive. And sober—in more ways than one."

"May I sit down?"

That brought a wisp of a smile to Nora's countenance, and she patted the edge of the hospital bed. Del eased over and rested against it, careful not to add too much pressure in case it would cause her discomfort.

Nora continued to gaze at the window. "Who found me the other day?"

"Tristan tried calling you—"

"Yeah," she murmured, "I vaguely remember that."

"He suspected you were in trouble, so he called Felicia, who called me. We met at your house. We shouted, we tried calling your phone, no response." He offered a bittersweet chuckle. "By the way, we owe you a new front door."

That got her attention. Her lips parted. Clearly puzzled, she squinted as the tease took effect. "What does *that* mean?"

"We broke down your door to get you."

"That must've been a new experience for you."

"It was a first. That's what happens when you hang out with young people, I suppose."

"Oh my—" Nora shook her head and rubbed her temples. She shuddered, then covered her face. "Oh, I'm embarrassed you had to go that far."

"Don't be." In one gentle sweep, Del removed her hands from her head. She gave him a sheepish look. "Do you want to talk about it?" he offered.

"I don't even want to *think* about it," she replied. "I lost control, Del."

"It happens, believe me."

"I mean I lost control over my *life,* as if it no longer belonged to me. I never cared about that Academy Award, but for some reason, it burned inside me. The passion grew. And soon, it meant everything to me."

"Everyone wants to be loved. Wanted."

"Well, it all scares me, Del."

He leaned in close, enveloped her hand in his, leaving room for the IV needle that was inserted into the top of her hand.

"I'm watching over you," he said. "From now on, you're not alone. I'm here for you."

He could tell that touched her. Her expression softened and a smile emerged.

"Del Corwyn, my guardian angel."

"Who would've thought, huh?"

Sincerity returned to her eyes. "Thank you for finding me."

"I lost someone dear to me long ago," he said. "I couldn't watch it happen again."

A pause, then Del rose from the bed and kissed the top of Nora's head.

"Try to get some rest," he said. "I'll come back later."

On his way to the door, he turned. "Do you want me to contact any family members?"

Nora folded her hands in her lap. "I don't have family, Del."

Del grinned, then shot her a wink.

"Now you do."

# CHAPTER 72

THE DOOR TO FELICIA'S OFFICE was open. A Bible sat open on her desk, along with a handful of other books from which she read, then typed brief notes on her laptop. Engrossed in one book, Felicia didn't notice Del's approach.

"May I come in?"

Felicia peered over her reading glasses, regarded him without expression, and then gestured to the seats in front of her. As Del sat down, she folded her hands atop the desk. Though she didn't utter a word, she studied him, giving him the chance to speak first.

"Are you busy?"

"I'm in the middle of preparing a sermon, Del."

"Do you have time to talk?"

She removed her glasses and folded her hands again, which Del figured might be the closest he'd come to a yes.

Aside from the day of Nora's tragedy, today was the first time he and Felicia had spoken since ending their relationship. And her current silence didn't bode well for him.

"It's a shame what happened," said Del. "To Nora, I mean."

"I feel so bad for her," said Felicia, who relaxed her shoulders. "I hate seeing people in those predicaments, where they feel they can't escape."

"We got there in time, though."

"Thankfully, God had His eye on her."

"It seemed like divine Providence, yes."

Del noticed Felicia had pulled her hair into a ponytail. He picked up a trace of her perfume, airy and floral. He still thought her beautiful. He regretted the unfair, self-centered outbursts he had made outside this building. Why had he lashed out at her that way? Even in the heat of the moment, he'd recognized she had sterling intentions.

"So where does that leave us?" he asked.

Felicia blinked. Otherwise, her face remained carved marble. "Us?"

"Well, sure. I mean, I'm here. You're here. The question is, what's between us?"

"I think you made it clear where you stand, Del."

She wasn't making this easy for him. Then again, why should she? He'd assumed she'd be willing to talk, but maybe she didn't want to see his face again and was too polite to say so. Maybe he was wasting his time here, but he couldn't let her go. He couldn't deny how he felt about her, or the way she'd drawn his heart to hers.

"I misjudged you," he said, "and I'm sorry for that. I've kicked myself ever since."

She stared at him, wordless. Okay, she wanted to hear more. Whether that was a good or bad sign, Del didn't know, but he kept going. After all, if he didn't try to win her back, he stood to lose everything.

"I admit, I'm settled in my ways," he continued. "I'm self-absorbed, and I don't even know why or how I got that way. Years have stacked upon years, crusted over, and calcified. That doesn't prevent a man from amending his ways; it just means change doesn't come without tremendous effort."

Felicia continued to stare at him, but the initial guardedness in her glare had begun to retreat. He might as well press forward and hope for the best, he figured.

"If you're looking for a perfect man, Felicia, you won't find one in me." Nervous, his belly fluttered. He craved a bottled water, if for no other reason than to occupy his hands, which had slickened with sweat. On the other hand, the bottle would have slipped from his grasp and spilled over her desk and into her lap. Del cleared his throat.

"This whole season—everything about it and all the individuals involved—has gotten me thinking about dreams. I've examined my life. Not the way an accountant analyzes things, but the way you examine your circumstances when you're stuck. When you find yourself in the middle of a forest and nighttime settles in. The batteries in your flashlight have died, so you try to navigate by feel, desperate to find your way. You hear wolves howl in the distance. Your breath goes short. You hope you'll make it through to dawn. That kind of examination." He paused. "The kind where you discover you took everything important in life for granted, and if you hadn't, you'd be spending the evening with the woman you love instead of wandering in circles in the woods."

"That sounds like a movie, Del."

"My life is a movie, Felicia. It's fiction," he replied. "I'm not real. I'm a ghost. Invisible. *I* know I'm here, but nobody else does. And so I surround myself with a fictitious world, complete with a plot, every day scripted, all the props in the right places. And when the production day wraps, all the players depart to their homes and loved ones and their broken lives, and I'm left alone with my dreams, the same ones that sat there unfulfilled when I awoke that morning." Now he fixed his eyes on hers, and they communicated in their mutual gaze. "All the fame and glamour, all those big dreams. And now, at seventy-eight years old, I've come to realize that maybe I've been dreaming too *small* all along."

Felicia pursed her lips. Fighting tears, perhaps? Her hands had parted. Her entire demeanor spoke of hesitation.

Indecision. The risk of getting her heart broken all over again. She swallowed, then exhaled, her eyebrows raised in resignation.

"I can't stop you from dreaming," she said. "If you want to rebuild your career—"

"Stop," he murmured, rising from his seat. "Please stop."

Del took a step forward, paused to allow his lower back to loosen—that nuisance, never hitting him at a convenient time—and eased around the side of the desk. She swiveled to face him. He reached for Felicia's hand, which she allowed him to take into his. He gazed at the sight of their intermingled fingers and discovered hers were as damp as his own.

Del lowered himself to one knee and held her hand with the care he would give to a large ruby.

"I don't want the material stuff, Felicia," he said, putting into his words all the affection his soul could muster. "I want you. Whatever that takes, I want you."

Felicia's eyes had grown moist. Her lips moved but no sound came forth. She blinked once. Slowly.

She pressed her lips together, bit back tears. And when she smiled, life traveled into her eyes.

She leaned forward, cupped Del's face with her hands, and stroked his cheekbones once with her thumbs.

# CHAPTER 73

DRESSED IN AN EXPENSIVE blazer and an Oxford shirt unbuttoned at the collar, Del sat in a bistro facing all incoming patrons, whose attire resembled his own. The bistro was known in town as an establishment where those who wielded power often congregated to hammer out deals. A restaurant with a faux-casual flair where you ordered all side items a la carte, French fries were thick strips of fried Yukon gold potatoes, and where the tips alone were more than a family of four in Del's hometown paid for dinner at their local diner. The atmosphere dripped with the aura of influence. Del felt the magnetism of limitless expense accounts.

Bernie Schulman walked in, dressed in a black suit and a power-red tie. He carried a small, black portfolio. Del lifted an index finger to signal his whereabouts.

"You certainly dressed for the occasion," Del noted.

"Gotta fly to Manhattan after this. I'm meeting with Clive Davis about a couple of recording artists for the soundtrack. Getting everything in motion so we're ready to pull the trigger on our little *Beautiful Mess.*"

"That's the reason I called the meeting."

"I figured as much." Schulman shook his linen napkin and folded it across his lap. "Don't worry, Del. Your role in the film is secure." Tapping his finger on the portfolio, he added, "I have the paperwork here, ready for us to seal the deal. Arnie and I worked out all the details. You made the right choice signing with my studio."

Schulman perused the menu. Del had lost his appetite. He wanted to press through this lunch and leave.

"I assume you saw the advance copy of the contract my assistant sent your way?" Schulman said, his voice half-absent as his eyes flicked from one entrée to the next. "I'm on a diet. Damn salads."

"Yes, Bernie, I saw the contract. And I appreciate the generosity." Del spoke to the guy's oily forehead. "But I'm afraid there won't be a deal."

Schulman didn't move, yet tension engulfed the space between them. A splotch of pink appeared on his brow.

The studio head placed his menu on the table and pierced Del with a glare that would have frightened Del on the set of *The Prince and the Showgirl.* At this point in his life, however, Del had advanced too far and matured too much to care.

"May I take your order, gentlemen?"

Schulman shot one hand, palm outward, in the waiter's direction. "Not now."

Without a further word, the server offered a slight bow, then spun on his heels and hustled away as fast as his casual stride could carry him.

Schulman's eyebrows knitted together. Grooves formed along his wide, oily brow. "I think I missed something here. Did you sign with someone else?"

"No, Bernie."

"I thought we had an agreement, Del."

"A verbal one. An understanding."

"When you and I were young, verbal agreements meant something."

"Let's say there's been a change in circumstances."

Schulman snorted, an understated smugness. "Is it a money thing? You want more?"

"No."

"A producer credit?"

Del knew how much Schulman craved this deal. No doubt, the studio chief could envision a competitor swooping in and stealing this once-in-a-lifetime opportunity from his lap. But screwing him over wasn't Del's intention. Del had made up his mind. He needed to protect Marilyn Monroe's memory, first and foremost. And to do so, he couldn't allow the public to see this script.

"I don't want anything from you, Bernie. I've simply decided not to make the script public. Period."

Schulman pursed his lips, scanned the tables in his vicinity, then drilled his eyes into Del's. Though he kept his voice subdued, the man's glare could have frozen a hot coal.

"Don't fuck with me, Del."

Del sighed in resignation. "That's not my intention. I've had a change of heart. It's a personal thing."

Schulman shook his head in disbelief. "I strongly urge you to reconsider."

"I can't, Bernie."

"I don't think you understand what I'm saying here." Leaning forward, making sure he had Del's full attention, he added, "You *need* this project to happen."

"I used to think so, too." Del's mind raced through the loss of income and what that would mean, and even now, anxiety threatened to enshroud his intentions. But when he thought of Felicia, Nora…and the friend whose reputation he sought to preserve today, it bolstered his resolve. "I've made my decision, Bernie. This deal isn't going to go through. Not for you, not for anyone."

Schulman pressed his lips into a thin line again. By now, his face blistered red, and the boil had spread to his brow, ears and neck, where loose skin betrayed his age. In an obvious effort to maintain his composure, he grinned and nodded, as though he still called the shots at this power meeting.

He jabbed a stubby finger in Del's direction, low enough so nobody except Del would see it. From the flesh of the fingertip, Del detected the aroma of cigars. *Expensive* cigars. Schulman's voice, though restrained, increased a notch louder.

"You're finished," Schulman hissed. "You can forget about your big comeback, Corwyn—now or ever. I'll personally guarantee you never work again—not for the rest of your miserable, washed-up life. I'm gonna kick your ass so sore, you'll be paying a fucking home nurse to rub it down with aloe."

And yet, Del remained at peace.

With one final glare just to communicate he meant business, Schulman straightened his tie. Slapping the napkin on the table, he arose, brushed the temporary wrinkles from his suit, and strolled toward the restaurant's entrance. The image of power—though Del noticed a few extra inches in Schulman's strides.

The telltale sign of a defeated man who wasn't accustomed to losing battles.

When the waiter returned, Del ordered a Cobb salad.

And a bottle of Dom Perignon for the hell of it.

# CHAPTER 74

DEL THOUGHT Arnie would have a heart attack when he reported the news about the meeting with Schulman—and the end of negotiations which his agent had worked so hard to hammer out.

When Arnie returned his copy of the script to Del, he did so with the solemnity of a man in mourning. After all, his career had come to an end, too. In the big leagues, at least. Not that he'd ever advanced beyond the status of a third-string kicker. Arnie would, in due time, return to making minor deals. Within a few months, the blame for this media debacle would rest solely on Del Corwyn's shoulders.

That night, Del ran his palm over both photocopies of the screenplay and sealed the stack with a tender, heartfelt kiss. It was the closest he could come to showing affection to his friend.

With a glass of wine in one hand, he carried the scripts to his living room, where a cozy fire danced in the fireplace. Miles Davis played on the stereo.

One by one, Del fed the pages into the fire. Flames licked the edges, which browned, curled and crackled as destruction crept toward the center of each page, turning it to ash which fluttered like dirty snowflakes to the bottom of the fireplace.

———

Darkness had set in. The Malibu shoreline had emptied.

Del zipped his windbreaker as a breeze rushed across the cold Pacific Ocean.

Tilting the vase toward the ocean, he sprinkled the ashes of the screenplay upon the water.

The atmosphere was silent, save the roar of high tide. The same tide Marilyn Monroe had loved to watch, once upon a time. Even now, Del could hear her giggle as the chilly water swept over her cherry-red toenails, then receded, leaving behind white foam that fizzled and dissolved around her.

# CHAPTER 75

**LOS ANGELES, 1961**

DEL ZIPPED UP the Pacific Coast Highway in his 1956 Chevy Bel Air. He was under contract with Columbia Pictures, and after two years of continuous—though minor—roles, he was no longer a starving artist. On occasion, he received positive mentions in film reviews. His career was on the rise. So he'd splurged and bought this convertible secondhand. His first major purchase since he'd arrived in Los Angeles, this car was a source of pride. A two-tone beauty of pinecrest green and India ivory.

He had turned down the vehicle's white soft top. Now he settled against the green interior and allowed his hair to whip in the wind. On the radio, "Travelin' Man" Ricky Nelson crooned about a Polynesian baby awaiting him in Waikiki.

Del's car contained a V8 engine, which he enjoyed pushing to its limits when he hit straight patches along the coast, pockets where he knew he wouldn't find pedestrians or police officers. In the passenger seat, Marilyn squealed with delight as he navigated a sharp curve around the mountain.

She wore large, dark sunglasses and a thin, stylish scarf on her head. Locks of platinum-blond hair peeked out from under it. For a woman considered a sex symbol, her manner of dress puzzled Del. She kept a conservative wardrobe—a tight turtleneck sweater today—almost as if she wanted to *hide* her figure from public view.

It was a Sunday afternoon, balmy beneath a gleaming sun, and Del wore a short-sleeve shirt with fat, vertical stripes. Marilyn guided him to an isolated stretch of beach in Malibu, where Del pulled off the road. It was a nook where they could park and savor the ocean with no one around to recognize her. Del shut off the engine but left the radio playing at low volume.

"One day, years from now," announced Del, "I'm going to live here."

"In Malibu?"

Call it faith, but Del felt invincible, as though the impossible were within his grasp. Victory burned inside his bones.

"Right up there." He pointed across the road to the mountain that hovered over them. "In a mansion, where the big-timers live."

"How wonderful!" She yanked off her sunglasses. "And we'll throw a party! A housewarming! With an open bar!"

"Careful," Del teased. "Don't spend all my money on this party. Gonna need to pinch every penny to afford that nifty house."

"Oh, pooh." She nudged his arm. "I'll take care of you. That's the way it is, isn't it? You and I? We take care of each other."

"Forever."

Curiosity filled her stare. Angling back, she regarded him the way she might have admired a Monet. Time stopped. Seagulls squawked, but Del paid them no attention. Marilyn drew near, laid her palm on his cheek, and kissed him. One kiss, long and full. Too stunned to return the gesture, Del froze as her lips pressed against his. He detected a trace of spearmint on her breath. He could taste her lipstick.

Del felt his loins stir and, in self-consciousness, tried to pull his shirt over his lap without disrupting the moment. How long had he dreamed of this, yet never expected it to manifest? And now that it did, he hesitated. So many people had taken advantage of her. He couldn't add himself to that list.

When she pulled away, she returned her attention to the rolling waves before them, as though nothing had happened.

Reaching for his hand, Marilyn bit her lower lip. "Have you ever been in love, Del?"

His heart trembled at the thought. Could he tell her the truth?

He wondered if he was the only one who understood her well enough to become the man she needed. Perhaps *she* didn't even know herself that well.

He loved her, he knew that much. But he couldn't wrap words around the affection he felt for her. Had he *fallen* in love, or did he love her simply because she seemed beyond the scope of possibility?

"I'm not sure I've ever fallen in love," he replied at last.

Del wanted to shed a tear.

*Just tell her. You don't know what tomorrow could bring. What if the opportunity vanishes?*

The radio station sounded its call letters in four-part harmony, followed by "Where the Boys Are" by Connie Francis. Marilyn hummed along to the dreamy melody as she gazed at the horizon, where a dolphin lunged in the distance. Yearning settled upon her face. Her eyes glossed over with tears.

Suddenly, she looked so fragile, like a wilting tulip, and the resolve to protect her emerged in Del's soul. As they sat in the car, their roles reversed.

Del was now *her* guardian.

"Are you happy?" he asked.

The corner of her mouth twitched.

"Of course I'm happy," she replied. "We always have fun cruising the coast together."

"No, I mean in life. Are you content?"

She glanced at him from the corner of her eye, then followed it with a look of confusion. She continued to stare at the great beyond, as though searching for a way to answer the call of the seagulls.

"I *should* be happy," Marilyn said, almost to herself, "but I can't say that I am. A moment here, a moment there, perhaps. But in general, sadness consumes me. Life is full of tragedy."

A tear escaped her eye, which she smoothed with her thumb. She wore no mascara. After all, she was with her friend Del, who didn't care how she looked.

"People see this bubbly woman on the silver screen. They read about the parties she attends and how popular she is. But inside, I feel like chaos."

She chuckled. A sad, absent laugh. Then she placed her hand on his and pivoted in her seat. Not one for sympathy, Marilyn Monroe was a woman of steel. She smiled through the pools in her sterling blue eyes.

"I'm a mess, Del. A beautiful mess, that's what I am." With a sniffle, she removed a white handkerchief from her purse and dabbed at her eyes. "But you, Del—you're a handsome, eager young prince with a full life ahead of him."

Marilyn searched his face, a vulnerable woman on a personal quest.

She was looking for joy. Del knew it. She was desperate to find it in his eyes.

She reached out, placed her hands on his face, one on each cheek. Her flesh felt warm. And when she had his undivided attention, her voice filled with conviction and hope.

"My little star," she whispered. "That's what you are, Del Corwyn. My bright, shining star."

# EPILOGUE

## FAMILY CONTINUUM

## JUPITER ISLAND, FLORIDA

DEL COULD TASTE the tropical flavor in the Florida sunshine. Contrary to his routine in California, where the Pacific always felt too cold for comfort, Del had come to love dipping his toes in the Atlantic bathwater.

Felicia preferred it, too. Much to their surprise, neither missed their former home.

Del leaned against the railing on his back porch and watched palm branches rustle in the breeze. Waves of emerald green danced beneath a horizon that stretched as far as the eye could see. Breathing deep, he allowed the scent of brine to soothe him. He swore his tanned arms had morphed to a different tone of copper here. Dryer. More casual.

He heard the glass door slide open. Felicia peeked out.

"They're here!" she announced.

Del nodded, removed his sunglasses, and wandered into the house. He followed the sound of chatter to the foyer, where he shook hands with Tristan and enveloped Nora in a heartfelt bear hug that lingered an extra moment. The visitors' luggage sat at the foot of the staircase.

"Why did you wait a whole year before getting yourselves down here?" Del teased.

"Del's talked about you nonstop ever since he moved down here," Felicia added. She approached Del from behind, wrapped her arms around his waist, and nuzzled her chin against his neck. He tilted his head and pecked her cheek with a kiss.

"Once production began on my next project, I hit the ground running and never slowed down," Nora replied. "This is the first breather I've taken ever since."

"You're happy though? Safe? In a good place?"

She responded with a playful roll of her eyes. "Yes, Del, I'm a happy camper."

Del gestured toward the hallway. "Come see the humble abode."

Del and Felicia led their friends through the den, the kitchen, and a few more rooms on the first floor. Within a few minutes, they entered Del's study, which contained a desk made of cherry wood, on which a laptop computer whirred, a soft leather chair positioned behind it. Cherry bookshelves lined one wall. Wallpaper wrapped the room in masculine tones of burgundy and navy blue. The office featured a nautical motif, with small model ships accenting the bookshelves.

"I'm so proud of Del," Felicia said. "He decorated this room himself. He even hung the wallpaper. It was finished before I ever moved in."

"Impressive." Tristan gave Del a jesting jab with his thumb. "A decorator? You've found your second calling."

Del grinned. This was his favorite room in the house.

And he'd embedded a secret upon its walls.

He'd ceased all negotiations for *Beautiful Mess*. As Bernie Schulman had threatened and Del had expected, the move had cost the actor his career, and had sealed his need to downsize to this home in Florida.

Del couldn't bear to destroy Marilyn's work or discard her memory. So he'd destroyed the photocopies he'd made, but not the original. But he couldn't keep the script intact. That put the document at risk of someone finding it. Moreover, Del feared the temptation to re-enter negotiations in the future. After seeing what a hoopla the script's discovery had generated, he knew the studios would jump at the chance to have another shot.

He'd yielded to that weakness once. He couldn't fall victim to it again, this time immortalizing the script on film and, in the process, destroying the Marilyn Monroe the public had come to know and love.

Yet he wanted to keep her with him.

Del needed a solution. And it came to him two weeks after

he'd settled into his new home.

He had moved to Florida in advance, to prepare the house while Felicia wrapped up final details with her congregation before her retirement. So while she resided in Los Angeles, Del picked the décor for this room and put his plan into motion. When he first moved in, the walls were painted white.

Using a Sharpie, Del blackened the information on the script's title page and, one by one, retracted the title in each individual page header to render the script anonymous. Next, using wallpaper glue, Del affixed each individual page of Marilyn's script to the walls of his study. He wasn't sure he'd have enough space to fit all the pages, but he'd wound up with a few square feet to spare. Once the glue dried, he overlaid the pages with the wallpaper his guests saw today.

He never told a soul. Not even Felicia. Though one day, Del promised himself, he would.

Nobody would discover the pages of the script. Given the amount of glue he'd used, if anyone tried to remove the script from the wall, they would need to scrape it off, which would reduce the pages to chips and shavings, rendering them unreadable. Del planned to remain in his home until the day he died. By the time that happened, those who had read the script and knew its premise would have retired or passed away. With neither title nor author visible on the pages, it would look like a random screenplay somebody had written. The fingerprints would mean nothing to them, but he'd blackened those, too, to be safe.

In the off-chance someone recovered the pages and kept them intact, Del had taken another step to protect his friend. The key document—the cover letter with Marilyn's matching thumbprint and explanation—would disappear. As the final gift she'd given Del, the letter remained precious to him. He couldn't bear to let it go. And when he died, he would take it with him.

He'd folded her letter—envelope and all—into thirds and sealed it inside a larger, pink envelope. Although he'd written nothing on the outside, the color would be easy to identify. Then he'd locked the pink, unmarked envelope in the safe that sat at the corner of his study.

Upon relocating here, he'd updated his will to include Felicia. In the updated document, he also provided the combination to his safe and left instructions regarding a pink, unmarked envelope inside. According to Del's specifications, the envelope was to remain sealed and join him in his cremation. By the time anyone removed the wallpaper, the final evidence of the script's authenticity would have vanished.

———

Sunset turned the sky sherbet orange. Although humidity hung in the air, the temperature had cooled. On the back porch, the foursome gathered around the table. Del had grilled their lobsters to perfection. The scent of the charred grill, lemon and melted butter stoked hunger pangs in Del's stomach. Felicia prayed a blessing over the meal.

"So how's married life treating you, Del?" asked Nora.

"There's a first for everything—even when you're almost eighty," he replied, drawing his wife close and giving her a tender squeeze. "And it's the best decision I've ever made. Why did I wait so long for this?"

Felicia opened the bottle of wine Nora and Tristan had brought and poured everyone a glass, which they lifted in unison.

"To new beginnings," offered Tristan.

Del lifted his glass an inch higher. Gratitude filled his heart.

"And to enduring friendships," he added.

The foursome clinked glasses.

Conversation came in such an effortless manner, Del felt as

though the passage of time hadn't left its mark.

The four friends chatted. They laughed. They teased. And they shed a few tears.

Darkness settled in. The breaking of waves seemed to roar louder as the hours passed and the tide crept farther up the shore, closer to the back porch.

The foursome remained at the table until late into the evening.

# BEAUTIFUL MESS

## JOHN HERRICK

## READING GROUP GUIDE

# BEAUTIFUL MESS
# By John Herrick

# READING GROUP GUIDE

## Discussion Questions

1. To which character did you relate the most? Why?

2. In Chapter 3, 4 & 10, Nora views herself as part of a continuum. *Beautiful Mess* treats one continuum—the art and evolution of film—as a microcosm of the continuum of life. It analyzes how random encounters in a large city can change lives across space and time. How do random encounters among the novel's characters impact each other? How does young Del's first encounter with Marilyn Monroe impact his life—and the lives of others—in the future? Can you recall a random encounter in your life that left you forever changed?

3. How does Del mature over the course of the story? What lessons does he learn about life and career? How do Felicia, Tristan and Nora help him grow? How does Del help the other characters mature?

4. In what ways to Del and Nora parallel each other? Del and Tristan? Del and Felicia? Nora and Felicia? In what ways do they contrast with each other?

5. How do ambition, emotion, sex and religion drive Del? Or do they? How do these factors drive other characters?

6. Nora's pseudonym, Jumelle, means "twin." In what ways is Nora Jumelle a modern incarnation, or "twin," of Marilyn Monroe? In what ways do the actresses differ?

7. Like her pseudonym, Nora's birth name, Tasmyn, also means "twin." In other words, although she changed her surname, she failed to escape her true identity. In what ways does Nora try to escape or alter her reality, both past and present?

8. Although Del is drawn to Felicia, he alienates her in Chapter 60. They end their relationship. With respect to Del, is this the result of self-protection, self-absorption, or both? Del reflects on this separation in later chapters. How does his response differ from the way he might have reflected on past romantic encounters when the novel began?

9. Both Felicia and Tristan provide guidance to others. How do these two characters differ in their approach, motivation and perspective? How do those factors end up preparing them—or not—for an emergency?

10. William Shakespeare wrote, "All the world's a stage, and all the men and women merely players." Marilyn Monroe brought her public persona to her film roles, yet that persona did not necessarily match reality. Prior to reading *Beautiful Mess*, what was your perception of Marilyn Monroe? In what ways do we all perform for those around us? In what ways might we all constitute a "beautiful mess"?

11. Do you have non-relatives you consider family? By the end of *Beautiful Mess*, in what ways might Del, Nora, Felicia and Tristan constitute a family? How do you define family? Do you have non-relatives you consider family?

## A Conversation with the Author

## How did you arrive at the idea for *Beautiful Mess?*

In 2010, I read a biography about Marilyn Monroe for pleasure. I had seen some of her films and loved them, but knew little about her. When I read that she had spent time—against her will—in a mental care facility, I was stunned. Imagine being fully functional and of sound mind, but losing your freedom through no fault of your own. I considered how frightened she must have felt, wondering if she would ever escape, pleading for someone to believe her. And all because she was misunderstood. Then I considered how such an experience might scar its victim. Would it change her perception of life? Would she grow paranoid of others, especially after those she trusted had betrayed her? As a creative individual, what might she find as a therapeutic activity to regain her confidence?

After all these years, I still couldn't shake my horror behind her predicament. I remembered she was once married to author Arthur Miller, who, I was surprised to learn, wrote and co-wrote some of her films. I considered their familiarity with each other as spouses. Did she observe Miller as he wrote? Did she read his drafts or offer opinions? Did she learn from him as a creative force? In that light, the idea of a screenplay penned by Marilyn Monroe seemed plausible.

The compelling nature of all those facts and questions led to the backstory behind *Beautiful Mess.*

Then came Del Corwyn, the main character. For American actors and actresses, it can become a stepping stone to better roles. For foreign actors and actresses, it can open the door to American film, which is considered the best and most successful in the world. But through the years, I've wondered about actors and actresses who receive Academy Award nominations—perhaps even win the statue—who immediately *disappear* from the box office. Think about it: Mercedes Ruehl, Juliette Binoche, and Jean Dujardin were all lauded after their wins.

But when was the last time we heard from them? It was in this vein that Del Corwyn was born.

**Marilyn Monroe appears in several flashback scenes. How did you prepare her dialogue?**

During my research, I found a terrific book called *Marilyn: Her Life in Her Own Words* by George Barris. Barris was a photojournalist and one of the last people to interview Marilyn Monroe. That interview formed the basis for his book. Along with photos from their session and the journalist's commentary, the book featured lengthy quotes from Marilyn as she told her life story in her own words. Because Barris conducted his interview in 1962, the year she died, but it also matched the time setting for *Beautiful Mess*. In other words, that was the way Marilyn spoke—*literally*—at that time. So I used her tone and word choices as cues to shape her fictional dialogue in my novel.

At the same time, some readers will know her only by her film appearances. So even though those roles were fictional, I tried to capture the essence of her language—as well as physical nuances—in a way that would remain accessible to those readers, too. The precision and poise with which she spoke was not a coincidence; it was a byproduct of her training with acting coaches, who hammered the importance of diction until it became habitual for her.

One interesting tidbit: In Chapter 48, Marilyn refers to her psychiatrist as "my Jesus" and explains to Del what she means by that. During my research, I stumbled across a documented conversation she had had with a close acquaintance, which captures that reference. Marilyn sought answers. Inner peace. As soon as I stumbled across that conversation, I considered my characters—Felicia is a minister and Nora is on a spiritual search—and knew the coincidence was too perfect to leave out of the novel. So I created a fictional conversation between

Marilyn and Del that captured Marilyn's view. So her view, that "my Jesus" figurative reference to her psychiatrist, is a documented fact. As also mentioned in Chapter 48 (and documented fact), her first foster parents were evangelical Christians, so spiritual seeds were planted in her life early on.

**Why did you select titles of Marilyn Monroe's films as subtitles for Parts 1, 2 and 3 of *Beautiful Mess*?**

That was a fun idea! It was an ode to Marilyn's career, as if it were a story arc itself. So each point in Marilyn's career corresponds with the relative point in the *Beautiful Mess* story arc. A hidden nugget for her fans. That said, the subtitles still hint at what will unfold. *As Young as You Feel* was one of Marilyn's earliest films and a minor role for her. It centers around a man who is young at heart but told he is too old for a career. That storyline resembles the disconnect between Del's self-perception and his reality.

*Gentlemen Prefer Blondes* is a film from Marilyn's heyday, the midpoint of her career. This section of the novel captures Nora—a Marilyn parallel—as her star rises. The title also foreshadows the novel's fictional Academy Award race: Nora is raven-haired; her competitor, Charlize Theron, is a blonde.

*The Misfits* was Marilyn's final completed film. Not only does that title signal the final pages of *Beautiful Mess*, but it captures the quasi-family bond that has emerged. All four characters are misfits in their worlds: Del is a misfit in his life stage and career arc. Some of Felicia's more traditional peers would frown upon her role as a female minister. Tristan is a life coach who lacks training or qualifications. And Nora struggles to find her place in an industry that adores her not for who she is, but for her portrayals of who she *isn't*.

Marilyn's final project, interrupted by her death, was the unfinished film, *Something's Got to Give*. I wanted to use the title as the subtitle for the Epilogue to indicate my characters' "family" relationship would remain in progress, but couldn't justify it. The title indicates tension, but an epilogue accomplishes the opposite: it ties up loose ends and brings the story full-circle. With a standalone novel, readers seek a sense of completion.

## Did you find any aspects of this novel a particular challenge?

My main character, Del Corwyn, is 78 years of age. In my own reading, I come across few protagonists in that age bracket. The most recent reads that come to mind are *The Wedding* by Nicholas Sparks and *Insomnia* by Stephen King. So I believed such a protagonist would lend *Beautiful Mess* a unique angle. My life never matches those of my characters, so it's always a challenge view life through their eyes. That said, living through my teens, twenties and thirties provided a reference point, albeit limited, for my previous main characters. However, in Del's case, I didn't have that advantage. Plus, I needed to take Del one step farther: He doesn't *see himself* as his true age. So after aging him physically and emotionally, I needed to pull it back a notch, tint his psyche with immaturity, and give him opportunities to behave like a man in his thirties or forties. That was fun. Here's a guy, Del, who feels so young and keeps fit, yet realities of life—lower back pain or retirement planning, for instance—prevent his complete escape into his fantasy world. Del maintains a youthful idealism, yet has endured enough punches in Hollywood to have grown savvy and cynical.

## What motivates you to select one book concept over another?

In general, three elements tug me toward a writing project, including a novel like *Beautiful Mess*:

1. The story emerges from my gut—I trust instinct.

2. Commercial and target-audience appeal.

3. Potential to inspire or encourage the reader.

The third element fascinates me: The same collection of words triggers diverse responses among readers. It can serve as entertainment for one person. It might inspire another to reach for his or her dreams. And that same novel could uplift someone enduring pain or contemplating suicide. It's such a privilege, and it's like fuel during my writing process.

**How do you view your connection with your readers?**

I believe the written word forges a bond between reader and author. When readers choose to buy a book, they've chosen to invest their valuable time in the story. If they decide to continue reading past the early chapters, a bond forms. At this point, I believe *the author* determines the depth of the bond. In other words, the greater my emotional investment—the more vulnerable I allow myself to become as an author—the deeper the reader will connect with what they read. If readers feel you've been honest with them and they're satisfied with what they read, a degree of trust results. And hopefully, by the end of the book, readers trust the author enough to invest part of their lives reading that author's next novel.

## Sketching the Story

"Whatever works!" That's the method authors use to plan their stories.

I sketch most books in advance, telling the story in synopsis form in a document that ends up 50 to 100 pages long. By capturing details early, it provides a roadmap and reveals where I need to fill holes in my logic. So most of my "creating from scratch" work occurs while planning—not when writing the manuscript! That means I can take advantage of momentum when I write the first draft, plowing through the narrative and minimizing roadblocks that cause delays. At that point, the manuscript process becomes a matter of mathematics: 1 + 1 + 1 as I write the novel day by day.

Because I'm in storytelling mode during the sketch, the action unfolds naturally and I record as much as possible. Much of the dialogue you read in my novels I lift from the sketch verbatim! The sketch itself is informal—a structured brainstorm, spilling everything I can onto paper—and filled with run-on narrative. Some of the details help me step into the character's psyche and are never mentioned in the manuscript. Why? By the time I start sketching, I've determined my characters, conducted research, and constructed their biographical information, but those details don't always propel the action.

That isn't to say all questions get answered in advance, or that things won't change in the manuscript! You'll find my sketch for Chapter 1 below, along with margin notations to myself—as I mentioned, the sketch was handwritten. Maybe you catch the links to the final product!

## Chapter 1

Fade in. Del Corwyn. Age 78 but looks and acts and feels much younger. Sunrise. Gets out of bed. He slept alone, but he sleeps in the buff (he would do that). Stands up, works a few cricks out of his lower back. Opens curtains of bedroom, slides open glass doors, and looks out at the ocean from his high hill in Malibu. It's so high up, from this angle, the balcony railing hides his body from drivers on the PCH—he's checked it out himself. He'd spent many nights stargazing in the buff. Now he feels crisp breeze rush over his body. —> Cool from rushing over cold Pacific Ocean. [Describe his trim, fit build.]

> What goes through his mind? He has partially
> convinced himself he's a young guy, and this isn't an
> honest moment for him.

Pours himself a cup of coffee (coffeemaker programmed to brew at ____a.m.)

Strolls around his house w/coffee in hand. [Describe house—RESEARCH CELEBRITY HOMES?—and tie in some good memories from a couple of rooms—a small group of friends (celebrities from late 1980s) getting together, a random sexual counter he recalls, etc.]—GIVE IMPRESSION THAT HE'S VERY WELL OFF.

Puts on track suit and goes out for his daily 5-mile run. He's done this for decades. When he returns, he showers and fixes himself a smoothie (like a young guy)—DESCRIBE INGREDIENTS, INCL PROTEIN POWDER, FLAX SEED, ETC—VERY HEALTHY AND FIT.

Sits at computer. First he logs into his Twitter account and tweets that he just finished his daily run, followed by homemade smoothie—ready for the day! 547K followers—he was surprised how easily he could learn the latest trends in social media and how to use—but he has plenty of time. After a cursory look at today's news, he turns to a site about latest Hollywood developments (not trashy—for people in the industry—deals made, etc).

> ***He lives on past royalties, and also investments (via financial guidance). However, market taken severe hit since 2008 and he's in deep trouble now—not enough royalties coming in to live on, and investments aren't yielding what they used to.

Del has been out of Hollywood spotlight for decades. He has public reputation for being highly selective; but the truth is, he hasn't been in demand since his career sank after a missed Oscar win. Industry people know this, but general public doesn't—so his public persona doesn't match his private reality. ***SHOW DEL CRAVING RELEVANCE TODAY. THIS PLANTS SEEDS TO MAKE HIM SUSCEPTIBLE! He holds

333

dreams of returning to glory with a final career comeback in a stellar role and that elusive Oscar win, and that when his life ends (he knows he's closer but also in denial), he'll die in glory and as a legend. So he only takes <u>rare</u> roles as a featured/spotlight char to maintain his reputation. He rose to fame during Marilyn Monroe era.

OTHER BOOKS FROM
JOHN HERRICK ...

# JOHN HERRICK

# BETWEEN THESE WALLS

## A NOVEL

"There is a heart and integrity
to Herrick's writing."
– *The Phantom Tollbooth*

# BETWEEN THESE WALLS

**Hunter is a Christian. Hunter is the man next door. Hunter Carlisle is gay.**

At 26 years old, Hunter Carlisle has a successful sales career, a devoted girlfriend, and rock-solid faith. He also guards a secret torment: an attraction to other men. When a career plunge causes muscle tension, Hunter seeks relief through Gabe Hellman, a handsome massage therapist. What begins as friendship takes a sudden turn and forces the two friends to reconsider the boundaries of attraction. Along the road to self-discovery, Hunter's secret is exposed to the community. Now Hunter must face the demons of his past and confront his long-held fears about reputation, sexual identity, and matters of soul. A story of faith, fire and restoration, *Between These Walls* braves the crossroads of love and religion to question who we are and who we will become.

"Herrick will make waves…with this tale."

— *Publishers Weekly*

"A compelling read from beginning to end … A sophisticated and deftly crafted novel … Very highly recommended."

— *Midwest Book Review*

"A story of secrets, self-discovery, and the triumph of the human spirit … A moving story of love's power to cast out fear."

— *Foreword Reviews*

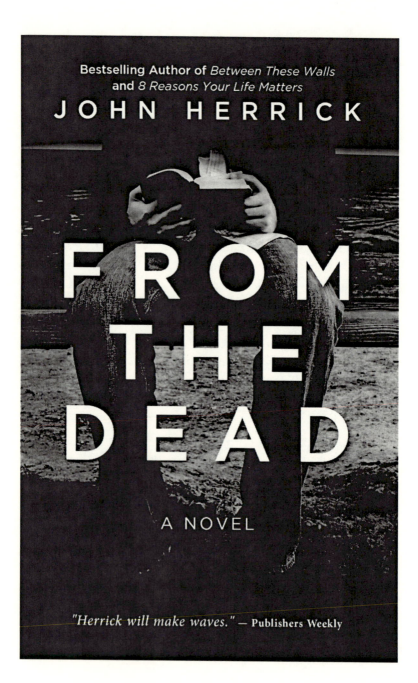

Bestselling **Author** of *Between These Walls*
**and** *8 Reasons Your Life Matters*

# JOHN HERRICK

# FROM
# THE
# DEAD

## A NOVEL

*"Herrick will make waves."* — **Publishers Weekly**

# FROM THE DEAD

**A preacher's son. A father in hiding. A guilty heart filled with secrets.**

When Jesse Barlow escaped to Hollywood at age eighteen, he hungered for freedom, fame and fortune. Eleven years later, his track record of failure results in a drug-induced suicide attempt. Revived at death's doorstep, Jesse returns to his Ohio hometown to make amends with his preacher father, a former lover, and Jesse's own secret son. But Jesse's renewed commitment becomes a baptism by fire when his son's advanced illness calls for a sacrifice—one that could cost Jesse the very life he regained. A story of mercy, hope, and second chances, *From The Dead* captures the human spirit with tragedy and joy.

"Eloquence with an edge. In a single chapter, John Herrick can break your heart, rouse your soul, and hold you in suspense. Be prepared to stay up late."

— Doug Wead, *New York Times* bestselling author and advisor to two presidents

"A solid debut novel."

— *Akron Beacon Journal*

"A well written and engaging story. It moves, and moves quickly. ... I don't think I've read anything in popular novel form as good as this in describing a journey of faith."

— Faith, Fiction, Friends

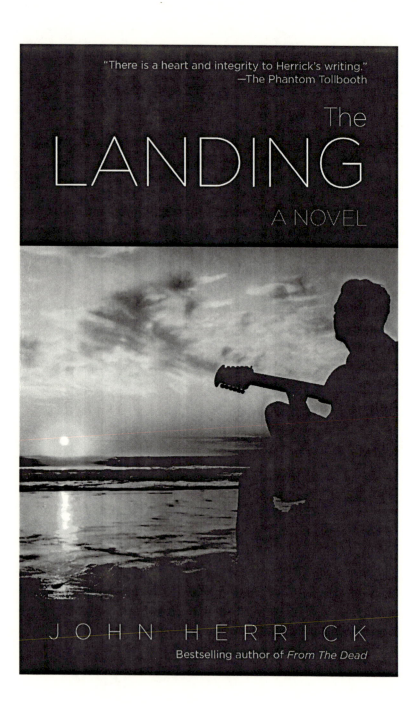

"There is a heart and integrity to Herrick's writing."
—The Phantom Tollbooth

The

# LANDING

A NOVEL

JOHN HERRICK

Bestselling author of *From The Dead*

# THE LANDING

**The power of a song: It can ignite a heart, heal a soul ... or for Danny Bale, resurrect a destiny.**

When songwriter Danny escaped to the Atlantic coast seven years ago, he laid to rest his unrequited affection for childhood friend Meghan Harting. Their communication faded with yesterday and their lives have become deadlocked. Now Danny, haunted by an inner stronghold and determined to win Meghan back, must create a masterpiece and battle for the heart of the only woman who understands his music. As memories resurface, Danny and Meghan embark on parallel journeys of self-discovery—and a collision course to seal their mutual fate. A tale of purpose, hope and redemption, *The Landing* is a "sweet story" *(Publishers Weekly)* that captures the joy and heartache of love.

"A powerful, absorbing tale, that will touch the heart and the mind as never before. A page turner."

— Doug Wead, *New York Times* bestselling author and advisor to two presidents

"Exquisite and honest. *The Landing* goes beyond language to pursue that elusive something that, when found, lingers and leaves you changed."

— Phyllis Wallace, Syndicated radio host

# 8 REASONS
## Your Life Matters

# JOHN HERRICK
Bestselling Author of *From The Dead*

# 8 REASONS YOUR LIFE MATTERS

### *"If I were to disappear, would anybody notice?"*

Each of us has asked that question in dark, honest moments.

In his first nonfiction book, *8 Reasons Your Life Matters,* bestselling author John Herrick combines personal struggles with biblical insight. Injecting eight chapters with humor, memoir moments, and a postmodern perspective on life, Herrick shares eight reasons your life matters:

Your Life is More Permanent than Your Struggles
God Sees You Differently than You See Yourself
You Have a Destiny
You are Remembered, not Forgotten
You Were Someone's First Pick
Your Absence Would Leave a Permanent Hole
People Need to See You Overcome
You are Loved and Valued
Eight solid reasons to give life one more chance. Eight reasons your life matters.

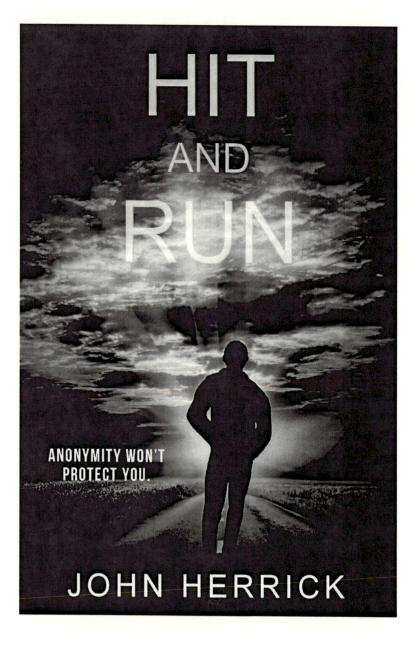

HIT
AND
RUN

ANONYMITY WON'T
PROTECT YOU.

JOHN HERRICK

# BONUS CONTENT

## *HIT AND RUN*

### A Short Thriller from John Herrick

*Anonymity won't protect you.*

On his way home from a much-needed respite in the Colorado Rockies, Gunnar Wakeman loses control of his car and dents a vehicle on the side of the road. When he sees no witnesses—and discovers a dead body inside the abandoned car—Gunnar flees the scene.

But the owner sees the incident. And records his license plate number.

Soon Gunnar finds himself stalked by a John Doe with an insatiable appetite for revenge. Jolted into a realm of paranoia, Gunnar must outmaneuver his enemy and engage in another hit-and-run—where the stakes have escalated and a wrong turn could prove lethal.

**Turn the page to begin the ride …**

# HIT AND RUN

## A Short Thriller

John Herrick

# PART ONE

# HIT

# CHAPTER 1

I save lives for a living.

I'm a good guy. I mind my own business. I don't cause problems for others. And I certainly don't wish them dead.

I realize not everyone operates like that.

Everybody starts out that way. Some people change.

When I say I save lives for a living, I don't mean I'm a paramedic or doctor or firefighter. I work under the radar. And technically, I haven't saved any lives yet—but one day, I will, if I can find the key.

Meanwhile, I'm a hero in the making. A warrior in disguise.

One day, you'll know me as a killer.

Of cancer.

You see, I'm a research biologist at the University of Nevada, a Reno man on a quest to find the cure for a curse. When I was eight years old, my grandfather died of bone cancer at the age of fifty-six. The loss devastated my dad, who was younger than I am today. Sometimes, late at night, after Mom and Dad thought I had fallen asleep, I would creep out of bed and tiptoe to the living room, where I listened to my Dad cry. And even though I was too young to understand his pain, I made a decision: I would never allow anyone to experience that type of loss again.

Even as a kid, I watched people. And I still do. You could

say I study them. I have good instincts.

The squeak of windshield wipers jerks me from my stream of consciousness. I grip the wheel and straighten my back. As I drive home, my eyes feel heavy.

*Pay attention to the road, Gunnar.*

Even a warrior—a man whose mission is to save lives—gets burned out. And so I cashed in a few of my vacation days and headed to the mountains of western Colorado, where my Dad's side of the family owns a cabin, high above the madness of the rest of the nation. Despite the altitude, the cabin is buried deep in the woods, at the end of a private road, where nobody can see you, and you can't see them. Peaceful. Isolated. We've owned it for generations. A lot of happy memories there.

Dad died in a car accident last year. He bequeathed the place to me. The truth is, I don't have the time or patience to maintain it, yet I don't have the heart to sell it.

My days on the mountain didn't bring a complete recovery, but they forced me to slow down. I've started to take deeper breaths. My blood pressure no longer feels like it's competing for first place at the Indy 500. Exhausted? Yes. But I feel normal again.

The only reason my nerves are on high alert is because my trek home is tense. I reached level ground a while ago, so my brakes are no longer fighting gravity. However, the weather remains unstable. A stationary front has remained in place since yesterday. Rain continues to fall, light but steady. The system ushered in a morning fog, which, against my hopes, has failed to dissipate. It's so thick, I can't see too far ahead of me. And unfortunately, I'm traveling along a two-lane road in God's country, where frequent twists and turns, when combined with the fog, prevent me from planning my moves in advance. It's the kind of fog that causes you to cling to the steering wheel with a white-knuckled grip without realizing it. Neither the defroster nor the headlights help. You move forward, as slow as possible, and roll the dice on whether you'll make it home safe.

I discovered this new route on my way here. According to my GPS, it's a shortcut, but it's also unfamiliar territory. And now, I wish I hadn't taken it. Saving those extra twenty minutes no longer seems worth it.

To make things worse, twilight has settled in.

Given a choice, I wouldn't drive in these conditions, but I need to return to work tomorrow. And I don't want to arrive home after midnight, rush to bed, and lose sleep, thus reigniting the stress I've spent the last few days soothing. I spent the whole afternoon waiting for weather conditions to improve, which didn't happen. So, eventually, I needed to bite the bullet, take my chances, and begin the trek.

The nearest town has a population of two hundred. If my experience is any indication, few vehicles travel this road: A car or two. The occasional eighteen-wheeler en route to who knows where.

Which is why I never expected a collision.

# CHAPTER 2

The dull thud of one car hitting another is one of the most horrid sounds on earth. I dread that noise. It signals circumstances have slipped from your control. It means you have, at minimum, a month's worth of headaches ahead of you. The only question is the shape in which they will manifest and the complexity of the maze through which you'll need to slog. And this evening, as I meander home, the memory of my accident has caused an acidic car wash in my stomach.

I shifted my eyes from the windshield so I could flip the defroster to full force. Just for a second.

But that's how fast your fate can change course.

The impact lurched me forward. My seatbelt locked in place and plastered me against the seat.

*What the—*

Because of the dense fog, I couldn't even see what I hit. It could've been a car. Or a deer. I prayed it wasn't another human being.

Pulling my car to the shoulder several yards from the accident, I turned off the ignition and closed my eyes, unable to move a muscle. Then, with a sigh, I unbuckled my seatbelt, reached for the door handle and climbed out of the car to unveil my fate.

To discover what—or, God forbid, *who*—I'd hit.

That was when my life changed forever.

That was when my worst secret, the one that will haunt me for the rest of my life, was born.

# CHAPTER 3

It was a car. A Chevy, maybe ten years old.

When I reached the vehicle sitting on the side of the road, I breathed a sigh of relief, thankful I hadn't stumbled over a body on the way to it. Nobody dead or injured on the road, and the impact wasn't forceful enough to have killed anyone inside a vehicle.

With manslaughter out of the picture, the yoke of what I'd done felt lighter already.

The lanes of the road were narrow, and so were its shoulders. More narrow than I'd realized, I discovered, as I took note of how far my parked car protruded into the lane. When I reached for the defroster switch, I must have veered toward my right and clipped the Chevy, which also hung across the solid line and two feet into the lane. The idiot who parked it there might as well have *asked* for trouble.

Once glance at the balding tires and rust along the car's edges told me this person didn't bother to maintain his vehicle. Getting hit might be the best thing that could happen to the owner. Quick cash. A newer replacement. Courtesy of *my* insurance. At least it wasn't a Porsche.

No one had emerged from the Chevy. Was the driver fumbling for an insurance card inside? Or calling the police? I could only guess how far we were from the nearest police station or highway patrol building. How long would it take an officer to arrive? So much for arriving home before midnight. Gritting my teeth, I counted to ten and forced myself to remain calm and cordial, even though this incident wasn't my fault.

Grimacing as rain pelted my body, I leaned toward the window on the driver's side of the Chevy, shielded my eyes from the precipitation, and peered into the car.

Nobody sitting inside.

Had I seen correctly? I peered again but, sure enough, saw no one.

I rapped on the window and peeked inside again. No movement inside. Had he run out of gas?

Pivoting at the waist, I continued to shield my eyes from the rain and gazed east, then west. The final hint of daylight lingered. Not enough for me to know for sure, but I spotted no silhouettes along the road. None that moved, anyway.

"Hello?" I shouted.

No answer. Beads of water scurried down my face and dripped from my nose and chin.

*"Hello?"* Louder this time. "Anybody here?"

Still no response. Not a sound, except the patter of raindrops hitting the leaves of the trees that bordered both sides of the road. Even the wildlife must have retreated to shelter. I couldn't spot any rodents or birds, but I knew they were there. I could feel their eyes on me.

*We saw everything.*

Grunting, I returned to my car and retrieved a small flashlight from the glove compartment, flipped it on, and discovered the batteries still had juice, though not much.

When I examined my fender, I found a small crack and some ugly scratches, but little other damage. At least I had something in my favor. Maybe it meant the other car wasn't damaged and I could continue my life as if nothing had happened.

Optimism morphed into dread as I sauntered back toward

the Chevy, studied its rear end, and shook my head in frustration.

The other owner wasn't as fortunate. He had absorbed the brunt of the collision. On the driver's side, at the corner of the bumper, I kneeled on the wet pavement and ran my fingers over a small dent. Tension oozed from my body as my muscles began to relax. Car repairs always cost more than you expect; that said, I guessed a small, non-union shop could repair this damage for a few hundred dollars. The only variable that might inflate the cost would be whether the repair required a brand new bumper.

*Why did this person park a car here?* I asked myself once again. Then again, maybe he hadn't parked it. Owner *abandonment* seemed plausible. But that wasn't all. Something else about the rear of this car was awry, too, but I couldn't put my finger on what or why. My mind was spinning too fast.

Fresh rain on foliage is one of my favorite scents. Under different circumstances, I would have stopped to savor it today. But I had no desire to stick around.

Thunder rumbled in the distance. I listened as the shower grew more intense. I was already soaked and had no way to blot myself dry. Now it started to pour.

Chewing on my lower lip, I gave the road one last perusal.

I still couldn't see much through the fog. I heard a crunch in the woods, which sounded like a small animal snapping a twig as it burrowed beneath a mound of leaves.

"Hello?"

Still no answer. Who was I kidding? I was the only schlub who had the patience—or integrity—to endure this. Aside from the nausea in my gut, I felt relieved.

How long had the car sat here? A few hours? A few months?

I shined the flashlight through the passenger window and, this time, scoured the entire vehicle for any sign of life. Inch by inch, though difficult from this angle, I swept the light across the interior of the vehicle.

When I checked the backseat area, I almost overlooked a man sleeping on the floor. Had he spent the night here? How could anyone have slept through the impact of the collision?

Rapping on the window again, I shouted, "Hello?"

Still no answer. Brushing the rain from the glass with my sleeve, I ran the flashlight up and down the man's body to get a better look at him.

Then I wished I hadn't.

This guy wasn't sleeping.

He was dead.

# CHAPTER 4

At the center of the man's forehead, I noticed a dark red spot, from which blood had trickled, dried and crusted. Blood had splattered the man's face and the fabric of the back seat.

I gasped.

Someone had shot him point blank.

Whoever had terminated this victim had stuffed a wad of white cloth into his mouth. The killer must have intended to gag the victim, but he had packed the cloth so tight, this man could have suffocated before the bullet ever entered his head.

The silver-haired man weighed a few extra pounds and donned a grey suit. Blue, nylon cords bound his wrists and ankles.

I fought the urge to vomit, too scared it would leave a trace of my DNA in the vicinity.

How long had the body been here?

Fear surged through my veins and sent me into an uncontrollable shudder. I'd never laid eyes on a corpse, aside from the occasional funeral where a family member rested inside an open casket—but those bodies never had bullet wounds in them.

I jumped away from the car, my eyes wide with shock, afraid to touch the vehicle more than I had. Creeping backwards, I glanced at the bumper again and realized why I had sensed something wrong earlier. The license plate was missing.

*No, no, no!*

Racing to the front of the car, I discovered the front plate missing, too. And when I checked near the bottom corner of the windshield, I noticed someone had scratched off the vehicle identification number.

Should I contact the police? My discovery could put me at the center of a murder investigation—a notion which scared me to death. I had no answers. Would they consider me a suspect? Or was *that* was the killer's plan? To set up a random passerby—me, in this case—to take the fall for the crime?

I pictured myself at a police station, sitting at a table in an otherwise empty, windowless room, stuttering my way through questions as two officers used the good cop-bad cop routine to manipulate me into a confession. I had no answers. Would that make me look guilty? Was *that* the killer's plan?

I panicked.

I have no other explanation for the choice I made.

The fact that I was sopping wet added to the pressure. As rain dripped from my clothes and face, I made one more careful, visual sweep of the area to make sure I hadn't overlooked any witnesses.

Just to be safe, I rubbed my sleeve against the bumper and windows, every surface I could recall having touched, in case the rain hadn't washed away my fingerprints.

Then I climbed into my car, started the engine, and left the scene.

# CHAPTER 5

That accident happened an hour ago.

I've been back on the road ever since.

I'm not a criminal. I'm not the kind of guy who flees the scene of an accident. I would've exchanged insurance information with the other party, but who knew when the owner would return, if ever? Was I supposed to continue standing in the rain, drenched, hoping for someone to materialize in the growing darkness? Spend the night in my car and wait for somebody to come along and rear-end me, too? I mean, I'd *shouted* for anyone who might be around. What else could I have done?

I suppose I could've written my contact information on a slip of paper and tucked it underneath the windshield wiper, but the rain would have destroyed it. And even if it didn't, although few cars travel along this road, who's to say *another* vehicle wouldn't hit that car—and inflict serious damage—without leaving *their* admission of guilt? My insurance might be on the hook for the entire bill.

Besides, it wasn't smart for the owner to abandon the car in the first place, was it? And I hadn't injured anyone.

That's what I've told myself ever since departing the scene of the accident and—*technically*—breaking the law.

# PART TWO

# RUN

# CHAPTER 6

Two months have passed since the car accident in Colorado. From time to time, the image of that Chevy comes to mind. Did the owner ever return? If not, is it still sitting on the shoulder of the road, a relic to which passing drivers will point and use as a directional marker for years to come, until it rusts and crumbles?

*"If you pass a run-down Chevy on the side of the road, you've gone too far. Turn around and hang a left at the gravel road."*

Despite the temptation to find out what happened to that car, I have no desire to return to the scene. The next time I retreat to the family cabin in the woods, perhaps I'll take the shortcut and drive past that fateful spot, just another anonymous traveler on his way to somewhere else.

For now, however, I fight the urge to doze. At the grumble of my stomach, I check the clock on the wall, then remind myself to fill my car with gas on the way home. It's well past dinnertime now, but I'm in the middle of some critical lab work. Peering into a microscope, I study a blood sample, a scarlet drop which, flattened between two slides, has taken shape of an amoeba.

Everyone else has departed for the day and left me alone in the lab. I spend much of my time alone these days, which suits me fine. Some people call it lonely or sad; I call it therapeutic. Solitude brings peace. Besides, as an introverted type, I've never felt the need to engage in small talk.

That drove my ex-wife crazy, the way I withdraw into myself, content when left to my innermost thoughts, without the need to verbalize my emotions.

*"Speak up!"* Bethany would blurt, annoyance evident in her tone. *"Tell me what you're thinking!"*

That's another thing about me: I don't trust many individuals. People have a way of abandoning you. Besides, you never know what's going on in the deepest recesses of anyone's mind. That person eyeing you at the airport or at your neighborhood IHOP could be a deranged psychopath with a short fuse, triggered when someone walks within twelve inches of their personal space.

My cell phone jumps to life in my hip pocket. The ringtone, Peter Gabriel's "In Your Eyes," is one of my all-time favorite songs, a masterpiece with few rivals: "God Only Knows" by the Beach Boys, maybe. "What's Going On?" by Marvin Gaye. But to be honest, the biggest reason I love "In Your Eyes" is because Beth and I danced to it at our wedding reception. And one year after our divorce, I still can't let it go.

Not just the song. Beth, too. Exasperated, regretting the day this emotionally stunted man ever walked into her life, she never wants to set her eyes on me again. But I still love her.

Retrieving the phone, I check the display. Ridiculous as it sounds, every time my phone rings, a part of me hopes it's Beth. I know it won't be her. She never calls. But the possibility helps make life solitude bearable.

Hey, never said solitude is *joyful* for me. I said it's therapeutic. It keeps me from hurting other people with my stunted emotional aptitude.

The call comes through as a private caller. No phone number. Weird. Probably a pollster trying to gauge the upcoming House of Representatives race. I'm on the cusp of my forties, so they consider me one of those swing voters who, according to statistics, should be a liberal who could start voting conservative at any moment. I get those calls all the time. But even telemarketers' phone numbers show up nowadays, so it must be an individual.

Perhaps it *is* Beth. Maybe she wants to talk, but she's not ready to share her new number with me yet. A guy can hope, right?

As soon as I answer the phone and hear the voice on the other end, I realize it's not Beth.

Or, more accurately, *he's* not Beth.

Goosebumps rip across my flesh.

# CHAPTER 7

It's not a pollster. It's not Beth.

"Gunnar Wakeman."

A statement of fact rather than a question. I swear, the man's gravelly, bass voice causes my phone to vibrate. I can feel it buzz against the surface of my ear. The man sounds hoarse, the timbre of a chain smoker or heavy drinker, but full of command. Before I utter a word in response, he knows he has me. He sounds too assured, a man who has the upper hand, as if he dares me to ignore him.

The hairs along my arms stand at attention. My throat tightens as I fight to swallow.

"This is Gunnar."

"You broke the law, Gunnar," whispers the grainy voice. Steady. Factual.

In control.

"Who is this?" I manage to ask, too stunned to utter anything else.

"What matters is I know who *you* are, Gunnar." The same matter-of-fact, don't-fuck-with-me tone. "I know who you are. I know where you live."

Moisture evaporates from my tongue.

"I know where your *ex-wife* lives."

I try to piece it all together. He knows I was married? And divorced? He knows my phone number too. And where I live, unless he's bluffing—which I doubt but feel too freaked out to ask.

"Who is this?"

"Does it matter? It didn't matter to you before."

I want to end the call, but fear prevents me from pushing this guy too far. Now I detect hints of anger in his voice, the sizzle of a flame eating up a fuse as it approaches a bundle of dynamite.

Struggling to keep my nerves steady, I swallow, then try to infuse my voice with intimidation, although I'm scared to death. "What the hell do you want?"

"Have you ever been to Colorado, Gunnar?"

The grin in his voice tells me he knows the answer. But how would he know? How *much* does he know? And why should he care?

"I've been there. Why?"

"Yes, of course you have," he said. "Do you remember the rain?"

My mind races back to my last visit. The one with the Chevy on the side of the road. But he can't be referring to—

"You hit my car, Gunnar."

Ice. My blood turns to ice.

"You hit my car," he repeated. "But you didn't stop. *You ran.*"

# CHAPTER 8

When I try to swallow, the lump in my throat stops halfway. My heartbeat doubles as I fight to breathe.

"I *did* stop," I manage to whisper.

"And then you ran." He breathes heavy. "You thought your anonymity would protect you, didn't you?"

"I don't understand," I reply. "No one was around."

The man chuckles to himself.

Dizziness oozes in. It slows my mind, which now treads in a pool of rubber cement.

"How do you know I was there?"

"I saw everything. Including your license plate number."

Shit. That's how he tracked me down.

Was he hiding in the woods? If so, I wouldn't have seen him in the fog. A hunter searching for prey in the rain? If so, he might have carried binoculars with him. How else could he have seen my license plate through the haze? But if he was there, why didn't he answer when I shouted?

Then again, he doesn't strike me as a rational guy. He's already admitted to stalking me.

"Who are you?" The aggression in my voice shocks me.

"You're in deep shit, aren't you, Gunnar? If you contact the police, you'll need to admit you committed a hit-and-run." He pauses. "And that you didn't report the dead body you found."

My staccato breaths return.

"Does that make you an accomplice to the crime?" the sinister voice continues to prod. "Maybe, maybe not. But it puts you in jeopardy, doesn't it? If you say something now, you'll risk prosecution. You could go to jail. All because you ran."

The man enjoys this conversation too much. My predicament is a game to him.

"I didn't intend to run," I insist. "Listen, what happened to your car, it was a small dent. Whatever the repair costs, I'll pay it. Just tell me how much and where to send the money. We could arrange a drop-off."

The man chuckles again. "No, it's too late for that."

Too late? Why?

Exasperated at the back-and-forth, I want this game to end. Then I want to change my credit card numbers and switch bank accounts. And get a new phone number.

"Just tell me what you want!" Wincing, I wish I could retract that remark. Who knows what will set this guy into motion?

"I don't want your money," the man hisses. "I want you."

I can hear myself swallow. A dry gulp.

"I'll be in touch," adds the man. "Don't bother trying to trace my calls. I'm using disposable phones, and I bought them with cash. I've spent two months preparing for today."

Fear and anger swirl together and send my adrenaline into a rush.

"Who the hell are you?" I demand.

The man breathes heavy.

"Call me Conscience."

And with that, a beep sounds.

Confused, I eye my phone's display. He ended the call.

My tongue tastes like copper and my appetite has vanished.

When switch my camera to selfie mode and examine myself, I discover the blood has drained from my face. A deathly pallor has chased it away. A cold sweat chills my neck.

I can't stop my hands from trembling. Glass rattles against metal as I remove the slides from the microscope.

# CHAPTER 9

I can't decide on my next move. Not that my options are limited. I'm just scared the wrong one will put me in greater danger.

My watch reads 8:26 p.m. Most nights, I would have started dozing by this time, but tonight, I couldn't sleep if I tried. My nerves are too frayed. I hope the alcohol will help.

Silence. Afraid my property is under surveillance, I sit in darkness, a prisoner in my own house and mind. Perhaps Conscience won't know I'm home if he sees no light in the windows.

Closing my eyes, I listen to the seconds pass on my watch, each tick a reminder that time for a decision is running out.

Maybe this Conscience guy is just a nutcase and will let up. I mean, revenge? Seriously? For denting his bumper? And the body—why should he care whether I reported the body or not? What difference does it make to him?

I take a gulp from my extra-large glass of cabernet. Should I call the police after all? No, I can't. Conscience is right: What if they seek charges against me? I'm not sure that's plausible, but I'm afraid to take to risk.

Even if I did call the police, what would I tell them? A body was in a car on a rural road in Colorado two months ago, but they probably won't find it now? The case wouldn't get solved. But my life as I know it might end.

# CHAPTER 10

My cell phone jolts me awake. Peter Gabriel serenades me again. Suddenly, I dread that song. Rubbing my eyelids, which have grown heavy, I brush my hand along the sofa but can't locate my phone. The sofa fabric is wet, which must mean I spilled my wine when I fell asleep. Sure enough, the glass has rolled against my body. No doubt, the wine has stained my sofa, but at this point, it's the least of my concerns.

Leaning on my elbow, I sweep my hand across the carpet and discover the phone has fallen to the floor. But by the time I retrieve it, the ringing has stopped.

I don't remember falling asleep. The wine must have worked.

The phone rings again. That same damn song. The harsh glow of the display pierces my eyesight in the pitch-black room.

Same identifier.

Private Call. No phone number.

It's him.

Before answering the call, I read the time. Eleven thirty-five. Tempted as I am to avoid talking to this psycho, I'm afraid not to. Answering the phone has kept the man at bay. As long as we don't cross paths, I'm safe, right? But how long can I keep that plan in motion? The rest of my life? The rest of *his* life?

And the body in that car still makes me shudder.

All I can do is think one step at a time.

When I answer the phone, I add a hint of severity to my voice, in the hope it will give this Conscience guy pause.

"Leave me alone. I said I'd pay for the damage."

"You don't seem to understand," the man wheezes. "I'm a victim here. A victim of a hit-and-run."

The buzz from the wine has worn off, but I rub away the sleep that lingers in my eyes.

"I know where you live. I know where your ex-wife lives," he reminds me. "And I'm coming for you. Tonight."

# CHAPTER 11

Fear shoots icicles up my spine. Before I can stop myself, I end the call and drop the phone like a hot coal.

This caller knew about the body too. Why hadn't *he* reported it to the authorities?

Unless *he's* the murderer.

Then it hits me.

I'm a witness.

This caller is twisted. He doesn't seek revenge for his car. During his prior call, when I offered to pay him, he told me it was too late for that. Now I know why.

*Too late, Gunnar. You can't undo what you saw inside his car.*

I had stumbled into a body I wasn't supposed to see. He wants to frighten me into submission before he eliminates the only witness to his crime. Few vehicles travel that rural road. *Nobody* was supposed to see that body. The killer must have been en route, transporting the corpse to its destination, wherever that was. Had he stopped along the way to take a leak in the woods? Was that why the car lacked a driver?

On the other hand, maybe I disrupted Conscience's plan the opposite way. Maybe I was *supposed* to stumble across the body and get framed for the murder, but the scheme fell apart when I fled the scene.

Regardless of the man's intention, I'm a witness to a crime.

If he is, indeed, a murderer—at this point, how can I assume otherwise?—and has tracked down where I live, then

376

I'm a sitting duck here at home.

*And I'm coming for you. Tonight.*

Panting from fear, I realize my clothes are soaked with sweat. I grab my phone and race to the bedroom, where I throw a change of clothes and a few other essentials into a duffel bag in a flurry.

On my way out of the bedroom, I stop, then run back to my closet, where I remove two wads of cash I've stuffed inside the toes of an old, grimy pair of sneakers. Ten thousand dollars I've saved for a rainy day. The hiding spot is my makeshift safe. I trust banks, but not enough to put everything in their care. I'm a scientist, a planner, but I've been paranoid my entire adulthood. ATMs have daily withdrawal limits, and I've always been afraid I'll need emergency cash when the banks are closed. Besides, who's to say this guy couldn't trace my ATM card use or charges to my credit card, pinpoint my location, and put a bullet through my brain?

*No more time to lose, Gunnar. Run.*

As an afterthought, I flick on a few lights inside the house, in case I can fool this Conscience guy into thinking I'm home. Chances are slim, but it's worth a shot.

You never appreciate the volume of your garage door opener until you hear the hum of its motor at midnight. It sounds ten times louder than usual. As the wheels of the door roll up the track, their creak punctures the silence of the neighborhood. Cringing, I glance up and down my street, but nothing appears out of the ordinary. No loiterers. No unusual cars. Relieved, I inhale the dry June air, which has cooled since sunset, and wonder if it will be the last deep breath I savor.

As I ease my car out of the driveway and shut the garage door, I take one last look at the street through my rearview mirror. Empty. I shift the car into drive.

And race to the freeway, ignoring stop signs at desolate intersections along the way.

# CHAPTER 12

After banging on her door for several minutes, Beth answers. Squinting beneath the porch light, she rubs her eyes and grimaces, a look that says she can't determine if she's confused or just pissed off. Unfortunately, she doesn't have time to decide.

"Pack your bag," I whisper, gesturing for her to hurry.

She responds with a grunt. "Huh?"

Precious seconds escape us as she hesitates. My stomach clenches.

"Don't ask questions, Beth. Just pack a bag. Come on, we've gotta go!"

She runs a hand through her golden, tangled hair, shakes her head, and purses her lips. Her expression tells me she thinks I still haven't let the possibility of us go. And she's right.

"Gunnar, it's over between us—"

She halts midsentence when I grip her arms and squeeze them tight. She stares into my eyes. The intensity she sees in them must frighten her because her pupils double in size. She tightens her lips into an O, her habitual expression when she calculates options. Tonight her options are limited. But she doesn't know it yet.

"I can't explain right now," I reply, releasing her arms from my grip, "but you're in trouble. I need to get you to a hotel. Now."

"You're beginning to scare me. I—"

Seizing her arms again, I lean my face close to hers and pierce her eyes with mine. "I need to listen to me, Beth. Are you listening?"

She falls silent and nods.

"I can tell you everything in the car." I eye my watch. We've lost a whole minute, dammit! "But we can't waste time right now. You need to go inside and pack a bag as fast as you can. Something to last you a day or two. Please, Beth!"

With that, I pivot her on her heels and, with tender urgency, nudge her into her house as she shakes her head, speechless and confused.

Three minutes and forty-nine seconds later, we're in the car.

# CHAPTER 13

"Gunnar, what's going on?" Beth is no longer tired or apprehensive. Now she's agitated.

"I'm taking you to a hotel. You need to stay put until I return."

"No way. I'm not getting out of this car unless you give me answers."

So by the time we reach downtown Reno, I've given her the gist of what has unfolded the last two months and the last six hours, careful to leave out details that might put her in danger. Like the corpse in the Chevy.

I explain the hit-and-run, the car owner who was nowhere to be found, and the guy who calls himself Conscience, a man whose dented bumper sent him into a rage. As expected, the explanation leaves her with a slew of unanswered questions—and obvious suspicions that I haven't told her everything—but she understands the severity of the threat she faces. And she's scared to death.

I hate to introduce fear into her life. Given a choice, I'd never do that to her, but in this case, fear might save her life. And *that's* the outcome I need to ensure. Whatever protects her.

I lost her once. I won't lose her again.

I pull into the parking garage of a huge casino hotel, an underground labyrinth where, if Conscience has followed us, we can vanish from his sight. At the elevator door, I put the car into park and unlock the door. Then, grabbing my duffel bag from the back seat, I remove a handful of hundred-dollar bills and force them into her hand. Her eyes go wide at the sight of her ex-husband peeling off cash by the hundreds.

"Check in to the hotel. Use a false name if they'll let you. Pay up front, in cash. Use cash for everything so your credit card won't be traced."

She casts me a glance of hesitation.

"Go!" I shout.

Her brow knit with concern, Beth climbs out and hurries to the elevator, which I refuse to stop watching until the doors close her in and I know she's safe. Then I race to the garage exit, insert my parking ticket into the machine, and pull out onto the downtown street. Checking my cell phone—and relieved to find no calls—I toss it on the passenger seat.

The killer can't track us both. Either he tries to locate my ex-wife in a twenty-story hotel and casino, or he tries to find me.

And I'm the one he wants.

# CHAPTER 14

Ten minutes later, I pull up to the 24-hour drive-through window at a Dunkin' Donuts, eyeing my surroundings on the way and catching sight of nothing unusual. Maybe we lost Conscience at the hotel, but the darkness makes it difficult to see. If he's here, he doesn't have his headlights on. I feel like one of those stationary, paper targets at a rifle range. An easy hit. But hunger pangs have started causing my stomach to crunch. Besides, I'll need to stay awake for who knows how long.

Putting the car in park, I order a breakfast sandwich and a large coffee with a turbo shot. I assume I'm safe while the cashier sees me, and as cash exchanges hands, I look for a security camera. Sure enough, it's affixed to the corner of the building, aimed at my car. Leaning my head out the window, I give it a wave—a long shot, but I want to be on record somewhere in the event I wind up missing.

My left foot is in a frenzy, tapping against the floor, as I will the cook to hurry. A timer near the cash register indicates a minute has passed since I placed my order. The desolate streets and parking lot bring an eerie tranquility to the environment. You know your life is operating outside the range of normality when you find yourself sitting at a Dunkin' Donuts in the middle of the night. I sip my coffee, which scorches my throat on the way down, and savor the taste of that smooth, rich creamer which seems to be a Dunkin' specialty. I swear I can feel the saturated fat clogging my arteries. If Conscience doesn't kill me, my guilty pleasures might.

Finally, the cashier hands me a toasty, grease-spotted bag that contains my sandwich, and I hit the road, catching the interstate ramp two blocks ahead. Although I could use some sleep, my catnap on the sofa has proven a lifesaver. That, and adrenaline.

At this late hour, the freeway is a paranormal universe, my neighbors a handful of vehicles and the ghost of my predator, so I floor it, setting the cruise control at twenty miles over the speed limit.

I have no clue where I'm headed.

Somewhere. Anywhere.

Someplace where I can think.

And formulate a plan.

# CHAPTER 15

Hours later, my nerves settled to the rhythm of my tires rumbling along U.S. Route 50, a couple of miles from Interstate 70. But I remain on full alert.

Wincing at the discomfort in my midsection wrought by a full bladder, I refuse to stop. As long as I move forward, I feel somewhat safe. On the radio, between crackles and bursts of static, I listen to the murmur of a female talk-radio host, for no other reason than I can use the company and it's the only radio signal that reaches me here. I'm in the middle of rural Utah, where, if I had the benefit of daylight, I'd find myself surrounded by mountainous terrain and wild vegetation that only a desert could love.

Although traffic is meager, the road isn't a dead zone, per se. Pairs of headlights speckle the flat pavement behind me, taillights dot the stretch ahead. Red and white, like ugly Christmas lights. Where the hell do people travel in the middle of the night?

A hundred bucks says I'm the only one on the run from a killer. And the wad of cash in my duffel bag is enough to cover that bet many times over.

My cell phone rings. Peter Gabriel's haunting voice. The display lights up. Private Call.

My gut wrenches as I click to answer it.

"You know better than to run"

"Leave me alone!" My voice is firm now. Resolve has begun to seep into my bones.

"I can see you, Gunnar."

"Why are you doing this?"

Calm and controlled, he ignores my question.

"You're merging onto I-70 right…" A beat. "…now."

An ice pick to my spine wouldn't have paralyzed me quicker. My arms stiffen as I grip the wheel until I can feel my knuckles turn white. My bladder would have emptied if I hadn't caught it in time.

"Just tell me what you want! Let's finish this!"

"All in due time," he wheezes in his sickening, scratchy voice. "You'll never victimize another soul. Not after tonight."

"I'm innocent!"

With his now-familiar patience, he continues speaking, as if I hadn't interrupted him.

"You can't run forever. When you stop, it will mark the beginning of the end. Your minutes are numbered, Gunnar."

Cursing under my breath, I end the call without another word.

My eyes flick toward the rearview mirror. Who knows what vehicle he's driven since he abandoned the Chevy? Hiding under the cover of night, I never would have caught him tailing me once I reached the freeway in Reno. Visible to the naked eye, yet he remains a phantom. He knew the split-second I entered I-70. A satellite tracker would lag as the signal beams to space and back. Which means, regardless of whether he's affixed a device to my car, he's on this freeway with me. Now that I know he's here, I'm confident he's one of the drivers behind me—any one of them. Which whittles it down to ten or so. The highway twists around the mountains, which seems like it should benefit me, but with only two eastbound lanes, my options for either losing him or identifying him are limited.

Conscience, he calls himself.

*Whose* conscience?

A thought occurs to me. Given the way the road bends, my pursuer will want to keep a close eye on me, won't he?

When I reach a short, straight stretch, I jerk into the other eastbound lane without using my turn signal. Ignoring the blast of a horn from the driver I cut off, I glance at my mirror to see if another car follows my lead. Coordinating this feat in the darkness makes me nervous—the next twist might appear with little warning—but I need to take the risk.

Nothing happens. No sudden shifts.

Shit, maybe he's not on this road at all. Maybe, once I'm in hiding and feel secure, he'll take his sweet time, GPS his way to my location, and plant a bullet in the back of my skull when I least suspect it.

I pull another abrupt shifting of lanes. The driver I cut off a minute ago, now pissed off at my aggression, floors his accelerator and zooms past me, out of sight.

My eyes dart to the mirror again—and see a car shift lanes about a hundred feet behind me. A casual slide. Discreet. Not a sudden jerk, but intentional, and without a turn signal. Is it him? Or just a coincidence?

I dart into the other lane again, an effort to make a spectacle of myself. Sure enough, two seconds later, the same car makes another casual lane shift. My suspicion grows.

A couple more twists, then the road stretches before me. I accelerate, hoping I don't get pulled over by a highway patrol officer. Then again, that could be the best thing that could happen to me.

But of course, how many cops would sit on the freeway before dawn? Who would they expect to pull over, a vampire racing to reach its victim before the sun rises? Vampires always travel by car, right?

After filling my tank yesterday on the way home from work, the fuel gauge assures me I have plenty of time to make a decision on what to do next. My pursuer didn't expect a car chase. Did he fuel up recently?

I'll keep running. This is the route I take to the cabin in the mountains, so I know my environment well.

Maybe better than he does.

# CHAPTER 16

At last, a glow bursts ahead of me as dawn begins to break. It looks as if the sky has caught fire. A cool, blue flame, the shade closest to the head of a burning match. And over the next hour, the highway comes to life as people begin to leave home. Not the beehive of activity you'd find on a typical morning in Reno, but sufficient for my purposes. Granted, the traffic volume will slow me down and reduce my mileage per gallon, but it also improves the chances of outmaneuvering my pursuer. It's easier to get lost in a crowd.

Unfortunately, the color of the killer's car remains a mystery since I saw nothing but headlights in the darkness. All I know is he drives a car, not a truck or SUV. And traffic volume has grown to where drivers shuffle across lanes to jockey for position. Keeping my eye on the parade of vehicles behind me, I try to determine which of them if Conscience, if he's still there at all. Who knows. But I need to assume he is. Once I get to a rural road in Colorado, I'll have my answer. Until then, I'll continue to shift lanes at unexpected junctures, try to blend deeper into the morning confusion.

Meanwhile, drivers exit the highway and even more drivers enter, adding fresh doses of chaos to the mix.

Before long, I'll reach the Colorado border and Grand Junction, where, if timing cooperates, I can try to lose him amid a heavier flood of morning commuters. Once there, I can conduct a few tests, exiting and entering the freeway at random, to see if anyone follows me. Maybe even get a chance to add fuel to my car. If I'm headed where I think I'm headed, a gas station won't exist for miles.

I've always considered the cabin a place of refuge.

A refuge from *what*—well, that has taken me by surprise.

If I can make it there, hide myself in the mountain, I'll have a chance to stop and formulate a plan. And I *need* a plan. Losing the guy in traffic will grant me a reprieve but won't guarantee my safety. If he's put a tracking device on my car, he can hunt me down at will.

But once I reach the cabin, I'll gain another advantage this crazy fuck doesn't anticipate.

I know what's hidden inside.

# PART THREE

# RESET

# CHAPTER 17

I've lost him. For now.

Who knows if I outmaneuvered him on the interstate or if he ran low on fuel, but I've departed the highway and now roll along on the rural road that leads up a mountain, closer to my family's cabin. The road is, for the most part, desolate. I'm alone.

I stop to get gas at a mom-and-pop station, my final chance to do so before my journey ends. Grabbing an old ball cap from the back seat of my car, I pull its bill low over my eyes. I make my payment in cash.

I still don't know if the killer can track my car. I need to assume he can. But in case he can't, I don't want to leave breadcrumbs behind. Should he find his way here and ask questions, the locals won't have answers for him.

I was never here.

Afterward, I wind another thirty minutes up the mountain, then weave through the woods along a gravel path overrun with weeds. Within minutes, I reach the end of the path, where foliage camouflages my family's cabin.

The deadbolt is stiff and in need of replacement, but I get it unlocked. Beside the door, pollen has coated the window, which could use a good cleaning next time I visit. If I'm alive. The doorknob creaks when I twist it. I enter the cabin and lock the door behind me. One prolonged glimpse through the window reveals I'm still alone.

I made it. The relief, though temporary, is palpable and overcomes my bones. Weary, I stumble into the bedroom and collapse onto a twin-size bed that squeaks beneath my weight. Worries turn to liquid and drain from my mind, and my final thought before falling asleep is how grateful I am for this flimsy mattress.

I have no idea what time Peter Gabriel disrupts my peace, but at first, I don't realize my phone is ringing. His voice sneaks into my dream, which, as far as I can recall, was a collage of incongruity, Beth and other acquaintances drenched in tones of grey and sepia.

When I realize it's my phone, reality hits me hard and I groan. Amid the scurry to hide, I forgot to plug in the phone. The battery is low. But when I read the caller ID, I wonder if I'll live long enough to require a recharge.

Private Call.

That menacing rasp.

"Enjoying the cabin?"

# CHAPTER 18

My adrenaline spikes. Without a word, I end the call.

*He knows I'm here? No one followed me the final hour of my drive!*

I jump from the bed, race to the front of the cabin, and gaze through the window, forgetting to hide myself. But it doesn't matter. The only car sitting outside is mine. Scanning the trees and brush, on careful lookout for camouflage, I discover I'm the only person in the vicinity.

No doubt about it now. He affixed a tracer to my car. Which means, unless I drive to town and manage to locate a bus station or taxi service—both of which seem doubtful in the middle of nowhere—I won't escape him for long. He doesn't *need* to follow me anywhere. He can come to me at a time of his choosing.

That metallic sensation returns to my tongue, along with the taste of bile.

But I can't remain here, miles away from another human being. He could show up in the middle of the night, kill me, and my body could go undiscovered for months. Longer, if he buries me here in the woods. I could buy or rent another car, but that won't help. He knows where I live.

I need a plan. I need to outsmart this Conscience guy. And I better do it fast.

I draw a breath and hold it in for a few seconds, an attempt to focus, to stop the churning of my brain.

Then I remember.

My grandfather had kept a small, loaded pistol, his old service revolver, hidden in a cupboard above the refrigerator, out of reach of the grandkids when we were young. We had dragged a chair to the refrigerator and climbed atop it, but with our young statures, the cupboard had remained out of reach. He had kept the pistol on hand for protection, in case a wild animal posed a threat. Today, I face an animal of a different kind.

Darting to the kitchen, I drag a over chair, climb on top, and sweep my hand inside the cupboard in the hope that none of my relatives moved it. In the corner, I feel cold metal.

Bingo.

Despite my awareness of its existence, this pistol hasn't touched my hands since I was young, under Gramps's supervision. It brings an onslaught of memories and feels heavier than I recall. Patting around the same corner of the cupboard, I locate a small box of bullets.

When I was fifteen, Gramps taught me how to load and shoot this pistol, but I haven't fired it since. I won't fool myself into thinking I can shoot with accuracy. And the thought of allowing the killer near enough to eliminate him from point-blank range sends chills up my spine. But now I've stacked two advantages in my favor: a weapon and the element of surprise. Granted, they don't constitute a plan. I don't know what comes next, but at this point, I'll take whatever assets I can muster.

Making sure the safety is on, I tuck the pistol into the waistband of my jeans and, on the off chance my pursuer is lurking in the woods and watches me depart, I cover up the weapon with my shirt.

One step at a time. I'm moving in the right direction.

We'll see if it keeps me alive.

When I emerge from the cabin, I pause on the front porch

and watch. Listen.

Birds chirping. Fluttering.

A rustle in the brush startles me. A cautious step upon dead foliage. To my left.

Sucking air, I catch my breath, consider pulling the pistol from my waistband. But the noise ceases. My heart turns into a jackhammer. I squint in the direction of the sound.

Sudden movement. In the corner of my eye. Rustling of leaves. I flinch, then reach for the gun.

A deer scampers away, no doubt frightened by the unexpected presence of a foreigner in its domain.

My heartbeat decelerates as I close my eyes and exhale. A gun in hand is useful. A gun in a twitchy hand, not so much. I hope I don't lose a toe in the process.

Locking the cabin door behind me, I scamper to my car, start the engine, and ease down the mountain.

# CHAPTER 19

Unpredictability. That's my key.

Don't go home the same way you got here. Make the killer wonder. Climb into his brain: Which route would he *least* expect me to take?

My gut clenches at the answer.

I open the GPS app on my phone, select my route, and don't look back. The last thing I want to do is return to the road where this nightmare began. But it could work to my advantage. Maybe it will give my pursuer a false notion of control. Let him think I've entered panic mode and started to make stupid mistakes.

It's early evening, but in the midst of June, I have plenty of daylight left. The twists and turns of this two-lane road look all too familiar. Tonight the mile-high air feels thicker than usual, the humidity palpable. Though the air conditioner would make my journey more pleasant, I roll down the window and allow myself to perspire. Comfort could prove dangerous. I need to remain alert.

Unlike the last time I traveled this road, the sky is clear, but cirrus clouds scratch its uppermost heights. According to a science teacher back in high school, cirrus clouds mean the weather is about to deteriorate. Careful to remain aware of the road—and its narrow shoulders—ahead of me, my sights enter a cycle of repetition.

Road. Rearview. Side mirror. Repeat.

An eighteen-wheeler approaches from the opposite direction, which, due to my higher altitude, I can see in advance. He must be on his way to a small town. Or lost. Or maybe he lives around here, though I can't fathom why he would want to.

Given the current state of my nerves and little room for error on this road, I grip the steering wheel with both hands, ease my foot from the gas pedal, and tap the brake as the truck looms nearer. Its license plates say Arkansas, but I suppose it's possible the vehicle is registered there and the driver resides elsewhere.

The monster steams past me, twenty miles over the speed limit, leaving in its wake a cloud of dust that sends me into a coughing fit. Grime sticks to the sweat on my neck and face. And though I look for a business name as the guy passes, I find the side of the white vehicle blank. Strange. Shaking my head as the dust clears, I glance in my rearview mirror. A car has approached from behind, close enough for me to catch not only its color, but its manufacturer's logo. A green Buick.

Paranoia gets the best of me. Is that the killer?

As I eye my surroundings, miles of forest overlooking the middle of nowhere, my stomach turns sour.

This was the vicinity of my hit-and-run.

# CHAPTER 20

This could be pure chance, nothing more than a field day for my paranoia. Then again, based on my limited experience, this road is, almost without exception, desolate. Two months ago, when the accident occurred, not a single driver passed the site the whole time I stood there. Suddenly I have company? In the vicinity where it all happened?

Another glance in the mirror. I catch sight of the driver. Male. Caucasian. Dark hair. Eyes fixed straight ahead as he takes a drag from a cigarette. He doesn't even check his mirrors. Just studies my car. Not in an aggressive way. More like I'm a specimen and he's curious to see what I'll do next.

Surely this is a coincidence. At this point, however, assumptions could prove fatal.

I'll give it more gas, speed up another five miles per hour. See how this guy responds.

A few seconds pass. Then the man follows suit. I check my speed and realize I've slowed down each time I've focused on the driver behind me. Maybe he just wants to pass me, but with all the curves obstructing his view, he can't risk the maneuver.

I press my foot harder against the gas pedal and accelerate another five miles an hour. He follows suit. Another five, ten, fifteen miles per hour. Soon my speed exceeds my comfort level for this rural road with its narrow shoulders.

The driver continues to pursue me.

This is not a coincidence. I'm looking at the face of Conscience.

My cell phone rings. I grab it from the passenger seat. No need to look at the display—I know who it is. The driver behind me has tossed his cigarette butt out the window and now holds a cell phone to his ear.

With one hand on the wheel, trying my best to maintain control, I answer the call.

"Leave me alone, you crazy fuck!"

With that, I end the call, slam the phone on the passenger seat, and almost lose control of my car in the split-second I've removed my eyes from the road. I swerve back into the center of my lane as a blend of terror, fury and adrenaline surge through me. When my eyes return to the mirror, I discover the Buick is almost on my tail. This guy intends to make his move sooner rather than later. And as long as I remain in his sights, he controls my destiny.

Whether he wants to kill me outright or leave me to die in a crash, I don't know. Either way, my minutes are numbered.

I'm at his mercy.

Unless I can outsmart him. And fast.

# CHAPTER 21

Determination turns to concrete within me.

Conscience wants revenge? He wants an anonymous murder?

He wants an accident?

He'll get one.

Checking my seatbelt to make sure it's secure, I eye the familiar terrain ahead of me. The accident site is up ahead. Landmarks don't define it, but the layout of the forest, the position of the trees and the curvature of the road, trigger in me a sense of déjà vu.

Sure enough, I reach another bend in the road, navigate my way around it, and recognize the spot where the accident occurred—not its physical features, but the foreboding creep that sends goosebumps across the surface of my skin.

As I recall, a straight stretch of road will follow the next curve. And then…

Sure enough, the horizon expands before my eyes. And as I scope out the half-mile ahead, just before the next curve, I find what I'm looking for.

A thick tree, a sentry whose roots protrude from underground and cause the earth to ripple above it. It sits too close to the shoulder of the road for comfort to drivers who don't pay attention.

One more glance to verify my pursuer is still close behind

me—and to confirm I have no other choice but to accept whatever collateral damage I'll inflict upon myself—I grip the wheel with both hands until the color drains from my knuckles. I tense my body to such a degree that the muscles become pronounced along the tops of my arms. My breaths have grown shallow.

As I speed toward the tree, which I imagine has withstood centuries of wind and snow and rain, I tense my stomach muscles, angle my shoulders forward, force myself to inhale deep.

And brace for impact.

Five. Four. Three. Two.

One.

At the last possible split-second, with Conscience on my tail, I discharge my biggest advantage—the element of surprise.

With a jerk of the wheel, traveling sixty miles per hour, I swerve to the right and crash into the tree, barreling into it with the same corner of my car that hit that fateful Chevy two months ago.

An air bag deploys with such force, it bruises my face. The engine shuts down.

The killer races past me and rounds the bend.

I feel a warm drip on my arm, and when I regain my sense of balance, I look down and notice several scarlet drops. My nose is bleeding. It feels broken. My wrists feel sore.

But I'm alive.

And ready to lure the fucker into Act Two.

# CHAPTER 22

I don't know whether the killer believes I'm dead or alive, but I expect him to return and find out.

And if he suspects I'm alive, I expect him to shoot me dead.

Which is why I intend to *play* dead.

One last look through the windshield to make sure he hasn't yet returned, then I slide down until I'm lying flat across the front seats, with my head on the passenger side.

The countdown begins.

Now that the car has ceased moving, the steamy temperature and lack of breeze are more prominent. The close proximity between the air bag and front seat turns the inside of my car into a coffin, stifling and sticky, which allows no room for error. The arm rest presses against my kidney. I wiggle until I'm resting on my left arm, which improves my angle and maximizes leeway for my right hand, with which I now hold the pistol. Sweat has drenched my chest and back. When the air bag deployed, I suspect it cracked my rib, judging from the sore spot in my chest. My hands feel grubby, but it improves my grip on the gun.

As an amateur gunslinger, my best bet is to attack my target at close range. And based on my position in the car, that will be the only angle at my disposal. But the unknown now works in my favor—as long as my pursuer believes the car crash could have proven fatal.

I wait. Listen. Not a sound except the rustle of an animal moving among the trees.

Thirty seconds pass.

Then I hear the tentative rumble of tires as a small vehicle approaches from the opposite direction. I shut my eyes when the vehicle eases to the side of my car. Its brakes squeak as it comes to a halt. The motor continues to hum.

Squinting, I try to make out the color of the car.

Green.

I tighten my jaw.

It's showtime.

# CHAPTER 23

Five seconds. Maybe ten. Then the car inches past and comes to a stop along what sounds like the shoulder of the road. I hear the open and shut of a car door, but the engine continues to run. Which means he doesn't plan to stay long.

My body stiffens—a head start on rigor mortis if I'm not fast enough. That metallic taste, like licking the gun barrel, returns to my tongue. I peek just enough to capture motion in front of me. I need my visitor to think I'm dead. Just for one second. That's all I need.

It must end today. I don't have a choice. Today, tomorrow, next week—Conscience will hold me in his grasp until I free myself.

One of us better be lucky. Nobody else is around. No one to hear me scream. Or see me put up a fight. Or watch him put a bullet through my forehead. If not today, then eventually.

Footsteps on the pavement, a firm clomp at a casual, yet intentional, pace. The soles sound weighty. Cowboy boots, perhaps. Or combat boots.

My heart pounds against my tender rib cage. I can hear my blood rushing in my ears.

I remove the safety on the gun. And listen.

The footsteps stop outside the open window on the driver's side. Through my squinted eyes, I can see his silhouette. Death in the flesh. I feel his eyes crawl over me.

And I hear the click as he releases the safety on his gun. My heart jumps. My breathing stops.

Panic erupts. Before I can stop myself, I jerk forward with a scream.

And thrust my gun barrel toward the window, too shaky to take aim.

The impact of the bullet sends the killer stumbling backward, arms flailing.

The force from firing the gun thrusts me backward. Because of my odd position, I pull a muscle in my back. Gasping, too stunned to move, my eyes flutter. My mouth turns to cotton.

Trembling, I punch the air bag, squeeze out of the car, and tread toward my prey. I loom over him, studying the man who hijacked twenty-four hours of my life. He lies flat on his back, arms and legs odd angles. His silver eyes, wide open, remain frozen in a permanent expression of shock. Slack-jawed, he must have spent his final moment alive fighting for breath. He wears a printed T-shirt, but a crimson blossom has overrun the artwork.

I consider the deadness of the man who lies before me.

No room for error.

I press the gun against his bony forehead and put a bullet through his brain.

# EPILOGUE

One year has passed. I'm not the man I was back then.

I'm bolder.

And I live with one more secret.

Under the covers, Beth draws near to me and asks what I'm thinking. True to form, I bottle up my feelings about the second incident on that rural road in Colorado. I've tried to forget that day but can't. Conscience endures. I guess we all live with our share of mutations.

Sometimes those mutations scar us; sometimes they inspire change.

Me? I've learned to open up to Beth more and more, allowed her into deeper recesses of my heart. I don't want to lose her again. But I refuse to complicate her life more than necessary.

I told her the killer, while pursuing me, misjudged a sharp turn, rounded it too fast, and sailed off a cliff.

She doesn't know the truth about what happened. But she knows she's safe.

The cabin no longer represents solace to me. I haven't returned to it—haven't even crossed the border into Colorado—since the day that grey-eyed man died. The closest I've come is eastern Nevada, where we are today.

Lake Tahoe.

Beth and I enjoy the weekends here. Plenty of tourists. We

visited not long after I brought word she was safe.

We decided to give our relationship another try, see if we can make things work this time around. A few weeks after that recommitment, we spent a several days here, which is also where we spent our honeymoon. Years ago. When I was the old me.

And on that first weekend after our recommitment, I acquired one more secret.

That Friday night—early Saturday morning, that is—I crept out of bed and out the door. I grabbed a small duffel bag from the trunk of my car and carried it to the lake. Beneath the moonlight, while Beth and the rest of the world slept, I donned a pair of latex gloves I'd brought from the lab. Removing my shirt, I used it to wipe my fingerprints from the gun and the box of bullets. When I finished, I wiped the items a second time. And a third to make sure.

Then I tossed the items into the lake.

This morning, I lay a kiss on Beth's upper lip and listen as she breathes.

The sound of life.

Like I said, neither my relatives nor I had registered the guns in our names. It still belonged to my grandfather, who died years ago. The last time I used a credit card in Colorado was the weekend of my hit-and-run. Two months before Conscience died.

Someone else found his abandoned car and lifeless corpse.

I won't track that lucky individual down.

And if he chooses, he can run.

# Did you enjoy
# *Beautiful Mess*
# or John's other books?
## *LET HIM KNOW!*

Visit John Herrick online to message him and discover his other books.

## johnherrick.net

 facebook.com/johnherrickbooks

@johnherrick

goodreads.com/johnherrick

CPSIA information can be obtained
at www.ICGtesting.com
Printed in the USA
LVOW11s1127020317
525904LV00001B/1/P